# URSULA OF ULM

# Ursula of Ulm

### DE RE DORDICA: BOOK TWO

## JB Jackson

Nantes       2024

Demonic sketches, from "A Case Study in Asuric Manifestation." *Chaturvarga*, no. 33, 2007, p. 15.

# DER SCHLEIM

# URSULA OF ULM

# DER SCHLEIM

*Translation by Randall Kelso from the German of an anonymous, undated (after 1628) manuscript. Original typescript on 4 onionskin leaves. Basham & Winstead (San Francisco). De re dordica: Treasures from the Seaberg Society. January 31, 1998. Sale no. 822, Lot 19. Provenance: Calvin "Cal" Calhoun.*

The scoundrel had been found cowering among the smoldering embers of the town house of Meister Durchdenmeer, alias "The Foreigner." He would only say he was Der Schleim, lately of Stab. Nor would he say what he was doing there. I paid off the watchman, the so-called landlord of the Green Frog, that I may see Der Schleim in his cell.

"My report is to be laid before the Rat tomorrow," I said. "Pray do not hinder me!" The watchman was too busy counting to respond. By the glow of an oil lamp he stacked the gleaming florins.

A steep staircase of worn stone went down to a maze of dank dungeon halls. I made my way in the gloom, treading into the echoes of my own footsteps. I came to a cell door upon which a bright red cock was painted. The mark of a fire raiser. Apart from my taper, the only light came from a smoky brazier of burning coals in a nearby alcove. I took a seat upon a small stool brought for the occasion. I drew my cowl close about my face. I opened the rusty iron grate. I adjusted my glove and placed within the dark opening an apple.

Chains clanked across stone. A subtle moldering reek filled my nostrils. The apple was removed. The fruit was replaced by the round, inquisitive eyes of Der Schleim. The prisoner would be heavily ironed at the waist and feet. Behind him would be an oaken bunk and perhaps a rough blanket. Next to that, a bench and wooden piss bucket fitted with a lid to eat upon. Naught else. As I well knew.

Der Schleim stroked the apple. He bit into it warily, as if it hurt his teeth. "You are the *Lochschöffen*, come to hear me?" he said eagerly, through a mouth full of pulp. His cheerful tone was at odds with the grim setting. Der Schleim dragged the bench to the door and seated himself with a grunt.

My answer was to withdraw a lightweight lap desk from my bag and unfold it. Der Schleim's eyes followed my hands as I seated my taper. I readied my goatskin, quill, and ink. Perhaps he thought I was the *Lochschöffen* and this visit a mere formality. The prisoner was quite forthcoming. One will do anything to break the abiding dreariness of being locked up alone.

"They are sending me to Turm," uttered Der Schleim merrily.

"Tell me about your hump," I said, lifting my quill. If they were indeed sending the wretch to Turm, it was because of his sickliness.

He bit into the apple. "Born a mooncalf, I was," he said. He snorted loudly but it was not enough to stanch the snot cascading down his beard. "My mother took one look at me and wrung my neck awry. A hook-maker hooked me out of the manure pit. He and his wife took me in. Most cruel, they were. Above all, the hook-maker. I stayed because of my feet.

"One fine day, the hook-maker was found upon one of his own hooks. The hook-maker's wife was locked up. No one thought to blame me. After her release, she swore never to speak my name again and sent me on my way. Kicked around, I was, a ward of the town. Friendless, penniless, bent neck. Since a young man has to eat, I became a thief. The good town folk showed me no mercy. If my hump and feet were not awful enough, they clipped my ears and took a finger from each hand. Der Schleim, they called me."

"And what of your nose?" I said. The holes glistened with his snot.

"Born thus, was I."

"What of your former jobs?"

"Hook-maker," said Der Schleim. He paused, as if trying to remember if he had ever earned his keep by honest means. "Hook-maker," he repeated flatly.

"Tell me about your partnership with Durchdenmeer and the happenstance of your meeting," I said.

"Caught was I, unlawfully partaking of the beekeeper's hives. Fancy that, would you? A man who thinks he owns the honeybees!" Der Schleim sniffed derisively.

"Flogged out of the dorf, I was. Back I went, torch in hand. From the rising flames came their woebegone screams. I rooted through their homes. My bags were bursting with booty. My pockets jingled with gold. 'Help me,' whimpered the hangman's daughter, her braids ablaze. With my cudgel of birchwood, I dealt with her lustily."

Der Schleim paused and looked at me hard. From two slits where his nose should be, he turned his head and blasted snot. The rough stone masonry of the cell was crusty with it. "Obrist Holky would have been glad," he said.

"Lost, I was. I wandered and found a little oakwood near Thennalohe. There I made my home. I learned to fend for myself. I became skilled at fishing and hunting with my bare hands. Cows, spiders, toads. The easiest prey, however, were other hunters.

"When I was spotted frisking a fresh corpse, I fled the little oakwood I called home. What was to become of me, I knew not. In Lambretzhoffen, I clubbed the bailiff once or twice and took his signet ring. The landlord has it now. I broke the back of a Jew as he drank at the fountain at Feylsdorf. His cloak and six ducats I kept for myself. From a bugler I stole four florins and a bugle. At the bottom of the Floß he lies."

"And of Durchdenmeer?" I said impatiently.

"Near the Schleegasse at Hersspruch I waited under a bridge. Against the gloaming I beheld a pointy hat. From my hiding place I crept, cudgel raised. My prey turned and grasped my arm. With dreadful strength he lifted me by my neck. As tall as a tree, he was."

In the gloom I beheld Der Schleim's bent stump of a neck and wondered how anyone could get a firm grip on it.

"I grasped at my prey's pointy hat and clawed at his beard. Having already taken what I swore was my last breath, I kicked with my club feet until I passed out. Yet I lived. When I came to, I was sprawled next to a campfire over which bubbled a cauldron. The wayfarer peered at me through a haze of smoke rings. His pipe was fashioned from a slender piece of bone. He pointed at the cauldron with it, whereby I joined him in a hearty meal of *Schnitz* with mutton of the likes of which I had never tasted.

"After supping my fill, I gave thanks and spoke my name. 'Durchdenmeer' he said. I took it to be a seafarer's name. When he saw I had but three fingers on each hand, he laughed like a kobold. I did not understand and laughed, too. Also like a kobold.

"As a newborn, I slept. To the sweet melody of 'Es wollt ein Jäger jagen' I awoke. The man stopped blowing his gemshorn and gave me bread. He then gathered his belongings and beckoned me to follow. We stayed for a spell at Stab. At the Inn of the Reichsapfel. Then to Nürnberg. At the Drei Kronen we dwelled.

"Durchdenmeer gave me lists of things to bring to him. At first, these things were easy to gain. Herbs and spices, and whatnot. These I supposed were for cooking though we usually took our meals together at the Tatzelwurm or sometimes the Ass. Some were stinky. Devil's dung I should not like to smell again. Nor *Hundskamille*. And some, such as savin and hemlock, are deadly poison.

"Into a cozy town house in the Barfüßer quarter we settled. Durchdenmeer I never knew to sleep. Indeed after dark, I often heard low murmuring, or bells tinkling. Sometimes spectral flashes of many colors danced beneath his door. Once, when I put my ear to the keyhole, there were voices other than the Meister's within. Never was I allowed to enter."

"Did you or Durchdenmeer ever hurt anyone?" I said.

"Once," said Der Schleim, "the Meister bade me bring him the spleen of a virgin. I asked not wherefore or whence I should find such a thing. By day, the

Lorenzer side of town I prowled. The Sebalder side after dusk. On the second day I wandered without the city walls as far as the old Rabenstein, wringing my hands. I briefly considered bringing him my own. The hangman's daughter had not counted, I reasoned. But on the second night along the Fischbach I reaped the spleen of an infant. This, I laid at the Meister's feet. Much vexed, he was. He accepted it nonetheless. For my trouble gave me a three-fingered punch ring. It fit my knuckles snugly.

"Charms I was given with which to bait the young women. How to wield them the Meister taught me well. Outside the pig market where whores like to linger I found the first luckless Fräulein, Hedwig with the flaxen hair. Such a ruckus she made all the way home. After the Meister took her into his rooms the noise was snuffed.

"Whensoever I should gladden the Meister with a thing hard to come by, he sometimes rewarded me. For Hedwig, he bestowed upon me new feet. For a nun, a trick coin which always came back to me. Until the landlord took that, too, Curse him! And his mother!"

"New feet?" I said quizzically.

With almost laughable effort, Der Schleim turned in his stool and held up both of his filthy feet for me to see. As were his withered hands, Der Schleim's feet were heavily ironed, but I could find nothing wrong with them. They were, in fact, the least afflicted aspects of his body. Nicely formed and oddly small and youthful for such an otherwise sickly person.

"To Hedwig I have always believed they belonged," Der Schleim said coldly. He looked down and sighed deeply. "Yet, I brought to the Meister the young women. He scolded me for stalking so close to home. For many of these came from the riding school on Schütt Island. Heeding his warning, I hunted as far as the Frauen-Thor. As with Hedwig, the young women were given to the Meister where they passed from all memory. But for one. The peasant wench, Ursula."

The name excited me. I stopped writing and leaned in closer, almost gagging from the stench.

"One night the Meister sent me to the church of St. Katharina. The old convent library was forgotten, he said, and its books would not be missed. Behind this place was a peaceful apple orchard. There I lingered with my jug and pipe.

"In a clearing lay a Fräulein, without a stitch but for her stockings. She rested upon her elbows, legs spread wide under the glow of the full moon. *Eine Hexe*! Never had I laid eyes on one before. Nor hands."

At this remark, I smiled sardonically.

Der Schleim licked his lips. "Enthralled was I by her long, dark hair. As a waterfall it fell upon her bare shoulders. Her milk-white skin was a snowy, rolling meadow dappled with moonlight and shadow. I would have tickled her gizzard then and there. But, like Venus come from the sea, the witch rose to her feet. She yawned and stretched as a person waking up of a morning well rested. I ogled her breathlessly. She brushed dirt off her backside and plucked leaves from her tresses. She pulled her kirtle over her head then deftly leaped over the wall. Alone was I now, breeches undone, pipe in hand.

"On the hangman's bridge I caught up to the witch and brought out the charms. She shook my wrist and said, 'Put those away.' I bade her come with me back to the house. So taken with her was the Meister, he kept her to cook and scrub. My bed she was given. In a vaulted undercroft where goods were stored I now lay my head. This sudden twist of fate unsettled me. The next morning, I cornered her in the buttery. She lay limp and dumb as I plumbed her depths."

At this I bristled but held my tongue.

"The witch had a way of getting whatsoever she wished. Brazenly she caught the indigo robe of the Meister when he came through the door of an evening. Soon she was allowed into the Meister's rooms. 'Tell me what you have seen, witch!' I begged.

"'Never!' she cackled. When I pinched her under her kirtle she lunged for a spindle then stabbed my ear hole. Into my other ear hole she hissed, 'You are a gruesome, thieving, snaggle-toothed *Wechselbalg*. You sicken me.' She said that should I ever so much as dream of her tasty cunt again she would cut out my tongue and add it to the *Schnitz*. I struggled to my feet. 'Away, black-brows!' I wailed.

"Henceforth I used the charms the Meister gave me to slake my lust. The witch would pay."

"What became of the women?" I said. This I knew well but I wanted to hear what Der Schleim would say. But he merely shrugged.

"Tell me more about Ursula, then," I said. "Did you love her?"

Der Schleim considered this question carefully. "I did not like to," he replied, at last. "When the witch fancied something, she plied me with white wine sweetened with flowers and herbs and was playful. Many times I found myself scouring the night pots, my loins aflame without understanding." Der Schleim rubbed his palms together thoughtfully, then crossed his legs.

"My itch for the witch would not be scratched. Of her keyhole I made good use. So careful was I not to give myself away on the creaky threshold I dared not breathe. At bedtime the witch took off her kirtle and faced the looking glass. From the bottles on her vanity she applied the scented oils. To her throat, breasts, armpits, and navel. And to her sex, upon which I descried the mark of the devil. Thus I spilled my seed at her door time and again.

"When the witch went to market, I often touched her things. Besides bottles of labdanum, aloe, and storax found upon her bench, there was naught of worth save a carved, boxwood comb. This I broke when I tried to run it through my rat's nest. I was scared. I tossed the comb out the window.

"Searching high and low, I at last pulled from under a floorboard a silken bundle. Manifold items it held: candles and incense, a small knife, a goblet, a talisman upon a chain. Witches' things. You know. A small book filled with queer signs."

"Did Durchdenmeer have any idea with whom he was dealing?" I said.

"A witch? If so, he did not say." Der Schleim paused to take another bite of apple. "Whensoever the moon was round and bright, the witch would sneak away to the convent grove and lie, un-Christianlike, as before. Always I followed.

"To München the Meister was called. The witch begged him to take her but was turned down. How I laughed in her face! As his friend I was to go but then he turned me down as well. Now it was the witch who laughed.

"As soon as the Meister had shut the door behind him, the witch clobbered me with the kettle. I stole her comb, she said. As a babe I had already ducked the clutches of Dunkle Großmutter. Without a fight I would not let the witch win. Limb from limb I would have torn her. But all of a sudden I had a clever thought.

"After the witch sneaked away, I sought the elder Meistersinger who lived nearby. A more God-fearing man there never was. From his dormer above the orchard he beheld the witch's snatch and bawled, 'What is the meaning of this?'

"'You see what I see,' was my reply, wherefore the Meistersinger sounded his horn. As his henchmen bore her off, the witch turned to me and shrieked, 'May your worthless God guard you! For dealing with me thus you will meet me again one day.'

"To my nostrils I held her still-warm kirtle." Der Schleim stopped speaking and looked away. He took another bite of apple, which he chewed pensively.

"Gleaming in the dirt, I spied the talisman from the witch's neck. This, I stashed carefully under a cobblestone near the sundial. With my trick coin I marked an *S*."

"An *S*?" I said, scribbling quickly.

"*Für den Schleim*," he wheezed. Here I noticed that one corner of Der Schleim's mouth is higher than the other in a sort of fixed sneer. "Back at the house, I lost no time picking the Meister's lock. It was my chance! To pry and poke around to my heart's delight. A nose I may lack, but that does not mean I am not nosy." Der Schleim grinned hideously at his own joke. His laugh turned into a harsh cough.

"What did you find within?" I persisted.

"Many tools lay upon a large table made of a thick quartz slab set on an oaken base. One I understood to be a distilling apparatus. Next to it stood an hourglass whose sands were in motion. Within a jar of toads I fancied I saw myself. Shelves sagged under the weight of books and scrolls, ancient and worm eaten. Whence the Meister came by these things I wondered greatly, for we came to Nürnberg empty-handed.

"Beyond his workshop, there was a smaller windowless room well-stocked with jars and phials bearing kelp, scullcap, or bark of the pussy willow. The label of one read, 'Tooth of a Khul.' It was empty. Others bore labels written in unknown words. A tun of Riesling stood in the corner. I lowered an empty flask within. Thus, I quenched my thirst and then some.

"My hoary old feet floated in an urn. Nearby, a cloth which, when removed, betrayed a glass box containing the head of Hedwig, mouth agape. Her flaxen curls swayed like river grass in an oily, opaline fluid. Of this I will say no more.

"A prism I pinched. The Meister would not miss it. Tempted was I as well by a ball of crystal. Swirling clouds beckoned. A curtain of green velvet concealed a door covered in studded leather through which the Meister would have had to stoop. This lock took much longer to pick. Beyond was a room of five walls. Empty but for a rack with straps within a circle drawn upon the floor in salt.

"To make the most of my luck, I carried on. At last I found what I had only hoped for: two glimmering ingots of purest gold. These I held to my cheeks. So cool to the touch were they! I cracked them together and judged their heft in my palms. A jig I danced! To Augsburg I would go, where they know well what to do with gold. How my heart leaped at the thought of beating the Meister at his own game." Der Schleim lowered his head and sobbed quietly.

"Too much I drank," he said almost inaudibly. "The Meister found me curled in the corner of his workshop, swathed in the velvet curtain. He lifted from me the prism and the gold ingots. He asked for Ursula. 'Taken away. she was,' I said. At this news, the Meister's face turned white, then red. He besought me to tell all lest he turn me into a toad. But I was afraid! He yanked me into the room of five sides and strapped me to the rack within the circle of salt. 'I'll straighten your neck, alright!' he bawled.

"Above the Meister's pacing I could hear mumbling and cursing. After days, he howled 'Der Schleim!' This was followed by a loud crash. He burst through the door with red-hot tongs. When he brandished them in my face I wailed."

Der Schleim retched pitifully. He waved me off when I leaned forward to get a closer look. He calmed himself and glanced at me sideways. Foam had collected on his lips. He wiped his mouth with his sleeve. "With the tongs the

Meister nipped me on the elbows and knees. 'Hark! How the devil whines,' he cried, until I told all. As I am telling you now.

"The Meister gagged me with a stocking and again forsook me. With my tongue I wiggled the stocking until it fell from my mouth. I yelled until I was without speech. The straps I pulled at until my wrists and ankles were raw meat. Until there were sores on my buttocks I squirmed. My lips peeled from thirst and my stomach fed upon itself. I soiled myself and stewed in it. Whether it was day or night I knew not, nor how many days had passed.

"Around my lovely new toes something came a-snuffling. A glimmer of hope, I had, when I was able to wrest one hand free. When the snuffler began snuffling up my leg, I waited. When it was within reach, I seized it and devoured it. Yet I hungered. Just when I could stand to live no longer, the Meistersinger came with his henchmen.

"I was unfettered then led into the workshop. 'Behold,' I said feebly. 'A sorcerer dwells here! From the convent the Meister has plundered these books.'

"'Liar!' came a shriek from behind. It was the witch.

"'Lift your skirts!' I barked. 'Show them the mark of the devil!'

"'I have come for what is mine,' she said. 'Where is it?'

"'Perhaps you come for the head of Hedwig. Whore of the pig market!' I said haughtily. The Meistersinger gasped, then pointed his bony finger at me." Der Schleim was now drooling abundantly, having consumed the apple's core, seeds and all.

"The Meistersinger's men set upon me," he slurred. "This nasty turn of events sapped my will to fight. When I regained my wits, I beheld flames. With my backside ablaze I made my way into the tun of Riesling and drew the lid shut. The wine stung my wounds. I feared my lungs might burst or that I would be boiled alive. For my last breaths on this earth, I buggered myself, then drank myself to sleep. Thus I was found before being hauled howling to this godforsaken tomb." Der Schleim winced as if in pain, then vomited. His breathing was strained.

"I was to be led away on the tumbril. Beheaded with a sword as an act of kindness on St. Walburga's Day." Der Schleim gulped audibly. "But it was the witch, I tell you!"

Now, I lowered my cowl to reveal my face.

"You!" said Der Schleim in an agonized croak. His bloodshot eyes bulged from their sockets. The wretch stiffened, his rotten teeth bared in an unwilling rictus. His convulsing body sank limply against the door with a soft thud. I put my gloved hand through the opening. With a forceps I warily recovered the apple stem from Der Schleim's slackened jaw. This I wrapped in a cloth and placed in my bag.

I gathered my belongings then calmly made my way through the maze of dank dungeon halls. I stepped from the staircase and murmured to the watchman. "*Male patratis sunt atra theatra parata.*"

"And a very good evening to you, *mien Fräulein.*"

The watchman did not look up. He was still busy counting by the light of an oil lamp the stacks of gleaming florins heaped before him.

Be careful, lest in casting out your demon you exorcize the best thing in you.

—Friedrich Nietzsche

Who is the fox? I am the fox. Who are you? I am me.

—The Hollies

Monday, May 9, 1977

Unless I am experiencing the final stages of Philly fever-induced dementia, the events of the last four months cannot be dismissed as paranoia. One need look no further than my bedside table for damning evidence. At intervals throughout the night, I switched on the lamp and glanced anxiously at the decanter. Beam's Choice. The Christmas collectors' bottle, purple with gold trim. A dozen were produced for *I Dream of Jeannie*. Most of their contents consumed by Larry Hagman, no doubt. How Sherwood acquired one is anyone's guess. I lay wide awake, mentally juggling nucleotides of mutant conversational DNA. Randy's toast: *"Por la razón o la fuerza!"* Wailing bagpipes. A name: Shagduk.

It hit me that I had to be at the information desk in five minutes. Scrubbed the Chilean flag off my face, along with trace amounts of shoe polish and dwarf blood. Just another day that ends in *Y*.

Hauled ass to the library. Almost collided with a Polyflex truck pulling into Lot C. With her usual air of sour disapproval, Dixie emerged from her burrow just as I burst panting through the saloon doors at the circulation desk. She frowned at her watch. For all she knew, I had been on time and was just now returning from a union-sanctioned nicotine fix after cataloging oodles of festschrifts. She said nothing about the ugly tie I had worn just to yank her chain, but I was in no mood to deal with her *yaje*, anyway.

The staff bathroom is out of order, so I had to use the public one. Someone entered the men's, cussing up a storm. At first, the talk was self-deprecating and suicidal. It then turned outward, targeting "they," whoever they might be, in threatening terms. Under the urine-pitted divider could be seen two filthy bare feet. Chanting could now be heard. A phrase from the fiction of H.P. Lovecraft, unless I am mistaken. The longer I waited, the more unseemly it would be when I showed my face. I do not know how long I stayed put. I thought the person would never leave and I could stand it no longer. At last, I exited the stall and fox-walked past the agitated paranoiac. Judd the Doom Hippie!

"Glad you could join us!" quipped the Bastard the moment I stepped into the workroom. He clicked his heels and gave me the three-fingered salute. Randy and I have been doing that lately, the salute. What began as a joke now seems more sinister. Moreover, Amber saw us and now does it, too. She has no idea what it means, of course. Not sure Randy and I do, either. Nor do I know why a kid is working at the information desk. But that is a matter for Dixie. Hedgehog logic, right there.

"Did you hear?" said Randy. "Maxine auditioned to be a Cowboys cheerleader."

After yesterday's savage treatment at the hands of the imp's pompatus, small talk felt almost perverse. My Adam's apple was still sore from the dwarf's velvet garrote. Until they get their hands on the "old tome," I fear their return. I offered a laconic grunt. Maxine is never cheerful. Instead, I told Randy about my encounter with the Doom Hippie.

"That Lovecraft dick," said Randy. "He always looks like he's fixing to go crazy. Wouldn't surprise me if he blew up the library."

"You've spoken with him?"

"Yeah," said Randy. "He says shit like 'wain't.' The past tense of ain't, I guess. As in 'I wain't doing nothing.'"

"Why do you call him a 'Lovecraft dick?'"

"I heard him reciting something in R'lyehian in the business school cafeteria before consuming a shaker's worth of salt. The strange and guttural language didn't feel out of place in that brutalist monstrosity."

"All that salt can't be good for his blood pressure," I said. "By the way, the Remington is still in the Rambler. Should I put it back?"

"Keep it. Guns get stolen all the time. Carlos knows it's missing by now. Returning it would be riskier than keeping it."

"What is the sentence for theft of a firearm?" I asked. But I have so many questions besides that one. Concerning the amulet, for example. *Amulets and Talismans* was unhelpful. It has chapters on Babylonian, Coptic, and Syriac, but not on whatever mine is.

Was supposed to have gone in early to help set up for the book sale. Having just returned from the Vault, Jo Ann and Amber greeted me at the information desk. "All done," said Jo Ann irritably. I regarded a pile of auction catalogs: Christie's, Parke-Bernet Galleries, Basham & Winstead.

"Ancient Marbles of the Marquess of Anglesey," I read aloud. "Who are these for?" I imagined the Marquess sitting on the ground, shooting his ancient marbles into a chalk circle.

Jo Ann slapped my hand away. "Those are for Mr. Burnside." She piled several boxes of microfilm into my arms and sent me on my way. I sat before the microform reader. Someone had managed to reverse the direction of the film on each reel. My train of thought was disturbed by a couple of co-eds chatting loudly on the mezzanine. Tried a *Shush* on them. Failed. As a librarian, I must master this spell.

Crossed paths with Diane on a nicotine break. She was on the patio, laughing hysterically. "Oh shit!" she repeated, falsetto. I sidled up to her and lit my cigarette. "What's so funny?" I stuttered. The words tumbled from my mouth like curdled milk. It was the oddest thing. Did I shush myself?

"Oh, nothing," said Diane.

I cleared my throat. "You," I began.

Diane gave me a sidelong glance. It seemed to promise something exciting and wonderful. She must purposefully time her breaks to coincide with my own. On this day our outfits matched perfectly: yellow pants and the exact same shade of burnt orange top. Except her top was a deep-vee'd blouse cinched in the middle with a floppy karate belt over lemon chiffon rayon slacks. Coincidence? Randy would suggest the witch was practicing some sort of sympathetic magic. To what end? As if she knew I was thinking about him, she said, "Tell me about that thing you do with Randy. With the three fingers." She attempted the gesture.

"You're doing the Boy Scouts sign," I said hoarsely. Surely Diane remembers the three-fingered hand from the hood of the Rambler. "It's just a private joke."

"A private joke you shared with Amber, a twelve-year-old girl, but not me?"

From the commencement ceremony on the quad came the sound of applause. "Yeah," I stammered.

"Oh, I see how it is," said Diane, in a hurt tone. But then she smiled that upside-down smile of hers. I took it to mean she was teasing. "By the way, Spunt's in the hospital. Appendicitis. There's a Hallmark card by the Mr. Coffee."

Uh, oh. That is Hazel's job, the Hallmark cards. For a temp worker on a special project, Diane has really insinuated herself into a position of—if not clout—a certain prominence.

After signing Spunt's card, I dawdled in the break room until Diane left so I could take some robins' eggs from a dish. "Those will rot your teeth," warned Doris in passing.

"Ugh," I spat. "Are these from this Easter or last?" The words were coming out a little more easily now. *Whew.* The Mr. Coffee machine slurped and hissed.

I returned some materials to the vertical file. I came across *Essentials of the Neurological Examination* and attempted a quick self-diagnosis. "The examiner should note if there are defects in the learned or cultural aspects of behavior." That is true of most of the people at Porteous. "Is the patient's clothing disarranged or food-stained?" Not that I am aware of. "Does he show eccentricities of dress, manner, or gesture?" On stage with the band, I do. "Is he cooperative?"

Was in the men's room again when someone barged in and said in menacing tones, "*Ph'nglui mglw'nafh Cthulhu R'lyeh wgah'nagl fhtagn.*" I froze. A second later, Randy's voice said, "It's me. I couldn't help myself."

"You bastard!" I cried.

Someone put a Mr. Yuk sticker on the display case in the vestibule. Tried to remove it with warm, soapy water, but a stubborn tacky residue remains. Carlos will know how to get it off.

A herd of parents and grandparents shuffled by, each clutching a sweat-soaked graduation program. "What does it mean?" said one, pointing at the Latin on the rafters. Just then, a horde of Kappa Mus streaked into the library, cocks in hand, chanting, "Shake the bottle!" One old lady shielded the eyes of a young, impressionable girl. Amber was not so lucky and saw everything.

"*A posse ad esse,*" I said cheerfully. "From being possible to being actual."

Tuesday, May 10

"The story of your life," it says in my diary, "will be most fascinating, intimate, and revealing. What a record of incidents, joys, sorrows, successes, failures, things attempted, things accomplished!" Turns out I have been using Sherwood's gift wrong. Mine is supposed to be a five-year diary. A page per day, each divided into fifths to accommodate each of the five years. I have been using whole pages. It means I will run out of space in one year, not five. One year is nothing.

James Jones has died. I made an impromptu memorial for him atop the card catalog, a stack of his books and criticism crowned with a Sons of the Republic of Texas coffee mug with a pencil in it that looks like a sunflower. A picture frame contained a Xeroxed obituary from the *Star-Telegram*. "X-roxed," as Dixie likes to say.

"Jones believed people are no different than animals," remarked Amber acidly. She was wearing a beaded Pocahontas headband with dyed swan feathers. "But he's terribly wrong."

"What sets man apart from animals is our detrimental ability to disregard our instincts," I said. "Otherwise, he's absolutely right. Sorry to disappoint you, kid."

Jo Ann was ill, so I was stuck at the information desk all morning with Amber. She took the good chair, so I got the lemon. While trying to adjust the height, it dumped me onto the floor. "Hey," I said. "I found a Dum-Dum."

"You don't know where that's been," she said.

"Some place worse than the floor?" I said. "It's wrapped."

Amber quizzed me on marine biology, which I know nothing about. When I repeatedly failed to correctly answer her questions, she suggested that Jo Ann was a "better librarian" than I. Ashamed to admit that got me slightly hot under the collar. "I'm a better speller," I countered fatuously.

"Okay," said Amber without missing a beat. "Spell *gewürztraminer*."

Fortunately, I got it. This shut her up. A student approached and asked what time we closed. "What day is it?" I replied, utterly confounded by this simple question. He said, "Monday," to which I responded, "Six." I then bade him "a gooden day." What the hell is "gooden"? Amber rolled her eyes. Before I knew what hit me, so to speak, she shot me in the center of the forehead with a sucker arrow. Mortally wounded, I slumped in my swivel chair, miraculously regaining consciousness when Dixie walked by. I yanked the arrow off with a soft *ploop!* A circular mark remained. For the rest of the day I told everyone it was my third-eye chakra.

I examined an issue of *A.C.L.A. Transactions on Aquarian Librarianship*. I then picked up a red pencil and ran my eye down the distribution list affixed to the cover with a paperclip. L.F.'s name was at the top, I noted. What on earth did he want to look at this boring rag for? Under his name were Dixie's, Jo Ann's, and my own. Typed neatly at the bottom were those of Diane and Amber. Next to mine I made a neat tick and tossed it into the wooden out tray. I shushed Amber preemptively. She knows I do not read any of this crap. I seriously doubt anyone else here does, either. Except Amber. She reads everything.

Two cops stood in the vestibule. They were speaking to Dixie. Employing evasive tactics, I hustled to the break room patio, really just a square of concrete by the back door.

"What's your deal?" said Randy. "What's on your forehead?"

"The fuzz," I whispered breathlessly. Lightning streaked across the sky.

"Relax," said Randy over the rolling thunder. "What are they here for?"

I made a small, hopeless gesture. "I'm not sticking around to find out." Randy wore an expression of bewilderment when I scrambled like a chimp up the wooded slope behind Church of the Nazarene. When I returned half an hour later, he was where I left him, opening a new pack of Marlboros.

"Following up on a report of a stolen gun," he said. "You were right to run."

"Son of a bitch! I knew it was a bad idea."

"They don't know anything. How could they?"

Was about to drive to Sherwood's and toss the gun into his well when I remembered the information desk. I found the Doom Hippie doing push-ups before a bemused Amber. She flashed me the sign of the three fingers. I carelessly reciprocated. "This gentleman has a question for you," she said. The so-called gentleman was wearing paisley bell bottoms, his taut, muscular chest bare beneath his customary fringed jacket.

"What can I do for you?" I said unctuously.

The Doom Hippie spat in the wastebasket. "Heard y'all have a book bound in human skin in the Vault," he said. "Is it true?" He stared at the curious mark on my forehead. What the hell? How in the world does the Doom Hippie know it is called the Vault? Only Randy and I call it that. Jenny must have overheard us and repeated it to the Doom Hippie. Pillow talk. But why, unless he brought up the subject himself?

"Of course not," said Amber. "Who would do such a horrid thing?"

"Anthropodermic bibliopegy," I said. "It's an uncommon historical practice."

"Practice?" said Amber dubiously. "More like anomaly. More prevalent in fiction than in real life, I should think."

"Well, surprise. We have one." I turned to the Doom Hippie. "Please wait while I retrieve it from, as you say, 'the Vault.'"

"What's the Vault?" said Amber as I rounded the corner to the elevator that would take me to the basement.

The door to the room I had heretofore considered my own private domain was wide open. Why even bother locking it anymore? I located the macabre object and brought it upstairs. I found the Doom Hippie whispering into Amber's ear. She giggled.

The Doom Hippie examined the skin-bound tome wide-eyed then took it to a nearby table. Once seated, he immediately began jiggling his leg and talking to himself. I found the constant movement and noise distracting. When he started mumbling, I tried a quick *Shush* spell. He looked up and glared at me, as if he knew exactly what I had just tried to do. The incident rattled me.

Amber observed us impatiently, oblivious to the subtext. "What about the white gloves?" she said. "Aren't you going to make him wear them?"

There were no gloves in the desk, so I had to go all the way back down to the Vault. Returned just in time to witness the Doom Hippie shove the book into his pants. With a leer of victory, he galloped for the exit.

I grabbed the walkie-talkie. Before I could say "Breaker 1-9," there was a ruckus in the vestibule. Boggs had the Doom Hippie bent over the display case. The punk's face was mashed against the Plexiglas, inches from an open page of the codex. If he only knew! The same two cops from this morning led the book thief away. He lunged toward me and spat, "You'll pay for this, Steven Miller!" In a sardonic tone, he then added, "Esquire!" Jenny must have given him one of my Hamcherry matchbooks. A word of power proved successful. The Doom Hippie howled in pain, the victim of *Invisible Wedgie*. He knew who sent it.

The commotion attracted staff and patrons alike, some of whom dawdled to gossip. Hey Now, who shouts when he is upset, happy, or afraid, shouted "Hey!"

"What I wouldn't give for a flamethrower right now," said Sarge. "That shit-bird's been nothing but trouble." He flexed his Extend-O hand irritably.

*More than you know*, I wanted to say. Everyone turned to look when lightning struck in the quad. Hopefully it hit the Doom Hippie. I glanced furtively at the shagreen-bound codex. It must be relocated.

One of the cops lingered for a statement from Boggs. As the latter departed, he scooped up a fistful of jawbreakers from a dish at the circulation desk. "My fee," he quipped. Boggs laughed heartily. "You have a great day, now!" bawled Boggs.

Made it to Pigg Auditorium for the book sale with twenty minutes to spare. I ambled down the aisles, examining the offerings upon each table. More tarot cards. Who keeps donating them? The *Satan's Scrapbook* from the hobbit room. Someone should have snagged that by now. Did see a few opera librettos I had to have as well as several Phase Four recordings of Stokowski, thanks to a dead music professor. One could write a book about the former's sonic wizardry. Evidently, Jo Ann and Amber had cleaned out the Vault pretty thoroughly.

A box on the ground caught my eye. It was full of serious items of an occult nature that could only be part of the Baumann Collection. Evidently it had escaped our attention until Jo Ann and Amber uncovered it.

"Hey, that's mine!" cried Turtle Man. He lunged for the box.

"Sorry," I said. "These things aren't for sale. They were placed here mistakenly."

Turtle Man threw a fit. We attracted Dixie's attention and I had to explain the whole thing to her. It was quite awkward. Of course, Dixie undermined my authority and let Turtle Man purchase a dozen items, some priceless, for the sum of one dollar each. I cannot imagine what his interest in an 18th-century German tome on the symbolism of fingers might be. What the hell is Dixie thinking?

Impromptu gig at the Knight Spot, a fern bar in the Green Oaks Inn. Sonny Side Up was warming up the clientele with an Al Jolson medley. The singer's pleasant, husky contralto and her accompanist's Oberheim SEM-1

Expander Module run through a ring modulator complimented the soft clink of china. I nudged Bonnie. "Check out that guy's gear. Is that a Freeman String Symphonizer?"

"Wow," said Bonnie.

Sonny Side Up had to leave early to play the wedding reception for the hotel manager's daughter. A noble excuse, I judged. By the time we took the stage, it felt improper to disturb the peaceful vibe with the violent power chords of "Rock 'n' Roll Insanity." But we did.

> *In the heart of the night, where darkness unfurls,*
> *There lies an energy that moves the worlds,*
> *A thunderous rhythm, a rebellious cry,*
> *In the realm of Rock 'n' Roll, insanity thrives!*

The vibrations from Dave II's drums toppled Sir Acorn, a mannequin in a suit of armor who shared the stage with us. I narrowly succeeded in keeping it from falling against the faux wattle and daub backdrop. Soon thereafter, we were asked to tone it down or pack it up. We chose the latter. "Horseshit," said Tim into a live mic. "I'm ready to get high and get laid. And I'm already high." He stormed off the stage, grabbing a handful of complimentary *hors d'oeuvres* from the buffet. I switched off the strobe light.

"I reject the theory that this gig was well-promoted," I observed as we loaded our gear into Tim's van. "What theory?" he said. "I taped fliers to the door of every room."

Wednesday, May 11

Observed Vee furtively from the kitchen window as she bent over her flowers. Could have joined her outside but I did not want to disturb her. Besides, I was content to just appreciate the view as she chattered and whistled "Dixie" to herself. Beauty and joy personified.

Dropped off one of my golden boots to Pablo for repair. We always take a few minutes to chat but today he only had harsh words for Videla's regime in Argentina. I let him talk.

"The censorship in the press," he said in his gentle, halting English. "The persecution of intellectuals. The raid on my uncle's house in Tigre. It is all too much."

Pablo speaks so softly. I often cannot understand him. You can only repeat "What?" so many times. On this day, he seemed sad, so I shook my head and frowned. My heart goes out to that guy and his family for enduring whatever it is they are enduring.

"What happened?" he said, gesturing to the puncture holes the thing in the tunnel made in my boot. The question caught me off guard.

"Lawn mower."

Pablo smiled warmly, then made a comment just below the threshold of hearing. I, too, smiled warmly.

Next stop, the courthouse for Professor Sherwood's death certificate. Had to wait over an hour to be told they had no records whatsoever of a James Marion Sherwood. If he had been born, died, or married in Tarrant County, I was assured, they would have had a record of it. L.F. lied. But why?

Lunch with Fred at Angelo's. I could not tell him what is going on. Everything that came out of my mouth felt like a bold-faced lie of omission. Even though I have known Randy longer, Fred is the one with whom I can make embarrassing confessions without judgment. Not even Randy knows I am a *virgo intacta*, as Randy would jokingly say. Nor does he know the truth about my relationship with Loretta. How it had been one of convenience at a time when I had to get away from Ron at home. How she preferred women over men and invited them into our bed. I got to watch her and her girlfriend Gabrielle get it on once but did not participate. It was not the thrill *Cosmo* would have you believe.

Fred was there when I got drunk for the first time. He introduced me to classical music. He and Bugs Bunny, that is. He turned me on to Eno and primitive art. He showed me how to get along with anyone regardless of their religion or politics. He showed me how to do a proper "Iron Claw." He taught me to be open minded. And here I am at my most open minded and I cannot even look him in the eye. Instead, I looked up at a big stuffed bear. Two kids were taking turns approaching it. Each time one of them got too close, it growled.

"What's eating you, kemosabe?" said Fred.

"Why is there sawdust all over the floor?" I said. I almost told him everything but then chickened out. With a discreet gesture, I made the bear take a swipe at one of the kids. They ran away, screaming. I could not help myself.

Fred walked to Omaha's Surplus to get a closer look at a howitzer out front. I waited by the Rambler like a party pooper. After dropping Fred back at the Novel Hovel, I returned to Collinwood in a pensive mood. Spotted a Mr. Yuk sticker stuck haphazardly on the rear bumper and peeled it off. How long has it been there? Am starting to believe the Doom Hippie is responsible for these. Has he marked me?

When not in the trunk of the Rambler, Carlos's Remington lives between my mattress and the wall. I take it almost everywhere with me as a precaution. After brushing my teeth and sprucing myself up, I headed upstairs for laundry at Vee's. Am beginning to look forward to these evenings, especially when Dawn joins us, as she did this time. After I innocently made Vee lose her place in *À la recherche du temps perdu* by removing her bookmark, we talked about Proust, Joan Crawford (who kicked the bucket yesterday), and Vee's upcoming trip to Rome.

"Are you sure you won't come with me?" said Vee flirtatiously. I take that back. She was not flirting. It is just the way she is. Before I could answer, the popcorn started popping. Everyone laughed at Figgy's short-lived astonishment. Vee offered him a piece. He bapped it around disinterestedly before grooming his butthole in front of all of us.

"Someday I would like to see the Rosetta Stone," I said. "Although I am happy enough to view a reproduction of it in a book."

"The Rosetta Stone's at the British Museum, not in Italia," said Dawn pedantically. I appreciated her mousy hair, the top of which is often disturbed. It looks like she has just come from a roll in the hay.

"Of course," I said. "I was just saying." I could have reminded her that in English we say "Italy" but I had suddenly become preoccupied. Talk of the Rosetta Stone got me thinking about the Sapir-Whorf hypothesis. There was a passage in the codex that made sense to me now and I needed to find it. I furtively searched for a pen and scrap of paper.

"What are you writing?" said Vee.

"Just a reminder to cash a check," I lied.

If Dawn seemed a little uptight, Vee did not, despite the Proust incident, about which she had every right to be irritated. Vee gave me a sack full of leftover popcorn. She then hugged me, crushing the bag between us. "My popcorn," I mumbled into her ear.

It was the Moody Blues on KPCD. *Are you sitting comfortably?/ Let Merlin cast his spell.* I was sitting comfortably, thank you. Though I had no intention of casting a spell, I located the passage I had been thinking of earlier. It is just as I thought. Solis's book is full of brilliant ideas, but his claim that words of power are "ancient and mysterious artifacts, derived from the language of the gods" is wrong. Many of them are, but I have seen them in the dictionary and even the Sunday morning Jumble. All you need is a command of phonetics, the mechanics of symbolism, and a basic knowledge of semantics and pragmatics. There is power in words, to be sure. But the rest comes from you. That is where the Sapir-Whorf hypothesis comes in. How the particular language one speaks influences the way one thinks about reality. Linguists have long disputed this claim, but they are applying it to everyday language and not magical languages such as Astarian or my own nascent Tarkusian, so-called in honor of Emerson, Lake and Palmer.

My mind was racing. I scribbled down as much as I could until my hand hurt. I set my pencil down. The Beam's Choice decanter gleamed on my bedside table. As much as I have fantasized about it, croaking the imp is out of the question. Keeping him bottled buys me time. Time for what? To find Sherwood? It remains to be seen how obedient he will be. What can I compel him to do? What is within his power? A chapter of *Beyond Good and Evil* offered some clarity. It also provided a wraith of insight into Diane.

Thursday, May 12

To the library early. From the display case in the Lysol-scented vestibule, I removed the original codex. Sherwood must have consulted the codex repeatedly, surely resulting in a crease, a smear, or some discoloration. I inspected its pages carefully at my desk but could detect no such marks. I gripped the tome by its covers and let it hang loosely. Toward the end of the book the pages separated noticeably. I opened it to this spot and examined the text. It was one of several "door" formulae—one I had yet to consider. A so-called aqua spell, like the others. Aqua, as in the color, not pertaining to water. The spells in the codex are organized by level of sophistication, indicated by color. At first, I did not understand what they meant. Sherwood's notes clarified the matter somewhat but for me the colors remain little more than a handy classification tool. At the bottom of the page was written in Sherwood's lovely cursive with crossed sevens, "Durch. 227-237."

For the codex's new hiding place, I chose the medicine cabinet in the staff bathroom. It should be safe there until a better spot suggests itself. In its place under the Plexiglas, I set one of Hogg's ostentatiously-bound sermons.

Before the meeting commenced, we chatted about the Colonial (or the others did, as I know zilch about golf), the price of coffee, and the Tandy subway. "You won't catch me on it," said Hazel. "All those flashers and chain snatchers." She reached for a donut. "Oh, I do love donuts. And bagels. In fact, I'll eat anything round with a hole in it."

"That's what she said," I mouthed to Diane. She stifled laughter. When I turned back around, Hazel was glaring at me hatefully. Guess she can read lips.

Thankfully the innuendo sailed high above Amber's head. "How do you think they got this huge table through the door?" she said innocently.

There was a knock. A woman's face appeared in the doorway. "Amber, your mother is here," said Hazel. Amber looked disappointed, no doubt because she could no longer play librarian. I thought her mother looked familiar.

Today's meeting agenda:

    Microform reader update
    New electric typewriters

New telex machine
A.C.L.A. conference report
Library Expo '77
New signage
Book sale
The book thief (a.k.a. the Doom Hippie)
Misshelved books problem
Card catalog prankster
Mr. Yuk stickers
Loud music in the library
Varmint control
Stolen firearm
Personal telephone calls
Display & exhibits policy
New duck & cover protocols
Suggestion box
All-staff campus retreat
Conservator position eliminated.

The meeting adjourned. Dixie motioned for me to remain seated. What now?

"You're losing your office," she said with a thin smile. "You will take the desk opposite Edith."

I emitted a low groan. "Can I keep my old desk?"

"Moving furniture around willy-nilly is against Porteous policy," said Dixie. "And didn't your desk used to be beige?"

"No," I said. "And who said anything about willy-nilly?"

I made a beeline for Randy's office. It was devoid of his personal belongings. Several books lay in varying states of repair. A scrap on the blotter bore in Randy's hand numerous palindromes in Dordic: "*Kapra nar pak*," etc. A surprising lapse of discretion, to leave that behind. I balled it up and put it in my pocket.

"Boggs escorted him from the building about an hour ago," said Hazel. That hedgehog sounded like she could barely conceal her joy.

"Thanks," I said. "Have you seen Guddu this morning?"

"Who?"

Spunt has bequeathed his appendix to the shenanigans dish. We were standing around admiring this supreme act of balls-out one-upmanship when Sarge rolled up. "What are you queers up to?" he said. "If you had listened to me, you'd all be lean, mean fighting machines by now."

I showed him the shenanigans dish. "But this is a library," I said.

"Get that thing away from me," growled Sarge. "Got a joke for you. So there's this crusty old brigadier general and he's really uptight, see? One night he's at a military ball and this beautiful young lady approaches him and says 'General, you look so tense. When's the last time you got your pipes cleaned?'" Sarge tapped me on the arm as if the joke applied especially to me. How would he know how long it has been since I have had my pipes cleaned?

"So the brigadier general says, 'I haven't screwed since 1950.' The lady says, '1950? That's so long ago. Come with me and I'll help you loosen up.' So she takes the crusty old brigadier general to the broom closet and he socks it to her real good. I mean, she's wailing Jesus's name and carrying on. She's seeing stars. You with me?"

Everyone nodded.

"When he's finished with her, she says, 'Wow! You haven't forgotten anything since 1950, huh?' The crusty old brigadier general replies, "I sure hope not. It's only 2130 now.'"

Monty laughed the loudest. "You're a riot, Sarge! You should do stand-up comedy."

"You are fucked up like a soup sandwich," said Sarge. "Drop and give me twenty!"

Monty got on his hands and knees.

Sarge regarded him with disgust. "At ease, maggot."

"C'mon, Sarge," begged Jenny. "Don't you have anything for the shenanigans dish?"

Sarge scoffed, then looked over both shoulders. "Thought I heard the brass coming," he said. When Jenny plaintively tugged his sleeve, he produced a cigarette butt from his pocket and placed it in the dish. It is hard to resist the Stone Fox when she does her puppy dog act. It is maddening that Jenny exposes her playful side to everyone but me. Just now, however, she seemed a bit too playful. Like she was on a Pez high or something.

"Say 'shenanigans,'" she said.

"Shenanigans!" roared Sarge, pounding his fist on his wheelchair's armrest before wheeling into the stacks.

"The shenanigans will continue until morale improves," I said in a Nazi accent. "Any of y'all seen Guddu?"

"Who's Guddu?" said Monty.

"What's Guddu?" said Spunt with unintentional prescience. He leaned in close. "*Psst.* Ever had a barium enema? They gave me one at the hospital. Highly recommended."

"I don't understand. Are you offering me one?"

"Almost forgot," said Spunt. He retreated into the workroom then returned with a t-shirt that had "Try It, You'll Like It" silkscreened on it. "My latest masterpiece. If you want any more, just bring me a blank tee." I refrained from asking him what it meant. I could only regret doing so.

As I returned to the information desk, Spunt yelled "Score!" It is a game, started by Spunt I suppose, whereby you touch someone's teeth whenever they smile or open their mouth. It has been going on for weeks. Spunt must have touched Jenny's teeth because she was laughing uproariously. She will laugh at Sarge's jokes and Spunt's childish games but I cannot get her to even smile. I have not even touched her teeth yet.

Changed into my "Try It, You'll Like It" t-shirt then headed to the Eagle's Nest. Randy was at the bar nursing a drink. "I'll have what he's having," I said to Jackie quietly.

"Haven't seen your buddy lately," said Jackie. "The bookworm."

"The professor? He's traveling." That much is presumably true, unless he is dead. Jackie has seen me reading piles of books at the bar many times, yet Sherwood is the one she rates "bookworm." Of course she is right.

Randy was clearly a few sheets to the wind already. We sat in silence as "Break on Through" throbbed from the jukebox.

"If the doors of perception were cleansed everything would appear to man as it is—infinite," said Randy. "True or false?"

"You seem pretty stoic for someone who was just fired."

"We've closed our minds. We see things through narrow chinks of our cavern."

What cavern? I did not know what Randy was talking about. "Did Dixie give you a reason?"

"Budgetary," said Randy. "Enrollment is down the sixth year in a row. Stagflation, dot dot dot. Horseshit. She simply repeated what Diane told her."

"Diane? Why do you say that? I suspect Dixie's motives, although this move reeks of incompetence more than anything else."

"Or malevolence."

"Dixie's far too occupied with herself to be malicious," I said. "Besides, incompetence sometimes appears as malevolence."

"This time it is," Randy insisted. "I'm positive."

Jackie deftly slid my drink along the counter. "Ugh!" I croaked. "Metaxa?"

"Hippocrates's grand elixir," said Randy. He cracked open a pecan. "Headed to California tomorrow. Staying with an uncle until I get settled. Staying somewhere, anyway."

"Dang, Randy. Do you have to go?"

"How am I supposed to pay rent? I can stay if you want to support me."

"Can't even pay off Southwestern Bell," I said. "I mean, I probably could but I don't want to. Besides, I've lived so long without a telephone that I'm used to it."

"Give me a ride to Grand Prairie in the morning?" said Randy. "I'm delivering a brand-new garbage truck to a company in Bakersfield. Gas, chow, and lodging are *gratis*. The catch is that I have to leave before sunrise. The delivery is already late."

"Gaw, Randy! When did you arrange all this?"

"Spunt caught up with me at the bus stop. His dad is the regional manager for the Metroplex." Randy's story sounded implausible but not impossible. Meaningful conversation is challenging with Spunt. But he would be the exact person to appear out of nowhere with a serendipitous garbage truck offer if there ever were such a person. I suppose I could ask him about it.

"Take care of my bettas?"

"Of course," I said. "What about all your stuff?"

"Sell what you can. Keep half the proceeds for yourself and wire the rest."

Once Randy makes a decision he will not be swayed. Our conversation devolved into small talk about the aerosol ban, the greatest guitar solos in the world, and whether the F-16 should be equipped with all-weather Sparrows. It was hard to concentrate, though, with Randy hitting me with all this at once. I held up three fingers to Jackie.

"Lip Service" issued from the jukebox. Steppenwolf's pathetic attempt to cash in on the disco craze. They must be having an identity crisis. The whole world is, evidently.

"You know, Diane is taking inventory of the Baumann artifacts, which is not what she was hired to do. It's highly suspicious. Or wouldn't you say? I must find out what she knows." I mentioned it only to make conversation but I now regretted it.

"Just ask her," said Randy.

"As if she would just tell me," I said. "If I could only get into her quarters."

"Are you sure you want to mess with her?"

"Aren't you curious? You should be breaking into her place with me. I thought we were in this together." The tone in my voice betrayed my hurt feelings at Randy's apparent desertion. This time it feels personal.

"In what together?" It sounded like one of his trick questions.

"You know," I said vaguely. "All of this."

Randy regarded me searchingly before continuing. "I can't stay here. I have my reasons. Sorry, dude." To the end of this statement, he added a full stop by way of downing the rest of his drink, then belching a few notes of "Capriccio on the Departure of His Beloved Brother."

"What am I going to do about Harvey?"

"In British folklore, if you name a boggart he becomes unruly."

In the corner, two old black cats were slamming dominoes onto a folding card table and swearing. We turned to look at them.

"The codex is missing from the display case," said Randy. "Where is it?"

*Ah ha*, the real question on his mind. "Hidden," I said. "By the way, do you know Amber's mother?"

"Gabrielle Nunn?" said Randy. "She's in the Women's Studies department. She's Dixie's daughter-in-law. Or ex-daughter-in-law, I should say. A real piece of work."

Randy and I wordlessly migrated toward the pool table. We called our shots into being. Instead of "eight ball, corner pocket," we would say shit like, "Kelso Fats will now attempt his famous Three-Fingered Filibuster" or "The Space Cowboy's going in for the kill with a Triple Dipple Ball Tickler."

"Try it, you'll like it," Randy sneered after sinking a double bank shot.

His leaving made me feel maudlin. The Metaxa did not help. While his news was unexpected, it is ultimately not surprising. After dropping Randy off at home, I realized I had missed rehearsal. I rolled up to find "Tim's Bolero" echoing throughout the wastelands surrounding the Mixmaster.

"Sorry I'm late!" I said as I rushed to plug in. No one stopped playing to acknowledge me. I simply joined in, pausing at intervals to tune up.

Tim put down his guitar. "I'm going to get tacos." Dave II went with him. Bonnie and I went outside to smoke. She shared with me a *Fortnite Weekly* review of our single.

*The A-side, "Journey to Dord," is a short trip on a long pier, the work of a band who has never heard of the Ramones, who make the same journey but faster and smarter. The B-side, "Hail Marys," had me making the sign of the cross and I'm not even Catholic. Bonnie Baxter's organ blams, and her repetitious furbelows test one's patience. Stephen Miller's bass sounds like if Chuck Barris were a bass. Somebody gong that sweathog! Tim Watson's self-indulgent arpeggios offer a specious argument for a return to quadrupedalism. What do you expect from a record that's not even round? Only the drummer, Dave McDermott, walks upright. C+.*

I flicked my butt into the street. "They misspelled my name."

"That's all you have to say?"

"They don't erect statues of critics," I said dismissively.

Tim and Dave II returned with a hundred tacos. "Ten for a buck!" said Tim.

We each ate three or four. When Tim threw one playfully at Bonnie, a full-scale taco war ensued. The shells are sharper than you would think. Tim and I both ended up with bloodied cheeks. Bonnie stopped everything so we could sweep up the considerable mess.

"Which songs rock?" asked Dave II.

We put our set list under the microscope. "Which songs offer a specious argument for a return to quadrupedalism?" I said.

"Return to this," said Tim, grabbing his crotch.

We selected twelve tunes from our arsenal. For when the management wants us to keep playing, we chose several covers. I suggested "Freedom's Inside Your Head" from a Moody Blues boot, but no one else knew it. "You and your Moodies!" teased Bonnie, though the sappy "Nights in White Satin" is okay in her book.

> "Subways of Your Mind"
> "Now You Know" (omitted in shorter sets)
> "Major Kong Overture" (omitted in shorter sets)
> "X Marks the Spot"
> "The Eagle Has Landed"
> "Up Your Hose (with a Rubber Nose)"
> "Rock 'n' Roll Insanity"
> "A Perfect Circle"
> "Hail Marys" (fast or slow, depending on audience vibes)
> "Psyche!/Prog Paradigm/Variations on a Theme by Ives" (medley)
> "Journey to Dord"
> "Andromeda Suite" (incl. "Tim's Bolero")

We figured it would be clever to each exit the stage after our Andromeda solos. Tim would return for some acoustic improv before segueing into "Lucky Man" on which I join in toward the end. For the encore:

> "Lucky Man" (insane Moog coda by yours truly)
> "Weeping Willow"
> "Astronomy"
> "Magic Man" (Bonnie on vox!)
> "Earth Hymn, Pts. 1 & 2"
> "Guitar Suite" (all hail Space Opera!)
> "Tush" (interpolating "Chaconne in D")
> "Es wollt ein Jäger jagen" (arr. Randy)

Studied the road atlas in bed, anticipating our route. Am excited to take a road trip but also filled with dread at the prospect of not getting to our gigs on time, and of failing on a technical or artistic level. Suppose I will have to take the imp with me. Wondered if he could make me a better bass player. If only there were a Geddy Lee spell. What would that be called? *"B" for Bass?* When I switched off the lamp, I could hear the DDT kid across the street, waving his flipper at passing cars and moaning hello. At this hour?

FRIDAY, MAY 13

Yesterday was so crappy, I wondered what Friday the 13th could possibly hold in store. Superstition is not my bag. Nor do ladders or black cats worry me. It is hard enough separating fact from fiction. UFOs? A profitless speculation. Bigfoot? Please. Demons? No comment. I ruefully regarded my new "Try It, You'll Like It" shirt, already ruined from taco shrapnel. But that is the consequence of Thursday the 12th shenanigans.

It was still dark when Randy and I passed Mrs. Baird's. "Smell that bread," I said.

"Hey," said Randy. "Remember when we took apart the Howdy King's Ford Falcon and reassembled it in the gymnasium?"

"You, Hot Wilcox, and Johnny Flournoy did. I helped carry parts."

"Crazy times."

"Yeah," I said. "Remember when we took those inner tubes and floated down the Trinity all day until we ended up in the Bottoms?"

"Where they always find dead bodies? I considered that when we went looking for the tunnel monster."

This stroll along Memory Lane had a whiff of finality to it. As if this was the last time Randy and I would ever see each other. I had thought the same thing when he left for Fort Lewis. But he came back. A completely different person, but he came back.

The sun was just beginning to peek over the line of shiny new garbage trucks. "Good grief," I said. "Do you know how to drive one of those?" Hung around for a bit waiting for a guy to show Randy which truck and sign over the keys. We smoked and stared at our watches. The guy finally arrived in a souped-up Road Runner, sliding to a sideways halt in the gravel. Randy accidentally flicked ash in my face. "Shit. I'm sorry, dude."

"One duffel bag, two cardboard boxes, and a sleeping bag," I noted. "No futon?"

"Too bulky," said Randy. "It's yours if you want it."

"This is all you're taking with you?"

"Possessions are diminished by possession. Not what we have but what we enjoy constitutes our abundance." Randy produced a skillet. "And this."

"The holy skillet," I said. "The one Julia Child sauteed onions in at your house that one time."

"That evening was alright," said Randy.

We hugged awkwardly with one arm.

"You bastard," I said.


Spent the morning moving to my new desk. It is old and wooden. That it is actually better than my last one provides some small consolation. Had I known I would be moving, however, I would not have spent so much time scraping the beige paint off my last desk. There was no place to put my Sherlock Holmes throne, so I wrestled it down to the Vault, along with the Bilby and my record player. Room 108 is shaping up to be a real bachelor's den. There are no bookcases near my new desk, so I do not know where Dixie expects me to put all the stuff I am working on. For now, I just made a huge pile.

Policy expressly forbids nails and tacks. Hazel recommended that I use a special adhesive putty to hang my failed National Library Week poster in my office but it left gummy, blue residue on the wood paneling. Carlos picked at it and said, "*Es de la chingada.*"

The queue snaked through the business school cafeteria. That is what I get for going to lunch at noon. Gobbled down my barbecue on a bun at a dirty table. Was just about to book it back to the library when Boggs sidled up to me. "My main man!" he said. "Hope I am not disturbing your meal."

"Of course you aren't."

"I'd like to ask you a question." Boggs cast a glance around the dining hall and leaned in close. I noticed his hair was turning prematurely gray. Unless he is much older than I thought. "Did you solve that problem of yours?"

"I did." Boggs's countenance suggested he knew as much.

"Good," he said. "I'm glad." As I rose to leave, he added, "Are you going to finish that meat?"

"We only get a half-hour for lunch," I said. "Have the rest."

Boggs shook his head. "Thirty minutes? That's not civilized. He began eating. "By the way. Mr. Burnside said he might transfer me."

"L.F. wants to transfer you?" I said. "To where?"

Boggs grinned from ear to ear. "Women's gymnasium."

"Moving on up! I can think of much worse fates, Boggs."


Spunt approached me while I was organizing my desk. "Do you party?" he said. I was dying to know what he and the Bastard talked about. I heaved a weary sigh. "You know I do, Spunt."

Spunt indicated the toothpick jostling in my mouth. He then produced a match and placed it in his own mouth. "Match is a lot cooler."

"Only if it's lit." Did Randy really confide in this freak?

"There is someone here to see you," said Hazel crossly.

I found Tim spinning the globe rather excessively. "Hey man, wait for me outside," I said. "I told you I don't get off until two."

"It's quieter than shit in here," thundered Tim.

"Don't make me shush you."

"I had to shush your mom last night."

Diane approached us. "Hey, Tim!" she said familiarly, even though she barely knows him. "What are you doing here?"

"We're going on a mini-tour," said Tim, providing pantomimed guitar for emphasis. "Tulsa, Shreveport, Port Aransas."

"The Big Three," I said facetiously.

"Where is Port Aransas?"

"Gulf coast," I said.

"Fun! Can I go with you guys? I really miss the ocean."

"Gas, grass, or ass," quipped Tim. Diane emitted a labial consonant. "Seriously, there's no room in the van."

*Keep your enemies closer.* Enemy or not, this was a chance to get to know Diane better. I doubted she had anything to do with Randy's dismissal. What would her motivation be? "She doesn't have any gear, though," I said. "It's not a big deal, Tim."

"If I had known we could bring our girlfriends, I would have brought mine."

"You have a girlfriend?" I said. "Besides, Diane's not my girlfriend."

Diane leaned forward and whispered something into Tim's ear. His eyes opened wide. "It's up to Bonnie," he said.

"Let me go back to the Fac and pack a bag," said Diane. "Oh! That kind of rhymed. I'll be waiting by the fountain. If you don't show up after ten minutes, I'll know I'm not wanted."

Never heard it called "the Fac" before. The only time I ever hear that word is when Vee and Dawn talk about their Sorbonne days.

Went into the staff bathroom to change into my driving duds. I found the others gathered outside. Boggs was lecturing Tim and Bonnie. "The library receives deliveries around back," he said. "Or, you can park in Lot D. But you cannot park your good times van on the sidewalk."

"Sorry, Boggs!" I said. "We're leaving."

"Do It In A Van," instructed the bumper sticker. I peered into the shag carpeted interior. It was crammed with gear. *Tim's done it in here*, I noted with disgust. The band took a vote to determine if Diane should tag along. Dave II was so enthusiastic that I wondered how and when the witch had gotten to him. A previous gig? I have witnessed at the library how she has a knack for getting her way. She even has some sway over the extraordinarily obstinate Dixie.

Dave II considered my cut-off sweatpants and said, "What on earth are you wearing? You look like Ben Gunn."

Bonnie smoothed out a map on the dash.

"Check out the highways that circle the Metroplex," I said, tracing my finger around the map. "They make the outline of a dick. See, Loop 820's the head."

"I see it!" said Bonnie. "And Dallas is the balls."

"'Dallas,'" I enunciated. "The Scrotum of Texas."

"You should pitch that to the Chamber of Commerce," said Dave II. "Sweet CB, by the way." He leaned forward for a closer look. "What's the harmonic suppression on that baby?"

"Twenty-five dB," boasted Tim. "It was fifty out of the box but I modified it."

"Why is there an exercise bike strapped to the roof?" It taxed credulity that Tim would allow such a thing.

"A girl's gotta maintain her figure" said Bonnie. Her bike was more sophisticated than Sherwood's. It had two gauges, which I assumed were a speedometer and tachometer.

"It better not scratch the paint," grumbled Tim.

Rather than direct Tim around the perimeter of campus to the Fac, we careened across the quad, nearly mowing down a couple of students playing chess. If Boggs complains, I will tell him Tim got lost.

Diane waved at us with her floppy, wide-brimmed hat. Her uncharacteristically colorful backless dress featured a plunging neckline fastened together by three brass rings. She squeezed between Dave II and me. "Your hat," I said, brushing it out of my face.

"Oops, sorry!" Diane produced a Tupperware container. "I made cookies," she announced.

"You made those just now?" I said. Or did she materialize them from thin air? There is no way I am going to eat a poisoned cookie a witch made.

"Last night, silly."

Bonnie's duties as navigatrix included finding acceptable radio stations. In due course we were all rocking out to Neil Diamond. "And no one heard at all, not even the chair!" we all screamed.

"What time do we go on tonight?" I asked.

"Eight," said Bonnie. "So you had better haul ass, Tim."

"Amarillo by mornin'," sang Tim.

"That's not on the way to Tulsa," I said pedantically.

Our route to the freeway took us past our rehearsal space. We stopped so Tim could get his wah-wah. He chucked it to Dave II. "It's gone flaccid on me."

"That's what she said," I said.

"Who? Your mom?"

Dave II examined the pedal. "The tensioner on the rack gear needs tightening."

Diane leaned in close to the Mormon drummer. "What's that?" she said. He fell under her spell. "This toothed gear rack rotates the gear on the pot when you move the treadle with your foot," he said animatedly. "Loosen the screw, push the tensioner against the rack gear and tighten it. It's also how you adjust the tone sweep."

"But what does it *do*?" said Diane.

Tim began howling wah-wah sounds like a deranged monkey. Dave II just grinned.

Once we were on the open road, Tim put the hammer down, making frequent lane changes and tailgating everyone. When I made a small gesture of protest, Tim said, "Offensive driving is defensive driving." We found ourselves side-by-side with a Taystee Bread big rig. Bonnie pumped her arm at the driver. He blasted his horn, much to our delight.

"A Kenilworth," I observed, referring to the truck's make.

"*Kenworth*, you ignorant slut," said Tim.

"Guess I was thinking of Sir Walter Scott." Should just keep my trap shut around Tim, who always has to correct people. He reminds me of Randy that way, except Randy is usually right, unlike Tim.

Dave II napped and did not awaken until Thackerville. "Are we still in DQ country?" he said.

"Yes, they have Dairy Queens here," said Bonnie.

"They have them in Southern California, too," said Diane. She does not seem like a California girl.

We chatted intermittently throughout the afternoon about triskaidekaphobia, the SST, and Texas Dolly's prowess at poker. We played a game called Categories. Each person takes turns declaring a category. Everyone responds with an example. If you miss you are out. Bonnie commenced with "Songs about Thursday," then offered the Jim Croce tune. Dave II and Tim submitted songs by Nilsson and the Strawbs, respectively. Mine was "Thursday" by Country Joe. Diane puzzled over the question, but then said, "In the tiny piece of colored glass my love was born."

"Donovan, right?" I did not need to be reminded of Shagduk in his colored glass prison under my seat.

Tim went next with "Bond Girls." Naturally, he chose Pussy Galore. Bonnie said, "Tatiana Romanova." Dave II said, "Vesper Lynd." I guessed "Honey Ryder." Diane said "Lisl Baum."

"Which show was she in?" said Dave II.

"I thought we were talking about books," said Diane.

I figured Dave II was going to stump us with Mormon mumbo jumbo. Instead, he chose "Moons of the Solar System," offering Io. Tim blurted "the moon." Bonnie said, "Deimos." I knew "Titan" on account of Pioneer 11.

"Miranda," said Diane.

"Who was raped by Caliban," said Dave II.

"It wasn't rape."

"Cows!" cried Bonnie. I thought that was the next category until I saw them.

Someone suggested the license plate game, but we gave up after about fifty miles. Everyone had Oklahoma plates.

At last, we found ourselves approaching civilization. "Wow. Is that Tulsa?" I said.

"Those be silos, retard," said Tim.

The Aztec Club was a squalid hotel lounge off the interstate. A rather moribund establishment that could not possibly be profitable. "Bar Cocktails, Dancing Sandwiches," said Dave II. "I could go for a dancing sandwich."

We parked and started unloading. Bonnie went in to announce our arrival. The windowless interior was dark and narrow, with a bar along one side and a billiard table in back. The beer was served warm in bottles by an affable bartender called Romeo. "Sorry, tap's on the fritz. Just brought these in from the shed."

"It's how they quaff it in England," said Dave II.

After unloading our gear, there was a lull during which everyone seemed to wander off. Romeo broke a five for me so I could call Jenny. I hung up when Mama Fox answered. I do not want to encourage her.

"Where's the stage?" said Tim.

Bonnie pointed at a worn rectangle of masking tape near the entrance. A tack piano occupied it. Tim tickled a couple of ivories. "What's better than roses on your piano?" he said.

"I don't know," said Bonnie.

"Tulips on your organ."

Dave II opened the lid and peered inside. He plonked out a bit of schmaltz. "Recognize it?"

"Should we?" I said.

"Nixon. Renaissance man. Scholar and poet. And he's got a piano concerto under his belt."

"Milhous?"

To fit into the tiny rectangle, we pushed the piano up front and put Bonnie's Minimoog on top of it. Dave II left his floor toms in the van. Tim and I stacked our amps on top of each other. As a band, we were now taller than we were wide.

Bonnie started cursing. "The mellotron's fragile, so I only brought the Minimoog. But I can't get it to function."

The formidable panel of knobs mocked one. "Did you turn it off then back on?" suggested Tim. Bonnie's eyes flickered.

"What about the piano?"

"Are you serious, Steven?"

"Well, it's either that, or nothing."

Bonnie dropped her cigarette and stamped it out. She experimented with mic placement, then said, "Hang on. This piano is a half-step flat." She played around for a minute, transposing the key. "It's more or less in tune with itself, just not with y'all. I'll figure it out." Bonnie's musical prowess is greater than she gives herself credit for.

Tim started pickin' and grinnin' Buck Owens-style. Dave II followed suit. I joined in the best I could in a style unprecedented.

"Screw it," said Tim. "Let's just play everything like this tonight. There's no one in here, anyway."

We all turned to Bonnie, who simply shrugged. Her defeated attitude was fully justified, I thought.

"Hello, Tulsa!" announced Tim. "We're Time Frame from Fort Worth! Y'all ready to whap a dang?" Tim made his guitar neigh like a horse.

"Rock 'n' Roll Insanity" sounded more like "Turkey in the Straw." Our brand of progressive rock was unsurprisingly ill-suited for whatever we were doing. Particularly the passages with odd time signatures, which we stumbled through or simply reduced to a turbocharged waltz. Remember Jeane Dixon's prediction that a modernized version of the waltz would be the big dance craze of '77? No one was dancing at the moment. During a particularly fried cowshit bass flourish, Tim gestured to me and announced, "Lady and gentleman, the Space Cowboy." When Randy calls me the "Space Cowboy" it does not bother me. When Tim does it, it gets on my nerves.

"Yee haw!" I yelled fatuously. My outburst was met with facetious finger pistols from Romeo. Diane cackled. Usually, her cackles are phony but this one seemed sincere. Despite sweating like a cartoon, I was having a blast. It recalled those summer afternoons on the porch with Randy, improvising interminable blues jams with ridiculous, inept solos. Tim sang with an exaggerated drawl which sounded oddly convincing. And where did he get that cowboy hat? The highlight of the set was when Tim broke a string during "Now You Know." He replaced it while still singing, then played a blistering solo in perfect tune. Effortless, B.B. King-level wizardry right there. Until he stepped outside the rectangle of tape and the string broke again.

I groped for my gig bag. A group of men on a stag weekend surged through the door. You could tell which one the bachelor was by his Flintstones-style water buffalo hat. He grabbed Tim's dead mic and squawked "Encore!" into it. "Ten bucks if you play 'Mustang Sally.'"

"We're a prog band," said Tim. "We'd butcher it."

"Twenty."

Tim plugged back in and began playing. The others reluctantly joined in. We turned it into an eleven-minute country prog odyssey that the groom's buddies ate up. They ponied up more money for us to similarly butcher "Louie Louie" and "Surfin' Bird." In this manner we made an extra sixty dollars.

"Romeo wants to pay us in coke," said Bonnie. "Is that alright?"

"You can have mine," I said.

We began packing up.

"Steven!" said a familiar voice. It was the Stone Fox's sister. She hugged my neck, then grabbed her companion's arm and said, "This is Troy." Troy shook my hand limply.

"How did you know we were here?" I said incredulously.

"Jen told me you were on tour. Said you'd be in Tulsa on Friday the 13th. Tulsa's a small town. There are only a few places you could possibly be playing, so here we are!"

"But why are you in Tulsa?"

"I'm visiting my dad," she said. "I'm from here."

"Is Jenny from here?"

"She's my step-sister. Same mom, different dads. What's your twenty, good buddy?"

"No telling."

"Stay at our house!" pleaded Shannon. "We have plenty of room."

"Okay, but we've all got to eat. All I've had since breakfast were Cheddar Taters." At the mention of food, Tim and Dave II gathered around us.

"Do you like Chinese food? Follow us!"

Tim almost lost them when Troy's Impala blew through a yellow light and he had to floor it. Dave II produced a flask. "Rumple Minze," he intoned.

"Fond memories," I said.

"My Rumple Minze memories are ones I fondly do not remember," said Tim. "If I did remember them, I'd never forget them."

We caught up with Shannon and Troy in the foyer of the Ricsha. "This place has terrific *lung harr gai kew*," said Shannon.

The waitress provided menus and lit our candle. I appreciated the imported hanging lanterns, silk screens, and fishnets. "I could live here," I said to no one.

During the meal, Tim and Dave II giggled and whispered to each other. They were hitting the sauce hard. At one point, someone's elbow came down hard on a plate, catapulting a sizzling hot noodle onto my forearm. "I've got a boner for these," said Tim, skewering a *won ton* with a chopstick.

"Don't stab it like that," cried Shannon. "To the Chinese it symbolizes death."

"*Ching chong ching chang chung*," said Tim, chewing with his mouth open. He whacked my arm. "You speak Chinese," said Tim. "Say something."

"Excuse me," I said in Mandarin to the passing waitress. "May I have another glass of ice water." She looked at me with fear in her eyes and scurried away.

"What are you doing?" said Shannon. "These people speak Cantonese, not Mandarin."

"Feet up." It was the waitress with a mop. We were suddenly the only diners left in the restaurant. The owner appeared. "You go now, round eyes!"

"I'm sorry," mouthed Shannon to the waitress as we filed out of the restaurant. On the way out I swapped a fortune cookie from a bowl.

"Let's see the Golden Driller," said Shannon.

The Golden Driller turned out to be a statue of a giant golden guy standing next to an oil derrick. His golden boots were a hundred sizes larger than my own. That he could leap over skyscrapers in them there was no doubt. Tim rubbed his palms together. "Drilling for gold nuggets!" he said lasciviously.

"*Liquid* gold, genius," I muttered.

"I am two seconds away from slapping you in the face," snapped Shannon. She and Troy must have argued on the way. The tension between them was felt among the whole group. It was like watching me and Loretta once upon a time.

"Troy has a headache," said Shannon. "Can I ride with you back to my house?"

The put-upon boyfriend gave a wave of exasperation. After Shannon dodged his peck on the cheek, Troy sped off in his Impala.

Shannon lives in a charming bungalow. Its manicured lawn stood in stark contrast to the adjacent property. The latter was divided by a sagging badminton net and a hot rod on blocks, its patchy grass littered with Dixie cups, beer cans, and neglected children's toys.

Unbeknownst to Shannon, her little step-brother Rodney was home. "But you said you were going to stay at your friend's!" said Shannon.

"We decided to stay here, instead," said Rodney. "What's the big deal?"

"Well, that's just great. Where are my guests supposed to sleep?"

"They can sleep in my room," said Rodney. "Harg and I can sleep outside on the trampoline. We're just going to play D&D all night, anyway."

"Harg?" I said. "That's an unusual name. Where's he from?"

"The City Afar," said Rodney. "I'm Yendor of Siluria."

"Oh, I get it," I said. "Like the books. That's cool."

It was decided that Bonnie and Diane would share Shannon's double bed. Tim and Dave II would share Yendor's bunk bed. I would sleep on the floor. "Rodney, go get your sleeping bag for Steven."

"I'm not Rodney. I'm Yendor."

Tim and Dave II fought over the top bunk. I returned to the kitchen for a glass of water. Shannon's fridge had one of those dispensers from which you could get ice cubes and cold water.

Join me for a smoke?" asked Shannon. She brought a box of ice cream. We perched on a low wall and lit up. For several minutes we listened to the music of the frogs. We then chatted about the neighborhood, the tour, and finally, Jenny.

"How are she and that scumbag piece of shit doing?" I blurted, surprising myself with my rancor.

The freckled teenager regarded me with pity. "His name is Judd and he's really nice." Guess Shannon and Jenny do not talk. She offered me a bite of Neapolitan. Without thinking, I opened wide like Shannon was my servant. She somewhat reluctantly fed it to me. Why did I do that?

Shannon scooped out the very last dregs before turning the carton inside-out and licking it. This, I watched in admiration and disgust. "Waste not, want not," said Shannon. Was she talking about the ice cream or Jenny?

After washing my face, I felt my way along the dank passageway. Yendor of Siluria's chambers were stuffy and smelled like a boys' locker room. Wished I had not forgotten my fan in the van. Tim and Dave II were already sawing logs. I quietly undressed. I then fussed with the sleeping bag's zipper before giving up. The Scooby Doo bag came up to my ribcage. It was evidently a child's bag, made for someone the size of Shagduk.

Shagduk!

I had not checked on him since this morning. Something grazed my foot. I recoiled from it with a jerk. I stood in the dark wondering what I should do next. Pulled my underwear on, then dug around in my mansack for the imp's genie bottle. I took the sleeping bag and returned to the bathroom. When you turn the light on, a noisy fan comes on, too. Better make this quick.

A faint shadow bobbed within the bottle. I tapped it with my fingernail. This was succeeded by Shagduk's muffled howl of impotent rage. "Soon," I said under my breath. I then placed the decanter on the counter.

Turned the sleeping bag upside down and shook it. An object tumbled onto the bath mat with a heavy thud. At first, I had no idea what I was looking at. A sickening sprouted mass with brightly colored appendages and a lurid mouth. And bulging eyes! Shannon's brother must have forgotten about his Mr. Potato Head. Grabbed a wad of toilet paper, then gingerly picked up Mr. Potato Head's remains and put them in the wastebasket. The zipper I worked on with soapy water until it finally loosened. Unzipped it all the way so I could examine the inside, which was not as bad as I feared it would be. The smell was not too awful. Got spud residue on my feet. I would shower in the morning.

I tossed and turned, unable to get comfortable. I recounted the day in my mind—Randy's sudden departure, Diane's rape comment, the tape rectangle. My language snafu that got us ejected from the restaurant. My fortune! I tugged at the drapes to admit a sliver of moonlight then cracked open the cookie.

*Confucius say trust you instinct. You never go wrong.*

I am not sure this is true.


Saturday, May 14

Slept poorly because the thermostat was set too high. The sleeping bag was too warm, as well. Sometime during the night, I heard someone showering. They then came into our room. The scent of herbs and flowers wafted through the air as the witch's silhouette floated over me. Droplets of water landed on my cheek. There was a rustle of fabric. What did she do? Was it a dream?

I got up to get a glass of ice-cold dispenser water. I inched my way along the pitch-black hallway toward the kitchen. The lights came on. Yendor and Harg stood near the breakfast nook, cheering and slapping each other five. I had sprung their elaborate trap. "Save versus poison," intoned Harg of the City Afar. He tossed me a die.

"This is called an icosahedron," I said pedantically.

"No shit," said Harg.

Yendor began rattling off the names of all the regular Platonic solids, Kepler-Poinsot polyhedra, and other tessellations. For some reason, I felt anxious. I cast the die on the cutting board.

"Ah, a one!" cried Harg.

"What does that mean?" I said.

"You're dead."

Yendor and Harg took their Pop Tarts out to the trampoline and resumed their game of D&D. How can they play that all night? Little did they know that Duke Mantee of Collinwood deals in real demons, witches, and pan-dimensional beings.

Bonnie joined me in the kitchen. We sipped our Sanka in silence. The linoleum was covered in dominoes, ping pong balls, and Hot Wheels. A Mayor

McCheese doll grinned stupidly from the hutch. The same one Jenny and Shannon had fought over in Jenny's room?

Dave II and Diane napped as we sped along the turnpike. Or pretended to nap. I felt Diane's presence strongly next to me. Our thighs were stuck together. Dave II seemed green around the gills. Probably hungover, unless he failed his saving throw versus the witch's poison. Bonnie buried her nose in *Zen and the Art of Motorcycle Maintenance*. How anyone can read in a speeding vehicle without becoming ill is a mystery. The book addresses two personality types, those who are detail-oriented and those who see the big picture. Hedgehogs and foxes? She read aloud various passages, such as "The range of human knowledge today is so great that we're all specialists." If I am a specialist in anything, besides cataloging festschrifts, it might be the Dordic language. Would hesitate to call myself a specialist in magic. It is no longer accurate to call myself an amateur, however.

Dave II yawned noisily and roused himself. "You look terrible," said Bonnie. "I feel terrible," said Dave II. He perked up somewhat when Bonnie read aloud from her book and proposed we play Two Kinds of People. Each player takes turns saying, "There are two kinds of people"; they must then complete the sentence. To set the tone, I opened with, "There are two kinds of people. Those who use bookmarks, and those who dog-ear."

Tim farted loudly. "In this world, my friends, there are two kinds of people," he said. "Those with loaded guns, and those who dig. Ya dig?"

"I dig," said Dave II.

"I'm not sure you do," said Tim. I sure as hell did not.

"There are two kinds of people," said Bonnie. "Those who make it a better place and those who make it worse." This shut everyone up as we each mulled over which one we were.

"Whenever I use a bathroom, I always wipe up whatever needs wiping up."

"Even if it's someone else's mess?" said Tim. "Why would you do that?"

"I don't Martinize it, or anything. I just leave it cleaner than when I found it. That makes the world a better place, does it not?"

"Worse," said Tim. "It sets unrealistic expectations for others."

"You sound like you're at the bottom of a well," said Jenny. "Where are you calling from?"

"A booth in the deep South," I said.

"I'm feeling lonesome."

"Is that right?" I said. I sensed a presence behind me.

"Buy me a cocktail, lover," cooed a woman's voice.

A huge pair of perfumed knockers mashed against my arm. I covered the receiver. "Excuse me, ma'am. I'm talking long distance."

The rollicking, buxom grandma looked me up and down then blew a stream of cigarette smoke in my face. It was all I could do to keep from busting a gut. She sashayed over to the bar, grinning over her shoulder as if to say, "I'll have you tonight."

"Who was that?"

"A Shreveport hooker."

"Was she pretty?" Jenny's tone was one of mingled jealousy and anger.

"She was old enough to be my grandmother," I said. "Everybody here is, come to think of it. People are all gussied up in ball gowns, zoot suits, spats, and feather boas."

No one spoke. The silence heightened the intimacy of the call, I felt. It was like I was lying next to Jenny in the dark. "I miss you," she said. The sentimental tone was unusual for her. After we hung up, I decided my absence had made her heart grow fonder. Not mine, alas.

We took our places. There was confusion about our booking. At last, Bonnie appeared and gave the thumbs up. Our numbers were received with polite applause. A few energetic couples jitterbugged during "Up Your Hose (with a Rubber Nose)." No one moved a muscle during Tim's bloody windmills.

During our set Tim engaged with an octogenarian heckler who kept maligning the Lone Star state. "Real quick, who's your favorite musician?" said Tim into the mic as the band vamped behind him.

"Gene Autry," blurted the heckler.

"Of Tioga, Texas? Or some other Gene Autry?"

"The Big Bopper, then."

"Sabine Pass, genius."

"Tex Ritter."

"All your favorite musicians are from Texas so shut the fuck up!" This outburst was met with boos and threats. Tim played the opening notes of "Deep in the Heart of Texas" on his Flying V before segueing into "The Eagle Has Landed."

It was only after we finished playing that we discovered the reason for the audience's skewed demographics—the headliners were supposed to have been Max Spaulding's Blue Bayou Orchestra. The event, which included ballroom dancing lessons, was hosted by the Art Deco Preservation Society of Louisiana. I had glimpsed the posters in the lobby (on which we were billed as "Time Plane") and assumed that event was at the hotel's other venue.

Bonnie explained the mix-up. The organizers had reportedly been upset by our appearance, but it was the venue management's mistake and we had a contract. In the end, the management apologized and we got paid. On the bright side, we introduced a generation of people to progressive rock who may not have ever been exposed to it otherwise.

As "Time Plane" playing before the wrong crowd, the opportunity presented itself to try a little musico-magical experiment. The instrumental "Up Your Hose" provided enough improvisational leeway in which to inconspicuously interpolate the required notes, themselves lifted from Warren and Dubin's "Shadow Waltz." The object—to make the octogenarian heckler dance. I suppose it was just an ordinary *Charm* spell. But without an explicit word of power, I succeeded only in making him suddenly exit the ballroom. Dave II glanced at me quizzically, as if he knew what I was up to. But how could he?

"Are we staying here?"

"No," said Bonnie. "We're at the Jo-Dan."

The Shreveport hooker tut-tutted me as I carted away my cabs. You just know she has a heart the size of Louisiana. I always feel bad when I have disappointed someone.

Girls in one room, boys in the other. Bonnie checked us in. Tim and I shared a joint. Dave II and Diane took a dip in the pool. Bonnie had the foresight to have brought bed sheets. We used them to conceal our equipment in the van so we would not have to lug it all upstairs. Bonnie dragged her exercise bike into her room so she could ride herself to sleep.

"Magic Fingers!" cried Tim. Dave II put a quarter in. The bed began to vibrate noisily.

"Turn it off!" I said. "You'll disturb the other guests." But we could not turn it off. We had to wait fifteen minutes for it to turn off on its own. Would have unplugged it, but we could not find the outlet and the bed was evidently bolted to the wall.

Perused the Gideons' Bible for a while before turning off the bedside lamp. It took forever for Tim and Dave II to settle down. They kept getting up for glasses of water, opening drawers, and going downstairs for candy bars and ice. I was curious to catch a glimpse of Dave II's special Mormon "temple garments" I had once read about. But when he kicked off his jeans, he was wearing some decidedly non-Mormon bikini briefs.

"Get a load of this," said Tim. Where two wood panels met, the patterns joined together to resemble a part of the female anatomy. Tim laughed like an imbecile. Dave II and I laughed, too, like imbeciles.

Around midnight, we were all startled by a peremptory knock at the door. Dave II answered it. A curvy figure was silhouetted by a sheet of lightning. Dave II had a brief conversation with the silhouette before shutting the door.

"Who was that?"

"Some gross whore. She asked for Pete." I wanted to know if it was the Shreveport hooker. At the same time, I did not want to know.

"Dumbass. *I'm* Pete," said Tim. "That was Two-Sack Sally. You should have asked her in."

"You told her Pete was your name?"

"I use aliases when I'm on the prowl," said Tim. "So what? Louisiana is one of four states I have never gotten tush in. And you screwed it up."

"What is that smell?" I said. "It's like a dead fish."

"I noticed it in the van, too."

We soon discovered the source. Tim was eating *won tons* on a Frisbee he was using as a plate. "Where'd you get those?" I said. Tim nodded toward a doggy bag. Dave II opened the window.

For the next couple of hours, Tim and Dave II flipped channels. They settled on *The Philadelphia Story*. At intervals, there would be a ruckus. "Commence bongos!" Tim would cry. He would then start beating Dave II like a bongo. During a commercial, I heard Tim say, "Beg your pardon, Gov'nor. Is my Johnson blocking your view?"

A librarian shushed Jimmy Stewart. Tim and Dave II thought it would be hilarious to start shushing me. "Hey, Librarian! Wake up!"

"Huh?"

"*Shhhhh!*"

When they finally turned the boob tube off, Tim said, "Good night, John Boy." Dave II replied, "Good night, Elizabeth." I grudgingly participated. "Good night, Daddy. Good night, Son." But who does that make me?

"*Shhhhh!*"

I offered a jocular malediction and turned off the lamp. I punched my pillow, then tried in vain to relax. The a/c turned off and it got very quiet. "What's that red light?" I said.

"Smoke detector," said Dave II.

"Aren't those radioactive?" said Tim.

"Hell yeah, they are. Loaded with Nickel-63."

With a loud sigh, I put on my cut-offs and turned on the lamp. From my gig bag I fished a roll of electrical tape. I then stood on a wobbly armchair and put a piece of tape over the offending red dot.

"What a pussy," said Tim, after I had lain back down. I could hear him furiously flicking his Bic in the dark. When it would not light, he hurled it against the wall with a loud bang.

The sands of sleep eluded me. It did not help that Tim kept getting up. At one point, I was roused by loud voices outside. Tim's in a plaintive tone, Bonnie's in one of remonstration.

"I have a *boyfriend*, Tim," said Bonnie. A few moments later I heard her say "Tim, that is enough."

In the deepest part of the night, I got up to use the euphemism. All was quiet but for the sounds of Tim and Dave II's gentle snoring. On my way back to bed I put a quarter into their coin slot. As soon as the mechanical digits began to carry them into the "land of tingling relaxation and ease," they both started cursing. The bed sounded louder than it had earlier. Weirdly, I fell asleep before the fifteen minutes were up. I think Tim and Dave II did, too.


SUNDAY, MAY 15

Kept waking up because it was too stuffy. Each time I got up to turn on the air conditioner, someone else would turn it off. Out of desperation, I opened the window, which admitted the sounds of traffic and coke dealers. I lay awake, worrying about everything, until sunlight streamed through a gap in the drapes.

Being an early bird, I showered first then stepped outside to smoke and think. I was stamping out my butt when I noticed the vent window of the Eagle was smashed. The van's back doors were wide open. Everything was gone except for Dave II's gas tank and some of his drum pieces.

I went back inside. "Someone broke into the van," I said.

Tim sat up. "You have got to be kidding." He raced across the parking lot in his underwear, Dave II right behind him. "Fuck a duck. They got my stash!"

Dave II held up a cymbal stand forlornly. He looked jacked up.

"Man, are you okay?" I said.

"My Egmond is irreplaceable," groaned Tim. "I mean, the action on the seventh fret. You need pliers to depress it. Still, that's the guitar I learned how to play on. For years it never even left my side."

"It is said Bo Diddley never put his guitar down," I said unhelpfully. "Not even to make love or go to the bathroom." I privately lamented the loss of my Pan, despite its smiling neck and truss rod problems.

When Bonnie saw the van she buried her face in her hands. "Should we call the pigs?" said Tim.

"No point in that," said Bonnie.

"Let me make a phone call," said Diane.

A flier flapped in the breeze under the wiper blade. I removed it and read it aloud. "Beloved, do not take any part in any of these components of Satan's spiritual structure. They are doorways to demonic possession: Freemasonry, Illuminati groups, yoga, Wicca, Urantianism, Rosicrucianism, Hare Krishna, astrology, tarot, Ouija boards, remote viewing, palmistry, voodoo, UFO worship, divination, meditation, lycanthropy, postmodernism, astral projection, necromancy, fire walking, levitation, mood rings, vampirism, marihuana, LSD, the Moonies, Dungeons & Dragons, est, satanism, fornication, and rock music."

"Tried all of these," I joked. "Except vampirism. Blood sucking's not my bag." All joking aside, the prospect of demonic possession is no laughing matter. Guess I dodged a bullet there.

"What do they have against postmodernism?" said Dave II.

"No idea what half that shit is," said Tim. "Without fornication, we wouldn't be having this conversation."

"Maybe the person who left the flier is the one who stole our stuff."

We stood around in front of the beauty shop smoking and kicking pebbles until Diane returned. "We're going to go buy new equipment," she said.

"Can't afford to replace my stuff," lamented Tim.

"It's taken care of," said Diane.

The others were oddly accepting of this development, so I went with the flow. If Diane wanted to be reimbursed later, I could always just turn everything over to her. Went back upstairs to make sure we had not forgotten anything. Saw the Gideons Bible and swiped it. I do not know why. Free book, I guess.

Del's Music was not open yet. Del let us in anyway. Diane instructed us to "get whatever we wanted." Only one more stop on this otiose expedition. Why not just go home? I proceeded tentatively, at once excited and humbled. Paused to flick an Arthurian table-sized gong with my fingernail, before noticing a sign that said not to.

A Baldwin Exterminator caught my eye. Del slapped his palm on the amp. "It has a real sweet spot when cranked and miked with a 57 on the right twelve," he said confidentially. As I searched for an ashtray, Tim snagged the combo for himself. His way of getting me back after being magically fingered in the middle of the night.

Scored a black double-necker in mapleglo. Haunted by Terry's admonitions, I had the 6-string pickups replaced with humbuckers. When I told Del I wanted to sound like Geddy Lee, he recommended an SVT with two V-48s for the bass pickup and a separate Sunn rig for the treble. I sniffed them, but the lure of Peavey is strong. In the end I chose the 400-watt F-800B with its exclusive slope circuit and overdrive. A pair of 412 cabs completed the rig of doom.

"Get the gong," I whispered to Dave II.

The witch leaned across the counter, her charms on display. She spoke in hushed tones to Del, who listened intently. I saw him tear up an invoice. What would Randy make of all this?

We loaded the van. When I stopped to tie my shoe, Tim slapped my foot off his bumper. He polished it with his sleeve, then bent over to kiss it. On account of my additional cab and Bonnie's sprawling ARP, our new equipment took up considerably more space than before. Those of us in the back seat rode with numerous synth modules across our thighs. Bonnie hugged a stack of nested toms. No one thanked Diane. It was as if nothing had happened.

"Were you guys having sex last night?" said Bonnie. "What was all that banging?"

"It was the Magic Fingers," explained Dave II. "You didn't turn yours on?"

"We did, but ours were quiet."

Just beyond the "Welcome to Texas" sign, an F-100 was lodged among the lower branches of a willow oak. The fuzz had pulled over and was writing a citation. "Only in Texas," quipped Dave II.

Lunch at a Nacogdoches sausage joint. We had to sit in the non-smoking section. Much was made of the sign that kept all that cigarette smoke at bay. "If you don't want to smell smoke, stay home," Tim complained. When Diane ordered a yard of ale, the rest of us followed suit. How could you not? Tim had several and by the time we left was drunk.

Tim let me drive. He took out his new Flying V and sang "Bell Bottom Blues" while looking at Bonnie, who happened to be wearing bell bottoms. "That was beautiful, Tim!" she exclaimed. She seemed oblivious, but I think the song was about her. Tim can be such a jerk sometimes, but he sure can make beautiful music.

The piney woods gradually gave way to prairie, then the endless marshes of the Gulf coast. It was dark when we took the last ferry to Port Aransas. The ferry was a novelty for everyone except Dave II, who said he had taken them in Maine. The ride made me seasick, so Tim took the wheel again. As we rolled into town, we observed a huge guy walking down the street in a denim jacket covered in Rush patches. "That's not a Rush fan," said Bonnie.

"A jacket in this heat?" said Tim. He cranked down the window. "Hey, you!" he yelled. "Lady doesn't believe you're a true fan. Quick, what's your favorite album?" When the guy hesitated, Tim roared, "Choose or die!"

"*2112*. Wait, no. *Caress of Steel*!"

"You live!" yelled Tim as he burned rubber.

"That was a true fan after all," observed Dave II.

"What's with the naked guy on Rush stuff?" said Bonnie.

"You mean the Starman emblem from the back of the *2112* cover?" I said.

"Some bands are naked chick bands, like Kiss. You know what I mean?" lectured Tim. "Rush is a naked guy band."

We double-parked in front of the venue and unloaded. Across the street was a shop with a colorful mural painted on the outside of palm trees, lizards, and Tahitian beauties. Diane tugged Dave II's sleeve. "Let's go inside," she said. I was curious, too, so I joined them.

The door stuck, so I forced it. It opened rather swiftly, causing some bamboo chimes to rattle violently. The man behind the counter squinted at us suspiciously. He put on a record at what was clearly the wrong speed. As I wandered down an aisle of tiki-themed tchotchkes, I recognized the song as "Quiet Village." The animal calls took on a monstrous rather than playful aspect at the slower speed. When I passed near him again, the man behind the counter said, "Good music goes slows." I recalled our slow version of "Hail Marys" and silently nodded. He continued: "This turntable has a variable-speed motor with pitch control. It can play anywhere from about thirteen to ninety r.p.m. Martin Denny's spinning at twenty-one."

The proprietor had grimy hair, greasy smile, and a stained aloha shirt with a droopy black turtleneck underneath. (In this heat!) He gestured to the merchandise. "Brought all this booty back from overseas." A rattan airplane hung from the ceiling. Powered by bicycle pedals, it surely did not fly. Along the walls were carved totem poles, snowshoes, and in a corner, a stuffed polar bear. "My wife loathes this shop and everything in it. I'm getting out. Everything's fifty-five percent off."

I beheld a shriveled mask in a glass vitrine. "Except for that," said the man.

"It seems familiar," I said.

"That was me," he said. The man reached for the grotesque mask. He caressed its delicate flesh nostalgically before strapping it on and gazing at me through tiny eye holes. "I'm someone else now."

"Glurpo," I repeated. "The clown? From Aquarena Springs?" The hairs on the back of my neck stood up. I remembered Glurpo well from when I was seven.

The whites of Glurpo's eyes were as yellowed as the skin of the mask. "Thus I inscribe myself on the heart of humanity."

I looked around nervously. Dave II and Diane had vanished. "Is this shrunken noggin the real McCoy?" I said, changing the subject. I joggled the macabre object in my palm.

"Mack, you wouldn't believe the crazy shit I've seen." Without answering my question, Glurpo went on to tell a story about his adventures among the treetop peoples of the Malay Archipelago. The tribe he was living with declared war on a neighboring tribe and he was expected to fight. "Snuffed sixteen mudmen that day," he said matter-of-factly.

"Gaw, that's something."

Glurpo inhaled sharply through the mask's tiny mouth hole. "But I have never felt so *alive*. D'you know what I mean?"

I puffed out my cheeks and nodded weakly. "Yeah, not really."

"The tribe and I partook of the rival chieftain as comrades in arms. I became no different than them." After a brief pause, he continued. "Paid my .453

kilograms of flesh. It was time to move on." I noted Glurpo's use of the metric system. But was he talking about actual or figurative flesh? Maybe the metric system is appropriate for certain calculations, I mused, but it is terrible for identifying proportions. The imperial system easily reveals halves, quarters, eights, and so on. Twelve units allows not only halves but thirds in whole numbers. It is visual music. "Quiet Village" warbled on hypnotically.

At twenty-one revolutions per minute, the animals' cries were revealed to comprise two or three notes simultaneously. I wished I could speak that way. Say ten things at once. I wish I could say all there was to say in one word.

From the back of the shop came a crash. Glurpo lowered his mask. "You break it, you own it!" he croaked. He was speaking to Dave II, who had evidently dropped a maraca.

"Listen, I gotta get out of here," I said casually. "Our band is playing across the street. Stop by, if you want."

"A musician, eh?" Glurpo reached under the counter and produced a small wooden trumpet. "A royal *nempiri*. This trumpet and the drums of the Selangor regalia were kept at Bandar by the former sultan in a galvanized iron cupboard in the middle of the lawn of His Highness's garden residence.

"His Highness himself informed me that the instruments had once been kept in the palace itself, but the servants vowed to leave and never return as they were the source of an uncanny evil when played. Go ahead, touch it."

"Why do you have these?"

"A fair question. Let's just say His Highness owed me one." Glurpo was beginning to sound like the Big Bopper at Fantasy's. I was not sure I believed him. He offered the trumpet. "For you, fifteen."

"Ten," I replied.

"Twenty," said Glurpo. "Toss in a shrunken head for free."

Before I knew what I was doing, I had pulled out three dixies from my wallet. Glurpo snatched them. He then carefully wrapped the *nempiri* in tissue paper and placed it in a paper bag with the shrunken head.

Dave II returned with Diane in tow. "This place gives me the willies," he said. "C'mon, they're feeding us."

"Y'all come back, now," said Glurpo.


Except for its bookcase-lined walls, the Library resembles lots of other small-town Texas cinder-block watering holes. Beyond a pinball machine stood a low stage with a Spirit of '76 banner draped behind it. The stage was flanked by card catalogs. They contained cards for some defunct collection.

Our arrival was unexpected but we were told we could go on after the Tightwads. Tim was nowhere to be found when J.W. the bartender served us diablo sandwiches. No one even saw him leave. He returned when we were finished eating. He was now wearing a white jumpsuit.

"You guys ate without me?" moaned Tim forlornly.

"We had no idea where you were!"

"After I changed, I went to look at the water," he said. "I told you but I guess no one listened."

"But you were gone for ages!" countered Bonnie. "And why are you wearing that?" she added. "You look like Pete Townshend."

"Or Evel Knievel's stunt double," said Diane.

"Fuck off, cunt." Tim scowled and turned to look at me. "I told you we shouldn't have brought her along."

"Damn, Tim," I said. "Seriously, what's with the jumpsuit? It's a simple question."

Tim pushed away the bowl of chili J.W. had placed before him. "Why don't you go look in the mirror?" he snapped. "All of you!"

It was still early. I explored the small commercial district with its warehouses on barnacled piles, empty wharves, and nets drying. From the harbor wafted the cries of seagulls and a rather fetid odor. Everything was closed up tight except for a few bars, from which revelers spilled into the streets. I found myself on a lengthy, seaweed-strewn jetty, hopping from one jagged chunk of concrete to the next, against which the tide ebbed gently. Before I knew it, dusk had set in. In the failing twilight I slowly made my way back to shore.

Outside the club, I observed Tim face down in the gutter, his jumpsuit peeled to his waist. He was soaking wet and covered with lacerations. As if he had been keelhauled. "What the hell happened to him?" I said.

Bonnie glanced at me remorsefully. "He ate that whole thing of cookies. Guess they didn't agree with him." Diane stifled a wry grin. Guess that is what you get when you cross a witch. Could have been worse. She could have turned him into a toad.

We waited in a makeshift green room. A waitress saw to our needs. She was a little bit flirty. You get more tips that way, I reasoned. Everyone watched as she bent over to pick up a bill that had fallen to the floor. The way Diane was glaring at her, she must have seen her as a threat.

"Mosquitos are eating me alive," said Tim. He was covered in bites. After a brief argument with him over how to pronounce Moog, he and I reviewed changes to "The Eagle Has Landed." I played an A. Tim strummed a G. We would stop and bicker for a moment, then repeat.

"I know it's a G because I wrote it."

"I know it's an A because that's how we have always played it," I countered.

Tim strummed the song in octuple time, glaring at me with bulging, crapulous eyes.

"I don't give a shit, but let me figure out how to play it the new way, first."

"There is no new way!" belched Tim boozily. "You may think you're irreplaceable, but you're not." I turned to Dave II for validation. He was snoring next to his kit.

Figured I would smoke a joint and check out the Tightwads. They were your run-of-the-mill bluesy frat guy cover band, whose "This Land Is My Land" was a particularly obnoxious parody of the Woodie Guthrie classic. The guitarist wielded an instrument fashioned from a toilet seat. Reverend Tightwad, a big lout in suspenders and a coonskin hat, whipped out a pair of nunchucks during "Tequila." He twirled them throughout the song, stopping abruptly each time he shouted "Tequila!" Kept praying he would whack himself in the nuts, but he was clearly skilled with the weapon. The crowd, chiefly students from A&I, ate it up.

They did "You Can Leave Your Hat On," but with a stripper beat. The frat boys went wild, hollerin' and hootin' and tousling each other's hair. The ladies drunkenly shrieked. Must have been the band's signature tune. "Baby take off your cardigan," the singer intoned, beckoning to a chick standing near the bar. She looked down coyly before removing her cardigan and waving it in the air like a flag of surrender. This elicited shouts of approval from all. "I say nobody needs a cardigan in this Gulf Coast heat." He talked like Foghorn Leghorn.

"Baby!" implored Reverend Tightwad. "I said *bay-bee*!" One fool responded by shouting, "WHAT."

"Baby," he said, pointing at one particularly busty sorority girl near the stage. I noticed almost every female in the bar was wearing a hat. The motley assortment of millinery, from tam o'shanters to sombreros, seemed contrived and suggested forethought, as did the cardigan.

"Yes, yes, yes!" slurred the sorority girl. Without being asked, she wiggled out of her dress and kicked it across the bar to thunderous cheers. In her underwear and deerstalker, she was lugged away by two blonde jocks who looked like Norwegian tennis pros. I have a feeling she and the tennis pros were paid in advance to do the lugging. The males of the species were hooting. A low sound, like a slowed down recording of excited gibbons. It, too, sounded rehearsed.

"You ladies! Y'all can keep your hats on, for now. We're just gettin' warmed up. I say, is it getting a little bit warm in here? It's a tad tepid." He licked his finger and held it up to test the air's tepidity.

The colorful dust jackets in a nearby bookcase beckoned. *The Occult Reich* caught my eye and I began to read in earnest before remembering what I was here for. I sorted the titles by genre until a waitress approached. "Don't touch the books," she said. This library has its own Dixie!

"You should get a job here," said Dave II observantly.

"No, thanks."

We took the stage. A huge drunk guy came up and said rather belligerently, "Y'all better be good." It was the true Rush fan from earlier.

"You had better be good," said Tim mockingly. No telling who was drunker.

Found myself glancing into the wine barrels just in case Shagduk was lurking in one of them. No, he was safe in his genie bottle in my mansack. My mansack! My heart skipped a beat. There it was, next to my amp. I recalled the last time the imp had discharged from a barrel at the museum. That could have ended badly. While the imp lives, I am a danger to everyone around me. Is it wrong that I like to live dangerously?

I plugged into my new F-800B. As I adjusted the EQ, I noticed an extra knob labeled "mojo" whose function was a mystery. I turned it clockwise while thumbing a few Es. Was it my imagination or did my bass sound more potent? I stared at my joint appreciatively.

Tim approached the mic. "Hello, Port Aransas!" he cried, snapping me out of my gloomy woolgathering. "We're very proud to announce that we just signed a contract with Columbia Records!" This turned few heads among the disinterested crowd. "Yeah, it's great! We buy eight records for a penny, and they send us another one each month! I'm Tim Watson and this is my band Time Frame. This first song is from my new album."

"My" band. "My" new album. Ha ha! Tim was thinking of Columbia House, but now was not the time to correct him.

The A&I students could not have cared less about us. Tim was in a mood and perversely ended every song with a shave-and-a-haircut couplet. No one seemed to notice when he experienced technical difficulties with a bad cable. Bonnie bravely improvised on her ARP. She acknowledged my encouraging nod with a confident smile. I then joined her on the recorder and the result, I felt, was lovely, though the crowd laughed at me.

We played "The Eagle Has Landed" Tim's way. Figured if I made any mistakes it would be his fault. It went off without a hitch. The song, with its myriad changes of odd time signatures, was understood by few. There was applause, but only, I think, by those who wished to pose as prog connoisseurs. One of them lay a dollar bill at Tim's feet.

"Ah, tips!" cried Tim. "Now we can eat." This facetious remark elicited a volley of nickels and dimes. "Ouch! No coins, please! Thank you."

"Up Your Hose" has a good beat and sometimes people dance to it. This evening was no exception. During the song, Tim nudged me. Diane was leaping about in the corner. Her moves were wild and primitive, a startling expression of untold urges and ecstasies. She knocked a tray of empty bottles out of the waitress's grasp. This brief moment of levity dispelled some of the tension between Tim and me.

The highlight of the evening was "Tim's Bolero." During Tim's windmills, achieved by playing repeated power chords and swinging his arm in wide, dramatic arcs, crimson droplets appeared upon his white shirt sleeve, which was unbuttoned and flapping loosely. A mist of blood, sweat, and spittle sizzled onto the floor lights. Despite the obnoxious haircut lick at the end, Tim's voodoo brought the audience around. The Spanish dance received a healthy round of applause. As he took his bows, all eyes were on Tim until Jerry Jeff Walker strode in and took a seat at the bar. Mr. Bojangles's voodoo is stronger than all of ours, combined. Except maybe the witch's. "*Sic transit*," I said to Tim. He did not know what it meant, but rightfully took it as an insult.

"I wanna hear y'all play a song by Rush!" It was the true Rush fan. Rush is not in our repertoire, but after whispered consultation we figured faking out the guy would be a slam dunk. "One more, by request," announced Tim. "Hope y'all enjoy it. It's a little ditty by a famous Canadian trio." It was really "Tush" but Tim figured the guy was too sloshed to know shit from Shinola. There is no way you could fool a true Rush fan like that so I figured I would help things along with a little hocus pocus.

"Lord, take me downtown, I'm just looking' for some Rush," sang Tim. The crowd did not give a shit. They were too busy watching Jerry Jeff Walker put ketchup on his fries. At the end of Dave II's concluding drum roll, the true Rush fan approached the stage. He shook Tim's hand, palming him a joint. "Y'all are the best damn band I ever heard," he declared. He then insisted on helping us load the van.

I occupied myself untangling what must have been the world's longest extension cord. Tim dragged his heels, sighing petulantly and avoiding eye contact. "Sorry for being a dick earlier," he said at last. "You were right about 'The Eagle Has Landed.' The guitar I used to play it on had standard tuning. But that doesn't excuse you for fucking around on stage."

"What do you mean?"

"When you thought you were playing the recorder? It was nowhere near your lips. You were just blowing into the mic."

I had been higher than I thought. Tim must be an idiot savant. One minute, he's Pete Townshend; the next, he's Baby Huey. How can you play in a different tuning without even realizing it? He was now getting into it with the bouncer. Evidently, Tim had tried to go back into the green room where I understood the Tightwads' retinue were making merry. "But I'm in the band!"

"Or these," said Tim. In one hand was his Toke-O-Matic. In the other, a wrinkled paper sack with enough marijuana in it to keep us stoned well into the eighties.

"Tim!" added Bonnie. "You could have gotten us thrown in prison. Do you have any idea of the sentence for possession of marijuana?"

Tim grabbed his crotch. "Let us consult the penile code," he replied contritely.

"Gene Chandler just got a year for heroin," I offered.

We were in the boondocks. "May as well go to the Tightwads party," said Tim flatly. That idea was preferable to wandering the entire length of the island, so Tim directed us to where he reckoned the festivities would be. We caught sight of a bonfire in the distance.

Dave II and Diane snuggled up on a driftwood log. Tim shared his Cheddar Taters and Gallo with a curvy brunette in a fez he introduced as Miss Low Tide. In front of all of us, he insisted she turn her "I'm with Stupid" t-shirt inside-out. Must have hit a nerve. "If you see the van rockin' tonight, you know what not to do," said Tim presumptuously. Bonnie joined me on the sand. "Tim has a woman in every port," she whispered.

"For Tim, every woman is a port," I said. "Give me some of that Rumple Minze."

The Reverend Tightwad gently strummed an acoustic guitar. "Isn't that a Fleetwood Mac song he's playing?"

"Yes," said Bonnie. "I think it's 'Born Enchanter.'"

"Fleetwood Mac's at the convention center tonight."

"You don't have to remind me. I had tickets to see them in April but the show was postponed until tonight."

We swigged the peppermint liquor in silence. "What's going on between you and Tim?" I said in a low voice.

"Your stupid guitarist told me he was in love with me. I told him this isn't Fleetwood Mac. I don't need this kind of drama in my band."

"Cupid's blind," I mused. "And so are his followers."

Tossed the empty bottle into the embers. One by one, or in pairs, people floated away, like figures in a dream. Some slept in vehicles, some in the open air, and some not at all. Bonnie stretched out on her bed sheets. Diane and Dave II hunkered down in a borrowed tent. I tossed my mansack in after them.

My feet sank into the sand as the waves lapped about my shins. Nothing better than pissing in the sea, I decided. I turned around to discover the waitress from the Library standing right there. Why else would she be there? I seized her in my arms and kissed her. We fell into the foamy surf. I roughly groped her as I fought against the tide with my legs. Love on the beach was more difficult than it looks on TV. Somehow, I managed to hurl my shorts toward dry sand. I tugged her apron aside. Just as I was about to penetrate her a wave washed over us. The force of the tide pushed me onto the scarp. I found myself alone, soaked to the bone, dick in hand.

There was no sign of the waitress. It seemed unlikely that she had been swept away. My eyes darted frantically to and fro over the surface of the shallow moonlit water. Not a single soul stirred along the deserted shoreline. The situation seemed as hopeless as it was puzzling. She had sought me out. How did she get here? How did she find me? Layup pussy snatched away at the last moment.

I made my way back to the tent and unzipped the flap. I reached inside and groped around in the darkness until I found my mansack. I dried my hair and face with my Ben Gunn shorts then put them on. I regarded Shagduk's bottle suspiciously then pressed down hard on the stopper. Making sure no one was watching, I buried the imp in the sand under the tent.

Sand is harder than you think. I tried and failed to conjure a pillow. Not that I thought I could. With the flap zipped it was hot and stuffy. On account of the imp's proximity, perhaps, I was tormented by lucid nightmares. Two shadowy entities vied for my attention, one beckoning, one mocking, both sinister. The dream landscape was at once familiar and strange. There was the windy cobblestone path of the previous dream, where everything was gray. I do not remember waking.

As uncomfortable as I was, the roar of the surf was an agreeable novelty. The crash of the largest waves made the ground vibrate. Gusts of wind buffeted the tent. Then I grew even more alert. The tent flap was open and a shadowy figure was crawling inside with outstretched arms. It was Diane. She positioned herself between Dave II and me. Some of her hair whipped me in the face. It was wet. I pretended to be asleep.

Diane would not settle down. After a moment I decided she was undressing. Above the din of the wind and sea I could now make out low chanting, underscored by the rhythmical slapping sound of thighs and haunches. At first, I was surprised that Diane and Dave II would make love in my presence. Or maybe I was still dreaming? But then I realized Dave II was asleep or unaware of what was happening. The witch's movements quickened. The chanting gave way to whimpers. They increased in fervor until they culminated in a banshee wail, made for, it seemed, my ears alone. She rolled off Dave II. Her fingertips brushed across my waist. An obvious attempt to discover if I was turned on. Mission accomplished, Diane. But what was the point of her sex magic? Not to make me jealous, I am guessing. Which, for the record, I am not.

Must get into her quarters at the Fac. Ask Boggs for the key? Steal one? Maybe I could pick the lock. How hard could that be?

Monday, May 16

Reveille came guised as Tim's gong. The instrument reverberated through my skull and across the gulf to Yucatán. When I saw the sheer number of men-o'-war about the beach, I was grateful for not having stepped on one. Tim challenged me to swim to a distant sand bar. It seemed like a good idea at the time. Until I lost sight of Tim, and then land. I looked about me for the floating body of the waitress I knew would not be there. Could she have been Diane who had taken her form to seduce me? It would not be the first time she pulled the old switcheroo. But how did she pull it off? A wig would not have been enough, nor an apron. Her skills are impressive, indeed.

I spotted a purple pillow. Surely not the one I wished for last night. Soon there were a dozen. "So this is how I die," I thought as the lethal organisms-closed in on me. It is unclear how my word of power influenced the outcome of the situation. But I did not die.

Our dip in the sea proved a poorly-conceived way of bathing. I waddled exhausted from the churning breakers, sticky and covered in sand. Tim tossed me a towel. I noted its bicentennial Mickey Mouse design. "Did you swipe this from Shannon's?" I said. There was sand in every orifice of my body. I brushed my teeth and gargled with seawater. I then sat on a plank and picked tar off the soles of my feet.

Movement caught my eye. It was Dave II, flailing away in the sand like a stranded turtle. Bonnie helped him to his feet and offered him warm Tab. He looked green around the gills but was otherwise conscious. I immediately suspected Diane, though he may just have the DTs. If I could only dissuade him from seeing her. But one is helpless in that regard. The witch was nowhere to be seen.

The Tightwads's crowd dispersed unceremoniously. Tim's van, we discovered, was stuck in the dune. Dave II watched we emptied the van to make it lighter. We sacrificed Bonnie's sheets and dug trenches for traction. Tim and I arrayed all our equipment like the photo on the back of the *Ummagumma* album cover. We hung the gong from the handlebars of Bonnie's exercise bike. I mounted it and started pedaling. Diane appeared, bright-eyed and bushy-tailed, having taken a morning stroll on the beach.

Tim looked at her, then looked at me. "Did y'all have a *ménage à trois* last night?"

I ignored his remark. "There should be more songs with gongs," I said.

"'Birds of Fire' by Mahavishnu Orchestra," mumbled Dave II. Attaboy!

A wrecker approached. "Tourists get stuck out here all the time," said the driver. "You're the first ones I've come across this morning so this one's on the house." After the van was back on solid ground, there remained the arduous task of dragging our equipment through the dunes so we could load it again. It was sweaty, miserable work that took much longer than any of us could have guessed.

Gas station coffee and danishes for breakfast on the mainland. Tim bought Chiggerex for his bites. I got one of those 76 balls for your antenna. We took turns freshening up in the bathroom. When Bonnie emerged, her hair was wet from having washed it in the sink. "Anybody have any change for the Coke machine?" she said.

"Coinage for some groinage," said Tim tactlessly.

Bonnie bought a Tab, which exploded upon opening. She held the bottle ruefully away from her, letting the foam flow down her arm. Tim gazed at her wistfully, clearly in love. Last night's conquest was all but forgotten, evidently.

Found myself making small talk with Diane by the ice bin. "You know, I was conceived not far from here," I said. She gave me an amused expression but said nothing. "What about our beaches?"

"The globs of oil made me feel at home," she replied diplomatically.

Wanted to ask her what her game was with Dave II. I know firsthand of what Diane is capable of and am afraid for the guy. Found myself wondering where she was conceived. Some people would have responded in kind to my icebreaker.

Tim pulled onto the highway. I felt a sudden uneasy pang. "We have to go back," I said. "I forgot something."

"Back where?" said Bonnie. "What did you forget?"

"A personal item," I euphemized.

"Your dildo?" said Tim.

"Just turn around, please." I spoke with an urgency so convincing that Tim obeyed at once, a move for which I will forever be grateful. Of course, he bitched about it the whole way. Everyone waited in the van as I searched the dunes for the bottle. There was no reason to recall the exact spot we had pitched the tent, and it took several minutes of frantic searching before I found it.

"Tell Jeannie to come out," said Tim. "I've got a command for her."

"Why did you bring that with you?" said Bonnie.

"It's a gift for my aunt," I lied. I have told more lies this year than I have in all previous years combined.

"An empty liquor bottle?"

"An inside joke."

"That's lovely," said Diane with great curiosity. "May I touch?"

Everyone was staring at me. There was no way to finesse this. "I'd rather you not," I said, looking straight ahead.

"Jet Airliner" provided a timely distraction. Kept waiting for Tim to make his inevitable hostile remarks, but he was too busy rocking out. "Don't want to get caught up in any of that funky shit goin' down in the city," sang the Pompatus of Love.

"Isn't 'shit' one of the seven words you can't say on the radio?" I said.

"What were the other ones?" said Bonnie.

"Let's see," I said. "There's shit, piss, cunt, fuck, cocksucker, and motherfucker."

"That's only six."

"'Tits,'" blurted Tim.

"Don't say that word," said Bonnie. "It's sexist."

"Don't give us that women's lib crap," said Tim. "Besides, that's what they are. Tits. What am I supposed to call them?"

"Breasts," said Bonnie. "Or even titties."

"That word's for babies."

"You can't say 'chicken breasts' on the radio? That ain't right. And what about 'dick' and 'pussy'? Those are perfectly acceptable?"

"'Fellator,'" I suggested.

"That's a Japanese monster," said Tim. "Fellator versus Mothra!"

"'Motherhumper,'" said Bonnie.

"'Matriphile,'" said Dave II woozily. "Sounds rather polite, doesn't it?"

"'Jugs,'" I offered.

"I love that word!" said Bonnie. "If I ever form an all-girl band, I want to call them the Juggs, with double *G*s."

"That's not sexist?" said Tim scornfully.

"Double *G*s," I said. "Like Two-Sack Sally. But why those seven words in particular, though? What about all the other ones?"

"What about foreign or antique cuss words, like *putain de merde, arbor vitae,* or *yaje*?" I said. Diane jerked her head to face me.

"In Polish they say *'Jebiesz jeze,'*" said Tim. "You screw hedgehogs."

"Now that is a grave insult," I said. "George Carlin made the list, anyway. I don't know if it's the law."

"Drop one on the air," said Tim. "I dare you."

"Everything I know about CB I learned from the song 'Convoy,'" I said. "Do I need a handle?"

Dave II coughed weakly. "You do," he said. "Mine's High Hat."

"Mine's Beaver Teaser," said Tim. "Bonnie's is Green Bean."

"Why Green Bean?"

"That's what my dad calls me," said Bonnie.

"I'm the Green Witch," said Diane. Of course she is, though I have difficulty picturing her using a CB. The mystery deepens.

"These all sound like the names of race horses," I said. "Except maybe Beaver Teaser. Do you have to register your handle? I mean, do you have to fill out any paperwork or pay fees?"

"You just pick one and start using it," said Bonnie. "When you're ready to talk, just press this button. Let go when you're finished."

"What do I say?"

"The first thing you do is identify yourself."

"But what do I say *after* that?" I grasped the receiver, then pressed the button. "Breaker 1-9, breaker 1-9. My handle is Bibliotudinous. Anybody got their ears on?"

"This is Motor Mouth," said a male voice. There was some interference by another, unintelligible vocalization.

"Biblio what?" said Tim.

"*Shhh*. What did he say?"

"Turn down the RF gain," said Tim. "And don't shush me." Bonnie fiddled with a knob, then passed me a cheat sheet of 'ten-codes' from the citizens' band operator's manual.

"Salutations, Motor Mouth. We're headed to, uh, the City Afar. We're on the lookout for any smokey bears."

"No one says 'salutations,' ignoramus," muttered Tim.

"10-9, Motor Mouth. You mean Austin?"

"Fellator! Matriphile! *Jebiesz jeze!*" I hollered.

"Sounds like we got us a three-fiver. Son, why don't you put your daddy on, or get off the air."

Bonnie yanked the receiver away from me. "10-100, Motor Mouth. Sending you 88s. We'll be 10-10 in the wind!" she transmitted. "Better hope there's no Kojaks with Kodaks!"

After I swore Bonnie switched off the CB, a low, guttural voice said something in what I swore was Dordic. I switched the unit back on.

"Steven, what are you doing?" said Bonnie.

"Listen!"

"I don't hear anything."

"I'm so hungry I could eat that roadkill," said Tim.

"How about a person?" said Dave II. "Could you eat a human being?"

"Hell, no. I would rather starve."

"That's gross," added Bonnie.

"You all could eat me," said Dave II meekly. "But only if I died first." By the looks of him, he probably will die first.

"That is so considerate of you, Dave," cooed Bonnie, before turning serious. "Don't take this the wrong way, Dave, but no thanks."

"Guess we would all starve, then."

"I would, if I had to," said Dave II. "Eat a human being, that is. Digesting someone's foot wouldn't be the worst thing in the world. I mean, it would be better than starving to death. Admit it." The rest of us groaned in disgust. "The legs are too sinewy," continued the cannibal. "That's working muscle—we're talking *osso bucco*. Could last all summer on all of your ribs, though. Mull it over."

"Remember that plane that crashed in the Andes a few years ago?" I said. "Those people ate their own brothers and sisters."

"Let's not forget Peter Stumpp," said Diane.

"That's going to be my porno star name," quipped Tim.

"Not porno," continued Diane. "The insatiable bloodsucker of men, women, and children. He ripped babies from the womb and devoured them panting, hot and raw."

"Badass," said Tim.

"Where was this?" I said.

Diane hesitated before answering. "In Germany. Many moons ago."

Aquarena Springs for lunch. Glurpo's old hunting grounds. My stomach was complaining, from having eaten restaurant chow too many times, and at times to which I was unaccustomed. Tim was still clamoring for roadkill and Dave II for human flesh, so we got off the freeway and made our way to a baseball-themed choke and puke.

Tim and Dave II excused themselves. Each booth had its own jukebox console. Bonnie and I perused the song selections. "Check out B-17," said Bonnie.

"'Please Mr. Please.' That's clever. My favorite Olivia Neutron Bomb song, by the way. Let's enrage Tim." I selected a quarter's worth of 'Magic Melody, Part II.' Nothing happened. I smacked it with my palm. The waitress gave me a dirty look. Tim and Dave II returned when the one-second, two-note song commenced. "*Dun dun!*" Tim talked over it, but before the second one, I knocked on the table: "*Dun dun da-dun dun.*" Tim paused and grimaced. I knocked on the table again. The third time, he glared at me then punched me hard in the arm.

"What was that song?" said Bonnie.

"Remember 'Magic Melody' by Les Paul and Mary Ford?" I said. "It concluded with the shave-and-a-haircut riff, minus the last two notes. People were pretty hacked off about it, so later that year, Capitol released a single consisting solely of the missing two bits. I think it's the shortest tune on record."

"Hey, don't bogart the syrup!" said Tim. "Get a load of that waitress. She's built like a brick shithouse." He wiped his mouth and stood up.

Bonnie frowned, then whispered into my ear. "Guess he's over me, now."

"Why a shithouse, in particular?" I said. The etymology of this seemingly unflattering phrase interested me.

"Shithouses are sturdy," said Dave II.

"They're not made of rickety planks with a moon-shaped window?"

"Not in Maine, they're not."

"Maine?" I heard what sounded like someone getting slapped. I turned to see the waitress glaring at Tim with her arms crossed.

"My family used to live in Moose River," said Dave II. "Do you care if I don't speak right now? My throat hurts."

"Didn't know you were a Maniac," I said, unsure of the proper demonym. Maine is not known for Mormons, but they have to come from somewhere.

Tim returned flaunting a slip of paper with a phone number written on it in loopy girl's handwriting. This he placed into his shirt pocket with a flourish. "The younger and hotter they are, the bigger asshole you have to be," he said. Bonnie flung the newspaper onto the table in disgust. "Anyone want this?"

"Naw," I said. "Don't usually read the paper, anyway. I just peek at the head-lines to see if the world ended. Did it?"

"Did it what?" said Bonnie crossly.

"End?" She did not answer me. I turned to a page at random. "The creator of this Doublemint gum ad has no idea what an ant-lion looks like," I said.

I was sick of being crammed in the back seat, unable to stretch my legs. Napping was impossible, but I tried anyway. I could not stop thinking about the snippet of Dordic I heard on the CB earlier. It could mean "I am the embod-iment of a dream, a dream for Yaat and the world." But it could also mean "This is a dream, Yaat's dream, part of the world." It is not quite the Dordic I know. Perhaps a dialect? Of course I am not fluent. As we approached the Austin city limits, I became aware of Tim and Bonnie arguing. "Women hurl their panties to you on stage," Bonnie was saying.

"Maybe people should hurl synthesizer manuals at you," quipped Tim.

I winced at Tim's cheap shot. He pulled off the interstate ostensibly to buy a pack of cigarettes. When he asked me to drive I realized he just wanted to drink his troubles away, whatever they might be. Tim's response to most conflict is to get small. I privately rejoiced at my good fortune. A comfortable bucket seat, leg room, and ball cooler vent all to myself. By the time we got to Panther City, no one had said a word. I took the Montgomery exit (so perfectly banked, what a joy that ramp is) and dropped myself off first.

It was pouring rain. I put on *An Hysteric Return: P.D.Q. Bach at Carnegie Hall* and started to unpack. I opened the back door and a few windows for cross-ventilation, then stepped into the shower. After toweling off, I emerged from the steamy bathroom. I stood before the fan, arms akimbo. The breeze felt cool. I watched the droplets evaporate from my bare skin. I went into the kitchen. There, I found Shagduk balancing on top of his bottle on one toe, his foot arched gracefully like that of a ballerina. Ballooning about his waist was a red tutu from which his dracontine tail emerged. Our eyes locked. No one moved.

"A command will put you back," I bluffed. How did he escape? I was not sure I could put him back. What is worse, I believe he knew it.

"Then command Shagduk!" he wailed defiantly.

Taking a cue from the cover of *Slave Lord of Siluria*, I boldly inspected the imp as if looking over a prospective purchase. His elongated, squamous head tapered to a horned snout. Vaguely ophidian features suggested a snake ready to molt. He looked smaller than I remembered him. Like an oversized *futbog*. I resisted the urge to kick a field goal. Efrén Herrera would have pooch kicked him. Cautiously, I proceeded toward the icebox for a cold Pibb. Should I offer Shagduk one? I stood naked before him and swilled my Pibb in one go in a display of macho insouciance. I then crushed the can and tossed it aside. It clattered noisily across the linoleum tiles.

All this bluster to buy time. A quick wit is not my strong suit. Now I faced a great test. While Shagduk flouted my authority, I got out the bologna and the mayo. The bread was stale but this was all for show. I opened the silverware drawer and removed a steak knife. I meant to demonstrate its sharpness by stabbing the cutting board. But the knife eluded my grasp and dropped, sticking into the top of my foot. The imp clapped gleefully, his eyes gleaming with malicious humor.

"Silence!" I said. Shagduk stopped clapping, still balanced atop his bottle. I withdrew the knife from my foot, which was bleeding profusely. "There are two kinds of emergencies," says Sarge. "Blocked airways and arterial bleeding. Everything else is a problem and problems can be solved." The chief problem now was not to pass out from the sight of blood. If that happened, my game with Shagduk would certainly be over. I considered the formulas I knew. Or thought I knew. I would show the imp who is the boss.

I had used a ventriloquism spell against Dixie once. When I attempted it now I discovered I had forgotten it. Every single word of it. An idea popped into my head. To white flour I mixed blood from my foot and mixed it into a paste. This I applied to my face. A sort of war paint, I guess. I then spoke the words of power. Shagduk spun slowly around on his toe to confront me.

"Answer me these questions three," I enunciated. I was still bleeding all over the place. "One. Who is your master?" The imp became agitated. "You will speak the truth!"

Shagduk uttered unintelligible syllables. The name I had read aloud from the codex? Uh oh. I hoped this would not blow up in my face. "Two. Why are you here?"

"To observe and report," said the imp.

"Three," I said. What is a third question I could ask? His response to the second one threw me for a loop. Report to whom? His other master, of course. Whoever sent Shagduk to keep tabs on me. "How do you find Kentucky on a map?" I blurted, for lack of a better question.

Shagduk flung his arm over his forehead melodramatically. "Steven already knows," he groaned. "He knows!"

"Of course," I said. "You will step down and bow before me."

Shagduk hesitated. Slowly, he raised his arms as if unfurling great wings. An attack seemed imminent. The imp deftly alighted from his perch and landed before me in a hostile crouch. Relying heavily on my Martin Solis exercises, I bore down upon him with my will. "Appear to me as Guddu."

The transformation was so natural, I did not even notice it happen. Guddu stood at attention, awaiting my decree. "I am your master, now," I said.

"Yes," said Guddu obsequiously.

"You will stay in your bottle until I permit you to come out."

"Yes."

I lifted up the decanter. It feels heavier when Shagduk is inside. Through the smoky purple glass I detected faint howling. I suppose he is throwing a tantrum. Let him! Mirthful sounds floated through the screen door. "What on earth?" said Vee. Her gaze roamed slowly from my floured face to my bloody foot. "You're bleeding!" she said. "Let me get you a Band-Aid."

Vee went into the bathroom. I dressed and cleaned up. "Sounds like a church in here," said Vee, meaning the P.D.Q. Bach. I tried to imagine a service at which they played *The Seasonings* and chuckled to myself. She applied the bandage to my wound. She stood and then reached for the decanter. I quickly snatched it away.

Vee looked surprised. "Rude!" she said.

"I know," I said. I repeated the story about it being a gift for my aunt.

"What a bunch of bull."

I put Shagduk in the icebox, then grabbed my foot. "Ahh," I moaned. Vee crossed her arms.

"What was all over your face?"

Rather than keep digging a deeper hole, I simply shrugged. Vee is much too intelligent to casually deceive. When I told her I had to get up early, she threw up her hands. Vee rarely frowns, and it pained me to see her do so on my account.

"I was going to invite you up," she said. I just smiled resignedly. "Keep that wound clean," she admonished, before disappearing up the back stairs.

Hoped the imp was uncomfortable next to the frozen peas but if he is really from Lansing, he must have felt right at home. In retrospect, "Where is Sherwood?" would have been a sensible third question. Sherwood would know what to ask! As for Shagduk's other master, why did he send Shagduk and not come himself?

I should probably be dead by now.


Tuesday, May 17

Imp ruminations kept me awake. How he abruptly appeared in the library three and half months ago, like he had always worked there. His eccentric ways. How no one at the library remembered him after I bottled him. What could I do with a personal demonic dogsbody? Guess I can put him to work. Dishes? But I enjoy doing those. Laundry is Vee time. He can scrub the commode.

The vestibule portrait of the Reverend Ralph Henry Pogue has been replaced with one of L.F. Wherever you go, his gaze follows. So do his jowls. Good thing it is not hanging above the information desk. The college president's harrying presence in Blanston Hall is already oppressive enough.

The Stone Fox punched in. "You're tardy," I said. She pressed a Mr. Goodbar into my hand. "It's from Mother," she said distastefully. Before I could thank her, Diane rammed the back of Jenny's heel with a book cart. On purpose, of course.

"Whoops! I'm so sorry," said Diane.

Jenny ignored her. "Notice anything different?" she said, batting her long eyelashes.

I looked her up and down and shook my head.

"I got my hair done yesterday."

"It looks the same," I said. "Why are you so dressed up?"

"Job interview," said Jenny. "Turkey Knob's hiring a circ desk supervisor."

"My neighbor works there," I said. "Not in the library. She teaches." It felt somehow dishonest to refer to Vee as my neighbor instead of my friend.

"The one who lives above you?" Before I could answer, Jenny touched my arm and said, "Let's go out tonight."

"I have to stop by Randy's after work," I said. "Come with me. We'll do something afterward." As soon as I said the words I regretted them. I was tired from the beach. A quiet evening curled up with *Successful Muskrat Farming* sounded pleasant. But so did the prospect of a little tail. I will never get any if I do not make more of an effort.

Jenny did most of the talking on the way. Details about the job she interviewed for, Carter's "Viet-namnesty," and the soap opera, chez Fox. She accompanied me inside and went straight into the bathroom. I fed Dorian, Phrygian, and the other bettas, then explored Randy's vast library and marveled at how casually he could leave it behind. Like my own, it was well-organized with little fat. I wondered where Randy was now and what he was doing. In the kitchen, an unopened jug of Palo Viejo beckoned. Jenny smirked when I opened it in the car. We each took a long chug from the bottle then passed it back and forth.

"I'm sweating like a pig," I said. We cranked the windows down. The handle came off in Jenny's hand. "Just stick that back on there."

The Rambler ran out of gas at the bottom of Burton Hill. Bouncing on the bumper gave us the extra few blocks we needed. Should really get that fuel gauge replaced.

Jenny examined a crumpled shopping list. "Why did you spell cat food like this?"

Now was not the time to tell her about how Loretta had written 'kat fud' on our grocery list once claiming the cat had written it. Since then, I have misspelled everything on my grocery lists on purpose. I still have not lost Loretta.

Jenny fanned herself. "I'm a terrible speller," she said.

"So was Scott Fitzgerald. Look at him now."

"Dead, right?"

"Afternoon Delight" tweeted from the speaker. "Did you know this group wrote 'Country Roads'?" I said.

"This is a super make-out song," observed Jenny.

"Why?"

Jenny blinked at me like I was an idiot. She tugged at her pantyhose. "I should have taken these off."

"Take them off now," I suggested. Jenny looked out the window. Had too much on my mind to have put much effort into our date or whatever this was. The prospect of making out, however, had me wishing for Chap Stick. "There's a Van Cliburn benefit recital," I said. "But I don't know what the program is. We could see *Young Frankenstein* at the drive-in."

"Let's go to Studio 6333," said Jenny. "Have you been yet?"

"I had no idea you liked disco," I said. "Why do you want to go there?"

Jenny's face clouded. "No reason."

"It's too early," I said. I tossed her the keys to the Rambler. "Let's go back to Collinwood."

I returned from the kitchen with a carton of spumoni and two spoons. Jenny presented no resistance when I lifted her up onto one of my speaker cabinets. I carefully removed *Selling England by the Pound* from its sleeve, cleaned it, then ceremonially cued up the third song of Side One. "This song is called 'Firth of Fifth.' A firth is like an estuary. A narrow inlet of the sea."

"I know what a firth is," snapped Jenny. She listened passively as I stood by. Time dragged. We finished off the spumoni. I watched fascinated as Jenny turned the carton inside-out and then licked it clean, just like her sister. Have not decided if it is sexy or gross.

"It's coming up," I said, tweaking the bass knob minutely. "Oops, too soon." At last, at about the seven-minute mark, the Taurus pedal kicked in. The Stone Fox gasped as her thighs rippled cymatically at 32 Hz. "Oh," she said quietly.

"The zenith of Genesis's career," I said.

Jenny yawned. I quickly touched her teeth and cried "Score!" She looked mildly irritated. Of course she busts a gut when Spunt does it. There was a knock on the back door. I peeked out of the blinds and spotted Hawlie walking away, Toby in tow. What do they want? I hoped they would go away.

Was fixing to put on the *1812 Overture* when Jenny motioned for me to help her down. For an instant, as I took her in my arms, she became supple. She immediately stiffened. It was as if she dreamed she was in someone else's arms, then discovered she was in mine. Her blouse had come untucked from her skirt. With my free hand, I fumbled to unhook her bra. The tight clasp sprung audibly and Jenny's boobs flopped free. She sighed. I relaxed my grip and she squirmed away. She glanced over her shoulder and gave me a look at once judgmental and encouraging.

"What's this?" said Jenny.

"Randy must have left that here on New Year's Eve. We've been hiding this in each other's houses for years as a joke." It was a Super-8 of *Scum of the Earth*. Jenny's eyes narrowed.

"It's not that dirty, really." I switched on the idiot box. It was a news story about a twister that leveled a Panhandle school.

"That's horrible," said Jenny morosely. "I'd rather watch the blue movie."

"No projector," I said.

We reclined side by side against balled-up pillows, our shoulders mashed together. I leaned in for an ill-timed kiss just as Jenny was about to get back up. She acquiesced, without fervor. Her lips were cold against mine. My own were numb. She stood up, then wiggled her butt at me. I unzipped her skirt, hesitated, then yanked it down. She stepped out of it then went into the bathroom. Slumber overtook me.

"Steven! Wake up!" Jenny stood at the end of the bed in her earth shoes and pantyhose. The peculiar soles make it look like she is walking uphill. Her pantyhose were hiked up to her armpits, which made it look like she was wearing a transparent body stocking. Mechanically cupping her breasts, her hips swayed like a bell in time to the *Kojak* theme blaring from the TV. "Is this what you want?" she said aggressively. She started boinking herself while I stared in alarm and fascination. The Stone Fox punctuates apathy and elusiveness with occasional frank sexual advances to confuse and excite me. A real prick tease.

I groped for my camera. "Who loves ya, baby?" I mumbled, then snapped her picture. Jenny lowered her eyebrow. She ceased gyrating and flopped limply onto the mattress next to me. The heel of one of her earth shoes dug into my shin. I winced and moved my leg.

Someone pounded at the door. Jenny and I glanced at each other. "What now?" I grumbled, rising unsteadily to my feet. An axe appeared through the gap between the panel doors and rattled up and down. "Avon calling," ululated Tim. I let him in. "Gotta shed a tear for Ireland," he muttered, thrusting past me in a cloud of Acapulco Gold.

"Don't go in there," I said as he burst into the bedroom. There was a shriek. I found Jenny with the sheet drawn up to her chin. She shot me a caustic look.

The commode flushed. Tim returned from the bathroom and took a seat on the corner of the bed. "Never refuse nature's call," he said. He and Jenny appraised each other. His foot was resting on Jenny's skirt, I noted with irritation.

"What do you want, Tim?" I said impatiently.

"I'm supposed to meet Vee." He glanced at Jenny knowingly. "I'll have what she's having," he said. "Guess Vee's running late. Help me unload?"

Unload what? I tagged Tim wordlessly to his van against which several airbrush paintings on black velvet leaned. They were similar in style to the eagles on the sides of his van. "Do these glow under black light?"

"Damn straight," said Tim. "Vee promised she was going to buy one."

"Did she, now?" I said.

Tim leaned in close. "Grade A," he said approvingly. "But you want to eat that meat elsewhere. You should get yourself a van. If she plants her toothbrush in your bathroom, watch out. You got to nip that shit in the bud, man."

As we entered the house, I expected we were taking Tim's artwork upstairs. Instead, he veered off into my apartment. "Let's show your girlfriend," he said.

We found Jenny in the kitchen unboxing a frozen pizza. She has reclaimed my ratty 'Dillos t-shirt. On account of her diminutive stature, it worked as a rather short dress.

Tim shambled about the kitchen, propping up his various velvets against every flat surface he could find. A lurid nude caught my eye. It was like Vee. I knew she had posed for Dawn but the latter is a real artist. While I was examining it, Vee walked in. Our eyes met. She smiled warmly.

The kitchen resembled an art gallery of sorts. Tim explained each piece but stopped talking when he noticed Jenny bent over the oven, fussing with the pilot. There was a flash.

"Are you okay?" I shouted, rushing to her side. I pulled her hands away from her face. Her eyelashes had been singed off.

"Can you see?" said Vee.

"I don't know," responded Jenny in a calm voice.

Tim turned the next piece around so it was facing me and Jenny. "This opus I call *Mushroom Manacles*. It's based on a dream I had." The surreal landscape featured the Polyflex building in the background. As viewed from a fungal pedestal in Sherwood's front yard, I judged.

"This is why we don't let you write our lyrics," I said. "If you don't mind, I need to take Jenny to the emergency room." Tim's eyes flashed but he made no move to leave.

Jenny leaned toward me and whispered, "I don't need to go to the hospital. I'm fine, really." Though I detected a note of panic in her voice, I trusted her judgment. Truth be told, I did not really feel like spending an evening at Fort Worth Osteopathic.

"Hawlie's here with Toby," said Vee, giggling the name I had bestowed upon Hawlie's slave. "You should ask him to take a look at your stove."

"Now is not a good time."

After lingering before her own portrait, Vee psychoanalyzed the other canvases. She honestly judged them to be good. I was afraid Tim's ego might go supernova after reaching critical mass. We finished off the bottle of Palo Viejo. By the time I hustled the odd couple upstairs, it was late. Jenny and I were too wasted to go anywhere. She got comfortable in bed. She left my t-shirt on. I turned on the fans. As I undressed, Jenny said, "I swear, if one ounce of air from those fans hits me, I'm walking home."

I positioned the fans so they would at least cool my feet, then stretched out next to Jenny on top of the blanket. Our bodies were illuminated by the sickly, blue cathode rays of *Coogan's Bluff*.

"I want to watch you fall asleep," she said softly.

These words, so ostensibly charming, simply made me feel self-conscious. I shut my eyes but felt my excitement grow under Jenny's gaze. Despite being too warm, I did manage to drift off but was jolted awake at intervals by pool hall fight scenes or the roar of choppers. Jenny lay on her side with her ass turned to me. I joined her under the sheet and pressed my body against hers. I gently kissed the back of her clammy neck. When I attempted some gentle probing she mumbled, "I.Y.D."

"I.Y.D.?"

"In your dreams."

WEDNESDAY, MAY 18

"Good morning, good morning!" sang Vee. She burst into the bathroom and playfully ripped open the shower curtain. Jenny dropped a bottle of creme rinse in surprise. I just stood there laughing uncomfortably. What else could I do? Vee thought it was hilarious.

The ignition key to the Rambler is missing. Its door key is still on the ring. Was tempted to call upon the imp for aid but the girls were here. He is probably the one who took it. I shuddered to think of Shagduk operating a motor vehicle.

"Your eyelashes," said Vee concernedly.

Jenny ignored her. I reached to zip her dress but she withdrew and did it herself.

"Knock, knock!" called Dawn. She bore an armful of sunflowers. "Can I put them in this?" She reached for Shagduk's bottle. I snatched it away. "Not this."

Despite my rudeness, Dawn demonstrated how to hotwire the Rambler. The engine gasped to life. A cloud of black smoke belched from the tailpipe. She got out of the car and circled it. "Do you ever change the oil?" she said, squeezing the 76 antenna ball.

"Not lately," I said. "Not sure I've ever changed it, come to think of it. Isn't that something they do when you choose full service?"

"Quite the seraglio you have there," said Jenny after we had gotten into the Rambler. She produced a compact and studied her face. "Crusty," she said. "Didn't bring my bondo bag. You're catching me without my makeup and hair."

"I dig you crusty," I said foolishly. In fact, the last thing I wanted was a crusty chick. What am I doing?

Jenny lowered her eyebrow, an expression I could never figure out. "So I'm crusty, then?"

You cannot win with Jenny. "That bee has been on the windshield since we left Randy's yesterday evening," I said, changing the subject.

"Steven, you have to drive him back!"

"Too late, there he goes." The insect flew ahead of us, impatient to get to his destination. I pulled up to the curb, scraping the wheels against it. "See you tomorrow," I said.

"Thanks for the ride," said Jenny coldly. Not "Thanks for the date." Admittedly, it had been a poor one in retrospect.

The oppressive humidity was a wet blanket over the whole day. After making numerous calls from a booth on campus, I finally found a bookseller to haul Randy's collection away to the tune of $180. I set aside the first Aldine edition of Catullus with Muret's commentaries. Surely Randy meant to take it with him? I boxed up the 24-volume *Children's Encyclopedia of Myths and Legends* for assumed sentimental reasons. There was a book I had given Randy for his birthday years ago: *The Pleasure of Ruins* by Rose Macaulay. I lingered wistfully over the inscription and placed it in the box, leaving a big sweaty handprint on the cover. I put the gaily colored futon in the trunk of the Rambler along with a pail of odds and ends.

Behind Randy's desk I had found an x-roxed sheaf of notes. One page concerned one of several so-called door spells of the kind that got the two of us in trouble. Randy's analysis made it all look so easy. One observation in particular gave valuable insight in how formulae like this could work in the first place. It supplied much food for thought throughout the day as I went about my business. It was careless of Randy to leave something like that for anyone to find. Of course, to a layperson it would look like nonsense.

Errands beckoned. First stop, Bruce Music for various musical implements needed for my musico-magical experiments—chiefly bells of various sizes, but also a triangle and a small gong. To Radio Shack for a treble pot, then Roy Pope for some Hamburger Helper and other sundries. Each time I pick something up from Pablo, I say, "What's the damage?" He seems pleased to have learned this idiom. Today he responded in his gentle Argentine accent, "Thee damage ees six dollar." More than what I paid for the boots to begin with. At home I touched up the repaired spots with a fresh blast of gold spray paint. I examined the trace of a puncture and shuddered at the memory of what caused it. Those undulating *plica fimbriata*!

General Tso's Cock from King Wok while watching *Nova*. "Yoo hoo!" cooed a feminine voice in the foyer. "We're doing laundry. Bring yours, if you have any." It was Dawn. Vee would have just barged right in. As I gathered my dirty clothes, I found Jenny's pantyhose draped over the towel rack. The heel of one was stained with blood from where Diane got her with the cart. I was going to throw them away but thought better of it.

"It's an Alamo," explained Vee. "Grapefruit juice and a jigger of Southern Comfort. This one has double jiggers."

"Why do they call it Southern Comfort?" I said.

"Who knows?" said Vee. "Maybe the South is uncomfortable."

If Dallas's motto is "Where the East Begins," where does the South begin? I looked to the east in wonder. The South seems so far away, not only in miles but in spirit.

The girls shared stories about their Sorbonne days. I was content to just sit there and listen. Vee put on some Tom Jones. She and Dawn sang and bumped hips, oblivious to my presence. After I joined them, I bumped Dawn too hard and she flew headfirst onto the couch. She somehow avoided spilling her Alamo. I suspected magic. It is everywhere, if you know what to look for.

"You never wear jeans," said Vee.

"I know," I said. "I'm burning up. My cut-offs were dirty so I changed into these."

"Let's cut those off!" Vee went into the kitchen and returned with scissors. "Stand up," she said. She kneeled down in front of me.

Dawn started griping about how hard it was to find a date. "Being single's like playing hide and seek," she said. "But no one is looking for you." Vee kept glancing up at me like she expected me to ask Dawn out on the spot, but that would have seemed reactionary instead of heartfelt. The scissors were cold against my balls. "Be careful!" I warned.

"Are you still sleeping with that girl, what did you call her, the Stone Fox?"

"Jenny Fox you mean?" I said. "It's nothing serious." How would Jenny characterize our relationship? Eyebrow up? Or down? If Dawn was bothered by the topic, she did not show it.

"All done!" said Vee. "Let me trim these strings off."

"They're too short," observed Dawn.

Vee eased into a chair and began to file her nails. We were talking about the Davis trial when the nail file sprang from Vee's grasp and vanished into thin air. "Did you see where it went?" she said. The three of us tore the place apart looking for it. "It can't have gone more than ten feet away," I said

When Dawn started hemming and hawing about getting up early I took the hint. Does she think I bumped her too hard on purpose? Maybe she is jealous of Jenny. What went on with Vee and Tim? I picked up the severed denim legs and wore them on my arms.

A shadowy figure greeted me downstairs. Guddu. He held a glass of chocolate milk. I cannot stand how he helps himself to my Nestlé Quik. I recalled what Randy had said at the Eagle's Nest: "If you name a boggart he becomes unruly." A boggart's ass I would simply kick. Guddu's ass is another story.

The imp in human form watched me put down my laundry basket and shed my denim arms. He cursorily inspected them then tailed me into the kitchen. I retrieved the ice tray and pressed the lever. Guddu watched closely when a cube leaped from the tray. I kicked it under the stove. I prepared a plate of leftover General Tso's Cock then figured it would be polite to offer him some. He accepted but did not eat. What was wrong with the food? Did I offend him somehow?

"Can I get you anything?" I said. Guddu just stared at his plate, forlornly. "Chopsticks!" I said. "Forgive me." These he wielded effortlessly. Perhaps he had spent time in the Orient? As we broke bread together, I fell into a false sense of camaraderie with the coworker I thought I knew. He took a bite, chewed, and swallowed, just like a normal, civilized, human being. Except he is not.

He put down his chopsticks then dabbed the corner of his mouth with a napkin. I tossed him a fortune cookie. He unwrapped it and broke open the cookie. "What is this?" The slip of paper was blank. Shagduk, who exists outside of the realms of fortune, returned to his bottle none the wiser. I could have kicked myself for letting me treat me that way. Has he forgotten who is boss? Or have I?

Sometime during the night I heard noises. Was someone in the house? I turned off all the fans. Remington in hand, I fox walked to the kitchen. The icebox switched off. All was tranquil. I sat in the corner with the weapon across my thighs and waited. There was a bump. A shadowy form crept from the trash hole. I switched on the kitchen light. "What the hell are you doing?" I demanded.

Shagduk squinted painfully, his pupils narrowing to slits. "Shenanigans!" he hissed.

"Stand before me as Guddu," I said. "I'm sick of looking at your skinny ugly gremlin ass."

The imp hurried forward in a servile crouch and in a blink became Guddu. "Guddu is just as his master made him," he said in a hurt tone.

Jesus. His master *made* him? How does that work? "Give me that," I snapped.

Reluctantly, the imp removed Figgy's bandana from his neck and offered it to me. On account of imp trickery, he did not untie it. The bandana simply passed through his neck somehow. I pretended not to care, but was privately amazed. "If you hurt that cat, you will rue the day your master made you," I said. "I'll send you straight back to Lansing!" This last word I pronounced facetiously.

Guddu's face fell. He returned to his bottle without asking. He must stay in his bottle by choice, not because I make him. He should choose to do so more often. His shenanigans are wearing me down.

The instant I settled back under the covers a cricket started chirping. Most likely the imp's doing. I resigned myself to a poor night's sleep but I whistled a melody. The chirping stopped.


Friday, May 20

Forgot to write in my diary yesterday, a first. Everyone is on vacation, so I had taken the opportunity to study at my desk Schubart's *Ideen zu einer Aesthetik der Tonkunst* in which the author examines correspondences between musical keys and emotions. I found his ideas inspirational and tried a few muskrat farming experiments. They were a resounding success. The only hitch was when Spunt sneaked up behind me and said, "Try it, you'll like it." Try what? A barium enema? My evasiveness only made him more persistent until I repelled him with a small bell. I had not wanted to do it. Magic is too risky when used impulsively. And I have been using a lot of it, lately.

In kindergarten I was given a diary as a gift but misunderstood its purpose. Instead of recording my life I used it as a catalog of things I hated: yellowjackets, stickers, canned spinach. People made the list, too. Bullshitters, cheaters, and show-offs. I fear I am becoming one of them. Adding to the list bummed me out. I began cataloging the things I loved: Mantovani, Bugs Bunny, and *Wallace's Street Guide*. In the rear were a couple of pages for autographs. These I filled with the names of classmates I liked. When I showed it to Dad, he opened it then merely said, "Who's Gam?" I had confused my cursive *S* with *G*. Alas, misunderstandings like these are emblematic of my approach to life.

Figgy had a meowing fit outside my door this morning. After I let him in, he immediately demanded back out. What's his game? I struggled to tie his bandana on while he squirmed in my lap. When Vee happened to come downstairs, I was compelled to explain what I was doing. I omitted the part about how a demon from beyond space and time had stolen it. Maybe she thinks it was me.

Found a Ben Franklin under my wiper blade. It was fake, which was Bullshit No. 1. Turned out to be a Jesus tract, which was Bullshit No. 2. Considered giving it to Guddu but it would only confuse him. He would ply me with questions. "Three bullshits and you're out," says Uncle Daryl. I do not know how many bullshits I am up to with Guddu.

I arrived at the information desk sweaty and irritable. Amber stood at attention and gave me the sign of the three fingers in a manner that recalled Betty Friedan's "equality" salute. "Don't do it that way," I said, though I prefer she not do it at all. Why did I not just say that instead? For the next ten minutes, she witnessed me fail to find a book that would explain how to pick a lock.

"Jo Ann would know where to find that information," she suggested.

"Some knowledge can't be gained from books," I said. "At least not in any Porteous has." Of course, there are other ways to break into a residence. I resolve to discover who the Green Witch is and why she is here.

The Stone Fox greeted me stiffly at the circulation desk. She was fiddling with a Pez dispenser. I thought she was going to inject one into my mouth so I opened wide. She ignored me at first but then said, "Hold out your hand, dummy." We crunched our candies in silence. Turtle Man approached with several treatises on eschatology then removed his library card from his mouth. I shucked the Gaylord while Jenny observed critically. "I would say 'enjoy' but—you know." My voice trailed off. Brutish chanting could be heard from the direction of the quad.

"Not a pleasant topic," admitted the Turtle Man.

"Almost forgot," I said to Jenny. I pulled her ripped pantyhose from my pocket. "Was going to throw them away, but figured you might want to try to repair them." The way she looked at me suggested I had chosen wrong. Again.

Diane sauntered languorously by. Her passage was like a caress. Why can't she saunter like a normal librarian? She has claimed my former office, which does not surprise me. The head games continue. Jenny watched me watching Diane and lowered her eyebrow. Dames! I do not understand either of them. I resisted the urge to ask Diane why she needs the privacy of an office since she is only a temporary consultant.

I leaned close to Jenny. "Your eyelashes are starting to grow back." She pinched my collar. "What's that?" she said. I went into the staff bathroom to get a closer look. Lipstick. I swear it was not there when I got dressed this morning. Witchcraft. Having come into contact with Turtle Man's saliva, I also washed my hands thoroughly.

Found Amber reading my diary. "Give me that!" I cried. I snatched it away from her. There was no way to ask her how she got past the glyph without rousing her curiosity, so I let it go. "Stay out of my mansack," I warned.

The ferns by the card catalog looked somewhat pendulous, so I watered them. "Those are artificial," said Amber, after I completed the chore. (She had watched me the whole time.)

"Of course they are," I said crossly. I have been watering them for months.

Amber sneezed. "You should say 'Bless you' when someone sneezes."

"But what if they're not religious?"

Amber shrugged. "The Bible says nothing about sneezing. Pope Gregory the Great believed that a sneeze was an early warning sign of the plague. He commanded Christians to respond to a sneeze with a blessing. The idea was that the prayer would protect the person from death."

"Apocrypha."

"Bless you," said Amber. "It's still a nice thing to say. It's a sign of God's beneficence toward all his children. It doesn't matter what you believe."

Amber resumed eating her cotton candy. It was unlike her to eat at the desk. She had chided me once for eating a banana. "Where did you get cotton candy?" I said.

"The Omicron Nus," said Amber. "They're sponsoring an event in the quad."


Two metal file boxes have surfaced in the thesis cage. That even the dregs of the Baumann material should have been so carelessly handled is typical of Porteous. The boxes contained letters, invoices, and ephemera pertaining to the Seaberg Society for the years 1968 and 1969, around the time of their dissolution. Seem to recall the Seaberg Society had corresponded with Sherwood before his disappearance. I wonder when they were reformed? Perhaps I would find something of interest. "Something of interest" being an euphemism for anything pertaining to magic. Or that might help me locate the professor.

An alarm sounded. Amber and Diane entered the Vault, succeeded by Lloyd, Hey Now, and Dixie. The new duck-and-cover protocols dictated staff should now take refuge in Room 108. Amber and Diane kneeled on either side of me holding Hogg's sermons over their heads.

"Is this for a tornado or the bomb?" said Amber.

"Only Bert the Turtle knows. But with Carswell A.F.B. a hop, skip, and a jump away, a rare book won't keep your face from melting off," I said. "Don't think they make a distinction anymore."

Two bells indicated we could return to our duties. On her way out of the Vault, Dixie noticed my Sherlock Holmes throne. "What is this doing in here?"

"It belongs to L.F., I think," I said. Given his penchant for outlandish chairs, the lie seems plausible.

Diane lingered to inspect my discovery. She regarded the metal file boxes with circumspect curiosity but asked no questions. She probably wants to look through them when I am not around. She must be close to her goal now. Whatever that may be. She went upstairs. I concealed the file boxes under a drop cloth. Whatever she is up to, I was not going to make it easy for her.

Rehearsal to prepare for this Sunday's benefit concert. While setting up, I referred to the F-800B owner's manual. Nowhere does it mention a mojo knob. I considered asking Tim about it but decided against it. If it was Diane's doing, I had better keep it quiet. Everyone's gear has sand in it. None of us felt the need to be there and the evening devolved into childish noise making. Dave II struck the gong for our attention. "Why don't we rockify a lengthy, difficult classical piece?"

"Now you're talking," I said. "You're looking much better, by the way."

"Two days in intensive care," said Dave II.

"Intensive care?"

"They didn't think I was going to make it. They said they had never observed such a low white blood cell count in a living human being."

The whole thing sounded fishy, but I did not press for details. "Nobody told me! Gee, Dave, I would have visited you had I known. Brought you flowers."

"Let's do *The Planets*," said Tim impatiently.

"'Mars' is King Crimson territory," I said dismissively.

"We could try Beethoven's Fifth Symphony," said Dave II.

"There's no way we could do it justice," I said. "How about Scriabin's

*Preparation for the Final Mystery?*" Of course I was not serious. The piece was on my mind lately, having considered it in relation to Zuberon's cosmological emanations as well as how music in general could serve magical purposes.

"Wholly unsuitable for the rock idiom," said Dave II, who evidently took my absurd suggestion at face value. "Honegger's *Pacific 231* contains some interesting material." When he explained it was about a train, I balked. "I don't play the blues, train songs, or songs about Mama." By the time we reached a consensus on themes from *Die Meistersinger von Nürnberg*, it may as well have been "Jimmy Crack Corn" because I no longer cared. Dave said he would have something arranged for our next practice. We discussed a new medley. Five songs in five minutes with all the best parts omitted. No, thanks. For reference, Bonnie put Rush's live album on the turntable. Lightning struck nearby and the power went out. Five glowing cigarettes appeared one by one in the darkness.

"Anyone seen Rush?" said Dave II.

"Saw them at the Electric Ballroom with Iron Butterfly," said Bonnie.

"Iron Butterfly was my first concert," said Tim. "No, wait. It was Jeff Beck at LuAnne's. Sixty-eight, thereabouts. He and Pete are my guitar heroes. But my first guitar god was Quick Draw McGraw." Tim brought his guitar down as if to smash it. "Kabong!" he yelled.

"Cool," said Dave II. He turned to Bonnie. "What was your first concert?"

"The Texas International Pop Festival, for me," she said. "My dad took me."

"I was there, too!" blurted Fred. "Man, Space Opera was tremendous. They blew Airplane away."

"High praise, indeed," said Dave II. "I saw Hendrix in Ottawa in '68."

"Mantovani at the Arlington State College Auditorium," I said. "My aunt took me. Sixty-five? No, sixty-six. I was deaf for three days."

Back at Collinwood, I got out the *Dictionnaire infernal* I had sneaked home from the library and casually compared it to the codex. No overlap, there, but Randy had prepared me for that. The *kakoi* of the codex appear in no other book that I know of. Still, it is interesting to consider not only that demons are real, but that they are so varied in appearance and ability. Where do they come from? And how is it that occult practitioners agree upon their attributes unless they have corroborated them? After a late plate of nachos, I studied, then dozed off to a gentle thunderstorm.


Saturday, May 21

Still thrilled about my quantum leaps in muskrat farming. If only the codex had a concordance, I could leap even farther. My own copy is already well-thumbed from trying to find passages. Did not make it out the door until almost eight.

Spotted a garage sale around the corner on Sanguinet. Must be that time of year. Since I had a little cash, I stopped and came away with a 1957 *Wallace's Street Guide*, the same one I used to have as a kid. Also snagged a trashed copy of Grand Funk's *Shinin' On* with the star-shaped 3-D specs. I wore them over my normal glasses all day. Now that I have observed Dixie's tie rule I can get away with all kinds of other shit.

"Oh, boy," said Amber. "Here comes Elton John."

"Get back, honky cat!" I snapped. Professor Ziglar shushed me from across the reading room.

"Did he just shush me?" I whispered. Amber giggled. At least we can agree that the professor has got to go.

"This eraser stinks," I said idly.

"Stop smelling it, then," said Amber. She drew a mermaid. I lackadaisically leafed through a new translation of *Beowulf* that just arrived. The 3-D lenses made it impossible to read. They must have affected my depth perception because I knocked the epic poem off the desk. It landed on a potted cactus, breaking one of its branches. I have always said that was a stupid place for a cactus. It has snagged my pant leg more than once.

Ziglar approached the desk and cleared his throat. "Degenerate art should not exist," he said in his reedy, didactic drawl. Was he referring to Amber's mermaid drawing?

"Who gets to decide what is degenerate?" I said.

The professor pointed heavenward as the sound of thunder rolled through the library. The synchronicity annoyed me. "Can't argue with you there," I said. Ziglar proceeded to talk my ear off about how the divorce rate in Tarrant County has doubled over the last decade. He attributes the increase to, among other things, declining church attendance. "Brides who don't attend church services expect white weddings," he said. "They treat churches as supermarkets and weddings as Hollywood events."

"True," I said. I smiled and nodded.

"Steven, don't forget to put your report on Mee Maw's desk," said Amber.

"Who the f—?" I blurted. "Right. My report." I turned back to Ziglar and said, "If you'll excuse me." Ziglar walked away muttering.

"Hey, thanks for saving me," I said to Amber.

"You're welcome," said Amber. "Professor Ziglar is certainly a chatterbox. I don't have the power to save anyone, however. That honor belongs to Jesus Christ, our Lord and Savior. I'm simply His humble servant who aims to bring light and hope to the world."

"That you do, Amber," I said. My tone was patronizing. "I'm going to slip out for a cig." On my way to the patio, I stopped by my desk and took the decanter from my mansack. When I was sure no one was looking, I released the imp. He took Guddu's form. A sign of obedience, I reasoned. If I leave him imprisoned too much, resentment will build up. Releasing him, on the other hand, will be seen by him as a magnanimous gesture on my part. To be repaid with voluntary favors instead of simply obeying commands. I am starting to understand Dixie's position better.

"See this cart of festschrifts?" I said. "Put these away for me. When you are done, you may sharpen these pencils." I refrained from saying "Witness, Shagduk, obey."

Guddu bowed with unctuous courtesy. His usual curiosity was not on display when he failed to inquire about my 3-D specs.

"I'm out of cigs," I said, patting my pockets. "Will you get me some?" I chose these words to see what he would do. If I was hoping to witness Guddu conjure up a pack of Kents out of thin air, I was disappointed. They materialized in his palm so quickly, I missed it. Probably could have done it myself, but spells require a certain amount of mojo and my reserves are not unlimited. Right now I am running on nacho fumes.

"Thank you, Guddu." I casually turned away like this amazing feat was the most prosaic thing in the world. Guddu has to believe that magic is nothing special to me. And that mine is far greater than his.

"Guddu is to be your dogsbody?" said Guddu. The question caught me off guard, as did his casual use of the word 'dogsbody.' Has he read my diary? Can he read my mind? "That goes without saying, does it not?" I said matter-of-factly. I extended no explanation and he did not ask for one.

The imp stood at the lectern, closely examining the dictionary. His English has improved since I first saw him. If only I could learn languages that easily. "What's the word of the day, Guddu?"

"The word of the day is 'muskrat,'" he said presciently.

He clearly knows this game. With my middle finger I pushed my glasses up my nose. "Buffalo buffalo Buffalo buffalo buffalo buffalo Buffalo buffalo," I said. Guddu stared at me in bewilderment. "It's perfectly grammatical," I added. Go ahead, diagram it. I did not tell him I could never make heads nor tails of the lexically ambiguous statement.

Closing time, Spunt approaches. "Care if I split?" he said. "Hot date in Dalworthington Gardens."

"Go ahead," I said. "I'll lock up." I could not tell if Guddu was invisible to Spunt, or if Spunt simply did not notice him. At any rate, he had no reaction to Guddu's unexplained reappearance in the library.

"Guddu, fetch me that flyswatter," I said. "Did you hear me?" He was still processing my buffalo sentence. With maddening deliberation, he obliged.

Guddu, Amber, and I stood in the vestibule ignoring each other like strangers. Like the rest of the staff, the kid typically shows no interest in Guddu whatsoever. To be that inconspicuous! There should be a formula for that. In Guddu's case, it seems more like an innate, chameleon-like power. A brass plaque I had never noticed before caught my attention. "The Christian and Eleanor Riddle Vestibule," I read aloud. "Must everything be named after a donor? Even the dang water fountain is the P. Harris Schlumberger Water Fountain."

"He speaks," said Amber facetiously. What did I do? The child librarian departed into the rain, unescorted.

Turtle Man ducked into the vestibule, soaked to the bone. "Do you have the key to the break room?" he said, panting.

"It doesn't have a lock," I said.

Turtle Man held up his Thermos. "Mind if I fill this with milk? That's my milk in the refrigerator. I brought it for the campus A.A. meeting."

"Knock yourself out," I said.

"What is an A.A. meeting?" said Guddu.

"A club for dipsomaniacs," I said.

"The dipsomaniacs meet in the William Lawrence Peebles Thrice Meeting Room?"

"Yes, but it's the William Lawrence Peebles *the Third* Meeting Room."

"There are three of them?"

So many questions. And, so long as I stand here, it is I who must answer them.

Turtle Man returned. "Thanks, buddy," he said. "I owe you one. By the way, there's a lot left. Wet your beaks, if you want."

Guddu and I were alone. What forces compel his uneasy servitude? Perhaps the genie bottle is unnecessary. His obedience could be a put on, so he could observe me more naturally. Or is he just biding his time? Until what?

"Where is Buffalo?" said Guddu.

"That's an unlikely question for someone who ostensibly grew up around the Great Lakes," I said. "Have a good evening." When he saw I had no intention of answering him, he hung his head down and exited the library. I locked the door behind him then took off the 3-D specs. Uh oh, my vision had become accustomed to the red and blue lenses. The lighted exit sign was gray. What about traffic signals? The rain was really coming down now. May as let my vision revert to normal.

Had no desire to encounter Boggs or Carlos so I headed to the Vault and locked myself in. I cracked open a Pibb, lit a Kent, and sat heavily upon my Sherlock Holmes throne with a sigh. With little else to do, now would be a fine time to farm a muskrat.

It only makes sense that one should practice a formula before using it in the real world. In this case, Door Number Two, so-called to distinguish it from the other. The thunderstorm was intensifying, evidenced by a pervasive, low rumbling that rattled the shelves. Even here among the musty old books, it smelled like rain. It is said in the Martin Solis book that one may take advantage of a storm's energy when employing magic. Further analysis is best left for the pages of my red notebook, but let us say that today's muskrat farming succeeded in that a door was indeed opened. An invisible one, discernible only by the way light bent subtly around its edges. This disturbance in the air revealed an oval shape as large as the trash hole at home. Into it I tossed several Hogg sermons, which subsequently vanished. After some careful thought, I decided not to pass through. There was just no way to know what was on the other side, or if I could even come back.

A faint whiff of sulfur tickled my nostrils. "Shagduk!" I hissed.

"Yes, Steven?" said a voice from the air duct near the ceiling. The imp's presence made me angrier than it should have. How much did he see? At this point it does not really matter.

"Even in a locked room one can't get any privacy," I griped. "How long have you been spying on me?"

"Guddu is not spying!" he squealed. I found it interesting he would refer to himself as Guddu in his impish form. "Please, what is a muskrat?"

"You know damn well it's the word of the day," I said. Shagduk somehow got hold of the codex and clutched it to his breast with his slender claws. When I lunged for it, he dodged me, like Figgy when I reach to pet him.

There was a clap of thunder. The lights went out. I acted quickly. With a gesture and a word, a sphere of illumination appeared around me as a pale, yellow bubble. Bright enough to glimpse the imp's legs slip into the air duct, the grill of which clattered noisily to the floor.

An observer such as Carlos might wonder greatly at the sight of a ball of light advancing up the stairs to the mezzanine. I ascended the ladder and found Shagduk huddled in the corner of the hobbit room. Shielding himself from my glamor, he shrank from me when I drew nearer.

"The book," I repeated. "Witness Shagduk obey!" I hissed. The imp obeyed. To be free of his *yaje*!


Space Opera is playing at the Ship's Wheel to raise money for one of the Blevins brothers. Doug Blevins, hyperrealistic painter of Texas landscapes, needs a transplant or something. If a witch has stolen his spleen, couldn't a witch also return it? Fred and Bonnie were there, as was Bonnie's sister, whose name I can never remember. She was wearing a homemade bear suit. Behind the stage a loop of film showed her eating bowls of porridge and testing out mattresses. I paused to see how it was possible to eat porridge through such a small opening. What a mess. I failed to see how the performance could be regarded as artistic. That it could be magical is a thought I would once upon a time have never had.

Fred and I snagged a spot near the P.A. The quartet stuck to mostly instrumental music, including two versions of "Guitar Suite." The first was played almost to the end; the second was played backwards to the beginning. Much of it was aleatoric and in that regard had more in common with free form jazz than what one knew from their album. Some of those in attendance lost interest and wandered away, leaving room for Fred and me to scoot closer. Fred dug it, of course. I, on the other hand, fell under their spell. The band would have seen me leaning in close, my brow furrowed in deep concentration. At some point during the performance, I had an epiphany. It became clear to me how to employ musical components in place of purely somatic ones in farming muskrats. Not only that, but my ideas concerning a potential relationship between music and language were now ripening on the vine. All that remained was to find an excuse to "speak" Tarkusian. At home on my guitar, certainly. But in the context of Time Frame, anything might be possible.

For the rest of the evening these theories raced through my mind. My scribbles filled a stack of cocktail napkins. Unable to hold a simple conversation, I was useless as a companion. I made excuses and left.

Back at Collinwood, I faced a pile of dirty clothes and an almost bare cupboard. Soon I had hunkered down on the couch with my last TV dinner, chiseled out like a relic from the Ice Age. Images from *Spectre* bombarded my retinas. Robert Culp dabbles in the occult and battles demons. It could be a movie about my own life. I watched it passively, without understanding. These, I passively received without understanding. My brain was just too fried. Like it felt after that one week where Randy and I spoke only Dordic to each other.

"Buffalo," I said to Figgy. He leaped deftly into my lap with a friendly, trilled meow. On account of semantic satiation, the word now held no meaning for me. I must take my mind off that dreaded sentence. Perhaps *Die Tür* might help explain the difference between Door Numbers One and Two. But reading Fraktur is maddening. And looking up compound words in a German dictionary is the pits. Then there are my musical theories. I nodded off next to my guitar.


SUNDAY, MAY 22

After last night I expected Shagduk to be difficult. Instead, I found him well behaved, if brooding. Much of the time he spends either in his bottle or another as yet undisclosed location. The trash hole? The hobbit room? As long as he stays out of my hair, I suppose it does not matter.

The ad specified eight. When I arrived at seven, people were already lined up at the gate. Some had even climbed over it and stood peering through the tripartite window on the front door. With difficulty I pushed past the crowd and into Randy's house, where I worked quickly to finish sticking colored dots on everything. Blue dots, five cents; orange dots, ten cents; red dots, twenty-five cents. Gold starred items were a dollar, but there were few of those. Whenever someone rang the doorbell, I clenched my jaw. Read the stupid sign! I admitted the crowd ten minutes early then had to endure the wrath of those who arrived at eight on the dot to discover people already inside.

"How much is this gas mask?" said a man who looked like Snoopy if Snoopy were a man.

"Put that down," demanded his wife.

"But it's only a nickel," he whined.

"You'll need a permit to do this after the sixth," snapped one busybody. A pair of dandies snagged a mysterious-looking idol. One of many given away by Atlantic Records to promote Led Zeppelin's *Presence*. A gold star item I had considered keeping for myself. But I did not want to end up like Bobby in that one *Brady Bunch* episode. Guess I am superstitious, after all. One of the dandies held up a chrome server for scrutiny. What was Randy even doing with one of those? It seemed a very grown-up thing to own.

"Oh, Dudley," he said. "Take a gander at this, would you? You can always judge an estate sale by what they're asking for the penguin hot and cold."

The couple regarded the red dot. It must have passed the test because they bought it. They also bought the giant wooden fork and spoon I gave Randy for his birthday.

By noon, the place had been decimated. No one wanted Randy's threadbare sofa at any price. Nor his brass trunk coffee table upon which the two of us had summoned a beast from another dimension. Other than that, only a spice rack and a gold-starred human skull remained, the latter which I kept. The bookseller picked up the remaining books in the afternoon without incident. I hung on to *The Morning of the Magicians* and *Lives of the Necromancers* for myself.

Guddu stood in the corner, pondering the skull like Hamlet. "You're awfully quiet today," I said.

"Steven has not commanded Guddu to speak," he said with a hint of sarcasm. It surprises me that he is capable of sarcasm. Or even understands what it is. The imp's obedience continues to impress me. I do not trust him. If only because of what he is. Is he a breathing creature like Figgy? He is quadrupedal the way a tree or a stone is not. He has two eyeballs, two nostrils, and one trap. Yet one would not find him on a phylogenetic tree nestled snugly between, say, Cro-Magnon and komodo dragon.

The ashtray held the world record for number of butts contained. Incense ashes filled a hubcap. These, I tossed out into a thick cloud, a move I instantly regretted. What I did not inhale now covered my face and arms. Neither Randy nor I own a vacuum cleaner. I made Guddu sweep the shag carpet with a broom. I wiped down and unplugged the icebox, then mopped the kitchen and bathroom. Sweaty work. Should have made the imp do it all.

On my way out, I slipped on some aquarium gravel on the porch. Guddu smirked. Was this his doing? I must be more careful.


Gig at the Rhinestone, a dazzling mega-saloon rivaled in size only by Billy Bob's. Twelve bands in twelve hours for a muscular dystrophy benefit or some such thing. Gratis, of course. I keep telling Bonnie we should hire a real manager. In our booth by the restrooms, we got blitzed on highballs served in fruit jars. As usual, Tim outpaced us all on liquor consumption. He almost got us all ejected when he mooned our waitress.

"Put your ass away," I groaned.

Unable to hear conversation or even my own thoughts over the din, I amused myself by watching people fly off the mechanical bull. Half the fun was watching the ladies try to hang on for dear life. You never knew when something was going to ride up or pop out. That I should discover this before Tim the pussyhound did speaks to his level of inebriation. What should have been drunken screams of excitement quickly turned into drunken screams of agony. One chick was KO'ed when she somersaulted over the horns. The mechanism came down on her face. Later, Bonnie's nurse friend explained the girl had suffered a traumatic dislocation of the eyeball into the maxillary sinus.

Roller Girl was next. She mounted the bull with her skates on. During her ride, she waved at me. Since I fingerbanged her at Spencer's, I figured I could get her to ride me later with little effort. But I am not sure I want her to. Getting laid should not be this hard. Especially in 1977. Why is it so important? I had come close a few times with Loretta but what she used to do to me was technically not intercourse. I had reached third base with Jenny. Or did she reach third base? I am not much of a baseball fan.

We went on at eleven but were asked to stop playing for a few minutes as someone was trying to load a real bull into a truck in the parking lot. The joint filled up with ropers. The highlight of our short set was when Roller Girl inserted a beer bottle into my mouth. I tilted my head backwards and chugged the beer while playing bass.

"Let the boot scootin' commence!" announced the emcee. Razzmatazz stormed the stage like a S.W.A.T. team. They launched into a country-disco hybrid of "Cotton-Eyed Joe." The tune elicited uncomfortable memories of having been forced to learn this dance in school. When the song was over, Al Dean's recorded version was still blasting from the jukebox, having been playing at the same time.

"Are you coming with us?" I said to Bonnie after we had loaded the van.

"I've had enough for one evening," she said wearily.

Roller Girl was waiting for me in the shadows. Time to choose. I put my arm around Dawn. "Ride with me," I said. Tim and I followed each other all the way down North Main, each honking, flashing our lights, and jockeying for position. The girls squealed out the window. That we made it to the Water Gardens in one piece is surely a miracle.

"This used to be Hell's Half Acre, for you history buffs," I said. "Sam Bass territory." No one was listening. We strolled around the park, laughing, drinking, and singing. From a terraced concrete knoll Dawn and I duetted "Mockingbird." It made me maudlin, as Randy and I used to sing it in the car in retard voices. "That bastard," I hiccupped. Dawn and I took turns pissing in the bushes.

We found Dave II naked in the quiet, blue meditation pool. He was singing "Ogre Battle" and using his Stretch Johnson as a tremolo. He seemed like a man possessed.

"You can get fined two hundred dollars for doing that," I warned.

Dave II shot me an undeserved bird. "Don't shoot the messenger," I said. "Dave doesn't act like a Mormon," I said softly to Dawn.

"Mormon?" she said. "No. He's Canadian."

Canadian! That explains much. I mouthed the words "come on." The two of us soon found ourselves on a broad polygonal carpet of soft green Bermuda. From the direction of the Mixmaster one could hear the soft roar of engine-braking semis. These competed with the shush of thin sheets of water cascading softly down the surrounding pebbled walls.

To amuse Dawn, I swung around a light pole like *That Girl*. The pole must have been corroded at the base, for it toppled, leaving a deep gash in the ground. I toppled, too.

"Oh my gosh, are you okay?" said Dawn. She reached down and pulled me to my feet. Sheets of lightning illuminated the sky, revealing an ominous dark wall of clouds to the west.

Dawn and I continued toward the active pool, which we found curiously unlit. We descended the spiraling cyclopean slabs amidst torrents of water crashing down the steep terraces. Figured we could sit on the edge and talk. Maybe more, if I was lucky.

"Take my hand," I urged. It was impossible to maintain a grip whenever Dawn stepped down. On the penultimate slab from the bottom she faltered in her Candies. She tumbled silently into the churning waters.

Since the "cooling oasis in the concrete jungle" had opened a few years ago, I had feared this Stonehenge of steps. When they featured in *Logan's Run*, I naturally assumed someone was about to die. Like the cold, murky depths beneath the diving platform at Burger's Lake, no one could tell you how deep it was.

The surface of the turbulent waters was beyond my reach. I looked about for something, anything, that I could use to fish Dawn out of the basin. A tree branch? The bald cypresses of the perimeter were out of the question. The fallen light pole was too distant, and too heavy besides. Bubbles burst to the surface, but no Dawn. The pumps would be pulling her to the bottom and holding her there. *Parting of the Waters*, one of the easiest formulae of all, would be useless here. I tried it anyway, in vain.

The wind picked up, as did the thunder. Among the bubbles there appeared two dark forms. They slowly materialized opposite me, one form laboriously dragging the other, larger one. I skipped to the other side, careful not to trip in the gaps between slabs.

"Get away from her!" I snapped. The imp perched on a nearby platform and watched as I attended Dawn's limp body. Her moony face was pale and clammy. I recalled the steps for artificial respiration. *Clear the mouth and throat. Tilt head jack and lift jaw. Pinch nose. Blow.*

"Green Bug!" sobbed Vee. She hugged Dawn, then threw her arms around me and covered my cheeks in kisses. Tim stood there grimacing. Not only was the spotlight on me and not Tim, but Vee was with me, not him. "It's not a competition!" I wanted to say, though in my heart I knew it had become one. Dave II slapped me on the back. "Great job, man," he said. He drew me aside. "Your friend Diane's a real bitch, did you know that?" he said, but did not elaborate.

The imp must have slipped back into the water. 1502 Commerce Street is the address Guddu had indicated on his emergency contact form. Is this where he goes when he is not with me?

The rolling thunder that echoed down Lancaster was now constant. Hail pelted us as we scrambled for our cars.

MONDAY, MAY 23

"Wave hello to the librarian." The toddler turned away and waved to no one. Jo Ann gripped her nephew by the shoulders and spun him in his baby walker around toward me. I waved back. So did Guddu. He stooped to pinch the cherubic cheek. The child immediately screamed bloody murder. Guddu shrank behind the ficus. When the child began choking, I saw Guddu give a snicker of wicked glee. To my relief, the child quickly recovered.

Inexplicably attached to his back were two white, feathery wings. "He looks like an angel," I said.

"That's no angel," scoffed Amber. "Angels' entire bodies, including their backs, hands, and wings, are full of eyes all around, as are their four wheels."

"Well, he's got the four wheels right."

"Their bodies are covered with eyes?" said Guddu with an expression of alarm. Amber and I ignored him.

Besides committing interminable mischief, the imp is here only to keep an eye on me, I now recognize. The work he does for the library is meaningless, a masquerade. This morning I caught him in the stacks juggling bound journals like a circus clown. If I do not give him tasks to perform, he busies himself with activities which upon casual observation appear legitimate. Upon closer inspection, however, they are damaging to the library. He types up catalog cards for non-existent titles only to misfile them. Or he removes books from the shelf. Of course, he then misshelves them. Staff are beginning to notice and complain. As he is more or less invisible to them, no one blames Guddu. I have neither the time nor energy to train and supervise him. Since I now lack the privacy of an office, I could only speak to Guddu in a low voice.

"Two things," I said. "Number one. Thank you for saving Dawn's life. And I really mean it." Guddu just glared at me. "Number two. Did you take care of that cart of festschrifts I asked you to put away?"

"Yes."

"I'll need more information because here is the cart," I said. "As you can see, the festschrifts are still piled high. By the way, Hazel has been blaming Sarge for your snafus in the stacks. You will cease at once. Do you understand?" It never occurred to me that Guddu would lie to me. Of course it should not surprise me.

"What is a snafu?"

"You, Guddu," I said. "If you really worked here you would have been fired ages ago. Your shenanigans can't be at the expense of people like Sarge. He's a good guy."

"Yes, Steven," said Guddu, in a hurt tone. "Guddu is a snafu."

*My own snafu*, I thought. "And put on a damned tie." I am starting to sound like Dixie.

Guddu stood, then scowled at me before turning to leave. Almost said something but held my tongue. I am going to have to be more careful about the way I speak to him. The imp is dangerous. Peace must be maintained.

"In case of emergency, break glass," read the plaque in the break room. I broke it and took the cigarette, then dropped the plaque in the trash. It was too hot to go outside, so I smoked in the men's room and glanced through a Sunday paper someone left behind. A piece on Jimmy Page caught my eye. The rock star owns an occult bookshop and lives in Aleister Crowley's former digs. Bet he can't perform an *Invisible Wedgie*.

Dixie spotted me traversing the reading room and called me into her office. "Shut the door," she said curtly. She slid a scrap of paper across her desk. "What is the meaning of this?" she demanded.

It was a catalog card for a book titled *This Is Bullshit* by Rantum Scantum. Published by Tallywags Press in Fort Worth, Texas in the year 1476. Guddu's doing, no doubt. "Is that a real book?" I said, stifling a grin.

"You tell me, Steven."

Clearly she thinks I am responsible. Why not Spunt? I rose from my seat and excused myself.

"You will wear a tie in this library," snapped Dixie. "This is your final warning." Crap! I admonished Guddu for not wearing one while not wearing one myself. I need to get my shit together.

*Witness Steven obey.* I stopped to check my cubby hole for mail. A memo from Dixie about the shenanigans dish and a parcel with no return address wrapped in plain brown paper. The latter contained a privately-printed edition of Ovid's *Ars amatoria*, the cover of which promises to teach one "how to meet her, how to get her turned on to you, and how to get her into the sack." Tucked within its pages was a spiral-locked letter I recognized as Randy's handiwork. The text was in Dordic. The Bastard's Dordic is idiosyncratic but when a word is not known he simply transliterates it. Toss in a little Nadsat and some private slang, this argot would be incomprehensible to everyone on Earth except me.

*Dude,*

*Made it to California in one piece. Dropped the garbage truck in Bakersfield then hitched to Frisco. Am staying at a youth hostel for hostile youth. They've got me camping in a courtyard in my sleeping bag. Preferable to indoors but I awaken covered in morning dew. Everyone here is high. This one scuzz was using my holy skillet. I said, "Where did you get it?" He said he traded it off a prostitute for a goofball. And I hadn't even been here an hour yet. When I confronted the prostitute, she stabbed me with a key. So much for the Summer of Love!*

*You are probably wondering about my sudden departure. All will be revealed in time but this was a journey I had to make by myself. You must trust me on this one. In the meantime, I would ask that you not speak to anyone about Sherwood. Do not attempt any more muskrat farming. Too much can go wrong in ways you can't even begin to imagine. Or maybe you can. I regret leaving you to deal with Harvey but I trust you are rid of him by now.*

*You can write to me here. They said they would forward my mail if I move on, which I intend to do soon.*

*Yr. obt. serv't,*

*The Bastard*

*P.S. Enclosed is a "how to" from the year 2 to help you keep your New Year's resolutions.*

The band rehearsed a new tune, "Masturbator von Nürnberg" (Wagner meets Porter Wagoner). Its four-part harmonies recall Shaker spirituals. It boasts a melodically extravagant section where I must play recorder and bass simultaneously. The piece is longer and more challenging than our usual fare, pushing the limits of our abilities. The only problem is the lyrics, which Tim wrote. Every line ends in "-ation" and one includes the word "stagflation."

"The Moody Blues do it," said Tim. "Besides, do you have anything better?"

"As a matter of fact, I do." I fished out my lyrics to "Evil Woman."

"Isn't this a song by E.L.O.?"

"Is it?" I said. "I always thought they were saying 'medieval.' By the way, what happened to your new guitar?"

"Chiggerex destroyed the varnish," said Tim gloomily.

We loaded the van. Tim and I got into it over who was the superior drummer, Bill Bruford or Alan White. As I was loading my cab into the trunk, Tim nudged me behind the knee. This caused me to drop it onto the fender, scratching it. If I had done the same to him, he would have lost his damn mind.

Everything that is good is compromised by Tim's choices, even though much that is good is on account of him. Then, there are the professor's disappearance, the witch's machinations, and the imp's shenanigans. I would quit the band if it were not for its potential for large-scale musico-magical operations. A potential that begs to be explored.

Stopped by Randy's on the way home to feed his bettas. They were floating belly up.

TUESDAY, MAY 24

Early to work. Had just left the elevator with my book cart when Carlos came stumbling from the Vault, his radio squealing. His eyes were rolled back into their sockets and he was drooling profusely. There was nothing to do but call an ambulance.

Throughout the morning, everyone whispered about Carlos being on drugs. How quickly people turn on the janitor. Not that there was any great love for him to begin with.

This much is certain: Door Number Two had remained open after Shagduk swiped the codex and I had chased him down. In the intervening time, anything could have come through. That had happened on Saturday. Whatever came through, Carlos evidently found it.

I had to see for myself. I tossed a Hogg sermon toward where the door had been. *Poof*! Gone. How to close it now? Previous efforts had failed. As urgent as the matter was, there was not much I could do but to lock the Vault and hide the spare key. Before doing so, I searched the room carefully. What was I looking for? The only thing amiss was the cover to the air duct. It was still lying on the floor where the imp had disturbed it.

With a sigh of resignation, I armed myself with the blade from an old paper cutter and made my way up to the mezzanine. From there, I crawled up into the hobbit room. I had to remind myself I was not simply yielding to paranoia. I was being careful. And thorough. A real muskrat farmer would not take chances at a time like this. A real muskrat farmer—is that what I am? Perhaps I am fooling myself. My own snafu was why I was in this situation. Randy would be appalled.

The claustrophobic space remained as it was. There was no obvious indication that Shagduk had used it in some time. I was preparing to leave when I came face to face with a dwarf. The panther's handler from Mayfest. He seemed as surprised as I was. As he scrambled into one of the vents, I grabbed his britches and yanked him onto the floor. He sprung to his feet and withdrew to the corner. "Why have you come here?" I demanded. The dwarf merely grinned. His golden chompers gleamed from his face of jet. He must have a good dentist. The last time we parted ways, his mouth was a bloody mess.

The dwarf raised his finger. I raised my own. Our evocations canceled each other out with a loud *crack*. Without missing a beat, the dwarf produced an axe and was upon me. I parried with my paper cutter blade. Its heft made it a surprisingly effective weapon until the dwarf disarmed me skillfully. A brutal punch crushed his larynx. Figured he was done for.

"You're in Fort Worth Osteopathic," said Diane. "What happened, Steven?"

"Give me my clothes," I demanded weakly. Diane called for the nurse. After I was sitting up and sipping Tang, I learned the dwarf had gotten me on the shoulder and the side of my head. Nineteen stitches, total. Not sure how the broken lateral malleolus happened. I struggled to recall our showdown. Unless I am mistaken, the dwarf got the worst of it. For the second time. Factor in my victory over the thing from Door Number One, as well as numerous fights in school, and I am at two wins and seven losses. My record is improving!

"Where's my mansack?"

"In your car," said Diane.

"My car?" So Diane had driven me here. Guess she knows how to hotwire the Rambler. She has probably found *Successful Muskrat Farming* and read it all by now. My thoughts were racing. Had the dwarf come through Door Number Two? He must have.

The nurse took my temperature. Yes, I could go home now. Diane offered to take me. When we reached the Rambler, she produced my keychain from her droopy denim handbag. The ignition key was present. "Where did you find this?" I said.

"What do you mean?" she said. I knew that either she had no intention of telling the truth, or I was crazy and it had been there all along.

Being alone with Diane in the car took me back to our Philadelphia trip. I reminded myself to watch my step around her. We stopped at a Town and Country (where Laws Brothers used to be) on the way for Anacin and a lighter. Diane made a wide U-turn in the parking lot. The fan belt howled in protest. It has been doing that lately. Next stop, 7-Eleven for Slurpees. She returned with only one beverage.

"This was their last cup so we'll have to share," she explained. I could taste her cherry lip gloss on the straw. Contrived intimacy. Typical Diane. I have given up wondering why.

She kicked off her clogs. She prepared an ice pack and propped my leg up with pillows. She then thumbed through the *Dictionnaire infernal.* "Where do they come from?" she said. As if she did not know.

"Who?"

She tapped on Eurynome, one of the horrid illustrations by Le Breton. It resembled Shagduk.

"I don't know," I said. That much was true. "How did we find out about them at all?"

"They sought us first," said Diane thoughtfully. What might she know about imps? Or dwarfs, for that matter. I kept waiting for her to ask me why I have a book on demonology. She removed the scarf holding her hair up, then playfully draped it over my face.

"Are you hungry?" I said. "I have a can of chow mein."

"I could bring back Pancho Villa's."

I love that place, but it is too soon to face the sting of another taco. "King Wok's right around the corner," I said.

We porked out while watching Jimmy Stewart on Channel 11. Diane used her chopsticks effortlessly and without thought. But she seemed more interested in Figgy than eating. She kept scratching his chin and whispering to him.

"Listen to that purr!" I said. "Looks like you've made a friend."

"Do you want to come home with me?" cooed Diane to Figgy. She turned to me. "How am I going to get home?"

"You can stay here, if you want," I said. She was going to stay no matter what. May as well let her think it was my idea. "Can you hand me my mansack?"

"It's so heavy," she said. "What's inside?"

"Manly things," I teased, reaching for the bag as casually as I could. LittLittle did she know what she held within her hands. I was beginning to think she did.

"Chap Stick?"

"And Dynamints and tickets to Casa Mañana. So what? Besides, nobody wants to kiss chapped lips."

Diane retrieved from her own handbag a mirrored case. "Fancy a bump?"

"Huh?" I said. Was she planning on staying up all night?

We watched *Mutiny on the Bounty*. Or I at least pretended to. It is difficult to focus on television with a sexy, treacherous witch sharing my bed. "Would you?" I said. The witch somersaulted backwards off the bed to adjust the rabbit ears. She did it a little to the left. The image was perfect.

"Do you have an extra toothbrush?"

"You can use mine," I said. "If you don't care about cooties."

Diane came out of the bathroom brushing her hair. Her lustrous curls tumbled about her shoulders like a soft, dark waterfall. She opened several drawers. "Got anything I can lounge in?" she said. "Whose is this?" She held up a skimpy garment.

"My ex's," I said sheepishly. Which was not even true. It belonged to my ex-girlfriend's girlfriend. "Why don't you put this on?"

Diane changed in front of me, pulling my ratty old 'Dillos tee over her head. Her torso is longer than Jenny's so it did not cover everything. She fell backwards onto the bed, then raised her legs toward the ceiling. Supporting her hips with her hands, she started pedaling. Anything for attention.

"That guy's getting keelhauled," I said, looking at the TV.

Diane seemed irritated that I was watching the movie and not her. "I'll keelhaul you, landlubber!" she said. "It seems that in a moment of exuberance, you stole two twenty-five-pound cheeses."

She straddled me and placed her palms flat upon my chest. I could feel my stitches stretch. I had a flashback to when she had dosed me in Austin as Ursula. But instead of tying me up and robbing me, she reached for a pillow and lowered it slowly onto my face. Inexplicably, I let her do it. "Bonk," she said playfully before rolling off me.

"That's not what keelhauling is," I said pedantically. I did not know the next line.

Diane collected our take-out mess and took it into the kitchen. She returned with a cup of liquid. "Drink," she said. If she was going to poison me, it appears I was a willing victim. Naw. She could have used witchcraft. I zonked out pretty fast.

WEDNESDAY, MAY 25

Awoke before dawn, naked and uncovered. *Black Forum* blared from the TV. My hands smelled weird on account of the rubber crutch grips. Diane had signed my cast, and pressed a perfect lip gloss kiss onto it. She had also left a note: "Call me at the library if you need me. I'll see you tonight." Talk about an early riser, unless she never went to sleep at all. I had already resigned myself to the probability that she had searched Collinwood thoroughly, but not so thoroughly she noticed I do not have a telephone. What a ridiculous charade this all is.

My head swam when I sat up. I felt like I had been keelhauled. *I drank the potion she offered me. I found myself on the floor.* Even the bits about the lady with the green eyes and long black hair trying to win me with her feminine ways rang true. I am living in a Cliff Richard song.

"Figgy kitty!"

"He's with me!" I yelled.

"Your car's not here," said Vee, bouncing into the living room. "What happened to you?"

Tried to preserve as much truth as possible, if for no other reason than to help keep my story straight. That, and because I am a terrible liar.

"Your job sounds hazardous," Vee decided. She reached down to pet Figgy. "Laundry tonight?"

"If I can," I said. "My friend is coming over."

"The Stone Fox?" she said, clicking her tongue suggestively.

"No," I said. "Just someone I work with."

"Mmm hmm," said Vee. "Give me your dirty things and I'll do them." She reached for my clothes basket.

"Vee, no!" I protested.

"Don't be ridiculous," she said. "I'll be back later!"

My place was now devoid of females, I noted. But for how long? Figured I had better write Randy. In Dordic. Took me all afternoon.

*Dear Bastard,*

*It's a relief to hear from you. Much has transpired since your departure. There is so much to tell that needs to be told in person. Everyone around me is insane, yet I'm the one with the invisible friend that no one else can see. Jimmy Stewart's character in* Harvey *makes sense to me now, although I am probably misunderstanding the entity's presence. I misunderstand most things. I keep expecting Alan Funt to step out of the closet amidst canned laughter. If I only had Amber's faith, for whom the Good Book provides a pat, if scientifically ignorant, explanation for everything.*

*The band went on a mini-tour. Our equipment was stolen in Shreveport. We went to a music shop where Diane told us to get whatever we wanted. Some would rejoice at an opportunity like that. But I like to be my own man.*

*Tim almost got us all busted in Port Aransas for unlawful possession. I don't know for how much longer I can play in a band. At least while Harvey is dogging me. I lose track of what is important. By the way, ELP is touring again. With a full orchestra. Yuck. Prog's last gasp?*

*Remember that fancy bottle on Sherwood's desk? Harvey lives in it now. Harvey does my bidding, if you can believe that. He's a mischievous little asshole, but he did save Dawn from drowning. I think he likes her.*

*I slipped at the library and broke my ankle. Diane took me to the E.R. then spent the night. Before you congratulate me, we didn't sleep together. Alas!*

*Your estate sale netted $226. I can wire it to you. They say never mail cash. I put your skull on the information desk at the library. It looks very poetic there. Am waiting for Dixie to notice. Amazing what I get away with so long as I'm wearing a tie. P.S. Remember the Eldorado West apartments? They razed them. We had a lot of fun times there, man.*

*Yours, etc.,*
*Duke Mantee, Esq.*

Read the first quarter of *The Morning of the Magicians*. I have acquired the new habit of reading several things at once, something I would never have done before. Nor would I have ever set a book aside, unfinished, before now. The part about Emperor Ashoka had me considering non-existent parallels between the Nine Unknown Men and the seven wizards of Vul Kar. To my horror, I discovered how easy it is to be receptive to ideas that under rigorous scrutiny are half-baked or even preposterous. The Doom Hippie would have had multiple epiphanies by now. He and I are not the same. Or perhaps I was just not high enough.

The witch returned. Moments later, Vee appeared with a clean basket of warm folded clothes. My mail was balanced on top. An envelope fell off. Vee picked it up. "Dollface!" she cooed. "Is it your birthday?"

"The 27th," I said. Vee handed me the birthday wishes. They were from Aunt Wanda. The envelope was festooned with colorful designs, smiley faces, and the words, "Happy birthday, Sweetie!" in flowery cursive. "Have you and Diane met?"

The girls exchanged knowing looks. "We're acquainted," said Vee enigmatically. "We had a nice chat." A nightmare come true. Like two exes comparing notes.

"Green Bug and I are going to the lake this weekend," said Vee. "She's house sitting for the sculptor Bill Blevins. You know his work—the big ear next to Ridglea Bank? Come with us. It can be a birthday bash extraordinaire!" Out of the corner of my eye, I thought I saw Diane make a gesture. Or maybe she just shifted her weight. Vee turned to her. "You're invited, too!"

Not only did Diane manage an invitation to the lake house but also a ride home from Vee. She always gets what she wants. Or does she?

I made popcorn and turned on an episode of *Nova* called "The Tongues of Men, Part 2." The narrator contemplated a so-called first language before Babel as a Pentecostal worshiper spoke in tongues. The resemblance of her glossolalia to my incantations was thought provoking. The segment on Leibniz's "algebra of communication" bugged me until the narrator said it is not something you can speak. It is only useful for logicians, mathematicians, and philosophers. He said "logicians" but with his accent it sounded to me like "magicians" and for the rest of the evening I was perturbed. By the time I nodded off I had filled my red notebook with pithy ideas.

THURSDAY, MAY 26

Carlos is back. Guess he still has a few brain cells. Parked next to his pickup on account of my foot. Boggs chewed me out about it. Dixie did the same, immediately thereafter. Had to hobble across the quad to an obscure service window in Comstock to apply for a temporary crippled parking permit. In front of Pigg Auditorium I observed a group of students who had chained themselves together. Some held signs which read "Down with Fluorocarbon Aerosols." To my dismay Guddu was among them. He sure knows how to push my buttons.

My lava lamp is missing. The imp, for sure. Also, my new IBM Selectric is acting up. Mysterial marks appear on the page at random intervals. This one is not Guddu's style. Malfunction or operator error?

X-roxed an old manuscript to send to Randy. It is right up his alley. An account in German of an odious fellow called Der Schleim. Tried to translate it myself but the handwriting is illegible. Oddly familiar, nevertheless. After placing it in the outgoing mail bin, I turned around and collided with Diane. She seemed uncharacteristically rattled. When I asked her what was wrong, she was evasive. Later, she was banging around in her office as if frantically searching for something.

'What is this skull doing here?" said Amber. "If it's real, its place is in a graveyard." Her remark led to a chat about Satanism and the occult. "It's common knowledge that the United States was founded upon occult principles," I said. Just to mess with her head, I pointed out the "all-seeing eye" on a dollar bill. "*Annuit coeptis*. Who do you think favors our undertaking? It ain't Jesus." Amber just grimaced and shook her head.

My ankle is killing me. Amber fetched me a glass of water so I could take my Anacin. An elderly faculty wife inquired if we would accept a donation of her late husband's books. I did not recognize his name. Someone from the Theater department. Tried to get her to describe the books but she would only assure me they were "scholarly" and "the very best." The last time I agreed to accept a gift sight unseen, I had to deal with three dozen boxes of nineteenth-century medical textbooks.

I popped the tablets into my mouth then reached for the glass of water. "My sea monkeys!" lamented Amber. "That's your water over there."

Spent the next twenty minutes trying to find out what sea monkeys were and if I needed to induce vomiting. Not a single book in the library mentions them whatsoever. Why is it the things I need to know the most urgently are not in books?

Evidently, my crutches left black marks on the tiles in the vestibule. Dixie made Carlos clean them with a broomstick with a tennis ball attached to the end. After "Happy Trails" sounded over the P.A., she approached me. "There are numerous boxes in the vestibule filled with damp *Playbill* magazines. Do you know anything about them?"

"Professor Slagle's widow probably dumped them there after I told her not to," I said. The way Dixie pronounces "vestibule" drives me insane.

"The library reserves the right to allocate gift materials without restriction," said Dixie. "You will dispose of them accordingly."

I pointed a crutch at Carlos. "Witness Carlos obey," I barked. Carlos stood with a blank expression on his face. There is a vague air of idiocy about him after his encounter in the Vault. Dixie huffed indignantly, but how am I supposed to carry a box? "By the way, the tennis ball on the broomstick? You should patent that."

Tim picked me up for tonight's gig at the Westerner. A drive-in theater, of all places. Bonnie summoned Car Boy, of all people, to find a way to get us and our gear onto the roof of the concession stand. The Bandido's treasurer succeeded by means of a clever system of pulleys, tubes, and ropes attached to cinder blocks. The latter toppled like dominoes. Up I went into Tim and Dave II's waiting arms. The exhaust for the bathroom fans blew into the middle of the makeshift stage. We were the backing band for the outrageous antics of none other than Turtle Man.

We played our usual set list with *Who's Afraid of Virginia Woolf?* as our backdrop. Turtle Man, in a 'Dillos football helmet and suit of cardboard armor, performed various shenanigans. For his first stunt, he tied a rope around his neck. He was then dragged around the perimeter of the parking lot by a chopper ridden by Car Boy. At one point, Car Boy looked up at me and mouthed something but I am not a lip reader.

During one of Tim's interminable guitar solos, Turtle Man climbed up on the roof with us. My job was supposed to have been to boot Turtle Man off the roof but my crutches and bass made that next to impossible. Tim was more than happy to oblige him, but I thought he kicked too hard.

For an encore we struggled through the twenty-minute "Masturbator von Nürnberg," the first time we have played it before an audience. To be honest we could have played anything and no one would have noticed or cared. Car Boy strapped a box of Cracker Jacks to Turtle Man's money maker. It detonated with a bang that shattered car windows and launched Turtle Man into the air. Car Boy draped Turtle Man's limp body over the handlebars of his chopper. The crowd applauded in a cloud of red, white, and blue smoke. "Is he okay?" I said.

"I'm sure it's fine," said Bonnie. "Art project."

We started to pack up. Bonnie and I kept looking at the big screen. "I keep trying to read the spines of George's books," I said. "I spotted Günter Grass earlier."

"What makes you think those are George's books and not Martha's?"

"Looky here at the women's libber," I teased. "Did you ever meet a chick who read Günter Grass?"

"You're a male chauvinist pig."

"You're calling me that with Tim standing two feet away from you?" I said. "Besides, don't forget I work at a library. I've seen who reads Günter Grass."

Car Boy left with his pulleys, leaving us stuck on the roof of the concession stand with no way to get down. For all that, we each were paid an order of cold chili fries. We could see it cooling on the counter below. Had meant to tell Turtle Man I had his tent, but never got the chance.

Another sleepless night. I read the Ovid book Randy sent me in its entirety. Its "simple, effective techniques" for manipulating someone into the sack might work if all one cared about was getting laid. However, Ovid's focus is ultimately on mutually fulfilling encounters. As is mine. Advice on "being wary of false lovers" and "trying older lovers" gave me pause.

FRIDAY, MAY 27

Last day of the semester. Hazel had blabbed about my birthday, so there was the obligatory celebration in the break room.

Spunt gave me a rather nice pocket knife. Amber's pet rock came in its own box with instructions: "Be sure you're willing to give your pet rock all the care it requires." With my luck it will go belly up like Randy's bettas.

Jenny took my hand. She slid a mood ring onto my finger. "What mood are you in?" she demanded.

"Either giddy or sullen," I said. "It keeps changing colors."

"Be serious."

"Green-brown. Dunno."

"Green-brown would signify ingratitude."

Time to reign in my dismissive tone. After summoning imps, casting spells, and battling creatures from other dimensions, this experience should serve as a reminder to keep my skepticism to myself. For all I know, the Lake Worth Monster is a Pisces and wears a mood ring on a chain about his spiny neck.

Guddu observed the proceedings wide-eyed. "What is a mood, Steven? What is a pet rock?" I drew him aside.

"What were you doing outside Pigg yesterday? And what the hell are we supposed to do without hair spray and deodorant? Did you not consider that?"

"Those products will still be available, Steven," he said. "Without fluorocarbons. Fluorocarbons harm the earth's atmosphere."

"What do you care about the earth's atmosphere?" I said.

Jenny's card had the crew of the USS Enterprise on it. "Happy birthday to a great human," it read. "You wouldn't make a bad Vulcan either! Love, Jenny."

It all makes sense now. The Stone Fox is an eyebrow-up, eyebrow-down Vulcan. She fed me a cupcake, which was annoying because I got frosting on my face. She tried to wipe it off, rubbing my mustache against the grain. Most illogical. All I wanted to do now was wash my face.

"*Charlie's Angels* is getting a fourth angel," announced Jenny.

"No shit?" I said, mustering what enthusiasm I could.

"An angel, all covered in eyes?" said Guddu. "What is an angel?"

Amber fielded this one. "An angel is a reflection of God and through all that is His, there is shining the image of God," she said.

"Which god?" said Guddu innocently. Bless his heart. But what if Amber is right?

"The ducks are back at Trinity Park," said Jenny. "Want to go visit after work?"

"Rats," I said. "I'm spending the weekend at the lake with friends. I would invite you, but it's not my house."

"School's Out" blared from the intercom. Spunt's doing, no doubt. Everyone assembled in the vestibule. When all were accounted for we dispersed into the sweltering heat. Diane was waiting against the Rambler, smoking a cigarette. She was wearing her floppy hat, Foster Grants, and an off-the-shoulder peasant blouse. Baggy, crepe-thin pants and gold sandals completed the ensemble. She looked like she had just alighted from a Lartigue photograph.

Avoiding Jenny's opprobrious gaze, I hobbled over to the passenger side. Boggs came jogging up behind me. "Steven!" he panted. "What did I tell you about parking here?"

"Please forgive me, Mr. Boggs," said Diane insouciantly. As we rolled away, I turned in my seat and witnessed Dixie bawling out Boggs. Jenny had already walked away.

If Diane had intended to alienate me from my colleagues, then she succeeded. But not without injuring her own influence over Dixie. Is her work at the library wrapping up? If she is ready to move on to the next phase of her fiendish scheme, I hope it does not involve me. Having gotten herself invited to the lake house, however, I am afraid it does. Why else would she want to go?

"Can we stop at a grocery store?" said Diane. "Promised Vee we'd pick up a few things." She ran into a Piggly Wiggly while I melted in the car. She returned with a sack of groceries from which protruded the obligatory stalk of celery. Like the ones housewives carry on TV. Like a prop one might carry to distract people from one's real motives.

"What's the celery for?"

"Casserole," she said blithely. Diane has an answer for everything.

At Cahoba, she did not know which way to turn. She must have divined correctly for we soon rolled up to a gate. It was partially open. Next to it lay a smashed lock and chain.

Bill Blevins's place stood at the end of a shady driveway. A Spanish Mediterranean affair, separated from an adjacent guest house by a swimming pool. The landscaping was wild. Patches of grass carpeted with daisies grew among scattered clumps of coreopsis and sage. Acorns littered a flagstone path leading to a secluded studio. Next to the studio, protected by a wall of prickly pear, stood one of Blevins's bronzes. The giant thumb suggested either general approval or a need for a lift.

Vee greeted us in a colorful crocheted bikini. It was evident her whistle had already been wetted. We left our things in the foyer lined in pampas grass. Vee took the groceries into the kitchen, her bare feet padding across the tiles.

"Poop," said Diane. "I forgot to get Tab!"

The kitchen counter was covered with bottles of vitamins and supplements. "Those are Dawn's," said Vee. "Take this. It's good for your bones." She offered me a tablet, which I swallowed dry. On the other end of the counter was a circular lid. It concealed a built-in dishwasher. I peered within, half-expecting Shagduk to leap from within.

Dawn came clacking into the kitchen in her Dr. Scholl's. Her hair sprouted from the top of her Aquarena Springs visor like an errant patch of grass. A one-piece gingham bathing suit contained her curves, poorly.

"Cute bathing suit, Green Bug!" said Vee.

Dawn tugged at the fabric around her crotch. "I've had this since my junior year of high school," she lamented. Dawn poked her head into the den where Tim was pounding out the coda to "Layla" on a baby grand. "Tim, be a sweetheart and go get me some suntan lotion?"

"And Tab," said Diane.

"We can make fondue if you get cheese!" chimed Vee. She tossed him a silver dollar.

"If I flip this coin, what are the chances of me getting some head tonight?"

"What?" said Vee. "I don't know. Fifty-fifty." When she realized what she had said, she blurted "You dirty dog! Hurry up so we can start the fondue. Chop chop!"

Did not know which room was mine, so I hobbled to the one nearest the kitchen. It was wood-paneled and dark. At the foot of the bed was a steamer trunk full of old-timey bathing suits. They probably belonged to Old Man Blevins whose portrait watched me as I hid the amulet in the pocket of one of the bathing suits. I tried on some belted wool trunks. I laced my espadrilles onto my feet and strutted poolside to applause and wolf whistles.

"Don we now our gay apparel!" sang Tim.

Dawn tailed me around the pool. She mounted the diving board and plunged gracefully into the deep end. Instead of the conventional light blue, the bottom of the pool had been painted black, with constellations, astrological signs, planets, even a space-walking astronaut.

Vee undid her top and stretched out on her stomach. Diane unfolded a beach towel and spread it out on the edge of the water. "Join me?" was printed on it in Old Hamcherry.

Her witchcraft worked. "Scooch," I said.

I watched as she squirmed around, her jugs wobbling under her open blouse. After I eased myself into position, she reclined with her head in my lap. With an indolent sigh, she pulled her floppy hat over her face. She ran her fingertips languorously over the surface of the sparkling water.

Why did Diane come? All this just to get her hands on the amulet? I now wished I had left it at home.

"Cute hat," said Vee over her magazine.

I nudged the witch. "Vee said your hat is cute."

"Vee says everything is cute," said Diane to me.

"Where did you get it?" said Vee.

"Myers," said Diane. "On lay-away." An unlikely story. Has she ever set foot in Myers? Like Guddu, some of the things Diane says sound like something a Martian would say to fit in among earthlings without arousing suspicion.

I watched Dawn climb out of the pool. We made eye contact and, for a moment, I felt as I had after the incident at the Water Gardens. Perhaps we both felt it. She smiled at me, then settled into a chaise lounge.


A B-52 roared overhead in a dramatic display of lethality. It banked toward Arkansas. "*Mors ab alto*," I said ominously.

Vee clapped twice. "Pool boy!" she called to Tim. "Peel me a grape."

"Huh?" said Tim. He was moving in circles in the water, trying to make a whirlpool or some shit.

"Bring me a Tab!" said Diane.

Tim dutifully emerged from the water, dripping, then disappeared into the house. He returned with Diane's Tab balanced upon a silver tray.

"Where's my grape?" asked Vee. Tim did not have an answer.

"Light my cigarette, then," said Vee. Tim did so, then remained at her side, fanning her with a ping pong paddle. "'The Academy of Mystic Arts invites you to become a witch,'" read Vee from her *Cosmo*. "'Age-old wisdom that brings you greater health, peace of mind, and opens the doors to the richer, fuller life you always dreamed of.'"

Diane smiled slyly at me, as if we shared a private joke. What could it be? She got up and went into the house.

"'Each lesson provides secret instructions,'" continued Vee. "'They will enable you to practice ESP, project your psychic body, and become a mystic master.'"

"Mind reading?" I said. "Hmm." I sometimes feel like Diane can read my mind, which is embarrassing. And alarming. Maybe she knows where the amulet is hidden. Maybe she is getting it now.

"'Release the ancient mysteries known only to sages and magi which have their origin in the Essenes, the Theraputae, and the Great White Brotherhood.'"

"Is that like the KKK?" said Dawn.

"Magi," I said. "Sages."

"What kind of person would fall for this horseshit?" said Tim.

Vee turned the page. "What a funny tequila ad," she said. "'It takes two fingers and one glass to turn strangers into friends.'"

"I can vouch for that," said Tim lecherously.

"It takes three to turn a friend into a stranger," I quipped.

"Did you get my suntan lotion?" said Dawn.

"Here you go," said Tim.

"It's a banana!" said Dawn. Meaning the bottle. She twisted off the cap and took a whiff. "Vee, will you do my back?"

Diane returned in a leopard-print string bikini. She reclaimed her spot with her head on my crotch. "Slide me that banana," she said. Dawn tossed her the bottle of suntan lotion. "Do me, pool boy." The witch was in seduction mode. I had seen it before. Did I detect a hint of cruelty in her smile?

Calling her bluff, I squirted an excessive amount of lotion into my palm and rubbed it familiarly onto her bare shoulders, arms, and nose. I lingered over the tops of her breasts and explored the broad valley between them. I did her stomach and scooped the excess from her navel. When my fingertips slid where the sun never shines, she did not flinch. I slowly pulled one of her strings until it came untied. With an irritated sigh, she drew her knees up and finished the job herself before casually re-tying her bottoms. I made a mental note of my successful sexual one-upmanship. Is this how Tim gets Vee? How the Doom Hippie gets the Stone Fox?

I stretched for Vee's *Cosmo*. Every issue is a newsstand grimoire, filled with secrets for giving women power over men. I turned to a page at random. "Get savvy about cars!" shouted a headline. "It's not cute to know zero about your car. It's dumb and dangerous." The brief article urges readers to inquire at their nearest Chrysler dealership about taking a free "Women on Wheels" course in automobile maintenance and repair. That must be what Dawn did. Heloise's hints, indeed. Bet the salesman who teaches that gets more ass than a toilet seat.

We watched boats sail by on the lake and took turns answering Vee's Proust questionnaire. Topics of conversation centered around her magazine articles.

These included dating advice, erogenous zones, and something called a "G-spot." The feeling was loose as our inhibitions slowly melted away. Vee and Dawn signed my cast with a Magic Marker. As Diane had, they also kissed it, much to Tim's consternation. Next to Vee's lip gloss impression, she drew a big asterisk. I wondered what omitted matter it referred to, but then remembered that I had told her about the time I met Kurt Vonnegut.

The sun set beyond the new bridge construction. We moved to the patio table. Vee tossed a delicious salad. Dawn served a casserole. Her determination with the fondue pot paid off and we were soon dipping skewers of bread into the gooey cheese. Tim placed his skewer directly into the Sterno flame. "Who wants to get branded?"

"Me!" cried Vee. She held out her wrist. I swatted the skewer away. Tim growled like a rabid animal.

"Happy birthday to you," sang Dawn. She emerged from the house with the cake, upon which burned a multitude of candles. The glow from these burnished her hair and cast shadows across her cherubic cheeks. To direct attention back to himself, Tim sang in a tuneless, operatic falsetto: "Happy birthday to you! You look like a Jew!"

Dawn presented to me a rather plain-looking ceramic vase. "Wow, thanks, Dawn!" I said. "You made this? Hey, there's something inside." A neat scroll tied with ribbon was a gift certificate to Western Auto Supply. "Thank you," I mouthed to Dawn across the table.

"Hold it up to the light," said Dawn. "The vase, dum dum! Not the gift certificate."

"What am I looking at?"

"It's a Rubin vase," she said. "See the two faces kissing?"

"Wait," I said. "I see them now. That's neat, Dawn!"

"It demonstrates the figure-ground distinction the occipital lobes make during visual perception."

Tim handed me a baggie of joints. "Happy beer day on your queer day," he said. "Wait, I almost forgot." He ran inside then returned with a large, blue capsule.

"There's no way I'm swallowing that," I said.

"You don't swallow it, retard," said Tim. "You add water to it."

He dropped the capsule into my drink, which was mostly just melted ice cubes. We watched as the capsule slowly expanded into a blue, spongy shape. "It's a cat," said Vee.

"Instant pussy," said Tim. "Speaking of pussy," he added, confidentially, "you should seize the opp while there's an opp to seize." Was he talking about Dawn or Diane?

Diane excused herself. Vee and Dawn did the dishes. I returned to my room and found the amulet where I had left it. I placed it inside an empty Chap Stick tube and left it on the bedside table.

The mosquitos had become a nuisance so we ended up in the den. The sunken conversation pit boasted deep goldenrod carpet. Strewn about were numerous cushions and pillows in brown and burnt orange. The surrounding terracotta tiles served as a place for drinks and elbows. "How do you get down there?" said Dawn. She circled the pit then leaped onto the cushions with an uncharacteristic squeal. She and Vee make such an odd couple. Like the TV show. But who was Oscar and who Felix?

Tim searched a closet for board games. "Get a load of that," I said. Above the mantelpiece a huge macramé thing threatened. "Looks like a spider web made of rope. Or something Cher might wear. Tim, you could use it to catch chicks."

"You're the one who needs it," said Tim. He produced several worn, squashed boxes for consideration. "We've got *Afrika Korps*, *Feeley Meeley*, and *Mystery Date*."

"I haven't played *Mystery Date* in years!" cried Dawn.

"Anything but that," groaned Tim.

"Afraid of getting your butt whipped?" teased Dawn. She opened the box and set up the game. For two, three, or four players, so it was just as well that Diane was missing.

"No, but you can kiss it," said Tim. "I know, let's play *Strip Mystery Date!*"

"It's not that kind of game. The object is to get ready for your date."

"My point exactly."

Dawn blew a raspberry. "When you open the door, you want it to be the guy you're ready for. The worst thing is if you open the door and it's the dud."

Vee prodded Tim with her toe. "Nobody likes an old fuddy duddy."

The dud jokes persisted throughout the evening. Tim begged the girls to play *Strip Afrika Korps*. He ended up tearing the house apart for a deck of cards. I dreaded the possibility that he would find another "weejee" board. Last time we fooled around with one, Dawn almost conjured up Krolok.

Dawn set up Feeley Meeley. "You take turns drawing a card," Dawn explained. "You then stick your hand in the box and try to retrieve by feel the object on the card."

A soft creak drew my attention to the ceiling. Shagduk's horned snout pressed against the skylight. Dawn saw it, too. "It's back," she said.

Had she seen it earlier? I tried to play it down. "There are possums around," I said casually.

In a bid to distract Dawn, I drew a card. "The elephant," I said. It worked. We plunged our hands into the box. My hand found Dawn's and gave it a playful squeeze. I then felt something sharp. Vee withdrew a bottle cap with the Gemini sign painted on it. I immediately identified Fred's artistry. At first, I did not understand. But when Tim produced the key to the Vault, I knew this all had to be the imp's doing. I furtively glanced at the skylight, but saw only darkness.

"I don't get it," said Dawn. "The pieces were all there when I set the game up." She moved to open the box. I slapped her hand away. "Steven!" she cried.

Diane sauntered into the room with a drink in her hand. "Are you all having fun?" she said with a smirk.

Returned to my room with the Feeley Meeley game under my arm. The lid indicated there should be a comb, a buffalo, an elephant, and so forth. Instead, the box held an assortment of objects, each charged with meaning. Figgy's turtle I recognized because I bought it for him. The sharp object turned out to be one of my *shuriken*. A nail file was most likely the one Vee lost. When I saw Jenny's sparkle-time crystal, my heart sank. How did Guddu come by it? Everything was coated with a stinky fluid originating from a small dead fish. One of Randy's bettas, evidently. Of the remaining objects, only a Weeble gave me pause. Whose was it?

My room had a waterbed but it was too late to do anything about it. Heavenly cold air rushed out of the vent directly above my head. Sleep eluded me, however. I hobbled my way into the kitchen for another slice of cake. I made a bunch of racket when I knocked over one of Dawn's vitamin bottles. Magnesium is good for your heart, I reasoned. And since this was Dawn's magnesium, I could use it.

The refrigerator motor shut off. The house was silent. I made my way back along the darkened hallway. I paused outside Vee's door and listened for any signs of depravity. A light shone under Diane's door. She was probably sitting up, alert as a Doberman.

Turned on the bedside lamp and reached for *Successful Muskrat Farming*. Randy bound it so tightly, I have to crack the spine to get it to stay open to the desired page. I placed the magnesium tablet on my tongue. It stuck in my throat, so I limped into the bathroom and put my open mouth under the tap. In a low, but forceful chant, I spoke the words of power. These also stuck in my throat. I stared at the door, as if Dawn was going to burst through in a negligee. When she did not, I felt somehow relieved.

A couple of well-appointed bookcases flanked the waterbed. Ended up reading half of Gombrich's *The Story of Art* before realizing I was lying in a puddle of water. The bed was leaking. The imp's way of socking it to me, no doubt. He must be furious that I am neglecting him. He would be dead by now if he were a pet rock.

A bare foot nudged me awake. Dawn hovered above me with a tray. "What are you doing out here?" she said.

"My waterbed sprang a leak."

Dawn was all dolled up in her too-small gingham bathing suit, lipstick and mascara. Daisies sprouted from her mousy, disheveled hair. "I'm your pool girl today."

In the sober light of day, I found the phrase "pool girl" off-putting. Dawn clambered into the conversation pit. She placed the tray in my lap as I labored to sit up in my belted trunks. She had made huevos rancheros. These were served with toast and a sectioned grapefruit on good china, complete with coffee and white cloth napkin.

When it became clear that Dawn intended to feed me, I humored her. She made small talk between bites. I could not always respond because I was chewing. When she offered me coffee, it dribbled down my beard. She dabbed it with a corner of the napkin but I could still feel it on my chin. I felt less like Murloc of Siluria and more like a sanitarium patient. Please let this not be magic, I was thinking. When I mentioned I was out of Chap Stick, Dawn sliced open a capsule and applied its amber goo to my lips. "Makes your kisser soft," she said.

As before, we spent much of the day basking under the brutal Texas sun. Vee and Dawn competed to see who could be the better pool girl. Diane may be ready and willing but she was nobody's pool girl. Vee kept Tim's drinks fresh, rubbed his feet, and towed him around the pool on a floatie. Dawn brought me birthday cake, sandpapered my calluses, and brushed my beard. She periodically saw to my lips. Without knowing for sure if my charm had succeeded, all I could do was follow her lead.

Tim wanted to have chicken fights. Vee let him mount her shoulders. They beckoned to Dawn and Diane but neither seemed interested in the other as a partner. I cursed my injuries.

By late afternoon, everyone was becoming restless. Vee read aloud from a *Cosmo* sex quiz but no one was interested. "Sex used to be taboo," I said provocatively. "Until it became ubiquitous. Now it's boring." Diane cast a furtive glance in my direction. I knew that would get her attention.

"Says the virgin," said Tim. His words stung. But how could he possibly know I'm still a virgin? "Hey virgin, my band's going to be on the *O.D.*," Tim said.

"Not the *O.D.*," I said. "*The Fringe*."

Dawn looked up from her sketchbook. "What's *The Fringe?*" she said distractedly.

Diane kept her distance and was engrossed in a paperback, though I am sure she was scheming. More than once she got up and glanced at what Dawn was drawing, as if it was driving her crazy. I started to worry. "Hell hath no fury," as they say. Tim ate a melted Marathon bar. His fingers were covered in chocolate. He was sloshed and bored and was now starting to mess with Dawn in mean ways. Vee even said so. I chucked a magnolia grenade at him. In retaliation, Tim dipped the corner of his towel in the pool and snapped me with the rattail.

"Check out this candy wrapper," he said. "It's got a ruler printed on it." He tried to measure Vee's aquiline nose. She swatted it away irritably.

We had forgotten to put the casserole in the fridge. Tim saved the day when he discovered a freezer filled with meat in the garage.

"What are we going to have with our steaks?" said Vee.

"Pesto," said Dawn, rising from her seat. "There's a rosemary bush by the driveway."

"You can make pesto with rosemary?" I asked.

"I'll get the grill going," said Tim. He returned moments later. "There's no grill."

Dawn found a brand new grill still in the box. I smoothed the instructions out on the patio and began assembling it. As I fingered a packet of toggle bolts, Vee shrieked. Two wolf spiders had charged through the open patio door. Tim scooped them into Tupperware and attempted to fry them up in a pan. This, we all objected to, shouting, "What are you doing?" and "Tim, that's awful!"

Once the grill was functional, Tim commenced tonging the meat. Vee made more fondue with the remaining Swiss. Unsurprisingly, the pesto was inedible as was the unripe prickly pear fruit that I picked. "Vile," pronounced Tim, rubbing it in. Dawn had made the dish with love so I theatrically swallowed a heaping spoonful. It is entering my lower intestine as I write this.

Dinner ended prematurely when the canned heat exploded, splattering everyone with boiling hot cheese. Dawn got the worst of it. Accident? Shagduk? Diane is certainly capable of such malice. Vee followed Dawn inside to help her get cleaned up. I followed so I could take a leak.

The others had gathered in the Texas-shaped hot tub. Vee produced a champagne bucket filled with ice. "I like champagne, so I like champagne buckets," she said in French, imitating a man's voice. She and Dawn then laughed. Perhaps they were sharing a private joke from their Sorbonne days.

I perched on the edge of the tub with one leg in the water. "He's a perfect stranger, like a cross of himself and a fox," sang Vee. Soon she and Tim were wrestling and splashing each other. "Stop hitting yourself," hollered Tim. "Why do you keep hitting yourself?"

I looked up at the sky, trying to locate Saturn. When I looked back down, Vee had removed her top. She whispered something into Tim's ear. He wiggled around then slapped his wet trunks down with a loud *smack*.

Vee peered down her nose. "I'm waiting," she said impatiently.

"Good things come to those who wait," said Tim, standing erect. "Colonel Mayer salutes you."

"Who's Colonel Mayer?" said Vee.

"Colonel Oscar Mayer, my b-o-l-o-g-n-a."

Dawn shrieked. I shielded her eyes but she pried my fingers away.

"At ease, Colonel," I said. Tim's boner became instantly flaccid. He looked straight at me as if he knew what I had done. I stared back.

Vee stepped out of her bottoms then twirled them on the end of her finger. Tim plucked them and hurled them, angrily I thought, onto the gazebo.

Dawn looked pleadingly at Vee. "*Pas terrible*," said Vee in her champagne bucket voice. "You're among friends, Dawn," added Tim. He made a magnanimous gesture with his hands.

"Am I?" said Dawn, her cheeks aflame. She squirmed out of her gingham one-piece without getting up. Out of politeness, I looked away.

"Your skin is so white!" teased Vee.

"Not as white as Diane's," I said. I turned to the witch and wordlessly held out my hand, deftly concealing the accompanying tridactyl gesture. *Witness Diane obey.* But I need not have bothered.

Diane's sunglasses concealed her expression. After hesitating, she stood up to face me. She unceremoniously dropped her top sopping into my palm. I placed it next to Dawn's garment. "For your collection," she said with a smirk. Now I felt like the tyrannical Murloc of Siluria. "Bottoms, too," I commanded. *Witness Diane obey!*

Diane stood with her hands defiantly on her hips. I never noticed how slender her fingers were. They made me think of candles. Dark shadows contrasted with waxen skin. Diane's legs looked as thin as ski poles. These were attached to skeletal feet which were translucent like those of a cave newt. Her stringy, chestnut hair clung to her puckered nipples. Was it a trick of the floodlights? Did I detect silver streaks?

This ghoulish striptease, if one could call it that, seemed to be for my eyes only. The formula was chosen to reveal truth. But which truth was this?

Diane stood as if waiting for a reaction. Because of her mirrored sunglasses, I did not know where to focus. My gaze darted from one lens to the other at my own reflection. However, if this was now a stupid staring contest, she could not win unless I participated. Not the reaction she had hoped for. I coolly reached for the radio and tuned in to *The Fringe*. In my peripheral vision I saw

Diane sit. Next thing you know, she spat out a cherry stem that had been tied into a knot. Must everything be a competition?

She must have forgotten that I had seen that trick before in Austin. Tim had been there that night at Mother Earth, but he has no idea Ursula and Diane are the same person. I carefully lowered myself into the bubbles, keeping my dry leg propped up in New Mexico. Due to the awkward shape of the tub, it took a minute to get situated. I leaned back against Dawn who casually embraced me.

After "Hangman's Dance" ended, there was dead air for at least fifteen seconds before the DJ spoke. "Whoa, I almost forgot where I was." This was followed by what sounded like the DJ gulping down an entire glass of water. "That was some far-out fringe from Fort Worth's own Bloodrock. Booger, the phone lines! You're on the air! What are you doing strange?" A succession of callers were asked the same question. There were words about the Film Club's Roman Polanski series and a PSA from the United Negro College Fund. At last, the DJ said, "Here's some fresh unsigned Cowtown Rock 'n' Roll from Time Frame."

"I saw Bloodrock a few years ago with Cactus," said Tim. I wasted a *Shush* spell on him right then and there. I did not care if Diane noticed.

> *In this twilight realm, where shadows whisper,*
> *With each step we take, the boundaries blister,*
> *With every heartbeat, new vistas unfold,*
> *As our souls seek treasures, yet untold.*

Vee rose like Venus amidst the foam, her white limbs spotlit by the underwater flood lamp. Briefly baffled by the lengthy intro, she gripped Tim's shoulders, then began to sway seductively as they touched foreheads. Frankly, Vee is much sexier when she is just flitting around being Vee. Now, naked, she was trying too hard. Dawn regarded her thoughtfully. Diane's eyes flashed with anger. When the drums kicked in, Vee raised her arms over her head and pumped her fists to the beat. I lit a cigarette.

During Tim's solo, Vee raised an arm and spun like a ballerina. For the spooky and appropriately nocturnal bridge, Vee caressed herself sensually. Tim ogled her appreciatively while I, too, savored the nectar of the moment. Dawn held a doobie up to my lips and I took a quick drag, now smoking two things at once. The tempo increased throughout the frenzied finale. Vee's hips gyrated wildly. When the song ended with a horrendous scratching sound, she collapsed into the tub, splashing us all pretty well.

"Bit of a hiccup there. One of the perils of overindulging in overnight delights. Something well understood by devotees of *The Fringe*. That was 'Journey to Dord.' Time Frame is—drum roll, please—Tim Watson on guitar; David McDermott on drugs, excuse me, *drums*; and the one and only Steve Miller takin' care of the bottom end. With me is the lovely Bonnie Baxter, keyboardist and lyricist. Bonnie, I have to ask, where exactly is Dord? Is it a country? Or a state of mind?" Diane whipped her head around to look at me. Dang it! Should have known he would ask that. While Bonnie continued, I studied my wrinkled fingertips.

"Our bass player came up with it. It's the name of an ancient city, I think he said. He found it in a library book." Before the DJ could continue, Bonnie shrieked. This was succeeded by a period of confusion.

"Speaking of strange. We had an uninvited guest with us here in the studio. Bonnie caught it with her bare hands and is disposing of it as I speak. Here she is now." My mind went straight to Shagduk. After a few boilerplate questions (and a couple of deliberately oddball ones) about our background, our sound, and our plans, the interview concluded. "It's 84 degrees here in the KPCR studio. Got a pair of tickets to see Heart with special guests Climax Blues Band on the twelfth. Fourth caller gets 'em."

"Look," said Diane dreamily. "How beautiful." She was referring to the moonlight reflected on the surface of the lake.

"It's waxing gibbous," I said pedantically.

"What the hell is gibbous?" said Tim. "That's gotta be a made-up word."

"No," said Diane. "Real."

"It means the opposite of crescent," I said.

"You don't need a college degree to shush people," slurred Tim. "You're a phony." He pointed at Diane. "And you're a phony, too."

Tim could not possibly know what Diane's game was. I doubt he would keep pissing her off if he knew who she really was. What the witch was capable of. He leaped unashamedly out of the water, Colonel Mayer at full attention. "Time to measure my donkey dick again," he said. "Where's that Marathon wrapper?"

"At ease, colonel!" I cried. For the second time this evening, Tim's boner went down like a lead zeppelin. His expression turned to panic. He stomped inside, followed by Vee.

Dawn struggled into her bathing suit before standing up. "My stomach's icky," she said. "I'm going inside."

I found myself alone with Diane. I was more than a bit shit-faced. While clambering out of the hot tub, I disturbed a yellowjacket nest with my crutch and got stung a few times. As she had in Philadelphia, Diane helped me to my new room, which was evidently the master bedroom. Next door to hers, of course. She turned on the bedside lamp. After I dried off, Diane dried herself off with the same towel. The soft luminescence of the lamp was much more forgiving than the harsh floodlights of the hot tub. Grotesque had become odalisque.

The witch examined her tan lines in the mirror. "Phooey," she said. She turned to face me, pausing so I could get a good look at her body. As if I had not memorized it by now. No stings, I noted. Had she provoked the yellowjackets as a ruse to get her hooks in me? Is this how she gets her kicks? She stared fixedly at my tube of Chap Stick. I snatched it up.

"My stomach doesn't feel so hot, either," I said. "Must be the fondue."

"Yes, that's what it was," said Diane. "The fondue." She stared at the tube in my hand. The wicker ceiling fan whirred.

Diane was gone when I finally emerged from the bathroom. Thwarted again. With the aid of a pocket knife, I stashed the amulet in the hollowed-out pages of *Slave Lord of Siluria*. It is a shame to wreck a book like that but you cannot fuck around with witches. With the aid of a Dixie cup, I listened at our shared wall for signs of activity. I could have sworn I heard tinkling bells and low murmuring. If her intention was to freak me out, then she succeeded. I will give her that. I settled down and prepared for a long night.


Sunday, May 29

The B-52s took off from Carswell at seven sharp. Their roaring engines shook the house. I turned over in bed and pondered Krolok's message. Afraid to sleep, I had fiddled with the radio. It had a "World Time Master" dial. I should have known that by turning it, I might tune into Krolok's voice. Or had it been a dream? My notes suggested I had been awake. I pored over them wide-eyed. Without admitting knowledge of Shagduk, Krolok had shown me a way I might banish the imp once and for all.

No one brought me huevos rancheros in bed, so I figured I may as well get up. I donned my belted trunks and stashed my dream notes in the piano bench. Ended up on the patio with the Gombrich and a cup of coffee. There was a warm breeze off the lake. Dawn joined me with her own cup of coffee and her sketchbook, her bed head in full bloom. "I had the most awful nightmare," she said. "It was so realistic."

I looked up from my book and furrowed my brow. Dawn hesitated before continuing. "The bed shook, like someone had lain behind me. Thought it might be you." Dawn averted her gaze and blushed. "It was dark. I dreamed I reached behind me and touched something clammy. I knew right away it wasn't a person." Her voice rose a quavering semitone. "In the dream, it trapped me under a net."

Dawn's choice of "it" suggests the imp took Shagduk's form and not Guddu's. "Under a net," I repeated. "And then what?"

She showed me what she had drawn. Compositionally, the sketch showed mastery of light and shadow. Executed with great *morbidezza*, depicting a crouching figure in a state of arousal. The imp's bat-like ears were unmistakable.

"This is superb, Dawn." Diane could have let him out of his bottle. Accidentally, I am guessing. How would she have known?

"Tell me it isn't real," said Dawn despondently.

"Did he rape you?"

Dawn looked confused. "Did *who* rape me?"

This was all my fault. For an instant, I yearned to tell Dawn everything. About Sherwood, my muskrat farming, and the imp. And for an instant, I actually thought she would believe me. So I lied. To protect her? Or myself? "It was just a dream. There's nothing in the world like this." Dawn removed her thick glasses and wiped a tear from the corner of her eye. She smiled tremulously at me, revealing the gap between her front teeth, then began shaking. I took her in my arms and held her close. She smelled like chlorine and gas. She evidently has not made the connection between the museum or the Water Gardens. I knew better than to bring those up.

"Guess seeing Tim's boner got under your skin," I teased. I made light of the situation for Dawn's sake but my blood was boiling.

"Oh my gosh!" Dawn choked back a laugh, then snorted. "My mascara's all over your shoulder." She licked her thumb and attempted to wipe it off. I took off my shirt so she could blow her nose. "You know, it reminds me of that day at the museum," she continued. "I just want to forget."

Uh oh. To discourage this line of thinking, I did not respond. "Can I have that?" I said, meaning the sketch.

"What? Sure." Dawn carefully detached the sketch of Shagduk. "What do you want it for?"

She probably thinks I am a freak now. Should have just taken it when she was not looking. "I'm a librarian, remember? I want to try to identify it."

"You said it wasn't real."

"And so I did. You could have seen it in a book."

Dawn showed me another drawing. The chicken pox scar was there, as were the stray beard hairs that Loretta used to say make me look like a hobo. Dawn captured how I always look, as if I am displeased, while also revealing the kindness in my eyes.

A red-winged blackbird (Dawn told me that is what it was—I am no good at identifying fowl) landed on the railing and side-eyed us.

"Poor thing, he's got one leg," lamented Dawn.

"Give him that crust," I said.

Dawn moved. The bird flew away. She scooted closer to see what I was reading. "She looks miserable," I said indicating the page upon which there was a reproduction of Cézanne's *Portrait of the Artist's Wife*.

"What a tactless thing to say!" cried Dawn. I now found myself in an incomprehensible argument. She went inside just as Tim came out with a beer in each hand and one sticking out of the top of his trunks. He spotted Vee's bikini bottoms on the gazebo and hooked them with a free finger.

Tim placed the cans on the mosaic table then pressed one against his forehead. "What's her deal?" he said, meaning Dawn.

"All I said was I thought Cézanne's wife looked miserable." Guess my charm has worn off. Unless Diane had something to do with it.

Tim glanced at the portrait and grimaced. "Someone's not getting laid this weekend."

"What makes you think I haven't?" Dawn had been in a receptive mood last night. I failed to act so Shagduk moved in.

"There is no way you have," said Tim with an air of utter certitude. I equated his comment with knowledge of Dawn's rape and felt a surge of anger.

"Come look at this," yelled Vee. Tim and I went inside. On the counter someone had built an imposing beer can pyramid. "When did you do this?" she said to Tim.

"I didn't," he said. Why fib about something a normal human being would be proud of? Obviously, it is another one of Shagduk's shenanigans. He does not seem to realize which ones are harmless and which ones are not. Nor does he give a shit.

"Don't look at me," I said disinterestedly. I was staring into the den. The macramé net above the mantelpiece was missing. I recalled my comment to Tim about how it could be used to catch chicks. I had put the idea out there and Shagduk had run with it.

The pyramid came crashing down. Cans flew everywhere. Tim had thrown a Nerf football at it.

I returned to my room. The genie bottle had been unstopped. I sensed a presence behind me and turned around. "I should croak you," I said.

Guddu furrowed his brow. "You cannot croak Guddu," he said. Did he mean that literally? Or that croaking him would be a mistake?

"Back in the bottle," I commanded. "Witness Shagduk obey!"

He went into the bathroom and shut the door. He eats, so it stands to reason he shits. I should issue him a citation for Failure to Obey. Scratch that. I recalled some of Murloc of Siluria's more nauseating torture techniques and smiled to myself. Or I could just keelhaul him under the Rambler.

Breakfast on the patio. One after another, B-52s, KC-135s, and F-111s traversed the skies. Could have sworn I spotted a B-36 on the horizon, but it was probably just Jimmy Stewart visiting the future from *Strategic Air Command*. Dawn did not eat or speak but merely gazed pensively across the water. She was clearly still upset. I put my forearm next to hers. We compared tans. Tim said Dawn looked like a Mexican. It did not help matters.

The mood was laid back. We spent much of the morning baking on the dock. I felt myself beginning to relax, as much as that was possible. Did not put on my watch nor did I glimpse at a clock or ask the time. No one was pool boy or pool girl. That game had become tiresome. I spotted Diane with the one-legged blackbird in her palm. She was speaking to it quietly. The blackbird cocked his head, as if listening. What was she saying to it? The incident was as mysterious as it was charming.

Tim bounced a ping pong ball on a paddle. It ended up in the lake. "I think I have heatstroke," he announced.

"Do you have a headache?" said Vee.

"Kind of."

"How about dizziness and confusion? Loss of appetite? Cramps?"

"The confusion is always there," I quipped.

"Fuck off. I'm just sober," he said gloomily. "Oh, say can you see!" he sang. Looked up just in time to witness him swat a bee with the ping pong paddle.

"How can you be so cruel?" wailed Vee.

Tim gave Vee a look that was at once withering and pathetic. Then he went inside. "What's eating him?" I said. Vee shrugged.

From the other side of the house came the sounds of loud machinery. We discovered Tim in a reflective orange vest, chugging along on an asphalt roller.

"Give me something to squash," yelled Tim over the sound of the engine. The rest of us looked around casually but saw nothing begging to be flattened. "Diane's hat!" shouted Tim. Diane frowned.

Vee went inside and returned with various items, including a tub of shortening and a can of Black Flag.

The bug spray cap flew off and stung my eyebrow. Crisco, birthday cake, and gravel stuck to the massive steel cylinders. The Nerf stayed squashed, which I found curious. I should have thrown Guddu in his genie bottle into the mix. If I cannot croak him, maybe I could flatten him. Where was he, anyway? We were so focused on the spectacle that no one noticed the beat-up Saab coming down the driveway.

The driver unfolded from the confines of Sweden's answer to the growing compact market. He was so tall, his shotgun looked like a toy. He had blond mad-scientist hair and his face had the color and texture of putty. We all put up our hands, except Tim, who could not hear us shouting at him to stop. Vee swatted his calf for attention.

Dawn stepped forward slowly. "I'm Dawn. I'm a friend of Bill's."

"Keep talking."

"Bill said I could stay here any time I wanted. He gave me the keys!"

"When did he do that?"

"At Justine's wedding," said Dawn. "I can go get them." She started to move but Putty Face motioned for her to stay put.

"Do that again and I'll blow all y'all's heads off!"

We all froze as Putty Face's threat worked its magic. "Bill doesn't even live here," he said at last. The cords in his neck pulsated when he spoke. "This is my mother's house. And she didn't say anything about you." He turned to Tim. "Get down from there." Tim wordlessly removed the orange vest then crumpled it into a tight ball. But he remained seated. His eyes were glued to Putty Face's shotgun.

I considered farming a quick muskrat. While it may have prevented Putty Face from eighty-sixing us, there would be an audience. "Sorcery must be done in utmost secrecy," says Randy. I do see his point, but how is that always possible? In this case, words of ordinary power seemed the only prudent course of action. Putty Face turned out to be Chris Petillo—Bill's step-son. The misunderstanding regarding our presence was on account of Dawn's lack of communication. Dawn seemed more indignant than embarrassed, though I felt embarrassed for her.

A cloud of smoke belched from the asphalt roller. Chris yelled and danced aside as the seven-ton machine lurched toward the thumb. The sculpture toppled, giving the proceedings a big thumbs down.

Tim leaped to the ground. "Don't you ever point a fucking gun at me, motherfucker!" he screamed. Vee and I held him back.

"Look what you did!" said Chris. He went inside. Diane followed. I feared the worst for the young man but when he returned, he had calmed down. He said his friends would be there soon, and grudgingly invited us to join them. This change of heart seemed odd for someone who had just threatened to blow our heads off. This was Diane's doing. She casually emerged from the house, smoking a cigarette.

We gathered our belongings. I contemplated the mess in the driveway and felt bad. When I crossed paths with Tim, I said, "Why do you do shit like that?"

"Something in me just snapped," said Tim. "Ever since Cu Chi, I can't stand it when things get too straight," he said. "I feel like I'm chained to a post. Besides, he pointed a gun at me."

"What happened at Cu Chi?" I said.

"Ran over a mine hauling diesel. I wasn't hurt. My buddies didn't make it."

"Damn, Tim. I'm sorry."

"For reasons known only to him, Big Otto spared me that day. My special purpose in life now is to debauch. You wouldn't understand. Then that asshole showed up acting like he owns the place."

"Doesn't he? Come on, you just had a whole weekend of debauchery."

Tim gave me a sly look. "It wasn't a complete waste. I did get a B.J."

"No!" I covered my ears. Somehow this confession was far worse than if Tim had simply banged her. Vee's an adult and can do whatever she wants. But why whip some skull on Tim? Because he's a stud? Because of what happened at Cu Chi?

"Plan on getting some tonight after our gig," said Tim.

What gig? Back at Collinwood, I searched the codex for clues that might shed light on Krolok's attempt to communicate. He who speaks my name? I spoke his name a month or two ago at Vee's, but so did Vee, Dawn, and Tim. Is Krolok trying to reach them, too? Recalling the details of Sherwood's map, I put two and two together. Krolok is saying hello. He recognizes me as a fellow muskrat farmer. If I go to Yaat and help him—do what, I wonder?—he will reward me. He urges haste.

Of course, this does not mean that Krolok knows where Sherwood is. Or has ever enjoyed the professor's tales of archaeological dread. Nor does it mean I can just drop everything and go to California. As for the imp—he saved Dawn's life. But then he hurt her. The imp must be punished. Or banished. Maybe destroyed.

I feel more tired now than I did before the weekend at the lake. I realized I had forgotten my dream notes. I would have to return for them, perhaps on my way to the gig. It was too early to leave, so I got comfortable on the couch. Dozed off during *Smile, Jenny, You're Dead*. Jenny would lower her eyebrow at me for watching it.

Vee woke me up with her pacing. The gig! Hobbled into the Fun Center with minutes to spare. A fire trap near the rock shop. A neon sign flickered "Beer." We were the first of nine bands booked, before Rhodesian Picnic, Nuk U, Bradly Skull, The Angry Retards, The Stick-Ups, Homo Erectus, and a solo act called The Animal which turned out to be Turtle Man. A man of many talents! The place was nuts to butts and I immediately felt claustrophobic. Someone offered me a McSpoon but I was too hungover. Where is all this coke coming from suddenly? The predominant fashion of the evening was ripped tees and leather jackets. No fringe in sight. I was the only one in a kimono. Saw Bonnie speaking to one punker chick in a spiked dog collar and a miniskirt made of pop tops. How does she sit in it? One guy had on a straightjacket, his arms tied uselessly behind his back.

No stage, just a corner. One outlet, but we were prepared for that. No sound check. For the occasion we decided to perform not as Time Frame, but as Aperture's anagram Rat Purée. We were told to keep it under twenty minutes. Our new song by itself lasts twenty minutes so we scrambled to shorten our set list. "Tush" is short, so we started with that. It was followed by a sped-up "Rock 'n' Roll Insanity" which segued into "Tim's Bolero."

People booed the instant Tim raised his pick. One oaf stood in front of me and aped my movements. Fortunately, I do not move around much, so he got bored and went away. I considered executing a mass charm on the unruly crowd if only to get them to calm down.

"Tim's Bolero" drew howls of derision and a volley of flying bottles. One ricocheted into Dave II's bass drum. I initiated my magic. I must have done something wrong because the crowd grew even more hostile. When someone finally pulled the plug on us, I immediately started packing up. What was I thinking, trying to charm a room full of angry punkers? I should have come prepared. I noticed too late that my mojo knob was turned all the way counter-clockwise. What if I had turned it up all the way?

Dave II was breaking down his kit when Rhodesian Picnic plugged in. They were a three-piece who shared a single Vibro Champ yet managed to be earsplittingly loud. The drummer banged on trash cans instead of a kit. "We put the *punc* in *punctual*! One-two-three!" their bass player shouted. His pawn shop bass was aposematically spray-painted red. Even the neck and strings. His boots and hair were also red. A "Nuke the Whales" bumper sticker graced his forehead. The songs were urgent and raw. The crowd response was also urgent and raw. Some even shouted along, including Turtle Man. Guess he has seen them before? Ten songs in under three minutes. "We're Rhodesian Picnic! Fuck all of y'all!"

"Theory in motion," said Dave II. "Eminently danceable." He sounded like Spock.

Tim got into it with the straightjacket kid. "Calm down," he was saying when I approached. "We're here for the same reason as you."

The punker, who I later discovered was the singer from Nuk U, got in Tim's face and bawled, "We're disgusted with your ornamental affectations and lack of purpose. You're nothing but a bunch of primping, posturing superstars!"

"Do we look like superstars?" I said diplomatically.

The punker spat. "The writing's on the wall, geezers."

The Animal approached the mic. He was wearing one of Spunt's "Try It, You'll Like It" shirts. "You're soaking in it!" he screamed. He then launched into a violent, one-chord diatribe against a lengthy list of *-isms*. For an encore, he crooned "In Every Dream Home a Heartache" to an inflatable sex doll. When it was punctured by shattering glass, the doll flew about the stage, bleating pathetically.

By the time we got paid, my ears were ringing. It was a relief to be back outside, where it was much cooler. Bonnie handed each of us three bucks. "I have a surprise," she said. From the back of her Pinto she produced a stack of gleaming shrink wrapped LPs. Tim stuck his head into the opening. "How do you and Bobby get it on back here?"

"We don't," said Bonnie. "As a matter of fact—this is a funny story—last night the cops caught me and Bobby behind the Iron Gate. They thought Bobby was raping me!"

If Bonnie's goal was to piss off Tim, she succeeded. He got into his van and burned rubber without his copies of the album.


I parked on the street near the lake house. Chris Petillo's Saab was in the driveway. So was a dune buggy. I suppose I could have rung the doorbell and said, "Hi, you will remember me from yesterday. I stashed some notes in the piano bench. You won't mind if I retrieve them?" That would be too easy. I could hear voices on the patio. The front door was unlocked. I readied *Evade*, but did not want to waste the energy unless it seemed necessary. No one stopped me. The notes were there.

"Hello?" said a female voice.

I turned around. A pair of big brown eyes were peeking at me from the conversation pit. "I, uh, forgot these," I said, holding up my notes.

Brown Eyes screamed.

I ran for it. By the time I made it to the Rambler, I could hear my pursuers shouting. Fortunately, I am getting pretty good at hotwiring. Chris Petillo pounded on my hood as I put the pedal to the metal.

That they would pursue me there was no doubt. I had no chance in the Rambler. The expected thing would be for me to take Quebec. Instead, I passed it. Under cover of a curve, I pulled into a long driveway and turned off my headlights. And I waited.

There was a knock on my window. I almost shit my pants. I rolled the window down.

"Can I help you?" said an elderly man with a rake.

"I'm looking for the Blevins' residence," I said.

"Blevins," repeated the man with distaste. "Around the bend. Look for the thumb." He waved the rake to indicate the direction.

"Thank you very much, Sir."

There was nothing to do but risk Cahoba all the way to Roberts Cut-Off. For most of the way, I drove without headlights. I turned them on for a passing car. It turned out to be a cop. I watched in the rearview as he did a one-eighty.

Curiously, *Evade* is one of those formulas you need a moment for. There was no time for that now. Chris Petillo might have called the cops. They might be on the lookout for a long-haired male Caucasian in his mid-twenties with a beard and glasses. Driving a '62 mint green Rambler. Figured *Open* might work. But I had never used it at distance. I used it now, putting a little extra *umph* in it. The cop's hood flew open. This bought me a little time. I sped around to Inspiration Point and parked. I walked through the Stonehenge of the scorched shelter house then continued along the trail. After such a stupid incident, I could use some inspiration.

I paused to take in the lights of the Air Force base. It is impossible to look at it without giving a thought to nuclear annihilation. Let it be a reminder of my own. The gentle sound of the spillway reached my ears. From now on, I vowed to be more careful and not so fucking casual. Especially when farming muskrats.

Back at the Rambler, I sank the blade of my pocket knife into the bench seat. In the gash I inserted the Chap Stick tube containing the amulet. No one would think to look there. I secured it with a glyph just in case.

Monday, May 30

Instead of another day at the lake, I found myself stuck at home with no pool girl and no a/c. I feel awful about what happened to Dawn. But is the imp's behavior any more reprehensible than my trying to magically seduce her? I took a cold shower. A thousand showers will not wash away this feeling.

Spent the morning trying to make sense of my dream notes. The good stuff went straight into my red notebook. Several hours into it, I had to stop. My back was aching and I needed food. I sat up to find Guddu observing me from the doorway to the kitchen. I played it cool, concealing my anger and determination.

As I took a package of bacon from the icebox, I figured I would cook enough for two but stopped myself. The imp serves me, not the other way around. He sees me limping. He probably thinks I am weak. I must convince him otherwise.

"Have a seat," I said casually. I lit the burner then shook out the match. With a pair of tongs, I arranged the bacon in the skillet until it began to sizzle. I then placed ends of the tongs into the flames. I reached for a pad of paper and a pen. "Watch me draw Australia."

Guddu observed with great interest as I traced the outline of the western coastline. "First, you draw a Schnauzer," I explained. "For the eastern coastline and Tasmania, you draw a cat barfing up a piece of popcorn." With perfect timing, Figgy leaped onto the table and sat upon the drawing. Of course, my incantation had no influence over him; he merely behaved as cats do. Tasmania popped. The black and white feline peeled out, sending the paper flying. I put down my pencil, crossed my arms, and leaned back in my chair. "*Qubuod uberubat dubemubonstrubandubum,*" I said in Ubbi-Dubbified Latin. "Now eat it," I commanded.

I have observed the effects this sort of psychological razzmatazz has on Guddu. For all his shenanigans, he has no conception of bullshit. In demon land, or wherever he comes from, I suppose bullshit does not exist because it would get you killed. Or worse. So when someone serves him a kernel of it, it messes with his demonic mind. As I knew he would, he mistook my factitious display for a bold power play.

"Witness Shagduk obey!"

Meekly, Guddu reached for the popcorn and inserted it cautiously into his mouth. He continued to watch as I slowly peeled a banana and ate it. When I was finished, I tossed the peel onto his face where it stuck. He wobbled his head in confusion. "Clean my house!" I snapped. I towered over him, now a Silurian slave lord.

Guddu started to speak. I casually put on an oven mitt, then seized the red-hot tongs. With my other hand, I grasped his throat, pinning all my hopes on this show of bravado. He reverted to his true form, lashing out with claws. One of them got me good on the face, but this was a fight I had to win. I increased the pressure around his throat. "Stick your nose into my business and you'll end up in an alley where the cat's looking at you," I said, borrowing a line from *Lady in the Lake*. I tonged his nose while he squirmed helplessly in my grip. Figgy watched from the doorway, unconcerned with the drama unfolding before him.

"But wait, there's more! If you so much as think about Dawn again, I will consume your flesh, blast your masticated remains from my anus, and deliver them to [redacted] in a flaming doggy bag."

I released the imp's throat. He dropped to the floor then sprang to his feet. I hoped by pronouncing the name of Shagduk's former master a second time a second imp would not appear. At any rate, he could see I was not afraid of anyone.

In retrospect, it is doubtful Shagduk knows what a doggy bag is. All the same, this halftime show of bullshit, bluffing, and balls of brass seems to have done the trick. He now scrambled around like a whipped cur scrubbing the commode, dusting the book shelves, and picking up lint and cat hair off the rug. In a burst of inspiration, I had him heal my broken ankle. That could have backfired but it did not. With his tail between his legs, the imp returned to his bottle. I sealed it with a glyph.

At dusk, I attempted a *Discover* spell to learn more about Krolok. Unlike the last one, this formula did not require something of Krolok's. Rather than mysterious mental visions, the answer came in the form of a voice. It seemed familiar somehow, like a blend of my own voice and that of someone I know. That the answer comes from my subconscious is a possibility that makes sense, but how can I know something that I do not know I know? The voice had this to say:

> *Krolok is calling upon you for a specific purpose. It may be that he wants you to help him acquire an ancient codex of dark magic, which is said to contain powerful spells and knowledge of lost Vul Kar. It is also possible that he is seeking your assistance in some other arcane endeavor. Whatever the case, it is best to proceed with caution when dealing with this enigmatic figure and consider carefully before agreeing to assist him.*

The advice, while being rather obvious, is sound. But there is no new information. Whoever responded to my spell knows as much as I do, though, which is disconcerting. What if it was Krolok and his words of caution were a sort of reverse psychology compelling me to help him?

TUESDAY, MAY 31

"What happened to your face?" said Jenny. I had made Shagduk heal my ankle but forgot about the scratches he gave me.

"Cat scratch fever," I sang. I could have answered in Dordic for all Jenny cared.

"You got some sun," continued Jenny, oblivious to any answer I might give no matter how outrageous. "How was the lake house?"

"A weekend of epicurean slave lording," I said. "I trespassed on private property, dined upon rosemary pesto, had a telepathic encounter with the mysterious being called Krolok, watched Tim run amok on an asphalt roller, and nearly got my head blown off."

Left out the bits about the nude hot tubbing and Dawn getting raped by a demon. In retrospect, I should have kept my mouth shut about Krolok as well. Jenny does not listen to a word I say, anyway. She regarded me with mingled confusion and pity. "Oh, they played our single on *The Fringe*," I added.

"Your foot," she said.

"The imp healed me."

"Wait, were you faking this whole time?"

Lies, the wages of sorcery. Even when I am telling the truth now, I am lying. "Why the third degree?" I said. "You should be happy for me."

"Tonight's Lobster Night at the Spanish Galleon," said Jenny acidly. "Want to go?"

"I have other plans." I had no desire to go on a date with Jenny tonight. Nor did she, judging from her tone. Too late, I realized she had wanted to celebrate my birthday. Is that all she wanted?

The skull is gone. Dixie is my prime suspect, but Amber believes the Doom Hippie swiped it. It burns me up thinking of it sitting on his mantelpiece. I should get it back somehow. The fan is gone, too. Guess I will have to bring my own from home.

Spent half the morning looking for a box suitable for sending Aunt Wanda our album. In the end I simply made one. The line at the campus post office was surprisingly long, so I decided to try again tomorrow.

Lunch in the break room. Hey Now was over in the corner, eating something stinky from a wad of tin foil. Periodically he would shout his trademark, "Hey!" Spunt sat opposite me. He chewed his Spaghetti-O's loudly, laughing his Muttley laugh at whatever visions danced in his head. I rose to leave. It was not that long ago Sherwood, the Bastard, and I ruled the so-called leisure chamber, when tomes were allowed and conversation flowed. Instead of listening to Jo Ann humming and talking to herself, it was to the professor's exploits in the Lost Caves of Murmiaz.

It was raining when I got off work. Boggs offered me an umbrella. Guess there are no hard feelings after the parking incident.

"Steven," he said. "Come over here a minute and let me show you what I found." He led me to his hideout whereupon he produced a tattered, moldy book. With trembling hands, I took it from him. The last thing I need is Boggs dabbling in the occult. Fortunately, it was only a copy of *Semi-Tough* by Dan Jenkins.

"People leaving books all over the place. Found this one in the quad." Boggs called my attention to the title page verso. "Says here, first edition. Is this valuable?"

"It depends, Boggs," I said, choosing my words carefully. "Condition is paramount."

"What happened to your crutches?" The way he was looking at me, I think he knew my little problem had not gone away after all.

Outside, a woman's figure approached, blurred and indistinct in the pelting rain. Diane came in from the storm, her clothes soaked and her hair plastered to her scalp. Boggs and I took in the absorbing sight. "Forgot my lip gloss," she said. When she was out of earshot, Boggs leaned in close to me. "You know, I seen Miss Bollinger with no clothes on."

"Welcome to the club, Boggs."

Boggs looked alarmed. "What club might that be, Steven?"

Diane returned carrying the aforementioned lip gloss. She held it up as proof. Of course it was all a ploy to get us thinking about her full lips. A trick right out of *Cosmo*. "It's pouring!" she said. "Oh, well. Have a nice evening, you two!" Our eyes were riveted on Diane as she ran shrieking into the cloudburst, boobs bouncing.

"She dropped something," said Boggs. I hesitated before retrieving the object. A key, attached to a keychain for the Women's Faculty Club. I pocketed it before returning to the vestibule. Boggs raised an eyebrow but I did not want to tell him what I found.

"Where did you see Diane with no clothes on?" I said to get our conversation back on track. Boggs must be her next mark. Unless I am, again.

"On the hill behind the library," said Boggs. "The way you like to take from the parking lot. I seen her in a clearing up there one night. Woman was trying to get a moontan."

"A moontan," I repeated, with an air of amusement. I lit a Kent and drew the smoke deep into my lungs. "When was this?"

"First Tuesday in May. That woman is the whitest white woman I ever seen."

"Yeah, she is pretty pale."

"You don't find this behavior unusual?"

"There is nothing usual about Diane," I said. I was dying to spill the beans but wisely refrained.

"You can't smoke that in here, Steven. What are you doing?"

"Sorry, man!" I buried the stub in the nearest ashtray. "Listen, I gotta get out of here. Have a nice evening."

Boggs's umbrella would not open. As I dashed after Diane, I chewed over the security guard's story. If I am not mistaken, the next full moon is tonight or tomorrow. Would have to see for myself if the witch makes a habit of moonbathing in the buff. Caught up to Diane outside her door. "Your key," I said breathlessly.

Diane twirled around. "Thank you, Steven! They charge five bucks for a replacement."

We regarded each other. Our sopping wet clothing clung to our bodies. My glasses were covered in beads of water and were fogging up. Diane did not ask about my crutches or my face. Not interested? Or omnipotent? Somewhere between the two, perhaps.

"I really have to pee," said Diane, clenching her knees together. I followed her into Room 4. "Make yourself at home."

Diane went into the bathroom and shut the door. Her furnished studio was one of six made available to visiting faculty and other academic dignitaries. Not sure how a temporary library consultant was able to snag one. The austere interior exhibited few traces of habitation. It was sparsely appointed in the Early American style. A braided wool rug covered much of the worn, speckled linoleum. Above an old desk hung a West Texas landscape in oil. The only modern elements were a Byzantine swag lamp and a polystyrene panel in avocado trimmed in rough cedar that segregated an unmade twin bed. A window above the kitchen sink afforded a view of the leafy boughs of a mature sycamore through which one could glimpse the campanile.

There is every possibility that Diane dropped her key on purpose, supposing that I would return it. I could kick myself for not making a copy first or just keeping it. A missed opportunity! The sound of a blow dryer commenced from the bathroom. Atop a desk lay *The Current Trend of Converting Dewey to LC Classification among Academic Libraries*. It seemed like a prop, like the books at that club in Port Aransas. A side drawer was empty. The one opposite contained a stapler. Just as I started to open the center drawer, the bathroom door swung open. I spun around and fumbled for a Kent. My breathing and heart rate quickened but I played it cool.

"There's a bottle of wine in the kitchen," yelled Diane over the blow dryer. She emerged barefoot. It was my turn to dry off. Lest its hinges squeak and give me away, I refrained from opening the medicine cabinet. Aside from a familiar-looking blond wig on a Styrofoam head, and a few unlabeled jars of what look like skin cream next to the sink, the bathroom was devoid of any personal belongings. Under cover of a loud piss, I undid the latch on a small window above the commode. The window looked like it was painted shut but there was no time to investigate.

The witch was waiting with two cups of Gewürztraminer. I gave my head a mulish shake. "No, thanks, no. I should really be going." The words stumbled out of my mouth. Diane must have sensed how nervous I was. She pressed one of the glasses into my hand and said, "Don't be silly. Tomorrow's your day off. Take a load off!"

It was so quiet I could hear my own heart pounding. Why did Diane lure me here? "I'm sorry," I said, yawning melodramatically. "Last night, I didn't get to sleep at all." This was no lie. Diane bore an expression of bewilderment. As Ursula, she had already gotten into my pants. Easily, too. Now I was on my guard. If she was disappointed that I thwarted her devious plan, she did not look it. She is a great actress, I will give her that.

There must be a store that sells muskrat-farming supplies. I looked up witchy shops in the *Yellow Pages*. Was surprised to find so many. I narrowed it to three. One on Bluebonnet Circle, one in Poly, and a superstore way the hell out on Precinct Line Road. I reviewed my red notebook. My latest scribblings were difficult to comprehend. But I feel I am so close to a breakthrough. To what, I cannot say. I continued with my musical experiments. With only a few instruments at my disposal, progress is challenging.

The wind buffeted the windows. I looked up "wind" in the encyclopedia. Concentration forsook me. I visualized Vee in her fluffy robe, curled up on the couch with Figgy, sipping tea and studying a male orgasm tutorial in *Cosmo*. She would welcome me, I knew. Nodded off watching *Gigi*.

Wednesday, June 1

Dr. Lanier removed my stitches. Should have had Shagduk take care of those, too, in retrospect. My lifelong pediatrician, who had also been Mom's, asked about the scratches on my face, then remarked upon my rabies treatment. I nodded solemnly. The less said about that the better. I asked him if my injury would prevent me from attending the campus retreat but he dashed that hope. "You're as healthy as a May morning," he said. But it is June.

To Bruce for another trombone mouthpiece, then Sound Warehouse. A few hours in a record store always cheers me up. *In Search of Ancient Gods* caught my eye. A prog album based on the works of Erich von Däniken. Bill Bruford is on it. Figured Fred might like it on the strength of its weirdness. The cashier smirked at my choice but said nothing. For myself I selected Judas Priest's latest.

"This one's heavy duty, man," said the cashier.

Dawn's gift certificate was burning a hole in my pocket, so I stopped at Western Auto Supply. Had to bring in the records so they would not melt in the car. I know nothing about cars so I found myself browsing for accessories. I regarded an air freshener shaped like Texas. To have that dangling in my face would drive me nuts. Ended up getting some curb feelers and an adhesive novelty switch labeled "Ejector Seat."

Splurged on a car wash. Watched a few cars get the hot wax treatment as I polished off a pack of Kents. The Rambler emerged with its antenna snapped off at the base. When I complained, the attendant pointed at some bullshit sign. Lunch at Old South, then off to the Equinox Gift Shop on Bluebonnet Circle.

Was surprised it even existed, until I remembered reading an article about "Fort Worth's occult underbelly." Never realized we had an occult underbelly, but if we do, its practitioners have to shop somewhere. In retrospect, I should have gone to the superstore, where they would have a better selection. And where there was less of a chance of being recognized.

Was disappointed to find a tidy, well-lit shop which despite its purpose exuded a veneer of respectability. A mixture of used and new books held my attention. Apart from Agrippa and Crowley, the subject matter chiefly dealt in tarot, palmistry, psychic phenomena, and sun signs. I lingered in each aisle, marveling at all the witchy stuff. Candles, incense, mortars and pestles, athames (thanks to Paul Huson for introducing me to this word), pewter chalices, and tarot decks graced the shelves. Herbs, powders, crystals, and the like are kept behind the counter. Wands, voodoo dolls, and talismans are locked in a glass case.

An endcap display featured the paperback edition of *The Sexy Witch*. I tossed one on the counter. A young woman with intelligent eyes emerged through a curtained doorway. Apart from the pentagram hanging from a chain around her neck, her conservative attire was less Endora and more Gillian Holroyd. Her hair and make-up however bore subtle qualities that marked her as a fringie. I studied her face as she glanced down at the book. Her eyes looked to the side then up to mine. When she realized I was studying her, I detected a subtle change in her demeanor. She would be more careful now.

The young woman took my list and read it. Again, I watched her face closely. She started to speak, but stopped. She then excused herself and stepped through the curtain. Muffled voices, the other belonging to a male, rose in volume before one shushed the other. The young woman returned. "These are rare and precious substances," she said with a smile. "Can you come back tomorrow?"

"I'd rather wait."

At five o'clock, the young woman stuck her head through the curtain. "It will be just a few more minutes," she said reassuringly. She returned with an invoice and began punching keys on an adding machine. She had unbuttoned a few buttons of her blouse to expose a full breast and white skin. One too many, so it would look accidental. But I knew better.

The bill came as a shock. My eyes moved from the adding machine's display to her cleavage. I swiftly met her gaze. Like a pro, she placed the tip of her pen in her mouth. All mannerisms designed to separate me from my dough. Is this what passes for magic these days?

"We'll have to special order some of the items on your list. Kindly write your name and telephone number here, please."

Felt wary of providing any personal information, so I did not accept the pen. I would have to pay by check, thereby revealing my true identity. I made a show of rummaging through my mansack and patting my pockets. "My checkbook," I lamented. "Can I pay tomorrow?"

"Of course," said the young woman. "I'll set aside the items we do have in stock."

I found her pushiness annoying. She was taking it for granted that her charms would work on me. But I would show her.

"Name and telephone number, please."

I met her gaze. "Duke Mantee," I said evenly. "No telephone."

The young woman knew I was full of it and tossed aside her pen, even though the telephone bit was the truth. "We'll see you tomorrow, Mr. Mantee," she said facetiously. Possessing only an awareness that there were rules without actually knowing them, I felt like I had beaten her at her own game. She would not know it until she looked in the mirror and saw the ink on her lips and blouse.

I slapped a fiver on the counter. "For the book," I said. "My list, please." I had no intention of returning. I will have to identify substitutions for the rare and precious substances. Hemlock and ambergris should be easy enough. Not sure what to use in place of a virgin's spleen. My own? Would an appendix do?

As kind as Vee is, I would not presume to go upstairs every time I need clean socks and underwear. Read three-quarters of *The Sexy Witch* at the washateria. The ideas behind the witchy techniques are sound. Many are even obvious. They prescribe a *modus vivendi* that promotes desired outcomes in everything from one's love life to personal finance. The paperback lays bare some of Diane's favored beguilements, which are not even magical but purely psychological. Does this represent the extent of Diane's power? Does she know any real magic?

The second-floor breezeway connecting Comstock and Pigg afforded an inconspicuous and unobstructed view of the Fac. Swarms of mosquitoes signaled dusk. I hunkered down with binoculars and a fresh pack of Kents. Boggs spotted me at once. We waved but fortunately he kept going. There were no other people about. The clubhouse, like much of campus at this hour, was completely dark. The constant, strident throb of crickets filled the warm evening air. Flood lights from the 'Dillos practice field cast diagonal shadows across the quad and afforded me with just enough illumination to finish my reading. I realized I forgot to mail Aunt Wanda's package.

The moon had risen above the quad and was now high in the cloudless sky. My patience was rewarded when Diane hurried out the door in the direction of her lunar trysting place. Leave it to witches, werewolves, and bartenders to know the precise dates of the full moon. I waited until she was out of sight. I did not follow. There would be little to learn from seeing Diane naked again. Soon I was shinnying up the sycamore. I made my way up a branch to a narrow ledge which ran beneath the upstairs windows. When I tried to open her bathroom window, however, I discovered it was indeed painted shut. After farming a quick muskrat, I was in.

Figured I had nothing to lose by turning on the bathroom light, as a flashlight could be easily noticed from outside. After checking the medicine cabinet, I continued my exploration. I turned on the swag lamp. An academic treatise on aging lay on the bedside table. Pocketed an antique-looking comb so I could have something that belonged to her, just in case. Intimate items are the most effective.

In the kitchen, I examined a wad of dried herbs. I decided not to disturb a clay vase sealed with wax. A couple of Mason jars bore the labels "Hundskamille" and "Asafoetida," respectively in Diane's foreign-looking cursive. A cookie jar caught my eye. It is the same one Aunt Wanda has had for as long as I can remember. I recalled that Diane had baked cookies and hoped there were some in there now. I lifted the lid and reached within.

*Snap!* A mousetrap got me. The last thing in the world I expected. Searing pain was followed by an interval of throbbing. Nothing was broken but there was a mark. Would Diane be looking for it?

Instead of cookies, there was a bundle. It was concealed under a glyph, which I have learned to recognize and dispatch. Wrapped within a square of perfumed silk were numerous items of occult interest as well as a letter to Randy that I had put in the outgoing mail bin myself. It had been opened.

Besides an athame and other obviously witchy items, I found a photo of Jo Ann, sliced from the pages of the *'Dillo.* A film canister contained either a putrified jumbo shrimp or Spunt's shriveled appendix. To be fair, it could have been someone else's appendix. But what are the odds? Among the stash was a passport for one Diane Nagy of California City, California. The photo proves the witch is a master of disguise; here she looks more like Ursula of Ulm than Diane Bollinger. The well-used passport bore recent stamps for West Germany, Spain, Japan, and Chile. I jotted down the address before putting the bundle back the way I had found it. I replaced the glyph to the best of my ability but I am not sure I can fool her. As I write this, I realize I forgot to reset the mousetrap.

In the freezer I found my billfold and my annotated x-rox of *Linguae dordica,* both taken from me in Austin by Ursula of Ulm. If I reclaimed these items  now she would know I had been snooping. Who was I fooling? She had practically handed me her keys herself. She wanted me to find these things. But why? I chuckled. Only a woman would hide something important in the kitchen.

I exited the way I entered, closing the bathroom window behind me. A torch-wielding mob rounded the corner. With loping gait, arms swinging wildly, they surged past me, chanting. Kappa Mus on a panty raid. Some wore panties over their heads, the lacy fabric stretched taut over their exuberant faces. Some wore them instead of pants, their balls hanging out the sides. I played it cool until they were out of sight. Hope no one saw me leaving Diane's window. Or recognized me.

Had to use up some ground beef so I made Manwiches. Stayed up until four transcribing the rest of my lake house notes, then contemplated Diane until the alarm went off. Since she has had my copy of *Linguae dordica* since Austin, I assume her knowledge of Dordic is sufficient to have understood most of my letter to Randy, except for the neologisms, slang, and word play. Time to find out who Diane really is. I shudder to think of what she is doing with Spunt's appendix.

THURSDAY, JUNE 2

"Why are you wearing that?" said Jenny. She was referring to my headband.

"That should be obvious," I said. "The a/c is either off or it's broken."

"Where were you last night? My roommate and I came by to take you out to Studio 6333. To celebrate your birthday."

"You mean Misty," I said. I recalled the time she handcuffed me with a plastic six-pack ring. "I must have just missed you." Guess I am out of the doghouse.

"We came back at ten."

"I was probably here at the library," I said, looking Jenny directly in one eye. A trick learned from Jimmy Stewart. "I forgot my mansack."

Jenny sighed. "Are you free this evening? We could have dinner then go to Studio 6333." It was the second time she mentioned the disco. What in the world is the appeal?

"Didn't they just get raided by the Alcoholic Beverage Commission for selling booze to minors?" Jenny did not answer. Casually, I lifted the lid from the shenanigans dish and peered within. As I feared, Spunt's appendix was missing. "It's a date," I said. When Jenny was not looking, I extracted her belly button lint from the dish. I toyed with the idea of a charm to make the evening's vibe more amorous. I recalled Dawn's encounter with Shagduk at the lake house, then put the lint back. The risk is not worth it.

Forgot to bring a fan from home. It is too quiet in the reading room. It is also too hot. Harrington approached the desk, his walker screeching. "I've taken a flat at the Chateau Villa." His English accent makes it sound like a real chateau.

"That's around the corner from me." Was curious about his walker but figured it was none of my business.

"Mock French Provincial across the way from quasi-Arts & Crafts bungalows. It will suffice for the nonce. There are washing facilities and a landscaped courtyard. Would you like to come round for a look?"

At first I thought he was coming on to me, but decided he was merely English. "I'm awfully busy, but sure."

"There is a pool."

"What time?" I blurted. "I mean, not tonight. But I'm free Sunday."

"Sunday it is, then," he said. "There is something rather important I would like to discuss with you."

"Wait, I can't Sunday. The staff retreat is this weekend. How about next Wednesday?"

"You are welcome any day," he said. "What is that device around your head?"

"It keeps sweat out of your eyes."

"I should like to have one. No one told me Texas was tropical."

"Here's an extra package," I said, reaching for my mansack. "I'm not playing hellball anymore, so I can spare them."

Sherwood's colleague accepted my offering eagerly. "That's kind of you," he said. His walker made more screeching sounds.

"Tennis balls would help dampen that racket," I said helpfully.

"What racket?"

Wrote Randy another letter, essentially a copy of the first one as I remembered it. This time in plain English. I attempted Randy's spiral-locking technique but only partially succeeded. I regarded the dismal-looking missive and sighed. I enclosed a fresh x-rox of the Der Schleim document before sealing it with a glyph Randy should recognize. I dropped it in the mailbox near the business school.

"You have a telephone call," said Hazel judgmentally. She waited for me to get up and then herded me toward the circulation desk where Jenny was assisting a patron. "Hello?" I said.

"It's me. Hope I didn't get you in trouble."

"No, it's fine." Hazel was glaring at me.

"There's a *Star Wars* party tomorrow evening. Would you like to go with me?"

"As in the blockbuster? What does that entail?" My heart began racing as I realized Dawn was asking me out. Now I wish I had asked her.

"Everyone goes as one of the characters from the movie," said Dawn. Jenny was now fussing with the Gaylord but I know she was eavesdropping. "Vee and Tim are going. She suggested I invite you." Was this Vee's idea or Dawn's? Maybe it is not a date after all.

"Can you check me out?" said Jenny. Evidently there is a policy about not checking out your own books. The book in question was an A.C.L.A. publication, *The Information Big Top: Applications of On-Line Computers to Library Problems*. I wondered if computers could solve my library problems. "Sounds so futuristic. "This is due in the year 2525," I said to be funny. "Your arms hangin' limp at your side. Your legs got nothin' to do. Some machine's doin' that for you." *Ka-chunk* went the Gaylord. No eyebrow movement from Jenny. Not even a smirk. And no questions about who I was talking to on the phone.

Spunt has seen *Star Wars*, so I sought him at his desk. After discussion, it was agreed that unless I shaved off my beard I should go as "Obi-Wan Kenobi." My monk robe and huaraches would suffice as a costume. "You'll need a lightsaber," he said. "On such short notice I can't do much for you. Put a water gun in your belt so you can party with both hands."

Jenny and I settled on Kip's that night. There was a waiting list and they asked my name. The rotating Graw McGraw Oldsmobile sign across the street caught my eye, so I said, "Graw McGraw, Jr."

"Right this way, Mr. McGraw, Jr." said the host obsequiously.

Jenny was neither amused nor bothered by my nomenclaturous shenanigans. After we had been seated, she reached into her Playboy Book Club tote bag and produced two wrapped gifts. I had forgotten we were celebrating my birthday! The first was a rather expensive-looking monogrammed crocodile wallet. "Now you can get rid of your horrendous one," said Jenny.

"It's so oblong," I said. Too oblong to fit in my pocket, perhaps, though I knew better than to criticize it. "Isn't crocodile illegal?"

"It's faux," said Jenny. The wallet? Or our relationship? "Save the wrapping paper. The ribbon, too. Now open the other one." It was a Texas Instruments digital watch. "It has five functions: Hours, minutes, seconds, month, and date."

Jenny was dissatisfied with what she ordered. She picked at her food but then started forking shrimps off my own plate. Much to Jenny's credit, she did not tell the waitress it was my birthday, so I was spared the humiliation of being serenaded by uniformed strangers. "What happened to your fingers?" she asked.

"I was snooping through a witch's things and sprang a mousetrap." I nibbled at a callus. One of the hazards of playing bass.

"Give me your hands," said Jenny. Thought she was going to read my palm. Instead, she pushed my cuticles back with her fingernail. "Ow!" I cried.

"You should take better care of yourself."

Words failed me. Since this was supposed to be a date, I held on to her hands when she was done. We were not holding hands, per se. It was more like I was cupping her fists. "What color are my eyes?" said Jenny, out of nowhere.

*Uh oh.* I leaned forward to get a closer look. I wanted to say "hazel," but forgot the word. The best I could come up with was, "They're the color of soup." I noticed they were dilated.

"Soup," repeated Jenny slowly. "Okay. What kind of soup?"

Certainly not minestrone. I could not think of any other soup names. "Cream of Chicken? Are you high right now?" She retracted her fists. Jenny paid when it was time to settle the bill. I let her since it was my birthday.

So much for the amorous vibe, I thought. But then I remembered the charm I had half-heartedly prepared at the information desk. If I want to get laid before December 31, I figured it could not hurt to try it now. I excused myself and went into the men's room. I had forgotten I had put Jenny's lint back into the shenanigans dish. It only provided a needless amount of specificity. Who else did I have a chance with?

It was early, so I called the movie hotline to see what was showing. Jenny wanted to see *The Sting*. I had already seen it with Vee. Of course I did not dare tell Jenny that. We ended up seeing *The Sentinel* at the Wedgwood. There was a scene where one of the lesbians boinks herself in front of Alison. The red leotard reminded me of Mama Fox. I squirmed uncomfortably in my seat. This was the kind of crap Gabrielle used to do in front of me when Loretta was in class. Jenny suddenly got the hiccups. The more she hiccupped, the more she laughed mirthlessly. She tried holding her breath. They say if you startle someone the hiccups will stop. I tried to startle her but with Jenny that is impossible. It is unfair to blame her, though. Her hiccups were probably a subconscious avoidance strategy. We stood up at the same time.

We paused before a Starscroll machine. Jenny turned the dial to Pisces, then inserted a quarter. The machine dispensed a neat plastic tube. She unfurled the scroll. We examined it together. The horoscope for today was "Alliances that aren't faring well should be steered clear of today. But relationships that are growing beautiful or loverly hold great promise." How beautiful was her and Judd's relationship? How loverly was ours? It certainly was not faring well.

I inserted a coin into the slot. "Now turn the knob," instructed Jenny. I did so but nothing happened.

"It's out of Gemini," said Jenny coldly. "You're supposed to check first." I started to walk away. "You can still choose a different sign." She said it so casually, as one who has no clue about the occult.

Traffic was backed up on Camp Bowie on account of everyone waiting to turn into the Studio 6333 parking lot. Each time the club's chrome-plated door opened, laser beams escaped and pierced the sky. Jenny became visibly excited. She peeled off her blouse then reached to unhook her bra. I helped her clumsily. Were those teeth marks? I was too shocked to ask. She unfastened her hair clip, letting her tresses tumble over her bare shoulders. She struggled out of her skirt to reveal gold Spandex hot pants underneath. Did she know we were coming here? She strapped on some gladiator sandals she had in her tote bag. She then put on a satin baseball jacket and unzipped it to her navel. "Is this too wrinkled?" she said rhetorically. Blue eyeshadow completed the transformation from beautiful library clerk to disco fox. "Carry my clutch," she said.

The parking lot was full, as were adjacent streets. We ended up circling the neighborhood until we found a spot in the driveway in front of the public library. Jenny removed my tie then unbuttoned a couple of buttons of my shirt. She then produced a paisley scarf from her purse and tied it around my neck. "It's a *foulard*," she said. "The French wear them."

"French fairies, maybe."

"This place is exclusive," said Jenny. "They don't let just anybody in."

We found ourselves at the end of a long line of hopefuls. I could think of better ways to spend an evening than standing around waiting.

"Stay here," said Jenny. As she approached the bouncer, I saw that the back of her jacket had the word "Trouble" embroidered across the back. Trouble, indeed.

I peered into the window of Say Chic and marveled that it was open at this hour. Evidently it was attached to the club. If your wardrobe did not measure up at the door, you could always spend two hundred dollars on one of their own fashion creations.

"I was a paratrooper," declared a triple amputee in a wheelchair. He was speaking to a group of chicks who were giving him a hard time.

"How do you get down?" said a curly-haired heartbreaker in a fishnet catsuit.

The amputee shrugged and offered her a flask. "My dick isn't grounded," he said.

"What is it?" said the heartbreaker. She held the flask away from her as if it were radioactive.

"Wild Irish Rose, which is twenty percent. Mixed with White Cobra. It'll put you right to sleep."

She handed it back to him. "Sweet dreams," she said dismissively.

I could not stop staring at the amputee's stumps. That poor bastard could have been me. At last, when he no longer amused them, the girls turned their backs on him. Guess he noticed me staring. "Mortar near Khe Sanh in '68," he said. "Did you serve?"

The heartbreaker pinched my elbow. I eyed the wide, plunging neckline of her catsuit. "Your friend is trying to get your attention." I could see Jenny near the entrance motioning impatiently for me to join her. She whispered something into the bouncer's ear. T-Bone! Porteous's former security guard. That hedgehog always had the hots for the Stone Fox. Who doesn't? As he unhooked the velvet rope for us, he looked me up and down in flagrant disapproval. He did not ask for the ten-dollar cover.

Jenny led me into the air-conditioned interior of the nightclub. As my eyes adjusted to the smoke-filled gloom, Misty came bouncing up to us, Jaclyn in tow, like a pair of goddesses. Misty looked ravishing in a short, belted tunic with a cat cartoon on it and satin heels topped with florettes. Jaclyn dazzled in a denim jumpsuit with slit neck and wide, sequined lapels.

There was barely enough room to stand without being jostled. Conversation was nearly impossible. A hairless boy in a satin vest pranced by with a silver tray laden with little baggies. Jaclyn hooked her finger in his waistband then whispered in his ear. After a brief exchange, he dangled a baggie in her face. "Disco biscuits!" she cried. We each took a snort off Misty's compact. We then ducked under a polished brass rail. The dance floor pulsated with constantly changing colors which made it difficult to stand, let alone move.

"A Fifth of Beethoven" blared from a state-of-the-art P.A. I winced at the senseless bastardization of this cornerstone of western music. As I do when obliged to dance, I made a complete fool out of myself. The Funky Chicken elicited cries of glee from the girls. They pressed in close, hips gyrating. The brief sense of euphoria provided by the Bolivian marching powder soon gave way to a hypersensitivity to the loud music and lights. I listened closely for any vestiges of Beethoven's original. E.T.A. Hoffman's review of the symphony crossed my mind. The "radiant beams that shoot through this region's deep night" came not from the loudspeakers but from the disco ball overhead which stabbed the darkness with blinding points of light. Likewise, the "climax that climbs on and on" that leads the listener imperiously forward into the spirit world of the infinite was now supplied by the incessant four-on-the-floor beat and the crush of sweaty bodies. The thin rayon of Misty's cat tunic glided over every curve of her swaying body. Every time I looked up, she was staring intently into my eyes. Was she coming on to me? Jenny did not seem to notice or care. She hustled half-heartedly, looking around as if searching for a face in the crowd.

"I'm going to powder my nose," said Misty. People Jaclyn knew waved us over to their booth. I sat on the end next to Jaclyn. Jenny ended up in my lap. She was jiggling her leg excessively, I thought. No sooner than I ran my hand up her goosebumped calf, she jumped back up. "Be right back," she said hastily, her mind elsewhere. I watched her hurry toward the door where the Doom Hippie was waiting. The two went outside.

Misty approached the booth but there was no place to sit. I pulled her roughly onto my lap. She threw her arm familiarly around my neck. "Did you know the bathrooms are unisex?" she said in a tone of amusement. "People are going at it like rabbits in there."

"They butchered Beethoven," I said. "Fate knocking on the door, indeed. Who's there? Hello, it's Walter Murphy the Psychopomp come to gently sever the last ties between civilization and its soul and guide it to the afterlife." I could not take my eyes off the smudge of white powder around Misty's left nostril. I myself was sweating profusely. If our mothers could only see their babies now.

Misty sniffed then licked her teeth. "You'd have more fun if you pulled that stick out of your butt," she said. "By the way, how'd your date with Dawn go?"

Uh, oh. She knows about the *Star Wars* party. But that is not until tomorrow. "What date with Dawn?" I said carefully.

"We saw you at the Water Gardens."

"That wasn't a date," I said. Who did she mean by "we" and what exactly did they see? "You do realize Jenny isn't my girlfriend," I added, perhaps ill-advisedly.

Misty blinked. "Does she know that?"

"Aren't she and Judd screwing?" I said.

"Maybe you should ask him. His dad runs this place, you know." She gestured toward a one-way window near the ceiling. I looked up, half-expecting Judd Sr.'s face to appear in the glass. Instead, I spotted Amber on the catwalk. She was dolled up in a slinky dress, heels, and lipstick. She looked like a child prostitute. *It couldn't be her*, I reasoned.

"I just might," I said. Confusion mingled with outrage. Why is a kid here? Roller Girl rolled by in a tinfoil bikini. She did not see me. I surveyed the room. A chick under a booth table was whipping some skull on some guy. I thought I recognized him as the painter Doug Blevins. Guess he must have found himself a spleen. The chick on her knees could not be more than eighteen. A good age for debauchery, I supposed. You can kill a gook at eighteen with Uncle Sam's blessing. "It's the principle of the thing," I said at length.

Misty swiveled around in my lap and snorted another bump. In the booth next to Doug Blevins, the lead singer from Pantego sat next to a middle-aged

Candy Barlow. For an old stripper, she still lives up to the legends. To her left sat Beau Price and Wildcat Murphy. "Can you believe this place?" I said. "Fort Worth's livestock and oil glitterati rubbing elbows with artists and entertainment royalty. All dressed to the nines. All with deviated septums."

Misty studied the scratches on my face for a moment, then began fiddling with my beard.

"Are you going to try to braid it again?"

"If you're lucky," she said loudly into my ear.

"Diz and Bird puttin' on the moan," crooned Bryan Ferry. "Tappin' out telexes to Tupelo." I considered doing something out of character. Something a shade reprehensible. I could tap out Misty's telex and be amusingly ashamed afterward. Jenny would find out and respond with mock outrage. She would then pout. Nothing is worse than being on the receiving end of the Stone Fox's pouts.

Amidst Misty's protests, I slid out from under her and made for the door. Across the crowded parking lot I could make out the Stone Fox leaning against Judd's dually. He stood before her talking animatedly. An uninhibited bray of laughter came from Jenny. That is the problem: I do not make Jenny laugh. Nor do I beat her.

I turned to go back inside. T-Bone thrust out his beefy arm. "But I was just in there," I said.

"It's time to give this beautiful lady a chance," he said. He unhooked the velvet rope and with a flourish of his hand admitted the heartbreaker from earlier. "*Excusez-moi*," she said as she squeezed by, her nearly naked tits brushing roughly across my chest.

As glad as I was to be out of that awful place, I felt I had unfinished business. A gesture later and I was back in, T-Bone none the wiser. I returned to the booth with two shots of Two Fingers to find everyone getting up. As belongings were gathered, skirts smoothed, and drinks signed for, I allowed myself to check Misty out. She is attractive in a sort of a stoner Natalie Wood way. Dark circles under her heavy-lidded, dreamy eyes indicated a dissolute existence. Her wild playfulness I find attractive, though. So unlike Jenny. "Quack quack!" sang Rick Dees. "Quack quack!" parroted Jaclyn. She and her friends headed back to the dance floor. "Come," said Misty.

I slid into the naugahyde booth and pulled Misty back onto my lap. She leaned back and looked at me dispassionately. We downed our shots. I drew her toward me and kissed her collarbone. Her perfume had a bitter taste to it. I pressed my lips against hers. She responded as if she had been expecting it. There was something rote about the way her tongue darted in and out of my mouth, like she had done it a million times before.

My calluses kept catching on the fabric of her cat tunic. I rubbed my knuckle over a nipple then opened her tunic a bit to expose it. It had glitter on it. I untied her belt and tugged it free. She adjusted her arm to hold her tunic closed. I reached down and slid my hand up her thigh. When I reached her bush, I flexed my cock: *dum dum-dum dum dum*. She flexed her bits twice in answer and her knees parted. But not enough. I determinedly pushed them apart.

It was time to turn a stranger into a friend. My fingers still hurt on account of the mousetrap but I sucked it up. Misty's quickening breaths were hot in my ear. "Deep in the heart of Texas!" chanted the crowd, their feet stomping to a disco arrangement of the classic tune. Misty began to squirm. Her mouth opened in a wide *O*. "You're hurting me," she whimpered. My callouses!

I stood up and roughly pulled Misty to her feet. Like a magician's tablecloth trick, I whipped off her tunic in one quick yank. With my *foulard*, I tied her hands behind her. I then looped her belt around her throat and with a sharp jerk led her toward the exit. She let out a stifled whimper. To a chorus of whooping and hollering, she emerged blinking in the bright lights of the parking lot. Her cheeks were pink from embarrassment. Or was it arousal? Her creamy white skin contrasted with her dark bush, rouged lips, and the rose florettes on her feet. I did not see if Jenny and the Doom Hippie were still there. Nor did I give a damn. The scene recalled the one from *Slave Lord of Siluria* in which Murloc attached a chain to the collar of the girl he had just purchased and paraded her, like an animal, naked through the market back to his chambers. In this manner I led Misty to the Rambler, stumbling in her heels along Bernie Anderson Avenue past a nonplussed jogger. When I was done with her, the seat was soaked.

I undid my scarf from her wrists, then tossed her wadded-up cat tunic onto her bare back. "Clean it up," I said. Guess Tim was right about women loving assholes.

No one said a word back to the Hacienda. I followed Misty up the steps to the room she shares with Jenny. She went into the bathroom and was in there for a long time. Meanwhile, I got comfortable on Jenny's bed. My hand encountered a cord. It was attached to a Prelude 3 electric massager. I experimentally turned it on. The moment I realized what it was for, Misty suddenly emerged from the bathroom. I quickly turned off the massager and shoved it back under the pillow.

Misty now wore a halter top over some terry shorts. She turned on a lava lamp and joined me on the bed. The room was bathed in its sickly, greenish glow.

"You're the carillonneuse for Porteous, right?" I said. "Maybe you can show me around up there sometime?"

"The biggest bell has a hundred-pound clapper," said Misty. "Feel." She flexed her delicate feminine biceps. I became conscious of loud hammering and the sound of clanging metal outside. Misty peeked out the window. "The Kappa Mus are building a Ferris wheel."

There was laughter in the hall. The door opened. Jenny and Jaclyn burst into the room in a cloud of perfume, chatting up a storm. They were discussing the Doom Hippie.

"Is he coming up?" said Misty, her tone fearful. Just the other day she wanted to "jump his bones," according to Jenny. What has changed? Why the hell does anyone give that guy the time of day?

"Nope," said Jenny glumly. "He's going to the Bunker." Misty leaped to her feet and pulled Jaclyn into the bathroom, no doubt to spill the beans about our tryst.

"Where's my clutch?" said Jenny.

"Shit," I said. "I guess I left it at the club. I'm sorry, Jenny."

Jenny opened the window and leaned over the sill. Her hot pants clung to her like a second skin. "Stifle!" she yelled. She took off Gino Vanelli and put on *Disco Assault!* "Frankenstein" gurgled from the speakers. Since when is Edgar Winter disco? "Come here," I said firmly. She joined me on the bed. I put my arm around her neck and held a doobie to her lips. "Where'd you get the lava lamp?"

Jenny exhaled a long stream of smoke. "The library," she said. "Someone threw it away. So wasteful."

Started to tell her it was mine but chose to keep the conversation mellow. "Look at the lava lamp," I said. I was starting to get high. "You know what it will feel like if you lick it. Imagine licking the typewriter. Or my cock." Jenny slapped my chest in protest. "Whether you have or have not actually licked these things, when you imagine it, your tongue knows. It knows. Do you know what I mean?"

"Close your eyes," said Jenny. I felt her soft lips press upon my mouth. I cannot believe she is using the same move I used on her when she told me she did not think of me "that way." Did her tongue know? She then licked one of my glasses lenses. Suspiciously playful behavior coming from her. Guess she has forgiven me for losing her clutch. She drew close to me, her hand landing limply on my growing hard-on. Was I going to get laid twice in one evening? It is as if a sex curse has been lifted. My charm must have worked. Jenny complained about Mama Fox and living at home, then about the noise and chaos of the Hacienda. So much for keeping the conversation mellow. I leaned in for another kiss but she stopped me. "If only I had somewhere else to go," she pouted.

"Hang out at Collinwood," I said stupidly. "Key's under the flower pot." Vee and I had put it there for emergencies. She would be miffed to know I had told someone about it. Rightfully so. Jenny sat up, having so easily gotten what she wanted from me. Which was evidently not my cock. She leaned over and licked the lava lamp. It erupted, spewing its creamy entrails upward.

Misty and Jaclyn emerged whispering from the bathroom. Jaclyn regarded me with a furrowed brow. Misty must have told her everything.

"Show her the jeans," said Jaclyn upon seeing Jenny. Misty located the jeans in question and changed into them in front of us. Jaclyn motioned for Misty to turn around. Instead of back pockets, there were clear plastic windows that showed skin.

"They're from Say Chic," said Misty. She and Jaclyn spent the next hour modeling outfits. Jenny and I provided scoring from one to ten, with commentary. Gradually, the girls settled down. Misty produced a package of chocolate donuts and we continued to snack and smoke until each zonked out.

Except me. On account of the Kappa Mus. I attempted a *Shush* spell but ended up disturbing Jenny. She sighed and nestled her face against my stomach. Could she not smell Misty on me? I lay wide awake listening to the *ratatattat* of a jackhammer. It chiseled apart my thoughts like concrete. At least there was a/c.

FRIDAY, JUNE 3

Beams of sunlight dissected the room. Misty and Jaclyn lay inert in the next bed. I groped behind me. The Stone Fox was gone. The events of last night came back to me in a flash. The charm. Since I had not been specific, I had sex but not with Jenny. As empty as the experience was, at least I ticked off one of my New Year's resolutions. I will never make them again. I quietly let myself out and headed to Collinwood for a much-needed shower.

I found Jenny's tote bag in the Rambler. I looked inside. A worn C-60 cassette bore the handwritten label "Jenny loves—" with a heart instead of the word "loves." The object of her affection had been scratched out. Whom had she loved? The label was faded from use. I contemplated her Betsy Ross Pez dispenser. The way the patriotic upholsterer's head tilted back to reveal a yawning neck opening I found unsettling. It was empty. Underneath a box of maxi pads were a few books—*A Thesaurus of Descriptors for Indexing Materials about Hippies and a Cumulative Index of* Far Out, *1968-1976*; *Design of a System for Automating the Circulation System of an Academic Library Using TAB Equipment*; and Peter Koestenbaum's *Existential Sexuality*. There was also a diary.

Six months ago, I would never have read someone's diary. As I learn to be mistrustful of others, I become less trustworthy myself. My word of power was too much for the shitty lock. It shattered. It occurs to me I know many formulae for destroying but none for creating. I told myself I was doing this out of concern for Jenny's safety. What was she saying about the Doom Hippie? For my betrayal, I was rewarded with the following passages from Wednesday's entry:

*Women see men differently than men see themselves. Take Steven. Simmering just under the surface is this fundamental masculine energy. Like most men these days with their cologne and neck chains, he doesn't bring it out. Or I don't bring it out in him, rather. God knows I tried! I was hoping to be the spark that ignited his lighter fluid of testosterone and wild physicality. His raw emotional intensity and strength, just from being larger and rougher than me, is just sitting there in check, waiting for the right woman to come along.*

*Judd, on the other hand, knows how to tap into that power and bring it out any time he needs it. Instead of trying to impress or flatter me, he has his way with me. I have never felt more like a woman than I do with Judd. Plus, he's a thinker. Steven just likes to talk about music all the time. He's just a tame house cat I can manipulate and control. If he ever wised up, I would reconsider. But I am not going to hand him the keys to the kingdom. He needs to be man enough to find it in himself.*

*Steven's off today. He went to the lake with the attractive woman who lives above him. Their doors don't have locks on them. She comes and goes as she pleases so I suppose they are sleeping together. Diane from the library went, too. She thinks she's a Breck girl or something. Steven made a flimsy excuse for not inviting me. It's too bad because I could see myself marrying him. Or someone like him. When he got back his foot was magically all better. Why would he lie about something like that? I asked him how the lake was and he gave one of his ridiculous answers. He seems so secretive now, especially after his friend Randy was fired. He probably thinks he's next but I don't see what it has to do with me. We were supposed to go out for his birthday when he got back but then he disappeared. He doesn't have a phone so it's hard to reach him. Neither does Judd but I can usually find him at the club after dark. Thank God for Judd and thank God for the B.G.'s. Without them, school and work would be too much.*

Judd, a thinker. Oh, brother! And what the hell are B.G.'s? Surely not the hit vocal group. A brass object gleamed in the bottom of Jenny's bag. At first I thought it was a trombone mouthpiece but discovered it was shaped like a tiny Hoover. A miniature worthy of one of Duchamp's *boîte-en-valises*. It was, however, just a device for snorting coke. Everyone does a little blow now and then but to buy accessories for it suggests more than a casual interest in the recreational stimulant. Probably a love token from the Doom Hippie. There was also a slim pink case that contained a strange object I assumed was a diaphragm. I had never seen one up close.

"Didn't expect to see you here," I said in a measured voice. Guddu did not respond. He was staring at a stain on my shirt. Chocolate from last night's donuts, no doubt.

"Do you know what will get blood out of poly knit?" Let the son of a bitch think I slaughtered someone. Guddu made a symbol with his fingertips, then gestured thrice. Without looking I knew that the stain was gone. I did not thank him.

Jenny was grateful when I returned her tote bag. She checked for her diary and gave a sigh of relief. I feel like scum for violating her privacy. Since she is clearly sleeping with the Doom Hippie, I guess it does not matter. Especially after last night. Not that it is any of my business.

The ghost in my IBM continues to type gibberish. I suspect the imp but it could be crossed wires. Was going to ask Spunt if he knew of a manual typewriter I could use but he had taken the day off. Hope Diane has not put his appendix to use yet.

At a quarter of, I changed into my *Star Wars* costume. Figured Amber might get a kick out of it. I found her talking to a foreign-looking guy at the desk. He did not look like a professor nor a student. I waited while he finished his sentence before saying, "Can I help you?"

"I'm Agent Ernst Dubochet with Interpol," he said. "I've already briefed your colleague on the reasons for my visit. In short, I'm here in response to a court suit filed by the government of Spain to recover antiquities stolen from an archaeological site near Cáceres. This young lady says you can take me downstairs to the Vault."

Should have told Amber not to call it the Vault, but she would only ask why. "I'm sorry, I don't have the authority to let you in there. You would have to speak to Dixie Womack, but she's away at a conference."

"Not a problem," said Dubochet. "I don't need permission. I just need you to take me to the Vault."

"As you wish."

Dubochet spoke little. I did not trust him but was not about to call Interpol. I would let him show me what his game was. He referred to a list he had removed from his coat pocket and unfolded. He seemed to know what he was looking for. I was not disposed to help him. I did not want him snooping around and finding another priceless codex I overlooked. The only sound was the soft rush of air from the ventilation system. "This is a designated shelter from tornadoes and the H-bomb," I said. Why was I making small talk? I just wanted him to go away.

"What's in here?" Dubochet tugged at the handle on the door of the thesis cage. "Theses," I said. He did not ask to be let in. He examined a couple of incunables then studied the book bound in human skin. "I've seen enough. Kindly unlock the display cabinet in the vestibule."

I led him upstairs. He placed his list on the case containing one of Hogg's sermons while I unlocked the display cabinet. I watched while he inspected the Venus figurine with the frog-like face and the Mississippian-era carved stone disc. The three-fingered gauntlet of unknown origin was missing, I noted.

After a perfunctory thank you, Dubochet exited the building and turned left, walking quickly toward the quad. He left his piece of paper behind. It appeared to be a list of stolen antiquities with detailed descriptions of each item. Among them were a carved soldier from Persepolis, Olmec jade masks, and Byzantine ecclesiastical articles. Nothing I recognized from the Baumann Collection.

"Why are you dressed like Jesus?" was all Amber had to say regarding my costume. I waited until everyone was leaving then said I had forgotten to turn off the Mr. Coffee. "Y'all go ahead. I'll lock up."

Polished off a bowl of Kentucky mints in the break room. No sign of Carlos or Boggs. When the coast was clear, I slipped into Dixie's office. Her file cabinet was locked this time. Utilizing a trick learned from a James Bond paperback, I was in. Found Diane's dossier. Figured I may as well take it and read it later rather than get busted by Boggs. I took Randy's, too.

Dawn's narrow gravel driveway off Westworth Boulevard is flanked by a concrete wall studded with ammonite fossils and shards of pottery. Hesitated at the gate, not knowing if I would have clearance to turn around. Six of one, I thought, and left the Rambler on the side of the road.

The doorbell disturbed a pack of dogs within. The door opened a crack, revealing a little Mexican boy. The dogs were going nuts behind him. They shoved past him and raced outside, jumping on me, spinning in circles, wrestling each other, slobbering, baying, snarling, pissing, taking dumps, sniffing each other's asses, and just being wild animals. Studio 6333 for canines. One of them raked a rough paw across my forearm, drawing blood.

As I prepared an incantation, Dawn whistled shrilly. The dogs stampeded back inside, berserk with excitement. "Simmer down, now!" she yelled. She let the dogs out the back door then appraised my costume. "No more crutches?"

"Nope," I said, dancing a jig.

"You're early," said Dawn. Her hair was done up like two cinnamon rolls. "Be a dear and keep Joaquin company."

Dawn went into a darkened hall. The house smelled like glue. I fell backward upon the sofa and contemplated the little boy. Does Dawn have a kid? Joaquin produced a Weeble out of thin air. "*¡Perro!*" he said gleefully.

It was not a *perro* at all but a reindeer. It was suspiciously similar to the one Vee found playing *Feeley Meeley*. It smelled oddly of fish. What's "reindeer" in Spanish? "*¡Cosa!*" I replied. Joaquin giggled. He grabbed the Weeble, then shoved it deep under the sofa cushions.

"*Discúlpeme, amigo,*" I said. I hid my hands behind my back. Joaquin was studying a booger. "*¿Dónde está?*" I said slowly in a mysterious voice. Had his attention now. "*¿Dónde está la mano de tres dedos?*" The child looked up at me, his eyes gleaming. "*Cuidado, mi amigo. Cuidado con la mano de tres dedos.*"

Joaquin pointed behind me and yawped a nonsensical noise, like "Da!" or something.

"Joaquin," I repeated ominously. "*Cuidado, mi amigo. Cuidado con la mano de tres dedos.*"

"Da!" Joaquin squealed with glee, still pointing behind me. I turned around but saw nothing. What was he looking at?

"*¿Dónde está la mano de tres dedos?*" I held up a menacing three-fingered claw. "*¡Dios mío!*" I snarled. Joaquin's expression grew dark. I tickled his armpit and cried, "*Disfruta la garra de hierro!*" Joaquin shrieked hysterically. Assumed he was having fun until I noted his face was frozen in a terrified grimace. Panicked, I tried my trusty *Shush* spell. It only amplified his caterwauling. Softly, I sang:

> *Sing...canta*
> *Sing a song...canta una canción*
> *Canta en voz alta*
> *Canta fuerte*

"What is going on in here?" demanded Dawn, with concern in her voice.

"Nothing!" I said. "We were just playing!" Joaquin was still blubbering.

Dawn gave me a dubious look. "Joaquinito, don't be sad," she said. The doorbell rang. "*¡Está abierta!*" said Dawn. A woman attired as a maid came in. She had an anxious look on her face.

"*¡Mijo!*" she cooed. She took the inconsolable child from Dawn and clutched him to her bosom. Joaquin sobbed quietly as his mother stroked his thin, black hair. She and Dawn conversed in hushed tones while I fished the reindeer from the bowels of the sofa. "*Tu Weeble,*" I offered plaintively. Joaquinito shrank away from me.

The mom and Joaquin took off. "Hey, that's not an ashtray!" said Dawn. She took the clay pot from me and emptied it in the fireplace.

"May I use your euphemism?"

"Through the kitchen."

Every flat surface in the kitchen was covered with bottles of vitamins. I paused to admire the blue and white geometric wallpaper. There were several doors in the hall. One had a beaded curtain, through which I saw a pink and orange room with flowers and pillows everywhere. A wad of rumpled clothing occupied the depression in a bean bag chair. I moved to get a closer look at a bookcase. Upon its shelves: *Ways of Seeing*, *Philosophy in a New Key*, and stacks of *Artforum* and *Interview*. A few slim volumes of Plath were cause for concern. Chicks who like Plath tend to be nuts. Loretta, for example.

Upon a vanity was make-up, perfume bottles, a case of curlers, and an open tackle box loaded with earrings and bracelets. A picture frame caught my eye. It bore an etched calligraphic message that casually resembled Dordic. Nope, it was just "I love you" but upside-down. I righted it. The photos within were taken from a photo booth of Dawn and some older guy making silly faces. They must have been taken a few years ago, before feathered hair was all the rage. I thought the guy looked an awful lot like Uncle Larry. I looked more closely.

*It was definitely Uncle Larry.*

Dazed and horrified, I fled Dawn's room just in time to hear her cry out in dismay. "You are so bad!" I found her examining a pair of panties whose crotch was now a large, jagged hole. "Did you see Buster do this?" she demanded.

"Huh? No!" Was I supposed to have been keeping an eye on Buster? I had the vague sensation of being in trouble. I tentatively reclaimed my seat on the sofa.

"Let me change into my costume and we can go," said Dawn, with a sigh. I still had to pee. My arm was still bleeding. She reappeared in a belted white robe and white leather boots. The robe showed her curvy figure to advantage. The cinnamon rolls were part of the costume, evidently. I reached over and gave them a squeeze.

Dawn regarded herself in the hallway mirror. "I made the robe and belt myself."

"Who are you supposed to be?"

"Princess Leia Organa."

"Wish people dressed this way always," I said. I wrinkled my nose. "What's that odor?"

Dawn led me into a low-ceilinged addition being used as a studio. "Fiberglass epoxy, from this." Upon a large work bench rested a length of rope that had been dipped into, or sprayed with, the epoxy and then arranged to form the outline of Texas. "For a client." Shelves were crammed with vases and other ceramic creations. Canvases leaned against the walls. A dog-eaten coffee table was burdened with coffee cans full of paint brushes. In the corner stood a creature fashioned from lumber and chicken wire, partially slathered in papier-mâché. Then I saw the photo. "Hey, that's me!"

"That's from the lake house." Dawn had captured me lying by the pool with *Slave Lord of Siluria* on my chest. The book was a nice touch. She popped open a L'eggs egg and removed some bills. These she tucked into her boot.

"My ex used to keep her stash in one of those," I said as if Dawn wanted to hear about Loretta.

We stepped outside. "Where's your car?"

"By the road." We trudged down the driveway in silence, Uncle Larry wedged between us. "What's worse than ants in your pants?"

"I don't know."

"An uncle in your pants."


The party was at a Ridglea apartment complex near the freeway. Tim and Vee arrived the same time we did. The girls squealed and patted each other's cinnamon rolls when they saw each other. "I was going to be Aunt Beru but it's too hot to wear a wig," said Vee.

"Are you supposed to be Jesus?" said Tim. He and I were similarly robed. Tim examined my costume critically. "Obi-Wan's garment opens in the front, like this," he said, demonstrating his own correct robe. "And he doesn't wear huaraches. Let's see your lightsaber." I showed him my water pistol. He sighed. "You can be my cousin, Ben-Wa Kenobi."

We had trouble finding the party. We finally asked a guy dressed like a gold robot. "It's Apartment 202 in Building B," he politely explained in the received pronunciation of an English butler. "Follow me, if you please."

"I like those gold cowboy boots," I said. "I have the same ones."

Apartment 202 was brimming with people gussied up as characters I recognized from the ads, including several Luke Skywalkers and guys wearing homemade white plastic armor. There were a few Obi-Wans but no other Ben-Wa Kenobis as far as I could tell. All the chicks were garbed as Carrie Fisher's space princess.

Dawn excused herself to speak to Vee in the kitchen. A Leia approached me. "Help me, Obi-Wan," she said sexily. "You're my only hope."

"No, I'm Ben-Wa."

She stared at me blankly.

"Ben-Wa Kenobi."

"I don't know who that is," she said.

Before I could respond, a one-armed Sleestak jumped between us and blurted, "*Negola dewaghi wooldugger!*" Something about the way he blurted it reminded me of Jimmy Durante and his trademark, "Ha-cha-cha-cha!" He, or it, flashed his blaster and slunk away.

Bombastic orchestral music blared from the stereo, which I understood to be the movie soundtrack. I wondered who the orchestra was. Tim held court by a wall unit. When we made eye contact, he beckoned to me. "Come, Ben-Wa! Meet my friends!"

I approached the group, and stood by patiently as they discussed the discovery of rings around Uranus. A hanging spider plant teased my neck. I struggled to read the yellow spines on a shelf above the turntable: Brackett, Weinbaum, Saberhagen, Fox. Sounded like the name of a law firm. At last, I spotted it—*Courtesans of Siluria*. One I have not read.

Introductions were made. Since everyone was clothed similarly—and I am terrible at remembering names—I figured I could just call them all Luke or whatever. A guy in a motorcycle helmet and black cape said, "I've been waiting for you, Ben-Wa. The circle is now complete." I shook his hand. He raised his visor and whispered, "How are your balls?" Everyone snickered. Must be a movie reference.

"I'm Luke," said one of the Lukes. "This is my Uncle Owen." Owen looked younger than his nephew by a few years. I was about to ask about that but then I remembered my own Uncle Larry. He and I could be brothers.

Someone in a bug-eyed mask joined us. "What's the word, Greedo?" said one of the Han Solos.

"T-Bird," said Greedo, his voice muffled by his rubber mask.

The Han Solo produced a bottle of Thunderbird and filled Greedo's cup.

"What's the price?" said Greedo.

"Fifty twice."

I marveled at the cryptic exchange. Dawn returned with a Merle Haggard collector's cup of orange liquid. The Han Solo smirked when he saw Dawn and said, "Well if it isn't Your Holiness." Dawn looked him over with aristocratic disapproval.

"Do you know him?" I said. Dawn shook her head. I drained my cup in one swig. "What is this?"

"Mad Dog and Tang, I think." She pointed at a large plastic wastebasket in the corner decorated to resemble one of the show's robots. Under its hemispherical lid were gallons of the beverage.

"It's like a sauna in here," I said. I fanned myself with a Texas-shaped trivet.

Dawn pinched my robe and made a face. "This is dacron poly, no wonder. Feel mine. She offered me a corner of her sleeve and I stroked it appreciatively. "It's *mousseline de soie.*"

The Han Solo from before kept ogling Dawn. I put my arm around her waist and drew her close. She did not resist. We took turns refilling each other's cups until we found ourselves lingering near the spiked Tang. Evidently, the orange beverage is the specialty of a "Mos Eisley cantina," whatever that means. Three Wookies started a yowling contest. With the music getting louder and the place getting more crowded, it became futile to have a conversation. Dawn said something I did not catch. As I bent to shout "What?" in her ear, I spotted Shagduk perched on a lampshade. Evidently, no one else could perceive him. I could not say anything because it would appear as if I were conversing with the lamp.

Something was crawling down my neck. A spider? I jumped, spilling Tang all over Dawn's white robe. She excused herself to clean up. I waited for her, mortified. The imp, of course, had made himself scarce. How many other minor misfortunes may be attributed to him? My scare tactics are wearing off.

Dawn and I topped off our cups and descended the stairs to the parking lot. It was cooler outside. There was no place to sit, so I suggested we take a walk. We made our way to Pershing Street. "My grandparents used to live nearby. Down by the ice place."

There was no sign of Shagduk. My dire warning about Dawn has obviously been forgotten. Or ignored. We found ourselves at a construction site for two high rise buildings. Without speaking, we entered one of the structures. The framework was in place but there were no walls yet. We made our way up a stairwell to the roof, which afforded an unobstructed view of the city. The cars on the freeway formed two red and white dotted lines that led toward the downtown skyline in the distance, itself outlined in white lights. A pleasant breeze blew up my robe.

There was a moon. Dawn and I cautiously seated ourselves along the edge of the roof, dangling our legs. It was at once terrifying and exhilarating. My stomach felt like it does when you ride the Monster Mouse. All we could hear was the soft hiss of traffic, punctuated by the occasional roar of a semi. Dawn produced a dandelion. She blew on the seeds, which blew back into her face.

"Where did you get that?" I said.

"I brought it up here."

I reclined, pulling Dawn with me. I propped myself up on my elbows and stared down at her. A peck on her cheek led to her lips. She did not stop me, but almost immediately, my arm hurt and I had to turn onto my side. We continued to make out awkwardly. With my one free hand I clumsily explored her curves over her Tang-stained robe. "Are you trying to seduce me?" she said.

"Do you feel seduced?"

Dawn grasped my water pistol and gave it several rapid squirts, which I deserved. After failing to overcome our amorous inertia, we gradually relaxed and just lay there, staring up at the stars. As I tend to do whenever I contemplate the night sky, I began to wax philosophical. I held forth on man's insignificance in the universe, the prospect of intelligent life on other planets, and the rings of Uranus. Dawn indulged my declamations, even making a few remarks now and then. I moved on to more mundane topics like Rhodesia and Anita Bryant. I spoke of the Baumann Collection, of Time Frame, and of which edition of Bill Martin's had the best hush puppies. It felt like I was speaking at Dawn, rather than with her, so I asked her questions. Her favorite band is Jackson Browne. Jackson Browne is not a band. I did not belabor the point. Learned she speaks fluent Spanish, which I have witnessed myself. She is also into photography, but does not know what she wants to be when she "grows up." Dawn is my age!

People are like chemicals. When they meet sometimes they form a bond. Others react violently. The latter would be "acid-base" reactions. If they react to create a solid relationship, that would be a "precipitation" reaction. "Redox" reactions involve an exchange of electrons. Despite my sex curse being lifted, I did not see any chance of an exchange of electrons this evening with Dawn.

We could not find Dawn's boot. As there were nails about, I carried her piggyback down ten flights of stairs. The descent was agonizing.

Tim and Vee had taken off. Dawn was sick in the bathroom. I asked Greedo if he would give us a ride home. In the back seat of his Delta 88, Dawn and I enjoyed a torpid and somewhat tentative makeout session. Spotted the arms merchant watching in the rear view. He grinned broadly. "May the force be with you!" he bade us, hands held in prayer, as we spilled onto the curb at Collinwood.

Dawn explored my pad as I brushed my teeth. "Why do all your books have bookmarks in them?" she said. I bristled at the question, recalling the time Loretta threw them all away. From shops all over Texas, some now defunct. I found Dawn with her heart-shaped ass in the air looking at my records. She selected *Ummagumma*, a serious make-out album. I winced as she put her fingerprints all over it. "Can I use your toothbrush?" She would be the second chick to use my toothbrush lately.

With a renewed spring in my step, I opened the windows, turned on the fans, and quickly tidied up. I was ready to tap into that wild physicality Jenny had written about but was reluctant so soon after Dawn's hideous encounter with Shagduk. When she came out of the bathroom, I gently removed her princess costume and we tumbled wordlessly into bed. "Can you point those fans away from us?" whispered Dawn softly as I kissed her bare shoulder. By the time I settled down, she was snoring.

I lay there staring at the ceiling, contemplating what Jenny wrote about me. I am not sure I buy a lot of it, but I want to believe she is right about my untapped masculine mojo. After studying *The Sexy Witch*, I understand well how energy like that could be harnessed and directed. There is plenty in reserve as I write all this next to Dawn's sleeping form.

SATURDAY, JUNE 4

Vee must have a sixth sense. She always butts in whenever I have a chick over. This morning was no exception. "Brought you a paper," she sang melodiously. She knows damn well we get it at the library. She threw open the curtains. Sunbeams sliced through the dusty air.

"Dawn's here," I said, pulling the sheet over my face. "She's taking a shower."

"It's about time!" She winked. I assume she was resferring to me and Dawn getting together. "Are you off today? I'm going to Traders' Village."

A day at the flea market with Vee sounded like heaven. Loretta and I used to go together regularly and it would be nice to reclaim the place for myself. "No, I'm going on a retreat for work. It's at the chancellor's ranch way out in Timbuktu." When I mentioned there would be horseback riding, Vee bounced upstairs and returned with some ornate chrome spurs.

"Take these," she said. She then barged into the bathroom. "Hey, Green Bug! Come with me to get Eagles tickets?"

"*Arrivederci*, Vee," I said forcefully, sweeping her out the door. An Alexander Hamilton lay on the rug. I tucked it into Dawn's boot. I reached for the paper and an ashtray. A story caught my eye: "Lost Pacific Continent Considered." It said that Atlantis may not be the only lost continent. That there is another one in the Pacific called Pacifica. Could it be Vul Kar? Dawn emerged from the bathroom, her hair wet and limp. She was wearing her Tang-stained Princess costume.

"Shit!" I cried. "We left the Rambler at the party." There was nothing to do but walk down to the gas station and call a cab. It took twenty minutes to arrive. Dawn accompanied me and paid the nine-dollar fare. We spoke little on the way.

While I hotwired the ignition, Dawn asked about the ejector seat. The engine sputtered to life. "Hold on," I said urgently, then flipped the switch. Dawn shrieked, then laughed. "You jerk," she said. It only just now occurred to me that the Rambler has a bench seat in front. We would both have been ejected. "Oh, I almost forgot. Can you model for my drawing class Wednesday evening? There's six bucks in it for you." I must have blushed. "You don't have to be nude. And you'll be doing me a big favor. Our usual model is getting married."

At Dawn's gate, I hesitated. "This car has no reverse." I pointed at the empty reverse button socket.

"I can fix that for you." Dawn came close to me, her lips parted, tempting, deliberately provocative. We kissed. It was soft and wet. "Last night was nice," she said affectionately. "Have fun at your retreat!" As Dawn stepped out of the Rambler, the belt from Misty's dress fell to the ground. I left it there. A quick search revealed Jenny's bra under the seat. I tossed it out, too.

Dawn's kiss left me feeling somewhat giddy. The flick of her tongue. How she had clenched my shirt. The butterflies recalled my first kiss in the fourth grade with Becky Ramirez.


For better or worse, I took Guddu's genie bottle but left everything else in an old guitar case sealed with a glyph. On my way to pick up Jenny, I snapped my fingers for the imp. Guddu appeared in the rear view almost immediately.

"We're going on a retreat," I said. "For Porteous. You are to stay close to me, and stay out of trouble. Do you understand?"

"Yes, Steven," said Guddu.

We rolled up to Mama Fox's house. "Wait in the car," I said.

Jenny was not ready to go. I winced when a boisterous voice called my name. "Mother!" screamed Jenny. "Leave Steven alone!"

"I'm not going to hurt him!" said Mama Fox indignantly. She sounded like she had been hitting the bottle, not that it would make any difference. "Besides, he gives good foot."

"Mother!" Jenny made her way slowly down the stairs with two overstuffed suitcases. I rushed to help her.

Mama Fox brushed Jenny's hair from her face. "You take real good care of Steven this weekend," she said. Jenny made an exasperated grunt and reached for her purse. "Kiss," said Mama Fox. Jenny stopped in her tracks and turned around. "Not you. Steven."

"Mother, I swear to God!"

"I'm just teasing," said Mama Fox. She turned to look at me. "Steven doesn't want a piece of this tough old meat, anyway. Or do you, Steven?"

"Goodbye, Mrs. Fox," I said.

"Ugh," said Jenny once she had settled in the passenger seat. "Don't encourage her, babe."

What did Jenny just call me? She did not acknowledge Guddu's head bobbing between ours in time to "Indian Reservation." Could she see him? How wonderful to blend into one's surroundings. Is there a formula for that? Or is it an innate ability, like horny toad camo?

Doris was waiting for us by the statue of Colonel Santos Benavides. Diane was with her. Why does this not surprise me? The two women were chatting in low voices. They got into the Rambler on either side of Guddu. Doris's telescope rested across their laps. She patted my shoulder. "Thanks for the lift. Wouldn't last ten minutes on the looney bus. Will everyone be there?"

"It is mandatory for everyone who is not on his deathbed," I said.

"It never used to be," said Doris. "What happens at the retreat determines who gets ahead at Porteous and who, well, let's just say you don't want to come last in any of their demented games. You've been to one, right, Steven?"

"Nope. I always managed to get out of it. Last time I went to that preservation workshop in Austin with Randy. We were *persona non grata* around Dixie for weeks afterward."

"Where is this place?" said Diane.

"L.F.'s Elephant Ranch," I said. "Out in the country near Santo." I turned to address Jenny. "You know how to get to this place, right?"

"I know how to read a map, if that's what you're asking," she said sourly.

"That is not what I was asking," I said. What a bitch Jenny can be sometimes. For once I would like to find a chick who is on an even keel. "Doris, are you going to let us look through your telescope?"

"Annie? Of course!"

"You named your telescope?"

"After Annie Jump Cannon, the astronomer. She developed the Harvard Classification Scheme, among other things."

"Star classification?" I said. "Like O, B, A, and so on?"

"Oh, be a fine girl, kiss me. Used to whisper that a lot in the dorms." Doris winked, then nudged Guddu with her elbow. He appeared confused. "It's a mnemonic device for memorizing the spectral classes. Like Roy G. Biv."

"Who is Roy G. Biv?" said Guddu.

"He speaks!" said Doris, who could clearly see and hear Guddu. "Red, orange, yellow, green, blue, indigo, violet," recited Jenny and I in unison. Everyone chuckled. Guddu grinned, but I do not think he knew what the hell we were talking about.

"All the colors in L.F.'s wardrobe," I added. Or the codex. "It's like HOMES, Guddu," I said. Anyone from Lansing would know the acronym by heart.

"Homes?"

"You know. Huron, Ontario, Michigan, Erie, Superior."

"Yes, Steven," said Guddu. "The Great Lakes. They are near Lansing."

"What's this switch?" said Jenny.

At last, she noticed. "Ejector seat." With a flourish of my hand I flipped the switch. It is my new litmus test for separating fox from hedgehog. Jenny watched, but said nothing.

"That's friggin' hilarious," said Doris. Thanks to her, the atmosphere in the Rambler felt festive. The radio was static, so she and I sang. Moldy oldies that she would know, like "Tom Dooley" and "Blue Yodel." Jenny joined in when she could. Guddu bobbed his head more or less in time.

*T for Texas, T for Tennessee. T for Thelma, that gal that made a wreck out of me.*

"In my case, it was H for Hazel," said Doris. Surely not the library's Hazel. "What's the difference between a pickpocket and a peeping Tom?" She took a leisurely drag off her Golden Lights menthol. "One snatches your watch. The other one watches your snatch." Everyone tittered like schoolchildren. Except Diane, who was now pensive.

"Steven, what is a snatch?" said Guddu.

"Go ahead, Steven," said Doris. "Tell him." Two of the snatches in this car I have watched, but I did not dare say so.

Doris regaled us with stories about the "good ol' days" as a rural librarian. I imagined a one-room shack with the Good Book on a lectern. She was born in 1899 in Kiev. Her family emigrated to the U.S. in 1915, settling in Sherman. Talk about culture shock. Her first husband was killed in the Argonne, leaving her a young widow with an infant son. Her second husband played with the Montgomery Wards Trail Blazers on WBAP. She had three kids with him before he was shot in both lungs during a game of hold 'em.

"You were married?" I said.

"Have you ever been a Jewish sapphist in North Texas?"

"Point taken." I regarded her menthol cigarette. "Give me a drag off that heater."

"It got easier when I came to the cit," said Doris. "Folks are more open-minded here. You've got your Bible thumpers who will shout in your face that you're going to burn in Hell. But then you have this whole stratum of artists, freethinkers, poets, and those who are just curious about your ducktail."

"Dixie calls them fringies," I said.

Doris chuckled. "Do you know what that old school marm calls me? A Lebanese. Either she can't or won't say lesbian. She thinks if she says it, she'll turn into one."

Guddu looked surprised. "You are Lebanese?" he said.

"*Lez-bee-un*. I like the ladies, Guddu."

"Then Guddu is a lesbian, too!" he declared. Even Jenny smirked at that one. Guddu grinned without comprehension, only pleased that he had made us happy. I clutched the steering wheel in anger in recollection of what he did to Dawn.

"Our kind always finds each other," mused Doris.

"Lesbians?" said Guddu.

"Fringies," said Doris, tousling Guddu's hair. "Like you and me."

"Deer crossing," said Guddu. After a pause he added, "Deer do not read."

"Yeah," said Jenny. "How do they know what the sign says?" Jenny is not Mensa material, but she cannot possibly be that dumb. She was probably just sparing Guddu's feelings. Little does she know he does not have any.

Clumps of tasajillo and red three-awn crowded the barbed wire fence posts. We rode in silence. I regarded the dark bruises across my fingers. What was I going to do, keep my hand in my pocket all weekend? I glanced at Diane in the rearview. She was looking at me.

"Hey, wasn't that Spunt?" said Doris. "Back there, on the ten-speed."

"That crazy son of a bitch," I chuckled. "He's going to die of heatstroke."

"So is your car," said Doris.

Smoke was now billowing from under the hood, obscuring my view through the windshield. To draw heat away from the motor, I turned on the heater. An Uncle Larry trick. Everyone groaned, except Guddu. He is probably accustomed to the flames of perdition. "The ranch isn't far," I said anxiously.

Soon, we were puttering along on a two-lane blacktop. Heat rose from the pavement, creating a mirage before us of a shimmering lake just beyond our reach. To our left and right, scrappy fields dotted with mesquite and live oak. "My grandfather taught me how to drive on this road," I said almost under my breath.

"Hmm?" said Jenny. I decided not to repeat myself.

After a few miles, we turned into a driveway and stopped before a gate festooned with puce and yellow balloons. Jenny got out to open it. "Ouch!" she yelled. "It's too hot!"

"Use the oven mitt on the nail," I said, recalling the instructions in the memo. We left the Rambler smoking by the road. Luggage in hand, we paraded through a forest of donkey pumps along a dirt driveway. The futon felt excessive, but it was too late now. At the pavilion, we took our place in line. Dixie acknowledged us with a scowl. She wore a cute costume in the style of Dale Evans, complete with hat and cowboy boots. And a fringe jacket, unwittingly marking herself as one of us. She thrust yellow jerseys into our hands.

Team Yellow included Miss Welch, Counseling Coordinator; Mr. Snyder, Manager of Procurement; and Miss Quigley, Instructor of Secretarial Science. All foxes, I noted. Team Puce's prickle included Maxine, Hey Now, and Carlos. All hedgehogs except for Diane. Where did her loyalties lie?

After registration, everyone gathered in the great hall of the rustic-looking manse. The place looked more like a ski lodge than a ranch house. Cowhide rugs and wagon wheel chandeliers adorned the hall. I scooped a handful of candied pecans from a dish embellished with cattle brands. "How darling," said Doris. Guddu picked up the dish and examined the various symbols upon it. He probably thought they were magical in nature. But who says they are not?

"You want to know what is not darling?" I said. An ornate pedestal bore a jar with an enormous horny toad floating in formaldehyde. The curvature of the glass made him appear larger than life. "Old Rip," read the plaque. Old Rip was legendary. Evidently, before this ranch house was built, there had stood an earlier one that burned down. Only the cornerstone remained. After L.F. had removed the Bible and other objects, he thrust his hands into the cavity of the cornerstone and carefully lifted out the dust-coated toad. When the college president dangled the creature by its hind leg before his bemused colleagues, its other leg twitched. Old Rip was alive, having emerged from twenty years of hibernation. Guddu tapped the jar. The bloated toad was clearly dead now.

"Where's your stuff?" I said.

"Guddu has no earthly possessions." I recalled Randy's words on the subject and wondered if he has moved on from the youth hostel for hostile youth.

People stood around gabbing in groups, anchored by piles of luggage, pillows, and sleeping bags. The Pompatus of Porteous stood up on the raised hearth before the grand fireplace and hollered into cupped hands. "Ladies and gentiles, may I have your eyes and ears!" Even though he was a hundred, L.F. was decked out in one of his trademark color suits. On this occasion it was orange. He looked like a spokesman for the Western Citrus Alliance. A hush fell over the crowd.

"Welcome to the Eighth Annual All-Staff Campus Retreat. Some of y'all have found the punch and pecans, I see." Some chuckled. "If any of you have not registered, please see Mrs. Garske yonder." Several unregistered guests groaned and pushed their way toward Mrs. Garske. L.F. continued, "For those of y'all who did register, note the name up in the corner of your dance card. This is the name of your tent where you will stay the next two nights. Refer to the map on the wall. In the meantime, you will take your dance cards and sign up for a total of four activities which include, but are not limited to: arts and crafts, archery, sailing, and horseback riding. We will convene at the pavilion twice a day for special, mandatory events.

"Please join me in thanking the organizers of this fine occasion: Eunice Neighbors, Betty Garske, Ned Finkler, and yours truly." L.F. tipped his hat then paused until the clapping subsided. Guddu held up his dance card. "The, um, Oriental fellow in the rear."

"Will there be dancing?" said Guddu. I could not believe what I was hearing.

"Indeed there will be. Tomorrow evening after the cookout. Your dance card isn't really a dance card. I can't fathom why Eunice refers to them thusly." Mrs. Neighbors, L.F.'s left hand, whispered into his ear. "Dang me," he drawled. "I'm in trouble now!" A few of the ladies nearby tittered.

Everyone scattered, talking all at once. "Dang me twice," yelled L.F. "Forgot to announce there will be a raffle drawing on the last day. Your dance card is perforated at the bottom. Tear off that bottom piece and place it in the milk can by the swamp cooler. The Trust Games begin in twenty minutes by the chapel. See y'all there!"

Guddu turned to me. "Steven, do we keep this part?"

I squared away Guddu. "Put it in the milk can, then keep this." I got a closer look at Guddu's dance card. It was blank.

"You are here," said Guddu. He fingered a grubby hole worn in the wall map. "Where are the elephants?" said Guddu with excitement in his voice.

"Seek and ye shall find," I said. "But perhaps not that which ye hath sought." Guddu regarded me with a somewhat worried expression. This is the way to speak to imps, I have decided.

The Stone Fox was a no-show for the Trust Games. They were much worse than I could have feared. You are blindfolded and made to fall backwards from a platform into the arms of people like Spunt. Players were scored based on the level of trust they exhibited when falling. I took my shoe off and pretended something was wrong with it. Mrs. Neighbors critically regarded my actions then wrote something down on a clipboard. No one bothered Guddu. He must have switched to invisible mode.

A group of us assembled by Crystal Lake—a glorified tank—for sailing. We would race around Ram Island and back.

"What did you ditch me for?" I said to Jenny.

"There was a long line to the ladies' outhouses," she said. "Do you know how to sail?"

When I responded with a doubtful stare, Jenny paired up with Monty whose captain's hat, if not indicative of maritime prowess, at least suggested the Ty-D-Bol man. Despite there being no wind to speak of, their boat was soon gliding along. No one else knew how to sail and, in due course, we were all flotsam. My partner was Professor Purvis.

"Avast!" cried Monty. Jenny's gay laughter floated across the tank. So that is what it sounds like.

We were slowly spinning in circles. "One could get out and push," said Purvis noncommittally. The water became too deep. I swam with one arm while towing Purvis with the other. Slow going. I paused to rest on Ram Island. The professor offered me a cigarette, as my Kents were now waterlogged. Was about to weigh anchor when I was hit from behind. The impact propelled me into the weeds. The ram was put out. I had intruded upon his domain.

Without thinking, I snapped my fingers and made a jabbing motion with my hand. Sparks flew from the ram's horns. The beast fell bleating to his knees, blood pouring from his nose. The odor of singed keratin reached my nostrils. "Whose island now, motherfucker?" I bellowed. The professor gaped at me in confusion. From her dinghy, Mrs. Neighbors observed me through binoculars. Guess she saw the whole thing. But what did she think she saw?

Despite our tribulations on Ram Island, Purvis and I managed to avoid last place. Jenny and Monty were celebrating like they had just won the Auld Mug. I dragged our craft ashore. Soaking wet, I turned to him and said, "One word from you and I'll have you seized up and flogged to the bone." I was quoting *Mutiny on the Bounty* but the Professor of English and Comparative Literature is evidently unfamiliar with that particular classic. He shot me a disgusted glance before alighting from the bow and waking away in a huff. I knew this glance well from when I was in his Modern Criticism class.

"Fletcher Christian!" I shouted after him. "*Mutiny on the Bounty!*" No response. I do not think anybody really reads.

An ectomorph in a plaid leisure suit and matching Luskey anteaters emerged from behind a shed. A protégé of L.F.'s, judging from his attire. His enormous embossed leather belt buckle depicted Jefferson Davis, Robert E. Lee, and Stonewall Jackson in the style of Mount Rushmore. The color of his skin suggested full-blooded Injun.

"Name's Boone," said the ectomorph. He spat a brown stream of chaw into the dirt. "Word to the wise. On account of bacteria, swimming in Crystal Lake is not advised."

The foxes' table included Mr. Valdez, the Physical Plant Director; Mr. Gooch, the Payroll Clerk; and some old bag from the History Department. Diane was the lone puce shirt. Our paper plates sagged under mounds of tamales, ranch-style beans, and something Mrs. Neighbors called Perfection Salad.

"I am hungry-ass!" exclaimed Guddu. He inserted a tamale into his mouth whole. I just smiled, unwilling to spoil the moment with grammar lessons. But I privately admired his novel use of the *-ass* suffix.

"You aren't supposed to eat the husk," scolded Doris.

"Like a damn Yankee," added Mr. Gooch, with a wink.

"What does a payroll clerk know about it?" I said impulsively. Guddu might not be my friend, but somehow he is mine.

Sarge wheeled up to the end of the table, a plate perched on his lap. In this informal atmosphere he was unusually forthcoming. "The grenade blew off a leg and an arm," he explained. "My other hand was fubar. They used tendons from my foot and leg to repair it. I'm the only person you'll ever meet who can get athlete's foot of the hand."

"Steven, please," said Guddu. "What is this?" He held up a ladle from which dripped a thick orange goo.

"Nectar of the gods," I said. "Hot dip made from diced chilis and melted cheese."

"What is its purpose?"

"Rotel is its own purpose," I said. Let the little shit wonder.

"Rotel," he repeated. He experimentally tasted some on his thumb before glopping some onto his hot dog.

"Rotel has a beautiful texture, Steven. And the flavor is most mouth-watering. It is certainly fit for the gods, as you have attested."

I pointed my fork at him and nodded in agreement. "I suggest you offer them some." Out of the corner of my eye, I noticed Diane stifling laughter.


Boone produced a huge ring of keys and opened the gun closet. "Anybody fire a .22?" Everyone nodded, including Jenny. "A gun is always loaded, except when the action is open," he continued. "All actions will remain open except when you are shooting at your target. Do not point your gun at anything you are not willing to destroy. In the event of a misfire, raise your hand. When I command you to fire, you will do so. You will then lay your weapon on its side. Do not point your gun at anything you are not willing to what?"

"Destroy!" cried Carlos.

Boone distributed the guns and ammo. A couple of scrappy-looking kids scampered downrange and hung paper targets. These depicted various animal silhouettes. "Hey, Carlos!" I said. "Is that a bat?"

"Screw you," said Carlos.

My target was a ram, which was no less disturbing than Jenny's fox. "Why not use beer bottles?" I said to Jenny. "There is a mountain of them behind the pavilion."

Jenny evidently knows her way around a .22, as do I. Diane was distracted. Guddu seemed to be enjoying himself a bit too much. Should probably have my head examined for arming a demon. Or whatever the hell Guddu is. A *kakon*, according to the literature.

"Is she keeping score?" said Wicker irritably. He cursed and tossed down his weapon, drawing the ire of Boone. I looked up to see Mrs. Neighbors writing on her damned clipboard.

We drifted to the pavilion for arts and crafts. Jenny made something out of popsicle sticks and yarn. Guddu solved various mimeographed cryptograms. I took a stab at fashioning moccasins from leather scraps, some cords, and a leather hole punch. Instructions would have been helpful, as would the requisite pieces. L.F.'s left hand appraised our every move over her glasses. I pulled on the moccasins then propped my feet up on the picnic table for her approval. "I've got you now," her expression seemed to say. "Suck my dick," said mine.

The last thing anyone wants to do while digesting a heavy, fattening meal is to be hunted in the dark like animals. So this is exactly what happened after dinner.

"On your marks!" hollered L.F. "Get set!" He fired a shotgun into the dusk, eliciting screams and laughter from fleeing yellow shirts. Guddu took off like a rabbit. Perhaps he thought the hunt was real. At first Jenny and I stuck together but she left me behind in the woods. My jury-rigged moccasins offered no support for my flat feet. I could hear Randy teasing me now: *He's got eyes like a bat, his feet are flat, and he always carries a purse.* "It's a mansack," I muttered.

The *trompe d'Orléans* sounded. Hounds bayed wildly for meat. Into the trees I hurried, determined not to be caught. The punishment was certain to be humiliating. Eventually, I came to the property line, marked by a fence of rotted, leaning posts and tangled barbed wire. Above the pulsating roar of cicadas was the occasional faint burst of shouting or baying. The longer I rested, the more I was beset by large blood-sucking insects. I must keep moving.

In a clearing I encountered Shagduk, perched Indian-style on a stump. He was smoking a whimsical pipe. Beneath him was a dark, sprawling form. It was Boone, the ectomorph. Dark patches on his plaid suit indicated blood. His throat had been ripped out. "He would not have hurt you," I said angrily. "It's just a game."

"Is this not how games end?"

"Take the corpse to a place where it will never be found." The imp stared at me with rheumy, icteroid eyes. "Witness Shagduk obey!" I cried. "And bring back nicotine." So this is how they play in demon land.

I continued to follow the perimeter fence, reasoning that it would eventually take me back to the pavilion. Along the way I spotted through the trees a windowless, imposing gray building. The railing along the roof recalled the Polyflex building. A low, electrical hum could be heard emanating from its walls. Upon a wooden palette on the loading dock stood a giant ear. I approached it. Bill Blevins's bronze from the Ridglea Bank. What was it doing here? The baying grew louder. I moved along.

"Where have you been?" said Jenny.

I shook my head, still out of breath.

"There are cold drinks at the pavilion."

I rescued the last bottle of RC from the bottom of a barrel of melted ice. Guddu appeared with a pack of Kents, indicating the morbid task had been done. He pressed a dog tag into my palm. It read "TENAYUCA BOONE A," followed by his service number, blood type "O POS," and religion, misspelled "MORMAN." So the Mormons got to him. Unless he came to them. "I don't want this," I said.

I guiltily lit a Kent, reflecting upon my callousness of asking for cigarettes in the same breath as the other thing. The imp aped my every move over my shoulder like a distorted version of myself. If mimicry is his primary means of fitting in, I am starting to wonder about what other beings he has been in contact with. I sucked down the RC in front of him. That rapist can die of thirst for all I care.

The hounds returned, playing tug of war with a bloody limb. Could be Boone's. Who else is missing? Some of L.F.'s hands appeared with whips to break it up.

L.F. addressed the throng through a bullhorn: "Those who were captured by your superiors, up against the fence!"

Doris ran her fingers through her ducktail. "You mean our equals!" she shouted. So Team Puce is superior? It all made sense now.

Nervous staffers made their way forward under Mrs. Neighbors's stern gaze. When no one else was forthcoming, L.F. continued: "On your knees. Like you do in a duck-and-cover drill. This time it's not a drill."

"Assume the position!" barked Spunt in a bombastic Nazi accent, which was met with much laughter and good-natured catcalls.

A dozen unfortunate souls assumed the position. Sarge refused to participate on the grounds he was in a wheelchair. Nevertheless, Mrs. Neighbors wheeled him up against the fence.

"To my esteemed colleagues, I salute your skill," said L.F. "Now let's find out how good your aim is. We have these here water balloons. If y'all'll please form a line. That's right. It's time to serve our malefactors some good old-fashioned Porteous justice."

The crowd erupted in cheers. "For what crime?" remarked Doris. "Wearing a yellow jersey?" She offered me her flask. I refused but she was insistent. I took a sip and tasted rum. "Ah, Doris, angel of mercy!"

"You may fire at will, Dr. Fullerton," said L.F.

The Vice-Pompatus of Student Affairs selected a water balloon as he would a fruit. He theatrically wound up like Fergie Jenkins, eliciting whistles from the mob. He then lobbed a mean curve ball right up Monty's asshole. The gentle, purple-haired library circulation assistant howled like the involuntary recipient of one of Spunt's barium enemas. A wet spot appeared on the seat of his shorts.

"Boot mistake," observed Sarge stoically. "Gotta tuck your nuts."

Following Dr. Fullerton's example, Spunt also wound up his pitch. But the intended *coup de grâce* sailed harmlessly over Monty's purple hair to a chorus of deep boos.

"Looks like Team Puce has it in for our Monty," said Doris. "I always liked him."

"He's not going to die," I quipped. Doris looked at me and drew her lips into a tight grimace.

Despite throwing like a girl, Maxine's missile connected with the back of Miss Welch's head, eliciting a blubbering wail from the charming Counseling Coordinator. Miss Welch had been so kind to me when I was a clueless under-graduate. I felt bad for her. The corporeal punishment continued in this vein until there were no more balloons. The humiliated POWs rose slowly from the ground, brushing dirt off their knees. Their teammates offered hugs and cold beverages.

Team Puce celebrated with a taunting chant. Its careless rhymes lent it an air of insincerity. *Wah wah wah, sis boom bah! Boo hoo, boo hoo, boo boo blah. Lickety split, elephant juice. Give 'em Hell! Go, Team Puce!* And I thought my lyrics were bad.


We gathered around the bonfire and sang "Kumbaya, My Lord," "Hello Muddah, Hello Faddah," and other lyrical platitudes. Some hurled twigs, dead batteries, and garbage into the rising inferno. During "On Top of Old Smokey," Monty harmonized *voce forte*, "All covered with *cheese!*" while holding up a chicken leg dripping with Rotel. What a good sport he is, all things considered.

Amber placed a turkey chick upon my shoulder, which promptly crapped on me. Before I understood what I had done, I roughly brushed the offending fowl into the flames. Amber shrieked. Jenny was staring at me in horror, a blackened marshmallow in her hand. And right behind her, Mrs. Neighbors and her damned clipboard. What is she writing?

Some of us wandered off to party in our own way. Doris was not the only one with the foresight to bring booze. Rumor had it the punch was spiked. People were calling it elephant juice. Reason enough not to consume it. We sat along the edge of the pool. Spunt climbed into the lifeguard's chair. I was sunburned, filthy, and dehydrated. I needed to drop a deuce. Could not get Boone's untimely demise out of my head. Someone passed me a flask of something.

Some jumped in the pool to cool off, not even bothering to change into bathing suits. The ombudsman hollered, "Cannonball!" before drenching everyone. A move right out of Tim's play book. I reclined on the warm cement, my feet dangling into the water. To my left, Monty was detailing his injury to a sympathetic Doris. To my right, Jenny had her back to me, explaining Elvis's sex appeal to a nonplussed Guddu.

"Elvis the Pelvis," said Jenny.

"Elvis the Pelvis," repeated Guddu. His eyes were looking at the Stone Fox, but mentally, he was staring me down. I do not know how else to explain it. Something I guess imps can do. Staring through a third party. It is creepy.

"Steven, watch out!" cried Diane.

The urgency in her voice compelled me to sit up. I turned around to see what she was pointing at. A dark queue of scorpions was upon me. Guddu's foul mood made manifest. I flung myself into the water. The others scattered, shrieking.

"One's in your hair!" someone yelled.

My best chance of survival, I decided, was to swim quickly underwater to the other side of the pool.

"Come here, buddy!" said Spunt. He fished the scorpion out by the tail, then flung it into the darkness. The other arachnids skittered pell-mell toward cover.

I struggled into a rotting ring buoy, then gracelessly treaded water near Guddu. I wanted to wring his neck. Jenny swung around and put her legs in the water on either side of my hand, accidentally kicking me in the face. "Whoops, sorry!" she said. "It was an accident." She swatted clumsily at a June bug.

"An accident on purpose?" I teased. I repositioned myself between Jenny and Guddu.

"I would never," she cried. The three of us made small talk. Jenny took several swigs of the flask before offering me some.

"Ugh," I said. "What is this?"

Jenny whispered in my ear. "I love you," she slurred.

Like the moron I am, I repeated her words.

"I said elephant juice," said Jenny dispassionately.

A flash from the pavilion, then cheers. Some cows stirred nervously beyond the barbed wire. "I have an idea," slurred Jenny excitedly. She pointed the empty flask at the cows. "Let's start a stampede." As soon as she said it, something spooked the cattle. They mooed anxiously and clomped away into the night.

Jenny leaned forward. "You look so handsome."

"Handsomer than Elvis the Pelvis?" I said mockingly. What did she want from me this time?

"I'm serious." Jenny's speech was almost incomprehensible. "You're a stud," she stammered. Diane smirked.

"Steven, handsomer is not a word," said Guddu.

"I am the maker of words!" I snapped. Guddu now bore an expression of one who has been chastised.

Jenny made grasping motions like a crayfish claw. "Come closer," she said flirtatiously. She lowered herself into the water with a splash. Her red bra was now visible through her wet yellow jersey. I glided away toward the deep end. "Don't go away!" she whined.

"Everyone out of the pool!" bawled Coach Grabowski. "Are you trying to get me fired? Move it!" I thought I detected a note of fear in his voice.


Most of the tents were named after Indian tribes. Each stood upon a raised concrete slab foundation accessible by steps at one end. The roofs were corrugated metal. Canvas walls could be rolled down for privacy or inclement weather. Doris got Wichita near the pavilion. Jenny and Diane got Caddo. The men's tents were at the top of a bluff.

We drifted toward our respective sleeping quarters. After saying good night to the others, I instructed Guddu to wait for me at the Old Guard Sleepatorium then accompanied Jenny to Caddo. I lingered beneath her cot while she retrieved a pack of Virginia Slims.

"I wonder if Mrs. Neighbors can read lips," I said.

We could hear her scratching out a note in the dark.

Jenny lit her Slim and collapsed on her cot with a dramatic sigh. She took a long drag then reached down to offer me one. "That's a woman's cigarette," I objected.

"Can you read my lips?" she said. She then mouthed, "come see me later," or maybe, "gum simulator."

I made an "OK" sign, not knowing if that was even feasible, nor what would happen once I got here. It was out of character for Jenny to be this wasted. What did she have in mind? The surroundings provided poor cover and I did not relish getting caught sniffing around the ladies' tents.

"Good night!" said Jenny loudly.

"Good night, Jenny!" I bellowed, with an exaggerated wave of the hand. "See you in the morning!" Anyone witnessing this convincing exchange would never believe that I planned to return later. "Good night, Diane," I added in a normal voice.

I scrambled up the alluvial wash that served as a trail. I found Guddu squatting on his cot, calmly herding scorpions into a jar. "Get rid of those!" I hissed. I pushed two cots together and unrolled my futon across them. A bed fit for a slave lord, in accordance with the dictums of Murloc. Nearby, Coach Grabowski was squeezing a hand grip strengthener. He was talking about an Omicron Nu he screwed to Vince Greco. "We made the beast with two backs, if you know what I mean," he said, winking. Does everyone know this phrase except me?

"Bullshit," said Vince. Guddu perked up at the use of his favorite word. "Heard she gave the whole lacrosse team trichomoniasis. If your piss turns blue, better visit a doctor immediately." The coach waved him off.

I changed out of my damp clothes and wrapped a towel around my waist. I wondered how much privacy we had with no walls. There were two other tents nearby, both filled with guys, so I suppose it did not matter too much. I regarded a wooden plaque upon which the rules had been engraved. Did they apply to adults?

Vince Greco was busy loading two dozen D-cells into an enormous cassette player. I introduced myself. "Vince Greco," he replied. "Athletics Department."

"I've checked books out to you," I said. One remembers a jock who reads Hegel. I did not introduce Guddu, nor did Vince look his way.

"What do you call a sunburned librarian?"

"No idea."

Vince poked my burnt arm. "Well red," he said. "Seriously, it must be great reading books all day." I must have made a face because he added, "Just messing with you, man."

"Nice boom box," I said.

"JVC," he said proudly. "Top of the line. Plays chromium dioxide." He inserted *Sin after Sin* and pressed the play button. Vince tossed me the cassette box. "Get a load of this next part. This, my friend, is called jamming." He turned it up and pantomimed the guitar solo.

"Jamming," repeated Guddu, like Frankenstein learning a new word.

Turn that garbage off, Vinny," said Coach Grabowski. Diane was now standing close to him. What was she doing up here? Not sure what the coach has to offer her besides a case of trichomoniasis. Or his life force. He has no idea who he is dealing with. Nor do I, really.

"Check out that trim," said Vince. He nudged me with his elbow. "Her meat's hangin'." I glanced furtively in Diane's direction. Her shorts were pretty tight, if that is what he meant. He turned to face the coach. "What's she doing here past curfew?" The coach wrestled the rules off the wall and stomped on them. He then glared at me and my futon, like Vince and I had both committed fouls.

"It's a futon," I said defensively.

The witch took his hand and led him away into darkness.

"That's not the co-ed he made two backs with, is it?" I said.

"Hell naw," said Vince. "The fox that rings the bell. Ever seen her? I'd like to ring her bell." I felt sick to my stomach.

The beans were starting to want back out. I was faced with the reality of using the outhouse in the dark. Did not occur to me to bring a flashlight, but I had the digital watch Jenny gave me, for what it was worth. It lights up when you press a button. I signaled "S.O.S." to Guddu but stopped before he could ask me what I was doing.

Beyond the open showers were a trio of rickety outhouses with moon-shaped windows. They were nothing like the fabled shithouses of Maine extolled by Dave II. Took care of business while concentrating very hard on not thinking about scorpions, or brown recluses, or anything with necrotizing enzymes.

Returned to my futon feeling like a new man. Would have finished the last volume of Schubart's treatise on musical keys but I needed better illumination for that. Gradually, the murmur of nearby voices died away. A Priest ballad rocked softly from Vince's boombox. Jamming gave way to crickets. I put on some clean duds. "Stay here," I whispered to Guddu. If anyone else saw or heard me get up and leave, they would assume I was going back to the outhouse. I made a point of moving in that direction initially before veering off.

Negotiating the rough trail in the dark was no easy feat, but I skidded down the alluvial wash in one piece. Encountered no one as I sidled up to Caddo. I located Jenny's prone form in the moonlight. I reached up and gently shook her hip. She slowly stirred, then rolled over to look at me.

"Steven?" whispered Diane.

"Huh?"

"Let me put some clothes on. I'll meet you by the pavilion."

Where was Jenny? I headed to the pavilion, hoping I would not bump into anyone. Diane soon joined me in her puce jersey.

"Traitor," I quipped

"What are you doing here?"

"Was supposed to meet Jenny. Thought you were her."

"She switched cots with me."

What the hell was going on here? Could not decide if Jenny switched on purpose because she was mad at me for something real or perceived, or if this was one of Diane's schemes. Either was plausible. Only one was likely.

The witch sighed. "Bum a cig?"

I patted my chest and thighs then shook my head.

"God, I'm drunk," said Diane. The meek, barefoot Diane before me now stood in stark contrast to the formidable enchantress. She sat heavily on a bench and wept. Yet another textbook attempt to manipulate me. It was not working.

"Why are we here?" said Diane.

"In the universe? Or the retreat? L.F. says it's to increase morale at work."

Diane laughed ironically. She complained about Jo Ann, then Spunt and his antics. I let her talk, amazed at her uncharacteristic garrulity. "And Mrs. Womack, that old harridan," Diane added, in a conspiratorial tone.

"What did she do this time?" I said, humoring her.

"When I first started working on the Baumann project, I misplaced a valuable object, a talisman. Mrs. Womack threatened to fire me if it didn't turn up." I detected a hint of quiet desperation in Diane's voice.

"And it will never turn up," I wished to say. It was safely hidden in the Rambler. "You should get some rest." Diane did not respond, so I slowly stood and withdrew. As I passed the pool, I glanced quickly over my shoulder. The bench was empty.

Sᴜɴᴅᴀʏ, Jᴜɴᴇ 5

Day two of the compulsory staff retreat began with Coach Grabowski freaking out. Vince later told me Wicker had given him a vial of methylene blue. Blue piss was the least of his worries, however, by the look of him. His pale, haggard appearance recalled Dave II's trials.

Guddu and I were late to breakfast. We each selected a box of cereal from a wheelbarrow. Unfortunately, the few remaining boxes were all Product 19.

Doris regarded an array of pill bottles before her. She noticed Guddu watching her. "This one makes you larger," she said. "And this one makes you small."

"What happens if you take them both?" said Guddu.

"Certain death," said Doris. She washed the deadly combination down with a carton of chocolate milk as Guddu looked on uneasily. They gazed at each other until Doris shouted "Boo!" Guddu recoiled. He probably thinks Doris is a powerful witch. She may as well be.

"Did you hear about Solomon?" said Jenny. "He's dead."

"Who's Solomon?" said Doris.

"The ram. He used to live at the petting zoo at Six Flags. When he got too old, he came here to live. It was in the news."

I instantly became alert. "What happened to him?"

Jenny's face clouded. The fucker deserved it. However, that I could unthinkingly harm a dumb beast filled me with remorse. Who am I becoming?

After breakfast, everyone took a short hike to a wooded area for the Obstacle Course. Guddu and I walked together in silence.

We arrived at a clearing filled with heavy-duty playground equipment. It was made chiefly from railroad ties and industrial pipes. The structures seemed contrived from components which had no recreational purpose. One of them was a rusted shipping container bearing the name Polyflex on the side. Tread marks from heavy duty vehicles led away into the trees. What goes on here? It is clearly not a working ranch, that much is evident. Would not be surprised if it was a front for something else. Wish I could talk to Randy about it.

Team Yellow competed first, which put us at a disadvantage as we could not learn from the mistakes of others. Snyder led us on an impromptu cheer:

> *Come on and shout for dear old Yellow*
> *We'll pummel our opponents into Jell-O*
> *For victory today cannot be won*
> *Without our songs, our cheers, our faith—yes, everyone*
> *Come on and fight for dear old Yellow*
> *We'll turn their smiles upside-down*
> *We pledge ourselves to be nobody's clown*
> *Hello, Team Yellow!*

Either the Manager of Procurement has a talent for improvisation or else he used to be a coach. What did he procure before he came to Porteous? The whistle sounded. Team Yellow climbed a rope ladder, then took turns swinging on a knotted rope from one wooden platform to the next. Putting her secretarial skills to good use, Miss Quigley succeeded with punctilio. She waited for the rest of us at the bottom of the slide. "Needs improvement!" urged Snyder, waving her on. Monty dangled helplessly over the dirt. Take away the book cart, reveal the man. Miss Quigley could not make it back up the slide to help the ninety-eight-pound weakling. *Other duties as assigned.*

"Looks like we got ourselves a powder puff team," chortled L.F. Mrs. Neighbors clicked her Bic excitedly.

Everyone encouraged Sarge as he was pushed, carried, and dragged in his wheelchair. We cheered Doris on, marveling at her attendance. Then I remembered she rides her bicycle to work every day from Poly.

Eventually, we got across. We proceeded to the part where one must squirm through a concrete pipe. This was succeeded by a rope net one must run through without tripping. Beyond that one negotiated a limbo stick above a freshly-hosed mud pit. Jenny tried to shimmy under it. The results were unsatisfactory, unless one asked Boggs.

"God bless the natives of Trinidad for the limbo," mused the security guard. His eyes were glued to Jenny's body.

The rest of us sensibly crawled. Jenny's back was covered in mud. Everyone else's front was. Boggs almost lost his shorts. He pulled them up at the last possible second, narrowly avoiding disciplinary action.

Of the remaining obstacles, only the wall required any actual teamwork. Yellow's approach was scattershot. Some people gave others a boost. Others climbed up cupped hands. Boggs stoically bore my muddy moccasins upon his shoulders. We reached the other side with only minor injuries, all of us a sweaty mess. Miss Welch nursed a split chin as a beard of blood soaked her yellow jersey. She would counsel no one this day.

"Four minutes and forty-four seconds!" announced Coach Grabowski. Boggs shambled over the finish line. He fell to his knees and buried his face in his hands. Mrs. Neighbors shook her head then wrote something down on her clipboard. Does four minutes and forty-four seconds meet expectations? Is it enough to save Boggs's bacon? To get my office back?

L.F. clapped his hands and shouted "Let's hustle!" from the sidelines like he was John Madden. Maxine sat this one out, fanning herself in a director's chair. Each time L.F. bent down to whisper in her ear, she smiled.

"Hey!" cried Hey Now at every new obstacle he conquered. I did not know he had it in him. Professor Ziglar demonstrated surprising athletic prowess. "*Hut hut hut,*" he chanted, guided through the gauntlet by the holy spirit. It was gratifying to see his pristine white Kinneys soiled. He soared across the finish line, his Fisher-Price hair askew. A toupée—I knew it!

Time stood still as Diane knee-highed the ropes. Her tits and ponytails moved hypnotically, commanding the full attention of every red-blooded male in attendance. When she fell, Coach Grabowski was first to her aid. He administered mouth-to-mouth liberally before massaging her chest. L.F. waved everyone back. He lifted Diane's head and felt her pulse. Two hands arrived with a stretcher and she was duly conveyed to the infirmary. L.F. lingered before picking an object out of the mud and carefully placing it in a bandana. He then looked to the left and right like a common shoplifter. What did he find?

"She fainted," declared L.F. "Nothing to see here, now get along." He seemed annoyed that Diane's performance skewed his team's stats. He counted out several bills and placed them into Coach Grabowki's outstretched palm. Were they betting?

"Good game," offered the teams to each other half-heartedly before dispersing. Some made their way to their tents to get cleaned up. Unwilling to ascend the hill, Guddu conjured up jodhpurs and a riding crop. I relented and conjured up my golden boots and spurs. Enough to remind Guddu of my powers. We found Dixie and Amber already mounted. By their comportment it was clear they were experienced riders. Amber had traded her Dune Diggers for Tony Lamas.

"Do you ride?" said Jenny. Her hair, now as fresh as a daisy and gathered by a black ribbon, lay tame and smooth upon her shoulders.

"Nope," I said. "You?"

"An Arabian called Peaches," said Jenny. "Used to ride almost every day. Between school and work, I haven't had much time." Horse chicks usually tell you about their horses on the first date. What else has she not told me?

"What about you, Guddu?"

"Guddu's grandfather and grandmother used to have a pet pony," he said. "Guddu used to brush him and feed him longan." I perked up. Another one of the imp's tall tales.

"This was in Michigan?" I said sarcastically.

"It is similar to rambutan or lychee," he said.

"That's not what I asked you."

"What was the pony's name?" asked Jenny.

"Chakkare."

"Aww! What a cute name! Do they still have him?"

"Chakkare was seized by thugs. They slew my grandparents."

"Oh, Guddu, I am so sorry!" said Jenny, horrified.

"Do not be sorry for Guddu, dear Jenny."

"Lansing sounds like a rough place," I said. For someone who is baffled by bullshit, Guddu sure can dish it out.

Mrs. Neighbors assigned to Jenny a healthy-looking Missouri Fox Trotter called Beau. Guddu got Nugget, a retired thoroughbred. I got an elderly quarter horse.

"How do you back up?" I said to no one.

Something spooked Nugget. Guddu howled with glee. Jenny and L.F. raced after them. For several minutes the rest of us swatted at flies, sweated, and complained about the heat. At last, Jenny and L.F. returned with the errant steed, *sans* Guddu. "Where in Sam Hill would an Oriental fellow learn to ride like that?" said L.F.

We rode single file on a narrow path which led into the woods. The soft clop of hooves I found lulling. The path converged with a fence. We passed a familiar rotten stump upon which a larkspur perched. Gone was the ectomorph's corpse and the gore-soaked duff. Boone, we hardly knew you.

The trail took us up a brief but steep incline where a creek cut through a hillock. Biondello faltered at the summit. I grasped at the horse's neck and swung under it, landing on my coccyx in a cloud of dust.

"Bild Yer Own Taco," said the sign, written in hillbilly letters with a backward *r*. "That sign is misspelled," observed Guddu. With great interest, he watched me build my own taco. "Always eat over an extra tortilla," I said. "When you're done, you get a bonus taco."

The table spoke of horses. "It's all so much leather fetishism," declared Wicker. "Dominance. Submission. The substitution of cruelty for the sex act."

No one seemed to be listening to the Rock Guy-cum-chemist. Except for Diane, who gazed at him as if seeing him for the first time. Beware, Wicker!

"Guddu, what do you have?" I said. He had just poured what looked like antifreeze from a glass jug into his cup.

"Elephant juice," he said excitedly. He downed the beverage in one gulp. "Spunt gave it to Guddu."

"I'd run that through a gas chromatography machine before consuming," said Wicker. "It's probably full of seven-syllable compounds that start with butyl-, and methyl-." I was loath to entertain the idea of an inebriated Guddu.

Jenny recounted Guddu's improbable sportsmanship as he looked on sheepishly. Evidently, she had witnessed Guddu acrobatically leap from the saddle and catch a tree branch overhead.

"Like one of the Flying Wallendas, eh, Guddu?" I said.

"This meat is tough," complained Guddu, in a bid to change the subject.

"Ground beef is not tough." I could not fathom what he was talking about unless he was trying to eat his paper plate. "Guddu, can you spell *tough*?"

"Of course, Steven."

"Did you know there are eight different ways to pronounce the four-letter sequence *-ough*?"

"No, Steven, there are eleven. *Chough, trough, doughty, furlough, dreadnought, brougham, thorough, hiccough, hough,* and *turlough*. And please do not forget the Greenough River."

"You have got to be kidding me," I said, under my breath.

Doris was busy scraping mud off Sarge's wheelchair with a stick. "Had a classmate once who spelled his name *Ptoughneigh*," she said without looking up. "He was quite eccentric." She proceeded to spell it until Guddu interrupted.

"Behold!" beamed Guddu. "Guddu has a bonus taco!"

Just then, Spunt leaped upon our table. He leaped off again, spilling my RC. We watched as he scrambled about upsetting people. L.F.'s voice could be heard over the din. "Do not chase Armando!" Everyone turned their heads to watch the spectacle. No idea what Spunt intended to do with Armando should he succeed in catching him. "Aren't armadillos carriers of leprosy?" I said.

Jenny complained all the way to Caddo. "Spunt should be ashamed of himself, terrorizing poor Armando." I wanted so badly to ask, "Why did you switch cots with Diane?" Since she was not mentioning it, I perversely waited to see how long we could go without broaching the topic.

We plopped down on the steps. Jenny reached for a honeysuckle hedge. She squirted a tiny drop of sweet nectar onto her bottom lip then blinked at me. The kiss was quick and inconsequential. Diane squeezed past us. She appeared a bit frazzled.


Jenny wanted to take a nap, so I headed to the Rambler. The Chap Stick tube containing the amulet was gone. The man in puce has it now. His shady behavior when Diane fainted suggests he knows its value. If so, he knows more than I.

Mugging L.F. would be impractical. The amulet would not be on his person, anyway. Figured I might try to infiltrate the ranch house. No time like the present! Broad daylight would provide the advantage of entering the building inconspicuously. If I cannot get the amulet back, perhaps I can find out why he wants it.

Mrs. Garske stood behind a desk speaking in low tones to a tall, skinny middle-aged man I had seen earlier. One of L.F.'s flunkies, no doubt. I headed over to the big wall map like I belonged there. Mrs. Garske did not acknowledge me at first, but when the flunkie took off, she turned her attention to me.

"May I help you, Sir?"

"Do you have anything for a migraine?" I said. "Mr. Burnside sent me."

Mrs. Garske concealed a look of exasperation. "Try the infirmary." She gestured toward the window through which could be seen a queue of wounded and maimed. Yellow shirts, each of them. I grimaced. Mrs. Garske seemed to take pity on me. "I think I have some elephant juice. Please wait here."

A narrow staircase beckoned. Admitting myself beyond the "No Admittance" sign, I skulked up the stairs, keeping my feet near the wall thereby minimizing creaks. Only the jingle of my spurs might give me away and I regretted not taking them off. There were several doors from which to choose. One had a window of frosted glass and a slot for mail. It was locked. I peeked through the slot and beheld a spacious wood-paneled study. Hocus pocus for ingress.

On display within were the trappings of position and wealth. A pair of ornate Geweihsessel chairs flanked the lone window. The bookcases gleamed richly with gold tooled leather bindings. There were crumbling books, too, I noted. A pillow balled on a chesterfield suggested L.F. napped here. I paused to admire Kolomoki Mound artifacts in a display case. A Ganesh the size of a Buick stood in the corner. It looked solid and I wondered why the floor did not collapse. An ancient and undoubtedly fragile vase stood upon a library book cart, waiting for someone to bump into it.

The amulet itself is possibly in a safe in the wall I discovered behind a dark canvas—a genuine Velázquez, unless I mistaken. The crude glyph protecting it was no match for me, but the combination lock was. A job for the imp.

L.F.'s unmistakable tenor wafted through the mail slot. I crept into the hall and peered over the banister. He was speaking to Mrs. Garske. Fortunately, my mojo was potent enough to do what I did next.

"Good lord!" roared L.F. Bubbles rose to the surface of Old Rip's jar, making a series of deep glugging sounds. The pair watched in confusion and disgust as the horny toad jerked in spasms. I slipped away undetected.

Resigned to the idea that swimming would be an organized activity that involved group participation, I was relieved to discover it was simply an afternoon of relaxation. The Stone Fox greeted me in a chartreuse bandeau bikini.

"Babe, can you go back to Caddo and get my suntan oil?" This I did. The witch's suitcase beckoned, but I left it alone. Back at the pool, I applied baby oil to Jenny's back and shoulders. Kept peeking down her top but could discern no fresh bruises. Guddu had changed into conjured antique trunks identical to the ones I had found at the lake house. Was he mocking me or simply mimicking me? He was now frolicking in the water as if he were part fish. For all I know he is part fish.

Some square with a guitar perched upon the lifeguard's seat, begging to be cannonballed. He played only Eagles songs, changing the lyrics to make them more biblical. "I was drivin' down the road, with the Lord at my side, I got seven verses on my mind," he crooned. I spotted Diane nearby with her floppy hat tilted over her face. She was probably eyeing me through the fibers of the visor. Guess she is feeling better now. She certainly looked a whole lot better.

"I feel so conflicted," said Doris, as Mrs. Neighbors herded us into the canteen. "Does Jesus want me to take it easy or to the limit?"

On a quest for a napkin, I encountered Guddu. I should have sent him to get the amulet back in the first place. "I have a task for you," I said. "I'll watch your Rotel." Less than five minutes later he returned empty-handed.

"Well?" I said confidentially.

"Guddu obeyed."

"Where is it?"

"It is in the safe."

"So you were unable to open it?"

After a provocative delay, he replied, "The safe is in the Rambler."

My blood began to boil. The imp evinces no concern for ordinary sensibility. "The amulet?" I said through clenched teeth.

"Yes, the amulet."

You have got to admire the imp's effrontery. I excused myself. I went out to the Rambler to see what Guddu had done. To his credit, the safe was in the trunk, as he said. It was so heavy, the rear end of the Rambler sagged noticeably. Nothing I could do about that at the moment.

A county deputy turned into the drive. He skidded to a halt in a cloud of dust. "You, with the beard!" he shouted through cupped hands. "I'm looking for a Mr. L.F. Burnside."

"You might try the pavilion," I said.

"Which one is he?"

"He has catfish lips and a complexion of boiled ham, weathered by a career of vanity and cruelty," I said. "What do you call what boxers get? Cauliflower ears—he's got those, I think. His mouth looks like a puppet's when he speaks. His jowls are disturbed tent flaps."

"What a monster!" said the cop.

"He's the one attired head-to-toe in puce," I added helpfully.

The fuzz on Burnside's turf could signify any number of things. He could be investigating a burgled safe. Or the slaughter of a ram. Or an employee's disappearance. No one had mentioned Boone since the Hunt.

I tailed him to the infirmary where a crowd had gathered. Coach Grabowski had passed away suddenly. "Trichomoniasis," I overheard L.F. say to the deputy. The latter doffed his cowboy hat and nodded solemnly. L.F. passed something into the deputy's palm. Hush money? Not a hush amulet, I hoped.

"Someone call the next of kin," said a voice. Mrs. Garske shoved past me, sobbing. Sarge played "Taps" on a bugle.

A blast of feedback issued from a bullhorn. L.F. addressed the sunburned diners. "The Great Race will commence shortly. But first, there is the matter of Team Yellow. As we all know, they were the losers of this morning's obstacle course competition. Team Yellow will not be participating. But idle hands are the devil's workshop, are they not?" L.F. gestured to a tractor behind which was a flat wagon. It was empty except for some shovels. Our very jobs were on the line.

L.F. led Team Yellow to the tractor and bade us sit upon the wagon. This must be where the duds from *Mystery Date* go. L.F. took a seat behind the wheel and drove us a short distance to the ranch house. Saw more of those stylized elephants on the shutters.

"What's with the elephants?" I said to Jenny.

"That's L.F.'s logo."

"Why an elephant?"

"L.F.-*ant*," said Jenny. "It's a rebus."

"That's not how rebuses work."

"Grab a shovel," directed L.F. He led us around the corner. A gravel path connected the parking lot to the rear entrance of the ranch house. Flanking the path were a dozen wagon wheels, each buried halfway into the ground.

"Dig these up and put them on the wagon." My eyes followed L.F. inside. He seemed preoccupied. Does he know about the safe yet?

We enthusiastically attacked the ground. It was atrocious work. No amount of wiping my face with my Team Yellow shirt would stop the sweat from burning my eyes. Too bad I gave my last package of headbands to Harrington. The shovel I had chosen was more like one a child would use. Too small to be very effective.

When I had dug as far as I deemed necessary to wiggle the wheel loose, I discovered that it was attached to a big chunk of concrete. Had to dig around and under the chunk quite a bit before I could get it to budge. Looked over at Jenny, who had not yet dug half as far as I had.

Festive music wafted from the direction of the pavilion, punctuated by laughter and cries of glee. "My blisters!" cried Monty. His purple hair was plastered to his forehead. Snyder swore and grunted with each movement. He had no cheers now for Team Yellow.

Evening came to the Elephant Ranch. At last, when all the wagon wheels had been exhumed, Jenny fetched L.F. He had traded his Stetson for a miner's helmet. "Hop up. Let's take these behind the stables." This statement was met with groans. It was past nine and the festivities were well underway.

There was not much room on the wagon for Team Yellow and the wagon wheels, so Guddu and I tagged along on foot. The trek to the stables took us past the festivities. Our appearance was met with jeers and wisecracks. Someone lobbed a water balloon, which hit Miss Quigley right in the kisser. May it bring her some relief from the sweat and grime.

L.F. brought the tractor shuddering to a halt behind the barn. "Toss the wheels onto that junk pile and you're done." I shielded my eyes from the blinding glare from the miner's lamp.

Great clouds of insects swarmed the festive lights. Doris flashed a flask tucked in her waistband. I accompanied her behind the propane tank. Poured the rest of my Tab into an anthill and Doris fixed me up. "Let the party begin!" I declared weakly.

"It has already begun," said Doris.

The dance floor was a raised plywood platform which bounced to the rhythm of the music. Live entertainment was provided by the Eagles guy and a couple of old fiddlers. Doris and I made fools of ourselves. We did the Hustle, the Texas Tommy, and other absurd steps. I do not pretend to dance well. But

I am arguably better than Jenny, who lurched about like a sick animal. Maybe she was sick. In contrast, Guddu's regimented movements recalled those of a Scottish Thistle Dancer. Ziglar stood by with a sawed-off yardstick, awaiting Dixie's edict.

Encomiums and congratulations were given throughout dinner. Trophies were presented, hands were shaken, and promotions awarded. The hedgehogs gathered in the winners' circle. "Special congratulations are in order for the star of this afternoon's Great Race," said L.F. "Everyone please give a round of applause to Maxine Doakes, our new Counseling Coordinator." Maxine approached the podium and shook hands with L.F. and Mrs. Neighbors. A cry was heard from among the hoi polloi. I turned my head to see Miss Welch dashing to the ladies' outhouses with her hand over her mouth.

"Boggs, comma, Curtis," pronounced L.F. "Your promotion to the women's gymnasium—." L.F. paused to locate the security guard's face in the crowd. "Is hereby denied." He brought a gavel down hard on the podium, like a judge. I looked around for Boggs and spotted him staring ahead stoically as if he had expected the news.

The Mayor of Santo regarded the winners with respect. Each time Mrs. Neighbors whispered into his ear, he presented a key to the town to one of them. I did not care. I felt a mixture of anger and self-pity over a life gone out of control. The absurdity of the retreat made me want to puke. Diane passed me Doris's flask. Maybe she can read my mind after all. But it was about to become even more absurd.

Someone turned off the festive lights. L.F. unrolled a screen while Mrs. Neighbors switched on an overhead projector. What followed was yet another boring presentation about L.F.'s pet museum project. We had all seen it before. But the real surprise was when he unveiled the baffling, soul-crushing design for the Olaf Pasquale-Rasmussen Book Tower.

"A book what, now?" I whispered.

"It makes no sense," said Doris. "Like the old Cincinnati Library? But those were just very high stacks, not towers." We all knew about L.F.'s wet museum dream but no one saw the book tower coming.

"Let me get this straight," I said. "L.F. wants to cut a giant circular hole in the floor of the reading room. He then wants to erect a giant tower composed of bookshelves which would hold all the books."

Doris nodded. "The tower would be accessed by a system of rolling ladders."

"Rolling ladders," I repeated incredulously. How much would it weigh? How would you hoist a loaded cart of books to the top?

"The museum would displace the reading room, the William Lawrence Peebles III Meeting Room, and most of the basement," added Doris.

After an initial hush of disbelief from the library staff, we murmured excitedly amongst ourselves. Jo Ann withdrew in a huff. Spunt loved the idea, naturally. Doris said it was the stupidest idea she had ever heard. Hazel just sat there with a smirk on her face. Of course, she does not comprehend what this would mean for her. For all of us. Dixie's expression was unreadable at this distance. She was seated at L.F.'s side which I took to be a gesture of solidarity. Or of ass kissing.

"Let us pray," said L.F.

"Let us vamoose," whispered Doris. We followed a dry creek bed past the obstacle course to a glade wherein stood a primitive amphitheater. "Chapel in the Woods" read a sign attached to an open-sided structure behind the pulpit.

The group dispersed among the pews. "Half-Breed" issued from Jenny's Toot-a-Loot. *The Indians said that I was white by law. The white man always called me "Indian squaw."*

A joint made its way around while we let the lyrics sink in. "Your flask," I said to Doris.

"That's not mine," she said, holding up her own, similar flask.

"Then what am I drinking?"

Guddu took the flask from me and sniffed. "This is elephant juice," he said. The second he said it, I remembered Diane giving it to me. It would not be the first time she dosed me. I suddenly felt woozy. Or was I just tanked?

Monty initiated what he referred to jocularly as the "Devil's Game." A variation of Seven Minutes in Heaven played with dice. My head was spinning. The icosahedron fell from my hand. "A one!" cried Doris. A finger hooked around my belt loop and tugged. I was led behind the structure. A body pinned mine against the wall. Before I could collect my wits, the Indian squaw's mouth was upon mine. Her fingers explored my body, pinching, squeezing, searching. Hormones took the wheel and I responded in kind. The squaw fumbled for my zipper. Her tongue slid from my ear to my neck. I pulled down on her ponytails. The lusty howl of cicadas was met with slurping sounds.

"Time!" called Monty.

"*Das ist schade,*" whispered a voice that was not a squaw's. The puce jersey should have given her away.

I leaned heavily against the back of the structure. There was a soft crunching sound of pulpy wood giving away. Something tickled my ear and I slapped it. There was a sudden realization that I was covered in crawling things. I ran. I found myself standing in the pool, wiping bugs off me. First scorpions, now these.

Boots sloshing, I emerged from the water and joined the crowd that had gathered around the telescope. Sarge was squinting through it. "We're studying the *Mare Cognitum*," said Doris. The people's astronomer looked me up and down. "Well?"

"Well, what?" I panted.

"You can tell Granny."

None of this was Granny's business.

"You got a big ol' hickey." Doris looked up at the sky. "You can see the stars so much better out here in the boonies."

"Isn't stargazing a dying pastime?" said Sarge.

"On account of light pollution, it may as well be," said Doris. "Professional astronomers don't know the night sky but know a lot about where those twinkly things came from. They stare at data. Boring!"

A commotion by the ranch house got our attention. More rules enforcers. They had Spunt up against the wall. One was shining his flashlight into a brown Buick Centurion. "What is going on?" people whispered.

"This belongs to you." Diane pressed a spur sharply into my hand. It is not mine, though. It is Car Boy's. As she had done before in the guise of Ursula, the witch had frisked me in search of the amulet under the pretense of playing Monty's game. It is only a matter of time before she discovers everything. If she has not already.

I scanned the crowd for Jenny's face. Considered stopping by Caddo but continued up the hill, having had enough excitement for one day. I passed Guddu taking a shower, a sight no one should have to see.

On my futon, I examined my thighs for saddle sores. My scratches stung from sweat. Caroline on *Little House on the Prairie* almost died when hers became infected. I went over the events of the day. I contemplated L.F.'s book tower. What would become of the Vault? My thoughts turned to *Successful Muskrat Farming*. I wished I could look at it right then to confirm a few hunches. It was not until two weeks ago that I even understood the logogrammatic aspect of its glyphs, or what the colored ink represented. If L.F.'s shitty excuse for a glyph is any indication, he knows a lot. But not what is in the codex.

MONDAY, JUNE 6

Two warring possums woke everyone up during the night. Shortly thereafter, something's awful screech held my attention until the horizon turned pale. An owl, I hoped. A mosquito bit me on the lip, which is more painful than one would think.

"Coffee," groaned Doris, as she plopped down next to me. Jenny took one look at me and said, "That's a hickey." She retrieved her bondo bag from Caddo. For the second time in as many months, she produced a concealer stick and applied it to the dark purple mark. Like she does to the ones Judd gives her. "There. You can barely notice it now."

"Owe you one," I mumbled.

"You should see Diane," said Jenny. "Her whole body's covered in poison oak." Jenny did not seem upset. If this was Diane's plot to drive a wedge between us it failed.

Everyone seemed languid, depleted, and indisposed to further revelry. Many were bright pink. Monty pranced by, covered in streaks of calamine lotion, followed by Mr. Lowell in a neck brace. "They dropped him during the Trust Games.

The drawing for the raffle was presided over by Mrs. Neighbors. "This is rigged," complained Mr. Snyder. He leaped from his bench and rushed toward her. "Let me see that clipboard!"

Mrs. Neighbors did not flinch as L.F.'s henchmen subdued Mr. Snyder and led him away screaming before his shocked colleagues. "My report is to be laid before Mr. Burnside tomorrow morning," asserted Mrs. Neighbors. "Just try and stop me!" L.F. Burnside himself sat nearby, oblivious to the proceedings. He was busy counting a huge wad of money.

If Mr. Snyder was right, it seemed rigged in favor of hedgehogs over foxes. This place is like a hedgehog training ground, I thought. A warren? There must be a special word. I recalled the imposing gray building in the woods and imagined L.F. in an apron and goggles scooping nascent hedgehogs out of a vat of bubbling gray ooze. The truth is probably far more sinister.

"If you were ever wondering how to get ahead at Porteous," said Doris ruefully. "This is where I learned to shun teamwork. These days I keep to myself."

"7548," intoned Mrs. Neighbors. Everyone looked down at his ticket. "Please come up to claim your Porteous paperweight."

"That's me," said Doris. "They make you pay taxes on raffle winnings in the state of Texas. I'm not paying taxes on a dang paperweight. If I wanted one of those, I would just snatch it off Dixie's desk."

Somehow Guddu won one of the drawings. I did not see how, a lowly fringie with a blank dance card. His prize: a Smith-Corona typewriter. He placed it on the ground with a grunt of exertion.

"What are you going to do with it?"

"Perhaps Guddu will write a book."

"I would read that book," I said. And I meant it.

Upon closer observation, the typewriter turned out to be my own. Unsurprisingly, it would not fit in the trunk. It ended up in Diane's lap. "Why is it that returning from a trip you always have more than you came with?" said Doris innocently. She knows nothing about L.F.'s safe, of course.

A couple of cops approached while I was hotwiring the Rambler. To discourage them, I mumbled every word of power at my disposal. One of them must have worked. They passed us by. In retrospect, I could have hurt someone.

No one said much on the drive back to Fort Worth. It was muggy and rained intermittently. We encountered a traffic jam. We moved at a snail's pace for miles. Finally we were able to pull into a Stuckey's to pee and take a break. Everyone had the same idea, so it was pretty crowded. The parking lot smelled like rain on hot concrete. The windshield was a mess so I had Guddu clean it. Must not let him forget who is boss. There was a line for the restrooms, so I decided to hold it. I longed for a real toilet, but no word of power could help me there. None that I am aware of, anyway.

Diane and I watched the wieners rotating under the burning red bulb. "That's what my shoulders feel like," I said. Diane smirked. Where was the poison oak Jenny had mentioned? Guess if I can have a magically healed ankle, the witch can make some pesky poison oak disappear. There is nothing to gain by asking her about it. I am just surprised Jenny did not confront her.

My Chap Stick had melted in my pocket so I bought another one. Guddu bought some Fun Dip and a Rangers cap. With what bread? Is Porteous paying him? Perhaps he just conjured up a bag of Krugerrands and paid with that. He put the cap on in the Rambler.

"You look like a real Texan now, Guddu!" said Doris.

"L.F. looks like a real Texan," said Guddu. "His hat is for cowboys."

"You do have a point," I said. "Do I look like a real Texan?"

"No, Steven. You do not look like anybody." Surely Guddu's comment was not intended to be an insult, but I took it like one. "The eyes of Texas are upon you," I said.

Guddu stared at me wide-eyed in the rear view.

The traffic jam continued. Eventually, we were routed onto the shoulder to bypass the scene of a horrific accident. "Look, it's Spunt," said Doris. He pedaled by on a ten-speed, a large bundle strapped to the back of his puce jersey.

"Did you hear?" said Jenny. "Someone broke into the ranch house. They caught Spunt sneaking around upstairs and detained him. They think he did it. Guess they didn't have any evidence so they let him go." So Diane has Spunt doing her bidding. Guess she is putting that appendix to good use.

We dropped off Doris at her house in Poly. I turned to Jenny. "Your mom's or the Hacienda?"

"Mom's is fine." After a pause, she added, "Don't you want to drop Guddu off first?"

It is strange to hear someone else speak Guddu's name. Proof that he is not simply a figment of my overtaxed imagination. "Are we dropping you off first, Guddu? Tell us where you live." Our eyes met in the rear view. Guddu did not answer. It is amusing to torment him this way. Of course, he could turn the tables by simply answering the question. Then we would both be in the doghouse.

"Sorry, Jenny. I have a lot to do before going back to work tomorrow. I'll catch you at the library." Fighting off Mama Fox was the last thing I needed right now. Jenny pouted the rest of the way. This is the reason Dixie set the rule against dating coworkers.

The safe is too heavy to move so I left it in the trunk. The rest of the afternoon I spent searching for a formula to crack it, to no avail. Nor can I sing my way into it. Yet. Maybe I could jam my way into it, like Judas Priest. Asking Guddu is out of the question. He must not suspect the limits of my power.

It was shady in the alley behind the Book Nook. "Kemosabe!" called Fred. "Are you robbing banks now? Seriously, how did you lift this into your trunk?"

"No questions," I said. "We have an agreement."

"It hurts my feelings that you won't confide in me. How long have we known each other?"

"Look, Fred. Let's just say I'm in trouble. If I told you anything about this safe you would be in trouble, too. It's to protect you."

"What if I don't help you?"

"Unless I'm mistaken, you owe me one." There is much I do not want Fred to know. But the amulet? I realized I have been referring to it as "my" amulet. It is not mine. Was L.F. not simply reclaiming it for Porteous, the legal owner? If his motives are questionable, what about Diane's? Until I discover what the amulet has to do with Sherwood's disappearance, and why everyone wants to get their hands on it, I intend to keep it. For all I know, it confers upon the wearer protection from demons. There is strong evidence that it saved me at Mayfest.

"I can probably get into it," said Fred. "But it will take time."

A series of metallic crunching sounds startled us. It was Wheeler. He was stomping around with two crushed Coke cans on his feet, a balsa glider crumpled in his fist. "What's happening, jive turkeys?" said Wheeler. Something about that kid is not developmentally typical. As much as I enjoy his odd ways, it is best to avoid him. I closed the trunk. "We'll have more privacy at my place," said Fred. "Let me lock up."

On the way to Fred's, he told me that after I had left the fundraiser, he got to meet Space Opera. "What happened to you?" he said. I had forgotten the lie I told Bonnie, so I just shrugged. Fred shook his head like I was retarded. We commiserated about Time Frame. Fred's complaint is that we are not experimental enough. This, coming from someone who listens to *Metal Machine*

*Music* for pleasure. Both of us agree Tim's ego is overinflated. "He always has to have his way," I said.

In the privacy of Fred's ramshackle garage we discussed how to get the safe out of the trunk without damaging the Rambler. "Happy birthday, by the way." Fred accepted the Däniken album with skepticism. It was obvious without even opening the shrinkwrap that it was warped from baking in the car for days. "It's in quadraphonic," I said. "Or it was."

"It can't sound any worse than an unwarped one," said Fred, glumly. But of course he has already heard it. What has he not heard?

It was decided to leave the safe in the trunk. Fred would get it open one way or another. Throughout the evening I watched him labor. We made small talk but our hearts were not in it. Could not tell if he was angry or just disappointed. On one of our cigarette breaks we split a can of chili enhanced with peppers and ketchup. Afterward, I thirsted for some carbonation. A trek to 7-Eleven would have gotten me out of that hot, stuffy garage and away from Fred, whose grunting and cursing became more pronounced the longer he worked. Each time he dropped a tool, I flinched.

"Ouch!" cried Fred. "Man, this is ridiculous. I've got other shit to do."

"Going to the corner for a Pibb," I said. Fred remained silent. When I returned with a six-pack, Fred had gone inside the house. The door to the safe was tantalizingly ajar. It was stuffed. A deposit bag contained cash, personal documents, and Polyflex stock. A small manila envelope held the amulet. According to various press clippings, a gold watch, an antique pendant, and a blue enamel latch box set with diamonds likely came from Montreal's so-called Skylight Caper, as did a small Rembrandt. Another small painting wrapped in newspaper, identified as the "Kwer'ata Re'esu" icon, was evidently stolen in Ethiopia by a British Museum agent before disappearing. A Pre-Columbian funerary mask of green stone grinned hideously from a Whitman's Sampler box. Its documentation suggested it had been stolen from the Río Azul site. I regarded the stash in amazement.

Fred was idly watching Shields and Yarnell with the volume turned down. "Our society is doomed," he intoned, his gaze fixed on the flickering screen. I offered him a Pibb, which he accepted. Middling, unadventurous space rock, sitting pretty firmly in 4/4, droned from the speakers.

"What are we listening to?"

"*In Search of Ancient Gods*," said Fred in an ominous voice. "Is that really Bill Bruford on drums?" he added skeptically. I popped a handful of candies from a dish into my mouth. "That's fake candy. Remember when I brought it back from Japan?" Fred's tone suggested his feelings were hurt that I had forgotten this fact.

There was no point in prolonging the tension between us. I briefly considered offering Fred some of the cash for his trouble but decided that it should be returned to L.F. I spat the candies into my palm. "Thanks, man," I said. "I'll see you."

Guddu was waiting for me back at Collinwood. He stood in the middle of the living room, assuming various poses with his riding crop. I just shook my head. "It's Fort Worth's birthday, today," I said.

"Fort Worth was born?" he said predictably. I curtly excused him and took a shower. I do not care what he does as long as I catch some zees. I lay sweating in bed, contemplating the events of the weekend, my damaged friendship with Fred, and my criminal activity. What is happening to me?


Tuesday, June 7

Arrived to work late to find a catalog card in my typewriter onto which was typed, in all capital letters, "KRLK." Guddu would not have typed that, nor Diane. Why would they? Talk about the ghost in the machine. A ghost that eschews vowels. Below that, an unintelligible string of numbers.

Hazel met me at my desk. "We're moving you," she said smugly.

"What do you mean?"

She led me to a spot in the hall between the William Lawrence Peebles III Meeting Room and the P. Harris Schlumberger Water Fountain.

"You have got to be kidding," I said.

"Talk to Carlos."

Jo Ann was out again, so I spent the rest of the afternoon with Amber at the information desk. Not sure why Amber needs me there. She does perfectly fine on her own. I found her examining a coin.

"Harrington gives them to me," said Amber.

"For what?"

"Scratching his back," she said. "And for taking him into the Vault."

"How?" I said irritably.

Amber produced a huge ring of keys, presumably her own. I give up.

The *New York Times* had a review of *Nyiregyházi Plays Liszt*. I checked the value of Polyflex stock but could make neither heads nor tails of the numbers. I looked up *chough* in the *OED* then presented it to Amber as the "word of the day." It is a type of crow.

"What's he doing?" said Amber.

"Installing a suggestion box." The two of us watched as Carlos tightened the final screw then shuffled away. Ever since the Vault incident, he walks like a lobotomized ape. Spunt emerged from behind the card catalog. He took a blank form, filled it out, then slipped it into the slot. After his ill treatment at the Elephant Ranch, Spunt must have plenty of suggestions.

The sound of a power saw sliced the quietude in two. Carlos was cutting my desk down to size. The drawers on the right side spilled their contents onto the floor. He unceremoniously shoved it into place in the hall.

I dialed Time and Temp. "It's ninety-nine," I said after hanging up.

Amber made a face. "It smells like ninety-nine dirty bottoms in here." She did not acknowledge my ill treatment but her expression bore traces of sympathy. To live with Dixie must come with its own scars.

"Sorry," I said. "Didn't shower this morning."

I called Fred at the shop. Wheeler answered. "Fred says he's not here," said the young boy.

"Can you take a message?" I said. "Tell him to meet me at seven o'clock tomorrow for coffee at Old South. Now repeat it to me." *Witness Wheeler obey.* "Good man."

Found a plate of peanut brittle on my chair. "Where did that come from?"

"It was there when I got here," said Amber. "May I have some?" She broke off a piece and held it to her lips. I slapped it out of her hand.

"Don't eat that," I snapped. What if the Doom Hippie made it?

A factory whistle tooted. It sounded like it was coming from the quad. "No more Happy Trails," said Amber.

"Since when?"

No response from Amber. She was still mad at me, I suppose, for slapping the peanut brittle out of her hand. Before we left for the day, I signed up to bring cowboy stew to the potluck.


Jenny sidled up to me in the vestibule. "Give me a ride?" she said sweetly. When I opened my mouth to speak, she placed half of a stick of gum in it. Spearmint. She knows I dislike spearmint. At least she should know by now.

On the way to Lot C, Turtle Man grabbed my sleeve. "Can I get into the break room? I'd like to get some of my milk." He grinned sheepishly and held up his Thermos.

I clenched my jaw. "No one's stopping you," I said.

"By the way, I left you some peanut brittle," said Turtle Man. "It's my grandma's secret recipe. Feel free to wash it down with some of my milk." I hate the way he says "some of my milk" and hope to never hear it again. I did not have the presence of mind to thank him or even acknowledge the kind gesture.


Jenny tried to get me to come upstairs. "Mother's not home," she pleaded. "Come rub my feet, would you, darling?" Jenny was starting to sound exactly like her mother. It was as if Mama Fox inhabited Jenny's body to get to me. I shuddered at the thought. But I also knew such magic was possible. "It can be sparkle time," urged Jenny.

Was tempted to stay for the a/c. Why did settlers ever stop in Texas? What pioneer stumbled into a dusty arroyo and collapsed, sweat streaming down his face, and said, "Home sweet home"? "We would need the crystal for sparkle time, would we not?" I said. I was hoping she would admit that it was missing.

"Sparkle time's a state of mind," said Jenny philosophically. "It's your loss."

I had said "No" to the Stone Fox. Guess her magic is getting weaker. What I needed most, I decided, was an Icee from the corner. They were out of blue, as usual. I chose red. The machine churned. A thin red fluid dribbled from the spigot. With a sigh, I headed back to Collinwood parched and empty-handed.

Vee met me on the front porch with curlers in her hair. "Dollface!" she sang. She then uttered the glorious words of power: "Come help me install this air conditioner."

*Witness Steven obey.*

I found Vee on her knees. White cotton balls were stuck between her freshly-painted toes. She was straining in a strapless terrycloth romper to shove a heavy cardboard box across the carpet. She glanced over her shoulder. "Are you going to stand there like a dummy?"

There is no stronger magic than tush. Together, we moved the box into her bedroom. She spread the instructions open on the bed. "Do you have a wrench?"

"Let me run downstairs." It took so long to find a wrench that I almost conjured one. I returned with the tool, out of breath and dripping with perspiration.

"This is not a wrench," she said. "Look in the toolbox under the kitchen sink. Listen to me, bossing you around!"

"Yes, ma'am!" I snapped, clicking my heels together and saluting idiotically before racing into the kitchen. There was no toolbox under the sink. Checked each of the cabinets. Even ransacked the drawers, even though a toolbox would not fit in them.

"There is no toolbox under the sink."

"Hmm, try the pantry, then."

Though it was obvious there was no toolbox in the pantry, I dutifully moved countless cans of soup back and forth. My efforts were redirected to the bedroom closet. Vee's closet was a disaster area. Dry cleaning sagged from a buckling rod. The shelf above was so crammed with stuff, there was clearly no room for a toolbox. Got on my hands and knees, and scooped out piles of shoeboxes, sandals, boots, slinky dresses, and dust bunnies. I felt a toe tickling my butthole. I shrieked like a schoolgirl.

Vee loomed above me, waving a wrench admonishingly. "*This* is a wrench," she lectured, looking down her aquiline nose at me with a smirk.

"Where was it?"

"Junk drawer in the kitchen."

Installing the air conditioner was not as onerous as I figured it would be. I felt like freaking Handy Dan. We did not need the wrench, after all. I plugged the unit in and Vee turned it up full blast. We stood in front of it, arms akimbo, heads tilted back in ecstasy, both making audible "ahhs" as the perspiration began to evaporate from our clammy skin. Nirvana attained.

The walls of Vee's sanctum sanctorum were adorned with various travel posters: Ireland, Mali, Vail. A Club Med poster leaned framed but unhung against an Art Deco vanity. A potted ficus adorned the corner, attached to the ceiling fan by a lone cobweb. The unmade bed was covered with a thousand pillows. Its rattan headboard matched a nightstand on top of which rested a dim globe lamp with a reverse tonsure of dust. Opposite the bed, under a burial mound of clothing, loomed a mamasan chair. Figgy and I watched passively as a Frederick's of Hollywood catalog slid off of it and onto the floor.

Vee led me into the kitchen. "Welcome to Margaritaville. Population: two!"

Errands beckoned, but there was no way I was going to turn my back on an alcoholic Icee, nor a chance to luxuriate in Jeannie's air conditioned bottle. After blending the booze, we toasted our success in front of the a/c. In imitation of the lass on the Ireland poster, I raised my glass and said "Slain-tay!"

"It's pronounced *slawn-che*," lectured Vee. She went into the bathroom, leaving the door ajar so we could still converse. Figaro rammed his head against the door which opened wide. Vee was on the commode, peeing loudly, romper pooled around her ankles. I looked away, blushing.

"Figs, you turkey!" Vee shrieked. She toed the door shut and finished her business. "Figs likes to be where the action is. Let's hang out in here, where it's cool!" she said over the flushing commode.

"The bathroom?" I said retardedly.

"No, Ding Dong," she teased, hiking her romper up. "Either the top is falling down or the bottoms are riding up." I regarded her outfit for evidence of her claim. Gone were the cotton balls. "Stay put," she instructed, closing the bedroom door behind her to seal in the cool air. This trapped Figaro, who immediately began pacing and meowing. Cracked the door for him but he just sat there, looking through the gap wide-eyed but not budging as cold air whooshed out. When I shut the door, he started meowing again.

"That New Black Magic: A Consumer Guide to the Occult" read the cover of an old *Viva* magazine. I stood there reading until Vee returned with two more margaritas, these festooned with paper umbrellas. The instant the door opened, Figaro impatiently shot through. Vee violently shoved aside sedimentary layers of magazines and panties so I could recline on the mamasan. My rear end sank into the depression, filling it perfectly. The a/c vents were now pointed directly at the back of my head.

"Was supposed to meet Blue Van at Spencer's but I'm having much more fun with you," said Vee.

We talked, drank, and listened to Bowie on a portable record player. Vee stretched supine on the rug, her feet propped up on the mamasan next to me. She held up the lyrics sheet to *Hunky Dory*, obscuring her face from mine. This afforded me an opportunity to appraise her pale, freckled body under conventional lighting. I noted the contrast between her Flowering Plum toenails and the filthy bottoms of her feet. Her romper fit snugly, revealing various tan lines. "*Brrr*! I'm getting goosebumps!" she said. "Feel."

When the blender was empty we switched to straight skunk piss. I joined Vee on the rug. One of us asked, "Could you ever kill someone?" We both said yes. But only in self-defense. Vee said she hated the shave-and-a-haircut knock. She said that when she was young, she thought the phrase "to pull the wool over someone's eyes" meant to have sex with them. She fingered my chicken pox scar then showed me where she was stabbed in the wrist with a pencil.

"What's this?" I said, running my finger familiarly over her arm.

"Smallpox jab."

"By the way, I've been leaving my butter on the kitchen counter like you said. I came home the other day and there was a groove from where Figgy had licked it. I've been eating cat butter!"

"You're supposed to keep it in a butter dish, silly."

The record began skipping: "If you stay, you won't be sorry," intoned Ziggy Stardust. Vee tossed a bra at the turntable. The needle ripped across the grooves of the record. "Whoops!" said Vee. "Didn't mean to do that!"

I stifled a yawn. "Do I bore you?" said Vee coyly, fluttering her eyelashes.

"Not at all," I said. "Just haven't been getting any rest on account of the heat."

"Flop here tonight," said Vee. "In the mamasan chair." She jiggled it with her foot.

Did not respond right away. Wanted to choose my words carefully. There were so many variables, I felt like I was doing algebra in my head. I would love nothing more than to pull the wool over Vee's eyes, fast and hard. But what we have is nice and I do not want to ruin it. For better or worse, I ended up saying: "Nah, I don't wear, uh, anything in bed."

"Me neither!" said Vee. "Besides, we've seen each other butt naked," she observed, casually and without a hint of lasciviousness. She sat up and scooped the rest of the clothes and magazines onto the floor. She stood, then paused, steadying herself.

"You okay?" I said.

She handed me one of her pillows. "A few good pillow kisses will help keep the demons away." I started at the unfamiliar phrase. I will have to remember to look it up in Bartlett's.

Vee laughed, then went into the bathroom to brush her teeth. "Did you and Green Bug have fun?" Chicks gab. Vee already knows I did not pull the wool over Dawn's Coke-bottle glasses. She did not wait for an answer. "Brought a bag of these back from Tivoli." She tossed me a toothbrush. It looked like it was made of faux marble. Did Blue Van, *et al.* each get one?

The Tivolian toothbrush was the "best I have ever had," to use one of Randy's catch phrases. Or is it Tiburtini? I gargled some Scope in case things got interesting. The television commercial is right—it did not taste mediciny. I lingered nervously in the bathroom before emerging to find Vee just slipping under the covers. "If it won't bug you, I'm going to read." She selected a book from a pile.

"Not at all," I replied, gung ho to appear hunky dory. "I'm an ardent supporter of librocubicularism," I added, stumbling on the last word. Vee either did not hear me or was ignoring me. I bent over and slowly untied my laces. Yanked the double knot the wrong way and ended up making a bigger knot. This dreadful tangle was not on Aunt Wanda's sailor knot chart. I forcibly removed my shoe. I then stood up and took off my football jersey, tossing it nonchalantly onto the edge of the mamasan. Turning my back to Vee, I unzipped my cut-offs. On a whim, I kicked them over my head like some sort of maniac. They flew onto the ficus in the corner. "Oops, sorry!" I said, inspecting its delicate branches for damage.

"Silly goose!" said Vee disinterestedly. Every move I made was conspicuous and foolish. Flopped heavily onto the mamasan. A sharp pain in my side turned out to be a tortoiseshell hair clip, which I mistook for a wolf spider. I frantically slapped it away and leaped to my feet. When I finally simmered down, I glanced in Vee's direction to find her absorbed by her book. The cover was yellow, so it was not *The Road to Oxiana*.

Vee had provided a thin chenille blanket. The a/c felt heavenly, but the mamasan was really cramped. On account of its shape, I could not lie flat. My feet stuck out beyond the hard edge of the rattan frame, which bit into my shins. "Good night," I said casually.

"Sweet dreams!"

Closed my eyes, but my heart was racing. Vee turned off the lamp. I immediately opened my eyes. The a/c droned on. It was going to be a long night.

It seemed ridiculous, but I kissed my pillow a few times. Gotta keep those demons away.

The room became frigid. Wrapped the blanket around myself like an enchirito and lay there, shivering. My nose started to run. Did not have any Kleenex so I used my shirt. I contemplated the events of the day. Moving me into the hall was a slap on the face I could not ignore. Things at the library have been topsy-turvy since the retreat.

Other people's thermostats are off limits. Should I crawl under the covers with Vee? Looked like a queen, or maybe a double. What if she minded? Should I wake her up and ask permission, first? Should I bump her hip with mine and whisper, "Scooch over"? She would probably let me and I could finally catch some zees. "Can I sleep with you?" Too ambiguous. "Can I sleep in your bed?" You mean *trade places*? My teeth began to chatter.

Inevitably, I had to get up to pee. A wedge of moonlight illuminated Vee's half-covered form. Though she told me she slept in the buff, she was now wearing her Gemini panties. Murloc of Siluria would pull them aside and have his fun. Headlights streaked across the ceiling. Someone had just pulled into the driveway. Blue Van? Tim? My heart sank. The lights went away. Maybe they were just turning around. Vee drew her knee up in a restless manner.

On my way back to the mamasan, I stepped on a flash cube and stifled an expletive. I gathered Vee's dirty things and piled them on top of myself for warmth. They smelled like her.

Wednesday, June 8

After a night of tossing and turning, I grabbed my clothes and tiptoed from Vee's cold boudoir, making my way downstairs. I showered and dressed. I then headed to the corner phone booth and dialed SEAL-ASS.

"You said you were going to come over last night," said Jenny drowsily. "Where were you?"

"Did I?" I said. "I was at Collinwood."

"I'm not sure I believe you." How would Jenny know, and why would she care? She has the Doom Hippie, does she not? Do not know why I even bothered calling.

Old South at seven sharp. Ordered coffee at the counter. Had not intended to eat here but the smell of bacon was driving me crazy. Thirty minutes passed, then forty. No Fred. Guess he is still hacked off.

Back at Collinwood, the witch's dossier beckoned, the one I boosted from Dixie's office. A resume identified her as Diane Bollinger. The address given was the Como Courts on Vickery, which means she was in Fort Worth before she applied for her job at the library. If a position at Porteous was her goal, she must have been pretty sure of herself to go ahead and move all the way out here from California. Her credentials include advanced degrees in Psychology and Library Science from Sequoia University. Her employment history includes library and archival work at the Collegium Adocentyn in Nuremberg and the Universität des Menschen, as well as a stint as Head Librarian at the Seaberg Society. In case of emergency, she lists Lotte Ziegenhagen of Los Angeles. Apart from a couple of early dress code violations, her record is clean. One would think her wantonly rebellious attitudes would have gotten her into more trouble. An offer letter indicates she was hired as a consultant, not as a cataloger.

Randy's dossier revealed nothing I did not already know. His background in the classics. His stint in Vietnam with his brother. He never speaks of either. His position as a security guard at the Amon Carter Museum and as a cook. For his emergency contact, he provides an uncle in Ojai, California. A report submitted by Diane on April 29 recommended the elimination of Randy's position. Dixie wasted no time! But why did Diane want to get rid of Randy? What did he ever do to her?

To Sound Warehouse for Nyiregyházi's IPA LP but they have to special order it. They did have *Hunky Dory*. To Mott's to mail L.F.'s cash and personal documents. C.O.D., of course. A Fort Worth postmark was unavoidable, but for the hell of it I put 1502 Commerce as the return address. Going to the police was not an option. What story could I possibly give them? As for the "Kwer'ata Re'esu" and Rembrandt, I would stash them in the thesis cage until I could think of how to best dispose of them.

Spent an hour at the Waffle House with the *Star-Telegram*. Ed Brice's column discussed the Kensington Runestone, an inscription upon which suggests Vikings were in America way before Columbus. Randy has a buddy who in the spirit of Kon-Tiki makes simple boats in which one may sail across the ocean, so it is not far-fetched to believe that the seafaring Vikings could pull it off. Hell, anyone with a boat and luck on his side. It was nice to sit around and do nothing. However, I soon got the nagging feeling that I should go home and do some muskrat farming. If only to rid myself of the imp once and for all.

The interior of the Rambler was like one of those microwave ovens. The prospect of going home to a sauna was an unhappy one. I decided to take Harrington up on his offer of the pool.

Parked at Collinwood. Figured I would walk the short distance to the Chateau Villa. The DDT kid beckoned from his lemonade stand across the street. "Get your ice cold lemonade!" he barked. His words of power were irresistible, so I bought a cup. As the thick, lukewarm liquid slid down my throat, I watched him stick his entire flipper into the pitcher and stir.

Harrington's door was ajar. I pushed it open with my foot. Within, all was darkness. The odor of mothballs and old people's medicine teased my nostrils. The professor floated from the gloom like a specter. He reached out with his bony finger then collapsed. I was quick enough to catch his fall and help him to a chair. The headband I had given him came in a package that included two wristbands. He was wearing one of the latter, but had somehow managed to stretch it around his forehead. When I pried it loose, it shot through the air like a rubber band. I am beginning to understand why Sherwood always called Bertie daft. As the blood returned to the professor's noggin, I surveyed the sparsely furnished digs. It was devoid of any personal belongings, save a bookcase which contained, besides books, objects of an anthropological nature such as fetishes, dolls, and queer stone carvings. On his coffee table among all the tea rings were the unmistakable trappings of sorcery.

Harrington's eyes shadowed my own to the trappings and back. The professor parted his lips to speak. "Never, ever, dabble in the occult," he uttered feebly. "Not only will you lose your mind, you will lose your soul, your sanity, your very ego. Jim used to get on my tits about it. He warned me I would get myself into trouble."

"Are you in trouble?" I said, loosening his ascot.

"My kingdom for a Guinness stout mixed with port," he said ruefully.

"Let's get you a glass of water, first." I found a banana, which I peeled and fed to him in pieces. I playfully stuck the Chiquita sticker on his sweater, then instantly regretted it. But any thoughts of Harrington's sense of humor or lack thereof were dispelled when he clutched my hand and said, "I don't want to die. I still like a toke and a toot and a poke and a root. Oh, to find the Fountain of Youth!"

The professor took another bite of banana. He stopped chewing, then vocally spat a pasty glob into his palm. Something gleamed among the masticated pulp.

A tooth? "A diamond in a banana!" I exclaimed.

The professor tapped his ear, so I repeated myself. He looked down sheepishly. "Bloody hell, I suppose I hid it there. Make an old geezer happy and scratch my back?" He pointed to a back scratcher nearby. I employed the tool across his trapezius. "Dermatitis ails me," he continued. "I would scratch my own back but a shoulder complaint prevents it. Aging is no bed of roses, as you Americans say. But having one foot in the grave has its advantages. I would normally avoid such a dreadful place, but the business school dining hall offers me a ten percent discount on meals." The professor mopped his brow with a handkerchief. "It is too warm here," said Harrington derisively. "I intend to write your council about it."

"You might remove your sweater," I said. "You know, when I was a child, a local department store had this huge chunk of ice in a bathtub. If you guessed how long it took to melt you won a bicycle. When no one was looking, I climbed into the tub and sat on the ice. My Aunt Wanda dragged me away by my ear but later I heard her laughing when she told my mother the story on the telephone. You may guess why I'm here. You offered the use of your pool."

"Indeed I did, Steven. You are always welcome."

The pool was refreshing. After a quick dip, I sat on the edge to let my shorts dry on the hot concrete. Harrington scooted up with tennis balls on the ends of his walker. I jumped up and met him at the gate. He wordlessly offered me a half-crown coin. I knew what it was for. On my way to Porteous, I realized I had forgotten to ask the professor what it was he had wanted to talk to me about. It must not have been urgent.

*The Fearless Vampire Killers* was showing at Pigg Auditorium. Parked on the outskirts of Lot D. Did not want to run into anyone from the library. Polanski had disowned the film, I understand, because of the dubbing and brutal editing it received at the hands of Martin Ransohoff. I found it entertaining, myself. One of my favorite scenes was the one where a guy drowns in a barrel of wine. But when I realized His Excellency was Count von Krolock, I became fixated on his name. Was my own Krolok trying to tell me something? After sitting through the credits where I learned of the different spelling, I decided the similar monikers were a meaningless coincidence. Still, it bothered me for the rest of the day.

Got a few errands out of the way before heading to the museum. Had a Sloppy Joe in the cafeteria. From the gift shop I bought some photosensitive paper. It was early when I peered into Dawn's classroom. She greeted me cheerfully. She showed me some of the sketches her students made, chiefly of still lifes and nudes, the latter a voluptuous young woman with a huge distended belly and plump breasts. She then produced her sketchbook which I perused as she spirited about setting up easels. A few quick charcoals of Shagduk surprised and disturbed me. The loathsome encounter is clearly on her mind. No one can blame her. As soon as she left the classroom, I tore out the sketches and stuffed them into my mansack.

Dawn returned with a stool for me. "You'll find a robe behind that screen," she said. Did not know how to broach the topic of attire, so I dutifully undressed for art's sake and donned the wrinkled ochre robe, which bore the monogram "LDG." Uncle Larry's initials? I tried in vain to recall his middle name. This ill-timed reminder deepened my already anxious mood.

The class was standing room only, attended chiefly by middle-aged women. The excitement in the classroom was palpable. Guess I am a breath of fresh air after months of drawing the same model. To my dismay, Mama Fox was among them. She gave my hand a friendly squeeze then scooted her easel and chair close to the plinth. Last to arrive was Diane. How did she even know about the class? Is she competing with Dawn, somehow?

Having to stay completely still for long stretches is harder than one would think. All hail the Slave Lord of Siluria! I felt like I held considerable power over this harem. In an attempt to contain it, Dawn presented a clear acrylic cube which she and Mama Fox lowered on top of me. Now I know how the Gutenberg Bible feels. We abandoned the pose when the case fogged up and it became difficult to breathe. So much for contemporary art, in which the power of the human form is compromised. I contemplated the roles of exhibitionist and voyeur. Plinth or stage, it is the same. Who wields the power? I decided I did, this time. But there is something unsettling about all those hungry eyes, feasting on my image. Care must be taken not to upset the balance in their favor.

Whenever Mama Fox was absorbed with some detail of my anatomy, I would steal a glance at her. Her voluminous wig was more air than hair. It reminded me of cotton candy. Her body was ample, but not fleshy. The Stone Fox in twenty years.

During breaks, I donned the robe and surveyed everyone's work. Diane's sketch was surprisingly small, as subtly detailed as a Dürer. He probably taught her, for all I know. The proportions exhibited in Mama Fox's drawing indicated some wishful thinking on her part but captured my tumescence in all its glory. She playfully smeared charcoal on my cheek. Dawn rubbed it off with a licked thumb. I found her application of saliva to my bare skin both arousing and yucky. She seemed annoyed not at Mama Fox but with me. Her irritation, along with seeing all those similar but not identical iterations of myself, put me in sort of an existential funk for the rest of the day.

Diane asked for a ride to the Fac. Along the way, she regarded her sketchbook. "What are you going to do with that?" I said. I shuddered to think of what sorcery she could accomplish with a likeness of me. She alone among the ladies had rendered my prick in its flaccid state. As if she had been afraid of the truth. Why did I feel like I had won this round? Maybe because she knows it had nothing to do with her.

"Hang it in my office at the library," she teased. "Seriously, you can have it." Not sure my distrust of Diane will ever diminish, but I took this as a sign of goodwill. She invited me up but I told her I was too tired, which was not a lie.

Home in time to catch the end of *Soylent Green*. Life in 2022 is unimaginable. Cars will be sentient and computers will make decisions for us. Horrible ideas for all the obvious reasons. You do not have to be Einstein to understand that technological progress is like an axe in the hands of a pathological criminal. I will be pushing seventy by then, unless World War III breaks out and we are all nuked into oblivion.

With a wet towel as my blanket, I positioned myself between two fans on high speed. A pan of water before each turned them into portable swamp coolers. There should be a formula for keeping cool. Or keeping one's cool. Guddu could probably alleviate my suffering, but there is no way I would ask him. I longed to be upstairs in Vee's air-conditioned boudoir again. But my thoughts kept drifting back to the witch.

THURSDAY, JUNE 9

After playing hooky from life yesterday, I was unprepared for what I had hoped would be an uneventful Thursday. Guinness and port in hand, I stopped by Harrington's to check on him and thank him for letting me swim. He did not answer the doorbell. An angry thornbush guarded his window. Hocus pocus failed to budge the spring-loaded pins in the door lock. My second attempt involved summoning an elemental to do my bidding. You do not perceive them, perhaps because they are too tiny. One can understand my reluctance to employ such methods, but it worked.

As my vision adjusted to the dim interior, my nostrils detected a sulfuric odor. I opened a window. The professor was crumpled on the floor next to the sofa. His mangled walker lay nearby, its tennis balls squashed. A case for Carl Kolchak! When I checked for signs of life, that is when I saw it. A huge, disembodied, hairy arm. At first I thought it was a trick of the eye, like a mirage on hot asphalt, seen only from a certain angle.

Upon my approach, the arm became animated. It then grasped wildly about as if to crush or choke anything it might catch. A ragged claw snagged my shirt and ripped it open. The buttons flew off. I beat the arm with a walker leg until it stiffened and dematerialized.

The old Englishman's face was ashen and gaunt. He had been brutally beaten. The floating arm? On the coffee table were obvious traces of a familiar operation. Working quickly, I gathered whatever books and papers I could find nearby and stuffed them into my mansack. Wiping surfaces for fingerprints, I reasoned, could do no harm.

There was a pay phone by the pool. I called the cops to voice my concerns about Harrington's well-being. "Name?" said the dispatcher.

"A concerned citizen," I replied and hung up.

Took a direct route from Lot C to the library. The factory whistle sounded. Late again! I arrived in no mood for anyone's crap. I donned a tight cardigan from the lost and found to conceal my ripped shirt. A ladies' garment, I am afraid. I now smelled faintly of jasmine. For most of the morning I organized my desk in its new location outside the William Lawrence Peebles III Meeting Room. I decorated it with a droopy geranium from the break room. What is next? Soon I would be out in the cold, so to speak.

In the reading room I found the information desk shoved against the wall. Amber perched upon it, her legs dangling over the edge. Professor Boynton stood before her, uncomfortably close, in my opinion. I regarded him with crossed arms and gave him a withering glance.

"Come see me in my office next week. I can show you that pelvic bone I was telling you about," he said. Amber regarded him with a smile as the professor of marine biology walked away.

"He has a whole sperm whale skeleton," she said excitedly. I doubted this very much.

Nearby, an old man on his hands and knees was inscribing in chalk a giant circle upon the floor. "He's measuring for the book tower," said Amber.

I entered the circle and observed the old man. He wore a Polyflex patch on his shoulder. "The circle is forbidden, Ace," he commanded. I now recognized him as the guy who said I could not park in the Polyflex lot.

It was one thing after another. Someone poured an Icee into the book return. A student tailed me into the men's room to ask questions about the Geneva Convention. Spunt dumped a pile of armadillo jerky onto my desk then explained the entire jerky-making process. Where did he get the armadillo is what I would like to know. Says he can get his hands on a manual typewriter, however. Does he mean to steal Guddu's prize?

"From where?" I said. After all this time I still cannot decide if Spunt is a hedgehog or a fox. A hybrid?

"Haven't you heard? I've been promoted. You may now address me as Manager of Procurement."

"Procurement," I repeated. "Isn't that Mr, Snyder's job?"

"Not anymore."

How in the hell did Spunt manage a promotion after what happened at the retreat? There is more to that guy than meets the eye.


Diane's office is empty. As in cleaned out. No one could tell me anything until I encountered Boggs in the break room.

"Damn, it's hot," he said, patting his brow with a paper towel.

"Diane's gone."

"That's right," he said. "The boss terminated her first thing this morning. Escorted her off the campus myself.

"Just saw her yesterday evening. Do you know where she went?"

Boggs looked out the window. "Felt kind of sorry for her. She charmed me into giving her a ride to a no-tell motel. The Caravan. You know, on Jacksboro Highway."

"Did she tell you what happened?"

"I'd rather not say."

"Don't tell me she's got you under her spell, too," I said dubiously. I gestured to the potluck sign-in sheet. "Are you going to this?"

"Potluck's mandatory," said Boggs. "It's the Porteous way."

"Could use a break from mandatory events," I said. "The retreat was worth it, though, if only to see Professor Ziglar gussied up like Bruce Jenner. Looked like he belonged on a box of Wheaties."

"Something's wrong with that man," chuckled Boggs. "Been meaning to ask you. Talked to my brother long distance. He says I speak with a Texas accent now. Do I speak with a Texas accent, Steven?"

"No, Boggs. You speak with a heavy Queens accent." I fanned myself with a newspaper. "Ugh, this humidity. I could go for a dip."

"In the old neighborhood a fire hydrant was our swimming pool. By the way, why are you sitting in the hall now?"

"Ask Dixie."

Today's meeting agenda:

> Museum and book tower
> LC conversion project update
> Microform reader update
> Library Expo '77 follow-up
> Parking complaints
> Staff bathroom renovations
> Bookworms in the basement
> Personal use of library supplies.

There was no discussion of my new work space in the hallway. My co-workers seemed to accept it as unremarkable. Debate over the controversial book tower dominated the meeting. Support for it was evenly divided between foxes and hedgehogs. "No one has ever had a book tower like this," said Hazel pointlessly.

I furtively devoured an ancient Whitman's Sampler. Amber noticed and indicated I should share. As I slid the box across the table Hazel stopped talking momentarily and regarded me with lambent disapproval. I stopped chewing.

"That goes without saying," I said, a cashew cluster melting in my mouth. "What if someone falls to his death? Is Porteous responsible?" Everyone agreed it would be. Hazel's solution was to switch to a closed stacks model. Having had enough of this *yaje*, I turned to Dixie and asked "What happened to Diane?"

Dixie uncharacteristically beat around the bush. "Miss Bollinger's services are no longer desired," she said unconvincingly. The LC conversion project is nowhere near being completed. Indeed, no discernable work has been done on it at all. So what did Diane do this whole time?

"Guess I get my old office back, then?" Now that the witch is gone, I do not see why not. Otherwise, I have a bunch of stuff in the Vault that I should probably take home. While the threats of dwarfs and disembodied arms remain, I am reluctant to go into it. Besides, there is an infestation in the Vault. Wicker collected samples. He believes it is *Trogium pulsatorium*. Sarge recommends we fumigate with Zyklon B. Says he knows where he can get some.

"It'll take care of the vermin and silverfish, too," said Sarge. "Whatever ails you," he winked. And any dwarfs, I hoped. Perhaps the pests came through the rip in the fabric of space and time I caused. Bookworms from beyond! Remind me never to take advice from him.

Spent the rest of the day cataloging an interminable supply of festschrifts, which seem to be multiplying. What a bunch of back patting! An entire series is unbelievably dedicated to Professor Ziglar. These I moved to the bottom of the pile. To my surprise, there was one for Sherwood, edited by none other than Bertie Harrington. *Hidden Archaeology: Essays in Honor of James Marion Sherwood*. I could have kicked myself for not having taken more of an interest in Sherwood's work. The volume was published during Sherwood's pre-Emeritus days when I was still in high school. It contained contributions from Professors Purvis, and Boynton, as well as the Reverend Ralph Henry Pogue and L.F. himself, each addressing the man but little else. "Minor Sexual Deviance Among Sorority Girls" could only have been a product of Professor Ziglar's deranged mind. Harrington's was the lone piece that had anything remotely to do with Sherwood's research: "Longevity and Mysticism in Pre-Macrobian Times: An Archaeological Survey," in which it is suggested that certain peoples lived in excess of two hundred years. I had read of this before in the Bible and put no stock in it. Now, I am not so sure.

Turtle Man passed my desk on his way to the campus A.A. meeting. Leaving "The Animal" to lock up the library does not sit well with me, but that is between him and Dixie, I suppose.

"Why are you sitting out here?" he said. If someone asks me this again I will scream.

What would it be like to make the rules?

Lingered before the Chateau Villa on my way to Bobby's. The police must have come and gone by now. Part of me wanted to go back in and snoop around, but I was afraid. I never want to see that hairy arm again. Or whatever it might be attached to. Poor Professor Harrington!

The bass tracks for our next single were laid down without incident. The A-side was "Prog Paradigm," a bold choice for these decidedly anti-prog times. I nailed it on the first take.

Bonnie unplugged something. There was a loud *pop*. "You'll blow the speakers, stupid!" shouted Bobby.

"I'll try not to blow anything of yours again," said Bonnie in a hurt voice.

The B-side was a radio jingle for Studio 6333. It was simply "Up Your Hose (with a Rubber Nose)" doctored up with a disco beat. Bonnie said it was to help pay for production costs. From my mansack I produced a bundle of mayweed. I worked quickly so I would not call attention to what I was doing. There was little I could do about the smoke and the odor.

"What are you doing?" said Bonnie.

"It stinks in here."

"Well, it does now."

Tim perked up. "Are you holding out on us?"

"It's not for smoking," I said. "Go back to sleep."

For the first time, I used magic to create magic. An idea that should have seemed obvious to Agrippa and his followers. But in all my reading I have only seen it addressed in the codex. I labored over my bass part. For the spell to work, every note must be perfect. And it was. Everyone congratulated me on a job well done except Tim, who hates disco. "Nice job," said Dave II. "Adding C sharp and F sharp as leading tones to that minor pentatonic scale was a smart move. Honestly, I didn't know you had it in you." For a moment, I was proud. But then I felt like an imposter. That was not really me playing, was it? The Doom Hippie's dad is supposed to come in on Sunday morning and dub the spoken word part, unknowingly taking part in the spell that would destroy Studio 6333 the moment it reaches the airwaves.


No amount of muskrat farming could have saved a botched batch of Hamburger Helper. I had no appetite, anyway. I did manage to eat half a piece of dried armadillo meat while half-watching *Kojak*. Harrington's papers beckoned. Want to figure out what he was up to when he was croaked. Maybe this weekend. On this evening my nerves were too shot.

Spent a couple of hours painstakingly recording two Judas Priest albums onto a chrome cassette. I eschewed Dolby in favor of careful equalization. Tape hiss is a reliable indicator that the source material has not been unduly fussed with; it is natural and good for you. Kept my fingers on the recording level faders so no peaks sneaked past zero. Was too paranoid to wear headphones, but I turned the volume low so I would not disturb Vee. Listening to good music and fiddling with knobs soothes the spirit. I rocked out to the solos and decided they were fine examples of jamming. After Priest's spell wore off, I made nice labels for the cassette with Letraset lettering, then carefully listed the song titles and their timings on the insert.

Was looking forward to a Pibb I had placed in the freezer. Alas, when I looked, it had exploded.


FRIDAY, JUNE 10

Another hundred-degree day threatened. Bubba the stuffed armadillo is AWOL from the circulation desk. When I questioned Jenny about it, she said robotically, "You'll have to ask Mrs. Womack." No, thanks. Did not want to start my day with an armadillo controversy. Spent the morning researching Piltdown Man. Porteous has a whole book about it but it is in the Vault. I had sworn off Room 108 on account of dwarfs and hairy arms, but my curiosity got the better of me.

A broad shaft of yellow light shone from the doorway of the Vault. There were clear signs of some sort of a struggle. My Sherlock Holmes throne was askew and my record player had come unplugged, as if someone had stumbled over the cord. With no other clues to go on, I tidied up a bit then locked the door behind me. I resisted the urge to sacrifice any more Hogg sermons. And I stayed clear of you-know-what.

There was nothing in Bartlett's about Vee's pillow-kissing maxim. Where had she picked it up, I wonder? Since Dixie was lurking about, recreational reading at my desk was not an option. Left my old wallet on my desk to make it look like I was around, then headed to the business school cafeteria. Boggs spotted me and monopolized my time talking about how much he hated its architecture. Of course, I had to agree with him. The newer the building, the uglier it is, I have found.

"There's a new Chinese place a few blocks from here," I said. "Have you checked it out yet?"

"No. I stick to regular food. By the way, Carlos gave this to me earlier." Boggs produced a Polaroid showing a hand opening the door to the library.

"What's this?" I said.

"It's his hand opening the door. He says he found it unlocked when he arrived this morning."

"Why couldn't he have just used words?"

"What was he doing here at four a.m. is what I would like to know."

"He's always jacking with the boiler," I said. "Don't know why he bothers. The building is never at a comfortable temperature. You know, Turtle Man was supposed to lock up after the campus A.A. meeting."

"Who may I ask is Turtle Man?"

"That's what Professor Sherwood always called him."

"How'd he earn that nickname?" said Boggs.

"We probably don't want to know."

"You going to the Chisholm Trail Round-Up?"

"Nope," I said. "What's that?"

"Country and western music show," said Boggs. "Fiddles, banjoes, and whatnot. I'm going this evening. Would you care to accompany me? It's going to be at the Water Gardens."

"Sorry, Boggs. I would but my band is having a record release party this evening at the Eagle's Nest. You should stop by. There will be progressive rock and roll music."

"What time? First, I want to go to the mall. There's a boot close-out at JC Penney. Thirty percent off."

"You're slowly turning into a Texan, Boggs!"

Boggs chuckled. "I reckon I am, pardner."

I returned to the library. Professor Boynton was coming on pretty thick to the Stone Fox at the circulation desk, asking her if she was "AC or DC" and if he could look at her flippers for a minute.

"I'll cover the desk, Jenny. Finish cataloging those festschrifts," I said. Boynton looked at me like I had just pissed in his Wheaties and walked away.

"Flippers?" I said, confused. "Even I haven't seen those."

"Thanks for saving me," she said. "I would have told him off but he's golfing buddies with L.F. You know what that means. He could make life hell for me."

"You should tell Dixie."

"She's the one who told me not to make waves."

"Imagine having L.F. as a boss," I said. "No wonder Dixie is meaner than a junkyard hedgehog."

Jenny withdrew a compact from her purse. A tiny mouse fell out and scampered across the circulation desk. Jenny shrieked. Hazel emerged from the workroom with a can of hairspray. While chanting "Die!" she sprayed it on the creature until it drew to a halt, well shellacked. Despite Jenny's pleas, it ended up in the shenanigans dish.

The factory whistle sounded. Headed to the Eagle's Nest early for the a/c. I was the first one there. I put a dime in the jukebox and selected "Evil Woman."

Nothing happened. "Hey, Jackie," I said. "Over here." She made me pickle and pimiento loaf sandwich as I waited for the others.

"Where's your friend Randy?" she said.

"California."

"What's out there?"

I was not sure myself. "Family," I said.

Several Lone Stars later, friends of Bonnie and Tim trickled through the door. Bonnie's sister showed up with her artsy cohorts. Bobby was there. Fred showed up with Wheeler under his wing.

"The kid can't come in here," said Jackie.

"This is no kid," whispered Fred. "This is a twenty-nine-year-old midget."

"My mistake!" she said, somewhat flustered.

Fred ignored me so I ignored him. He brought an antique Soviet-made dumpling gun or some shit. Guests were passing it around and pointing it at each other. Some chick's bored husband sat at the end of the bar, staring into his beer. Felt bad for him, so I introduced myself. Gus is an auto mechanic. Over a couple of Flaming Mr. Pibbs we spoke about tropical fish, about which I know nothing—although I did mention Randy's bettas.

Guddu appeared out of nowhere. It is like he issued from the jukebox speakers. He just walked out of "Just Got Paid." He kept his distance, nursing a cigarette which never grew any shorter. His imp trickery gets on my nerves. What comes so naturally to him is difficult for me. No one spoke to him or even seemed to notice his presence. "Is that a joint?" I said.

"It is a marijuana doobie," said Guddu.

"Spoken like a true narc."

"Steven, what is a narc?"

"You are."

Hipgnosis never responded to Bonnie's inquiries, so Tim designed the album cover himself. The title appears in Shatter typeface opposite Bonnie's Time Frame logo. A black and white line drawing of a man in a straightjacket stares down a striped corridor which recedes into a single point in the distance. Tim said his inspiration was the old Leonard's subway. More likely it was one of his magic mushroom visions.

Tim examined one of the LPs. Bonnie relayed the story about how she caught a huge rat on live radio. "What the hell is this," asked Tim. He was squinting at the message in the runout groove.

"It's Dordic," I choked. I had forgotten about this! "It means 'To Irr, long they traveled through the, uh, dreamlands.' Cryptic messages in the runout groove is a tradition. You know how on The Immigrant Song it says 'Do what that wilt shall be the whole of the law'?"

"That's fine if you want people to think we're freaks."

"Heaven forbid people think *that*," I said, clutching at invisible pearls.

Tim shrugged and turned to face Jackie. "Put this on," he commanded. Jackie wordlessly took the record from him. Tim popped open a bottle of Almaden and sprayed it all over the place as the thunderous riff to "The Eagle Has Landed" split a few eardrums. "Get ready, y'all," he bawled. "We're going platinum!"

Hank the bored husband digs country. He showed no interest in our album other than to say the guitars are "too loud." He is right, but they do sound good. Bobby doubled Tim's tracks by having him play an octave lower or higher, which give them a meatier sound. At intervals I noticed the bass is either too low in the mix or missing altogether. Tim must have gotten his flippers on the faders.

We played a short acoustic set. No psychedelic light show, so Fred sat this one out. Bonnie played tambourine. Dave II negotiated an elaborate array of percussive instruments including celesta, glockenspiel, and gong. He dampened his snare with a banana peel. During our performance, I was distracted by my latest ideas concerning magic and music. When I missed a change, Tim shot me a withering glance.

Car Boy crashed through the front door on a chopper. His old lady clung to his torso like Velcro. It is not the first time that has happened at the Eagle's Nest. The crowd knew the drill. They grabbed their drinks and parted like the Red Sea. Careening through the tables and chairs, Car Boy rode up to me and pointed at my spurs. "That's Car Boy's," he growled.

The biker dismounted and balled his fists. Before I realized what was happening, he threw a hook which, had it connected, might have knocked me out. Instead, his brass knuckles froze mid-swing. His face bore an expression of confusion. After a brief tussle with an unseen force, he then punched himself in the nose. The blow knocked him backwards over his chopper, which crashed against the jukebox. I had seen similar stunts countless times on *Gunsmoke*. But this was no stunt. Through the glare of the stage lights, I spotted Guddu in the corner, dumpling gun in hand. Cheers to the band for continuing to play throughout all this.

We finished the song then played a few more. At intervals I spotted Car Boy glaring at me, a bloody cocktail napkin dangling from his nostril. When I could stand it no more, I implemented the *Death Stare*, a formula based on the Fear turned outward. With enough mojo behind it I suppose you could kill someone, hence the cool name I chose for it. This neat trick was made possible by the techniques learned from the Martin Solis book. At first, Car Boy looked mad, like he was going to try to punch me again. But then his face turned ashen. He slapped his lady on the arm, then got up and made a hasty exit. The look on his face as he glanced over his shoulder told me all I needed to know. The formula worked. I then gave Guddu a little taste, to let him know I did not need him to fight my battles for me. He cowered behind the cigarette machine. Good.

"Are those really Car Boy's?" said Bonnie.

"Yes," I said. "Vee got them from him. I don't actually know if he gave them to her or if she pinched them. I just know that if Vee asked me for my spurs I would kneel and put them on her boots myself."

Bonnie clutched my arm. "You have to give them back," she said urgently.

"They're mine now," I said firmly. "Car Boy took off."

Boggs approached. "My main man! That was quite the show, if I may say so. Just wanted to shake your hand and offer congratulations." He then produced a copy of our album and a pen. "Would you do the honors, sir?"

"You do know we're not famous, Boggs."

"You never know. Someday you might be. Then this record is going to be worth a penny or two. And I can say I was right there that night in 1977 at the Eagle's Nest. Fort Worth. Texas."

Almost bumped into Fred on the way out. "Hey," I said. "You didn't show up at Old South. Wanted to meet so I could apologize."

"But I did show up," said Fred. "Wheeler said seven o'clock."

"Well, I stuck around until almost eight. I had to leave because I had a bunch of shit to do that day."

"What do you mean? What else did you need to do at eight in the evening?"

"Eight in the *morning*, Fred. Nobody drinks coffee at night."

"Man, that's the only time I drink coffee. I don't even wake up until ten or eleven. You know that."

Fred and I stayed until closing. He accepted my apology but I can tell something has changed between us. I decided not to tell him about Sherwood or muskrat farming. It is probably for the best.


SATURDAY, JUNE 11

Encountered Carlos in the vestibule when I arrived this morning. He bore a small casket. He opened it up revealing a plush interior within which reposed a regal amphibian.

"Old Rip!" I declared. Guess my spell had finally worn off.

"Pneumonia," said Carlos, crossing himself. "May his soul rest in peace." To my ears, Carlos's speech was a bit off. Slower and more deliberate, like someone leaning to speak again after a stroke. Was going to ask him if he was okay but figured it was none of my business. I watched him install Old Rip in the display case and wondered if this had anything to do with L.F.'s museum plans.

"Carlos, what happened to you in Room 108? What did you see in there?"

"What are you doing?" said Dixie. "That's not your job." What is she doing here on a Saturday? There goes my day of R&R.

"Nothing," I said sharply. "I was just talking to Carlos."

"Your department and his have nothing to communicate."

Dixie waddled away. When she was out of earshot Carlos looked at me and slowly muttered, "*Ay ay ay.*"

The factory whistle sounded. On a Saturday? With Amber manning the desk, I settled down at my own station in the hall. Someone swiped my old wallet I had left there. It was relatively peaceful except for a constant stream of people using the water fountain and Carlos's muffled sawing and hammering in the staff bathroom.

Forgot my lunch so I walked over to the business school cafeteria. I was so used to Randy and me ordering under fake names that I gave one now, Mr. Sleeve Lint. Then, I waited. And I waited. When no one called "Mr. Sleeve Lint," I inquired at the register. "What's the name again?" said the bored lunch lady.

"Mr. Sleeve Lint," I said sheepishly.

"Sorry. Nothing for a Mr. Sleeve Lint."

"Is there any unclaimed egg salad?"

"No."

"Are there any unclaimed orders at all?"

"No."

"You have been most helpful." I felt like I no longer existed. At least under the name Mr. Sleeve Lint. As Steven Miller I felt as massive as a black hole. Everything that enters my orbit is slowly ripped apart. Surely that is not the case. How much easier life would be, to not exist.

Amber was just hanging up the phone when I arrived to relieve her. "Who was that?

"Another crank call," she said. "He said his name was Krolok."

"What did he want?" I tried to conceal my surprise.

"He said a bunch of jive talk. I told him to stop calling but he won't." I noted Amber's use of slang. It seemed out of character. Where is she picking it up from?

It will not do to have occult entities calling my workplace. Good grief, first Shagduk and now this guy. I do not even know that he is a guy. For all I know he could be a brain in a jar. I must put an end to it somehow.

There was nothing in the pantry and I did not feel like going to Roy Pope. Found a half-empty box of fish sticks in the freezer encased in a chunk of coarse ice. These would have been fine had I not dropped the baking sheet as I was removing it from the oven. The fish sticks melted the linoleum, which evidently stuck to the food because I could taste it.

Among his papers I found Harrington's own version of a door spell. What did he think was on the other side? The formula was followed by scribbled notes in Harrington's own cipher. It took me all of five minutes to crack it.

It was time to put my latest musical schemes to the test. The attempt had to be something I could immediately and easily verify, and simple enough to translate, so to speak, into a melody. Parting the waters would involve filling up the bathtub. Too easy. Charming Vee was out of the question. Invisibility? If I was going to put that much effort into it, I may as well try Harrington's formula. What is the worst that could happen?

Preparations took several hours. Fred's *Oblique Strategies* deck helped me overcome a couple of obstacles: "Remember quiet evenings?" and "Discard an axiom." I hope I do not become too dependent on the cards. At last, I picked up my trombone and got comfortable on the couch. There was nothing left to do but begin. In retrospect, I cannot pinpoint where it all went wrong. Perhaps it was the discarding of that axiom. Or the wow and flutter introduced by the tape recorders. To produce harmonic complexity in the absence of other musicians, I had employed two Scully 8-track units for a slap back effect. A trick I learned from Fred. Next time, maybe Bobby would loan me his Echoplex. At any rate, I now found myself standing in a vacant lot, staring at what used to be my house. In place of Collinwood, there jutted obscenely into the nighttime sky a bouquet of jagged, cyclopean shapes. The sky itself comprised myriad mirrored shards, each reflecting upon the other flashes of familiar scenery: the bright lights of the Showdown, All Saints' steeple, even a glimpse of Farrington Field some two and a half miles distant. The Rambler was barely recognizable as a mint green polyhedron, like one of those D&D dice. The ground beneath my feet was merely a jumble of geometrical abominations. Vertigo quickly gave way to panic as I struggled to discover which way was up.

When all seemed lost, I caught a fleeting glimpse of a man. His robe flapped wildly about as he, too, fought for composure. He lifted his staff and shouted a word. His image separated into colored beams that merged and vanished. I, too, collapsed into a singularity, like a TV screen when you turn it off. Then it was all over. I was once again sitting on my couch, trombone in hand. An odd reek hung in the air.

The accretion of several ideas, none in themselves decisive, had informed my decision to act. I just needed to see what would happen. At least I did not get the hairy arm. The ordeal drained me. Had the mysterious robed figure not intervened, I might not have survived.

Sunday, June 12

Woke up feeling like hell. It was cooler outside than inside, so I stepped onto the porch for a smoke. Found the new phone book in the bushes. I know I am not in it, but I checked all the same. I took a seat on the porch and looked up everyone I knew. Randy did not have a phone. Diane would not be listed under any name. Sherwood's number is no longer in service. For the life of me, I could not remember Vee's surname. Ah, there she was: Veronica Brooks. Loretta's name irked me, if only because she is the one who ran up my bill by calling the west coast all the time. I spoke her name. I do not know why.

Vee's door was fastened, which is somewhat unusual. After tapping twice, I heard a muffled shout, "Come in!"

Vee was not in the front room or kitchen. I made my way to her bedroom, where I found her in bed with Blue Van. "Oh!" I said involuntarily. Vee sat up, clutching a sheet to her bosom. "Whatcha doin'?" Blue Van just lay there smoking, staring back at me.

"Was thinking about mowing the lawn," I ad-libbed.

Vee shook her head. "Not with that piece of junk in the shed! Would you hand me that bag on the mamasan chair?" She dug around in it then produced a little date book. She flipped through it, said "Call the DDT kid's mom." She read the digits aloud. "Or you could just cross the street, knock on their door."

"Got it," I said. Is he even old enough to operate a lawn mower?

"Is that what you came up here for?" Vee smiled sweetly at me, like I was a child who had just brought her a dandelion.

"Thought you might want to show me how to care for Figgy while you're in Italy."

"Come back in half an hour." Blue Van looked pissed. He was probably ready to pull the wool over Vee's eyes and I was cramping his style. "*Ci vediamo allora!*" I blurted. "Nice to see you again, Blue, uh, Van."

"What did you call me, faggot?"

"Keith!" cried Vee, glancing at me apologetically as I turned to leave.

Blue Van was gone when I returned. Vee was up and about. She showed me where Figgy's food and medicine was and provided instructions. "There's a cat carrier in that closet, in case there's an emergency." When Vee started telling me about bonus water, I wondered if I should be jotting this all down.

"Steven, you're a real dollface for doing this," said Vee. "I really appreciate it."

"No problem," I said. "Figaro and I are pals, aren't we, Figgy?" The cat had his back to me. He licked his paw. "Go ahead. Ignore me!"

To Roy Pope for groceries. Checked the circular rack for Silurian paperbacks to take my mind off yesterday evening's near catastrophe. A brief thunderstorm cooled things off but also made it more humid. Was headed back to Collinwood when I spotted Loretta going west on Camp Bowie. Eerie how you can say someone's name aloud and then they appear. If only that worked for Sherwood. I had dreaded this moment but I was now hopeful. Loretta waved and I made a peace symbol back. We caught up to each other in the King Wok parking lot.

We got out of our cars laughing and hugged. I looked down into two pert, sparkling eyes under a coarse fringe of dirty blond hair. Time heals all wounds, as they say. We chatted like old friends until I made an off-hand remark about the heat.

"Come to my place," said Loretta. "You can take a dip in the pool. We can have some tea and catch up." When I hesitated, she added, "I have a/c."

I parked on the street then tailed Loretta up the metal steps to her garage apartment on Dorothy Lane. She entered without unlocking the door. It used to drive me crazy when she left our door unlocked. She tossed her keys into a fruit bowl. "Ninety-five a month," she said, anticipating my question. I immediately spotted my antique roll-top desk which had once belonged to Governor Jester. And there, on the mantelpiece, the lucite lady, a classical statuette that Loretta and I had fought over. That *Golden Age of Piano Virtuosi* album? Mine. Bet she does not even listen to it.

A Leon Redbone album caught my eye. "Remember when we hung out with Leon Redbone in his trailer?" I said. Loretta and Leon talked about Fats Waller and Mongolian throat singers into the wee hours. I just sat there sweating and trying not to fall asleep. Loretta could charm the socks off of anyone.

"It's rented," she said when she saw me turning knobs on her color TV. "From the 7-Eleven on Hemphill. Shall I give you the grand tour?"

The lovely apartment consisted of a large room divided by an ornamental elbow-high wall, a tiny kitchen, and a bathroom with adjoining dressing alcove. Loretta clearly lived alone. I wondered if she was still sleeping with Gabrielle. Fresh daffodils adorned the small table at which we used to share our meals. I lingered by a bookcase, looking for any of the titles that Loretta ended up with when we divvied up our library. Instead of Flaubert and Zola I was now seeing Betty Friedan, Kate Millett, and Germaine Greer. And then, I spotted it. A pink Princess telephone. That such an innocuous object could cause such a surge of anger through my body was remarkable, but I held my tongue. Because of Loretta, I have been living without a telephone. Frankly, that has worked out just fine. "Where are you working these days?"

"Polyflex," she said. "I make hooks."

"Hooks for what?" If Loretta and Tim can work there, they cannot be that serious an organization, I decided.

Loretta's face clouded. "Do you do business with Polyflex?"

"I don't even know what they do," I said. I raised my finger to my mustache.

"What are you doing?"

"Blocking a sneeze by applying pressure on the trigeminal nerve."

"That doesn't work," said Loretta with a dismissive wave. "If you want to cool off in the pool, I'll put the kettle on."

"No Lipton?" I said. "When you said tea I thought you meant iced tea."

Loretta made a face, like she used to do whenever I put on symphonic music. "Conductors don't do anything," she used to say. It drove me crazy. I resolved to leave if she started that shit again. I found myself staring at her. Everyone looks like somebody. People say I look like the drummer for the James Gang. Loretta does not look like anyone else. Her nipples protruded through a men's tank top. I noticed with some amusement that she no longer shaves her armpits. "Chamomile," she said. "Tea for grown-ups."

"If Lipton's good enough for Don Meredith, it's good enough for me." I said. I had no intention of letting her know she was getting under my skin. She put the kettle on, then disappeared into the bathroom. The second she closed the door, I grabbed *Golden Age of Piano Virtuosi* and the lucite lady and tossed them out an open window into the bushes below. Petty, I know. I also yanked her pink Princess telephone cord out of the wall. I should strangle her with it. When she returned, I asked her if she had a bathing suit I could borrow.

"Just wear what you're wearing."

"How do I get over there?" I said, looking out the window.

"Not my landlord's pool," said Loretta. She indicated a different window. "That one, by the pagoda. Take as long as you like. The kettle needs to boil and I have a few bills to pay."

"That's a grim pergola."

Loretta sighed deeply. "A grim pergola? Why must you always—" Her voice trailed off. "Never mind."

"That's what it is," I asserted. This might have been a good time to ask her to pay my phone bill, but we were getting along so well. The pool turned out to be a tiny plastic one for kids. I slaked my thirst on scalding hose water before filling the pool. I took off my shirt and sat in the water. Despite feeling like a child, it felt refreshing. Loretta always had a way of making me feel like a child. I regarded her car, a Monza hatchback with racing stripes. Guess she is making her car payments on time for once.

Removing the cellophane from a fresh pack of Kents, I considered everything I knew about my ex-girlfriend. My first thought was how this information could be used against her. What does that say about me? Except it could not. She is too self-assured to be ashamed of any past deed. In the meantime, she ostensibly knows more secrets about me than Fred. Secrets I have worked so hard to forget.

A passing driver blared his horn. Spunt in his hearse. I flipped him off but I do not know if he saw. My anger returned. Why was I here? Why would I risk subjecting myself to Loretta's infuriating *yaje* after all that had happened?

My wet shorts squished when I got behind the wheel. I sped away without saying goodbye. The lucite lady gazed up at me from the passenger seat. The piano LP had another ten minutes, tops, before it would warp from the heat. In the back seat were my wilting lettuce and melted spumoni, which I had forgotten were there. My stomach ached from yesterday's linoleum fish sticks. Or maybe I was developing an ulcer. On my way home I examined my feelings about Loretta. I still tend to deal with people passively and let resentment build. Speaking my mind should have been one of my new year's resolutions.

My encounter with Loretta, followed by an afternoon of unsuccessful musk-rat farming, put me in a funk. After boiling my bass strings, I took a shower then headed upstairs to Vee's. I found her sitting under the hair dryer in a towel. "You scared me!" she cried. She regarded me in my red satin tux. "Oh my god, is it time to go?"

Vee fluttered about getting dressed. She hunched over her vanity, applying false eyelashes. She then stood on the bathroom scale. "Shoot, I've gained three ounces!"

"Must be the dress," I quipped. "That's quite an outfit for Z Boaz Park. Are you sure you want to wear those heels?" Funny, I never figured Vee was the calorie-counting type. I reckoned the deep cleavage was for Tim's benefit, but I guess that is none of my business. "Where's Dawn?"

"She had to go to a memorial service," said Vee. "I think I hear her pulling up now." Vee put on earrings then made some pharaonic poses in the mirror.

Dawn was attired conservatively in black. "Who died?" I said.

Vee cast an admonishing glance my way. "Steven!" she said.

"Sorry!" I said. "Vee just told me you attended a memorial service. Guess I heard the words without comprehending them."

"It's alright," said Dawn. "Otis passed away. You may have met him at the museum after the rodent incident." Her expression became troubled.

"Oh, no! I'm so sorry, Dawn," I said. "Who is Otis again?"

"The janitor."

The person she called to deal with Shagduk. I wonder if he died from any-thing the imp did to him? Three months is a long time to suffer.

Vee retrieved a shiny garment from the mamasan and tossed it to Dawn. "You can change in the car," she said.

"What about my shoes?" moaned Dawn. Vee tossed her a pair of stilettos.

There was no time to acclimate our bare thighs to the hot vinyl. We rocked in our seats and bore the pain, as one does. We turned onto Camp Bowie. Vee fumbled around in her purse then said, "Can we stop for smokes?" I peered at Dawn in the rear view squirming out of her skirt in the back seat.

Traffic around Z Boaz was heavy. We had to park on the shoulder of Benbrook Boulevard. Families in Time Frame t-shirts filed past with folding chairs and coolers. What was going on?

We got out of the car. Vee squealed with laughter at Dawn, who was awkwardly adjusting the outfit Vee had loaned her. Her mousy hair was charmingly disheveled. I recalled our last kiss and looked forward to pulling the wool over her eyes soon.

"You're wearing it upside down!" said Vee.

Dawn looked down in confusion. Indeed, Dawn had somehow put the silver Lurex bodysuit on so that the crotch served as a strap over one shoulder. A narrow shoulder strap threaded between her thighs like dental floss. The mistake made more sense when I understood the garment was asymmetrical.

"That's hot stuff," said Vee. "But you can't parade around in that!" Vee guarded Dawn while she put the bodysuit on correctly behind the Rambler's open door.

"The people in that helicopter can see you," I said teasingly. Nearby, the Channel 8 news team emerged from a van with tripods.

"Oh no!" cried Dawn. "This thing got me on the ankle. It ripped my nylons."

"That's a curb feeler." I leaned down to examine it. The little ball at the end had been scraped off, resulting in a sharp point.

We moved slowly on account of Dawn in stilettos. When we finally reached the stage, the band was preparing for a sound check. Tim greeted me with a glare. He wore a Team Puce t-shirt. Where did he get it?

I plugged in my bass. There was a horrible crackle from the speakers. Tim almost jumped out of his skin, as he does whenever there is a sudden loud noise. "Let there be sound!" I announced dramatically into the mic. Then there was no sound. Bobby got to work sorting out the problem.

"The reviews are in," said Bonnie, holding up copies of *Buddy* and *Fortnite Weekly*. "'Prog rock scum set to bum you out,'" she read aloud. "'Unspeakably pompous offal that lacks much of the human dimension one usually associates with music. Why play three chords when you can play three hundred?'"

"Why do they hate you so much?" said Dawn. Thought I detected a hint of disgust in her voice.

"Do they?" I said. "Look at all these people!"

"The reviewer takes a shot at Fred. 'Lacking any mentionable instrumental proficiency, Fred Knox claims he 'treats' the other musicians' instruments, though the end product of his efforts would have to be classed as indiscernible.'"

"To the untrained ear, perhaps," I said. "What does the other review say?"

"'A *tour de remorse*,'" continued Bonnie. "'The cover says *play loud* but *Subways of Your Mind* is equally damaging at any volume."

"No one appreciates serious music anymore," said Tim. "Meanwhile, they praise the Ramones. What do those guys have that we don't, besides fake names and identical jackets?"

"I have a surprise for all of you," said Bonnie. "We're opening for Kansas on their upcoming tour to support their new album. It was either Crawler or us and they chose us!"

The gig was another one of Bonnie's sister's charity events. For what, I never discovered. She must be raking it in. There were carnival games and food: hamburgers, hot dogs, and homemade ice cream. All of it cost tickets. Band members were given five each but then a beer cost five tickets. Vee and Dawn volunteered to wait in line for us.

We took our places on stage. I was sweating my ass off in my tux. Evidently, the corrugated fiberglass shade canopy had not been replaced since the tornado, so we would have to play in direct sunlight. There was a commotion stage left. Tim was getting into it with some huge bastard who looked like an FBI agent. The huge bastard belted Tim in the ear, then said, "Count your lucky stars that's Tony's cough and not Ozzy's."

Bonnie and I rushed to Tim's aid. "Tim, who was that?" cried Bonnie.

"Said he was Black Sabbath's counsel."

"How did he know about the cough?" I said.

"I sent a demo to Vertigo," said Bonnie.

Tim turned to look at me. "That cough was your dumb idea," he said.

"No, it wasn't," I said. "It was Fred's."

There seemed to be some competing magic in the air. The negative reviews, the lawyer from Vertigo. And the huge audience. What did it mean?

Throughout almost the entire set, fueled by Tim's arrogance, I found myself vying with him on stage for the girls' attention. Whenever he thought they were cheering me on and not him, he would start showing off. He spun his guitar around his neck. He embellished songs with Baroque flourishes. Soon he was racing around like Pete Townshend on speed. He certainly knows how to excite the crowd's awe. All eyes were now on Tim. Even Boggs, who I spotted under a mesquite. He was wearing a Time Frame t-shirt. Where are people getting them?

We decided to end with "Masturbator von Nürnberg." Time for some muskrat farming! With the whole band playing in unison, it should be a piece of cake to charm one or more people in, say, a twenty-foot circle of influence, to cheer wildly for me and not Tim. That the tune was in E major, a key associated with joy, was serendipitous.

The occasion called for the royal *nempiri*. I miked it through the F-800B. For good measure, I turned the mojo knob all the way up. Unfortunately, I failed to realize I had no experience playing the cursed trumpet. At the climax of my solo I reached for the mallet and struck the gong. At the exact same instant, Tim broke all his strings at once. Did my orphic victory charm cause that to happen? Or Tim's bloody windmills? We took a break so he could put on new strings.

Took this opportunity to run to the restroom. Of course there was a line. As I was washing my hands, I heard amplified bass guitar. "What the hell?" Before I could reach the stage, the band had launched into "Green-Eyed Lady," a Sugarloaf song Tim and Bonnie used to cover in Aperture. The crowd went nuts.

My jaw hit the deck when I saw it was Jack Chuck playing my Rick. Had he asked politely, I would have agreed to let Tim and Bonnie's former band-mate join in. Guess he is back from Alaska. His new artificial leg looks very convincing, I will give him that. When the song ended, they launched into "Journey to Dord" right in front of me. That of course made me madder. How did Jack Chuck even know it? Unless he was just faking his way through. Some musicians are just that good. His bass solo was amazing, naturally. The way Tim was stink-eyeing me, I was afraid he somehow knew about my musical hocus-pocus.

"Let's boogie," I said into Vee's ear. If Tim thought he was getting a piece of Vee's ass tonight, he can think again. As the girls and I wended our way through the crowd, Vee twisted her ankle. She put her arm around my waist for support. Tim would not have known about her ankle, of course. From his point of view, it looked like she and I were together. Damn, that motherfucker is going to be mad.

Had intended not to look back, but I could not help myself. With a gesture, Jack Chuck's amp fizzled out. As with most petty revenge, I regretted it at once. I ended up disappointing hundreds of people who had been enjoying themselves.

"What about your stuff?" said Dawn.

"That's all Diane's property," I said. "Except my trombone. Tim can shove it up his ass."

"What do you mean it's Diane's property?" said Dawn suspiciously.

"It's a long story," I said.

The girls waited by the playground. I trudged along Benbrook Boulevard to retrieve the Rambler. The car would not turn over. I had to walk all the way back and get Dawn. It took her an instant to diagnose a broken fan belt. It took another to peel off her nylons and resolve the problem.

"Where did you learn how to do that?" I said. I examined her quick fix and noted her use of a triple bosun's knot.

"Hints from Heloise!"

"Really?" I said dubiously. "Heloise does engines? What else does she do?"

The Rambler limped back to Collinwood. Dawn and I helped Vee upstairs and deposited her on the couch. Was tempted to linger but when Dawn made to leave, I decided to call it a night. I was determined to figure out if Jack Chuck's appearance was my doing. I saw Dawn out. As she pulled away, she rolled down her window. "I'll come by in the morning to fix your fan belt." She made it sound like an obligation rather than a sweet favor for a love interest.

Did not notice the white dually parked around the corner. Muffled sounds of partying issued from my bedroom. The Doobies blared from the stereo. Jenny's voice could be heard singing along: "Take me, take me..."

I burst into the room into billowing clouds of incense. I found the Stone Fox and the Doom Hippie sitting on my bed with a million lit candles. Guess I should have seen this coming. "What the hell?" I demanded.

Jenny scrambled to adjust her hot pants. Judd rose to his feet and turned up the collar of his jacket with a *snap*. Clipped directly into the flesh of his bare, bleeding scalp was what appeared to a fox tail. I bristled at his choice of species. In a macho display of bravado, he ripped my phone book in half. His rough, hairy forearms bulged from the effort.

"Get lost," I said.

"Wain't bothering nobody," said the Doom Hippie indignantly. He fingered the bell on Jenny's black ribbon choker. "Besides, I'm a guest here."

"This is my house and I am asking you to leave."

"Or what?" said the Doom Hippie balefully. He moved closer so his nose touched mine. "You'll turn me into a toad?"

I could not have this asshole talking to me like this in my own home. Especially in front of the Stone Fox. I put up my dukes. The Doom Hippie put up his own and we began feinting around the bed. I threw the first punch. Judd, clearly an experienced fighter, deflected it easily. He then slugged me hard in the solar plexus, briefly knocking the wind out of me. Soon, we were rolling around on the rug, tipping over candles. Uncle Daryl had educated me on striking first and striking hard. "Go for the eyes, the nuts," he said. "The aim is to maim." Is that the goal of a brawl? Or is it to subjugate? To kill? No one told me the rules. I bit Judd hard on the Adam's apple. A taste of his own medicine. He screamed and shoved me away. Once back on our feet, he looked at me like I had hurt his feelings. "What are you, a vampire?" he muttered.

There was a click. The Doom Hippie was flicking his Bic and sniffing the flame. He thrust it threateningly in my face. The Remington was on the other side of the room, as was Tim's axe. Circling closer to the window, I reached for my Brannock device. Judd kept looking at it in my hand, trying to figure out what it was. He found out when I smashed his ear with it. He pulled his gun.

For this, I had a formula. Must have worked, for he shoved the useless item back into his waistband. I dealt him a palm to the spleen. He gasped in pain. Spittle formed at the corners of his mouth. "I'm going to burn this sucker to the ground!" he shouted. I grabbed him by his jacket and dragged him out the door. Tossed his Thermos after him. There was the sound of burning rubber.

Jenny was huddled behind a pillow. I bade her stand and come forward. She was scantily clad and wore a lot of mascara. I refrained from commenting on her Dorothy Hamill haircut. Not that I cared. I was in no mood to hear her excuses, which I knew would only exasperate me further. And coming from Jenny's trap, they would not even make sense. Could never decipher chicks, but Jenny's code was always the hardest of all to crack. An untroubled and outrageous personality whose depths I have not even begun to plumb. "My key," I said. Jenny retrieved it from her purse. "You should leave, too."

Jenny pursed her lips. "Give me a ride?" she said without a hint of remorse. I expected that question to be uttered sheepishly, at the very least. Her manner indicated everything was perfectly hunky dory. I thought I had even detected a seductive note in her voice. One last attempt to manipulate me.

"Take the Huffy. Go out the back door. It's under the steps." The Stone Fox hesitated then gave me a withering look. I cannot believe I was kicking a body like that out of my bed.

Jenny left her coke vacuum on my bedside table. I opened some windows and turned the fans on. I put the spare key back under the flower pot. If Dawn had stayed she would have witnessed all this *yaje*. I turned on a lamp then extinguished what remaining candles were upright. Wax was all over the rug, the bedside table, and even the wainscoting. A wine glass lay in pieces upon a red stain. By the commode I found one of the decorative colored bottles I keep above the kitchen sink. It was partially filled with butts, even though I own numerous ashtrays. I cleaned up and fantasized about the Doom Hippie's demise. With all the recent advances in forensic science, it would probably be impossible to get away with it. I have a motive and, thanks to the author of *Successful Muskrat Farming*, the means. Had I croaked him just now, one could have argued self-defense. But the legal fallout would be intolerable. Not to mention living the rest of my life knowing I killed a human being. Something tells me the flame sniffer's pop is already mourning him from his disco offices.

Stayed up late listening to Steely Dan while researching ways of croaking the Doom Hippie. Instead, I found a formula that would certainly work to get rid of the imp. If only Randy were here. Aspects of its almost theatrical execution baffle me. The spell I had used on the Doom Hippie worked almost effortlessly, despite its casual execution. Often, I get bogged down in minutiae and nothing works. Or it backfires.

I could not fall asleep. When I am not preoccupied with memorizing formulae, I am anxious about everything that has been going on. I left my royal *nempiri* at Z Boaz. I will get it back from Bonnie. What a reliable friend she is. There are times where my mind is relaxed or empty, or when I am thinking about something pleasant. Reveries of romantic prospects offer only confusion and doubt. I did something I never do and looked at the clock. Two-thirty, the deepest part of the night. Which meant that if I nodded off right now, I would get three and a half hours of sleep.

Something has got to give. It may as well be Time Frame. It has become impossible to participate in the band and keep up with muskrat farming. I have become so disciplined lately. And hitting the books is paying off.

I got up for a glass of water. I turned on the kitchen light. The robed figure from before was sitting at the table. Again, his face was obscured by a hood. He was smoking a slender pipe. Before I could speak, he vanished. I just stood there staring dumbly at the dissipating cloud of smoke.


Monday, June 13

A cursed day. The 13th was, that is. I am writing this down on the 15th whenever I can find the odd moment to myself. Monday began innocuously enough. Dawn arrived early to fix my fan belt, fulfilling her promise. With skepticism I watched as she removed her filthy nylons then replaced them with a new pair. "This is temporary, right? I said.

"The old ones were control top," said Dawn. "These are sheer energy. They'll last a long time." She slammed the hood. "You're leaking oil," continued. "Some cat litter might soak up these stains." At first I thought she meant me, that I was leaking oil. Afterward, I made coffee and we shared a cigarette in the kitchen.

"Was wondering if you wanted to do something this Sunday," I said. "Maybe go to the zoo or planetarium."

"I'm pretty busy that day," said Dawn. "And that evening I'm going to see Journey. They're playing with R.E.O. and Priest."

"Wow, that's a great lineup." I did not want to invite myself, and was somewhat hurt she did not ask me to go with her.

"What's this?" said Dawn. She pointed at one of the ripped halves of my torn phone book. I attempted in vain to tear one into quarters. She looked at me through her Coke-bottle glasses like I was a retard. I tossed the phone book aside and took her face in my hands. She squirmed away from me. Without a word, she went upstairs. Ostensibly to say goodbye to Vee, who is leaving this morning for Italy.

Despite being 'Dillo Day at Porteous, the library was in a vile mood. Carlos has begun cutting through the floor in the reading room to accommodate the book tower. He yelled at a pack of feral co-eds who had knocked down his illegible sign. The noise and dust are unbearable. Knowing him, he will complete the circle and fall into the Vault. I do not dare go down there to see what they have done.

With so much on my mind—strange wizards in my kitchen, and now Dawn's behavior—I had forgotten to bring or even make the cowboy stew. Hopefully, no one would notice. Encountered Hazel in the break room. She was removing cling wrap from a cheese and pineapple hedgehog. The culinary horror gave a more bitter impression of hate than one of Dixie's sharp rebukes. Too bad Randy was not here to witness it. He would have busted a gut.

The word of the day was "oust." Which is fitting because Monty was ousted first thing this morning. No one seemed to know anything about it. It pained me to think the gentle soul was let go without just cause. I will miss his purple hair and our opera chats. Doris was next. Boggs kindly led her through the vestibule. I expected she would shout something pithy. Instead, her countenance was one of utter defeat.

Jenny and I were both wearing matching white slacks. I joylessly thrust my hip toward her. The Stone Hedgehog declined to bump, the slut. How the worm has turned.

"Why do you sit in the hall now?" she said. Before I could scream, she continued. "Your friend Turtle Man is missing."

"How do you know?"

"Spunt told me. No one has heard from him since Thursday."

"Boggs told me he found the library unlocked the following morning," I said. "Turtle Man was supposed to have locked up."

"You forgot this," I added. I put Jenny's coke vacuum into the small cloisonné shenanigans dish where it joined Sarge's butt and a shellacked mouse. I looked at her and waited for one of her four basic expressions. She now bore a fifth, one of complete indifference. Guess she is over me.

The information desk now sits by the globe. On my way to it, I took the opportunity to write "Mrs. Womack is a hedgehog" on a slip of paper and put it in the suggestion box. I do not think Amber saw me, nor do I care. "Here he is now," Amber said, speaking on the telephone. She handed me the receiver. "Is it the crank caller?" I whispered to her. She shook her head.

"This is Steven," I said. It was Abner, a debt collector from the Nationwide Accounts Systems calling about a check that bounced back in April. For a couple of hideous ties purchased in defiance of Porteous's antiquated dress code. After fees, $5.98 had now ballooned to $14.44.

"Refusal to pay will result in immediate and appropriate adverse legal action," said Abner threateningly. He wanted me to send it by "express mail," which sounded unnecessary and expensive. "Don't nickel and dime me!" I howled over the roar of Carlos's electric saw. "I'll send it to you but you'll get it when you get it." I then hung up on him.

"Your voice is so deep," observed Amber.

"I can go deeper than that," I said. I sang a few bars of Figaro's aria from *The Barber of Seville*. Amber stood with arms crossed. Speaking of Figaro, I must remember to feed the finicky feline when I get home.

"I didn't say I liked it."

For the rest of our shift, Amber and I took turns answering the phone *basso profondo*. To make oneself heard over the noise, one almost had to. That kid is really something. It is hard to believe she is related to Dixie.

One of the calls was Misty. I made knife gestures across my throat. "Tell her I'm not here," I whispered.

Amber thrust the receiver toward me. "I won't lie for you," she said.

"This is Steven."

"I was just wondering," said Misty cheerfully. "Since you said you wanted to see the campanile, I thought I might show it to you today on your lunch break. I made us some po' boys." Rather presumptuous of her, I thought. She should have asked Vince Greco from the Athletics Department.

"There's a potluck today," I said. "I'm stuck on the desk until one."

"Come after the potluck," she said. "I'll wait."

Amber was gone when I hung up. I was relieved not to join the others. Just when I thought I may enjoy some peace and quiet, a guitar and bongo tune in D-sharp minor penetrated the walls of the building and pecked at my brain. Every fear, every hesitation of the shuddering heart, oozes out of that horrible key.

Only one person was sitting near the globe. I recognized him as Ron Wooten. The same guy who sucker punched me after school in the fourth grade after a game of Truth or Dare in which Becky Ramirez and I kissed. He must have been jealous.

The chatter of the bongos rose and fell, rose again. Each time I looked over at Ron Wooten I got madder. I wondered if there was a formula I could use just to get back at him. None of the ones I knew were appropriate in this scenario, except maybe *Dental Liquefaction*.

Ron Wooten got up and headed toward the men's room. I nonchalantly strolled over to where his belongings were arranged on the table. He had a Dataman, one of those latest Texas Instruments jobs. Impulsively, I glided back to my desk with it. I popped open the bottom panel then ripped out its guts. I had just replaced it and returned to my seat when he reappeared.

Ron Wooten tried to turn his Dataman on. Of course, the screen was dead. He turned the switch off and on. He then checked the battery compartment. The crestfallen look on his face was worth it. Revenge is best served cold. Ron Wooten's was served frozen.

"How was the potluck?" I said to Amber. She did not answer. The bongos vied for my attention. I moved to the window and looked out at the late spring green of the trees bordering Lot C. The Doom Hippie sat before a statue of 'Dillos football legend Bobby "Bull" Dozier, playing guitar and singing. Some waifish chick accompanied him on bongos. Wanted Jenny to witness this but did not want to be the bearer of bad news in case he is cheating on her. I do not know what the hell I am doing. All I know is that I hate the Doom Hippie. The world would be a better place without him. He suddenly looked up and waved in my direction. Amber was now standing at my side. She waved back.

It was all too much. Headed up to the stacks where I wandered aimlessly. The Vault having become a dangerous place, I had nowhere to go to get away from all the *yaje*. The hobbit room was always an option. I paused at the bottom of the ladder and gazed upward, unsure of what to do.

A clinical voice crackled over the outdoor P.A. The last time that happened was during the student riots. "Would Team Yellow please assemble in the quad?" I recognized the voice as Mrs. Neighbors. The message was repeated.

"Steven," said a different voice. This one came from behind me. It was Hazel's. "Mrs. Womack wants to see you in her office."

The head librarian was seated behind her desk, upon which rested the suggestion box, its lid in a raised position. "Please close the door and have a seat," she said portentously. Numerous slips of paper were spread before her like a tarot reading. A thin sliver of pizza draped over a paper plate. A paper towel had been placed on top of the pizza to soak up the grease. Another paper towel bore a stack of pepperonis.

Dixie read the suggestions aloud. "Porteous can kiss my—." She stopped reading and set that one aside. That could have come from anyone. She read another one: "The library is a bunch of fascists." Am guessing the Doom Hippie wrote that one, as he is the only person I know who uses that word with any regularity. One suggestion was rolled up into a neat scroll tied with a ribbon. Dixie took a moment to unfurl it. "Please, more superb tomes by Rantum Scantum."

Dixie read more suggestions. An exercise in tedium! My eyes wandered around her office. It was devoid of photos or a fern. Even her paperweight was a Porteous one and not the butterfly one everyone has. Behind her hung a portrait of Charles Ammi Cutter, of Cutter number fame.

"Are we done here?" I said impatiently.

Dixie held up a minatory finger. "Take this job and shove it," she said. "This is your handwriting, is it not, Steven?"

"I don't recall writing that," I said.

"It brings me no pleasure to tell you this, Steven." She provided me with a formal letter of dismissal detailing a lengthy list of scurrilous accusations, a rap sheet as long as my arm including: numerous dress code write-ups; consorting amorously with co-workers; the lava lamp incident; playing loud music; disappearing on the clock; taking personal phone calls at the desk; the Mr. Coffee incident; various cataloging irregularities; numerous parking violations; unauthorized travel expenses; unexcused absences and tardiness; personal use of library supplies; unauthorized use and abuse of the dean's x-rox machine; allowing unauthorized personnel into the basement; insubordination; miscellaneous policy violations; mishandling of antiquities from the Baumann Collection; Professor Whipple's missing cushion; and various shenanigans.

I whipped off my tie and threw it into the wastebasket. "Is that all?" I said indignantly. "You forgot: entering the library if unclean or suffering the pox; imbibing alcoholic spirits in the library; napping on the job; behaving without couth; partaking of pipes, cigarettes, and tobacco; destroying and defacing books, newspapers, and other library property; bringing livestock into the library—and demons; gross negligence; indecent exposure; disorderly conduct; shoplifting; breaking and entering; burglary; grand theft of a firearm; assault and battery; blasphemy; making filthy remarks to Hazel; and sabotaging Ron Wooten's Dataman."

Dixie opened her mouth to speak. "Are you detaining me?" I demanded, rising from my chair.

"You will clean out your desk and gather your personal belongings," said Dixie, with a sigh. "Mr. Boggs will see that you stay out of trouble. He will also escort you off the premises."

Boggs was waiting outside the door to the hedgehog's airless burrow. Carlos's racket had resumed. "My main man," shouted Boggs forlornly. "This ain't right." I found my desk covered in tottering piles of festschrifts. Where did they all come from? The one on top bore the title *Try It, You'll Like It: Festschrift in Memory of Professor Roy G. Biv*. Boggs provided a carton for my belongings: my pet rock, a drawerful of pens, piles of personal books brought from home. Boggs looked the other way when I pinched the Antioch Chalice.

"Gotta drain the lizard," I said. The staff bathroom was cordoned off with masking tape, which I ripped away. The walls bore fresh wood paneling. There was no sign of the medicine cabinet. I tapped along the wall, listening for hollow spaces. Did Carlos remove the cabinet first? If so, he would have discovered the original codex stashed within. It seems unlikely that he just covered the cabinet without even looking inside first. But then again we are talking about Carlos, the most incurious human being I know. Especially after his encounter in the Vault. With what, the dwarf? Or worse? He is lucky to be alive. I traced a glyph upon the paneling. Something I should have done earlier.

"I have some personal items downstairs in the Vault, including an antique chair. You may recognize it. It's the one that looks like a throne."

"Oh, I don't go in there, Steven," said Boggs. "Besides, the basement is all torn up on account of the book tower. These people are out of their minds."

"If you can have Carlos set it aside for me, I would appreciate it."

We headed for the exit. I checked my cubby hole in case Randy had written. Could really use his guidance right about now. There was some mail and a bunch of memos. I would sort them out later. The hedgehogs stared at me as if I were being led to the scaffold. "Hey!" shouted Hey Now. It sounded like an accusation. Sarge alone saluted me.

As Boggs held the door for me, a woman entered the library. "Gabrielle, right?" I said. Evidently, Loretta's ex is Professor Nunn. Small world. "Steven?" said Gabrielle. "How are you?"

The first time I met Gabrielle, I had walked in on her and Loretta. Gabrielle had introduced herself like everything was hunky dory. My recollection of that moment caused me to blush and look away. "Nice to see you again," I said. I was looking at Old Rip when I said it.

"You, too," said Gabrielle.

Amber and I made eye contact. I am terrible at reading lips, but I understood when she mouthed the words, "*Yubu're fubired.*" I nodded, then tousled her hair.

"So long, kid."

Boggs and I made our way against the grain of foxes heading toward the quad. We made room for Doris who was pushing Sarge along in his wheelchair, Jenny and Monty in tow.

We regarded a Polyflex truck parked near the loading dock behind Blanston Hall. Two men were loading it. Among the piles of boxes stood my Sherlock Holmes chair. Boggs caught me staring at it. "Best let it go, Steven," he said gently.

Boggs helped me load the Rambler on the outskirts of Lot C. In a rare unguarded moment, I let him catch sight of L.F.'s empty safe. Of course he would not know what it was or even care, but the slip disturbed me. I slammed the trunk and turned to face him. "It was a pleasure working with you, man."

"You as well, Steven." We shook hands. Boggs looked all about, then added, "Sometimes I don't know about this place."

I gave a concurring grimace. "No women's gymnasium, then?"

Boggs shook his head. "They're sending me to the business school cafeteria. They're about to award our demotions in the quad. Unless I'm on the chopping block. Better get over there. Be cool, now."

*Team Yellow. You will assemble in the quad. This is your last warning.*

The carillon tolled one. I gazed up at the campanile and was blinded by the early afternoon sun. Misty would be waiting for me on her blanket, naked with her po' boys. How long would my charm last?

As I turned onto White Settlement, a speeding white dually almost took off my bumper. The Doom Hippie! Looked like Jenny in the passenger seat. What does she see in that sicko? *Cosmo* would have something to say about it.

The Eagle's Nest was dead. Or was it just Randy's absence? Jackie must have been off as the other chick was behind the counter. The one with the ape hairdo. Her huge costume earrings looked like magnolia grenades. When I ordered Harvey Wallbanger after Harvey Wallbanger, she served me wordlessly. You could always count on Jackie to ask you what was going on and cheer you up.

I pawed through my mail from work. Nothing from Randy. But there was a telex. Spunt must have printed it out for me.

> RECEIVED 13 JUN 1977, 9:23 AM
> ITEM MATCHING THAT DESCRIPTION STOLEN IN DECEMBER FROM OUR OWN
> COLLECTION. WOULD LIKE TO COME SEE IT. PLEASE ADVISE.
> SENDER: M. TATE, INSTITUTE FOR ORIENTAL STUDIES
> RECEIVER: N. SPUNT, LANGNER LIBRARY, PORTEOUS COLLEGE

That the Elephant Ranch is a front for trafficking in stolen antiquities makes perfect sense. At least it did to a very drunk Steven Miller, Esquire on this fine June evening.

Must have memorized every license plate on the ceiling by the time I left. Where did they get Yukon plates? I stumbled out of the Eagle's Nest, tired, wasted, and angry. It was dusk. The automatic street lights on Camp Bowie came on one by one as I passed them. As I approached Collinwood, I noted a squad car and medical examiner's van parked out front. I kept going and parked behind the Showdown. No squad cars there, for once. My thoughts raced. Did they come to arrest me? Had something happened to Vee? I was dangling from my kitchen window when another squad car screeched into the driveway, its headlights spotlighting my kicking legs.

"You dumb bastards, I live here!" I blurted while being roughly subdued. On the way to the cooler, I recall making arrogant demands. Spells to break free fizzled, though I did manage to flatten all four cop tires. One of them referred to me as a fringie. More than once he uttered the phrase "get the chair." The electric chair? Dread gave way to vertigo, then blackness.

*Vee, no!*

No.


Came to on a hard, concrete floor. My mansack! They must have taken it. The cell was empty but for a bunk bed, a sink, and a commode with no seat. Bits and pieces of the evening came trickling back into my brain. The way people had been talking, they must think I did it.

As much as I felt like giving in to despair, I did not let myself break down. All I knew is that I had to escape this cell at any cost. There are maybe two dozen formulae I always have ready, should I need them, including:

> *Shush*
> *Parting of the Waters*
> *Tie/Untie*
> *Ventriloquism*
> *Invisible Wedgie*
> *Discover*
> *Open*
> *Hinder*
> *At Ease*
> *Kents*
> *Light*
> *Evade*
> *"B" for Bass*
> *Command*
> *Strike*
> *Truth*
> *Charm*
> *Unmake*
> *Iron Claw*
> *Dental Liquefaction*
> *Death Stare*

Most are aqua or purple spells. Some are orange. *Death Stare* is blue. After blue there are brown, green, red, tan, and gold. Gold being the most complex. Why the colors do not correspond to Roy G. Biv, I do not know. *Open* failed. Guess I lacked the mojo for muskrat farming at the moment. After two more attempts, I must have dozed off. When I awakened, Guddu was standing in the corner, smoking.

"You killed Vee, didn't you?" I cried. My thumbs quickly found his windpipe. I squeezed hard. He choked back an exclamation of protest. He escaped my grasp easily enough by simply changing into Shagduk's form and scampering through the bars of the cell. The imp is impossible to kill. Or so he said.

"Anger is an Energy" is the title of a chapter in the Martin Solis book. It taught me to channel my anger into something useful. In this case, clarity of thought. "Get me out of here," I said through clenched teeth. "Do so and I will free you." I suppose I could have gotten myself out of there. In fact, I am sure of it. But if I could convince the imp to do it, I would be back in control. The bargain could only have worked had he truly believed I was his master.

Shagduk eyed me dubiously. "Your freedom for mine," I repeated.

"It is bullshit," he said.

"Have I ever lied to you?"

The imp's tail twitched like Figgy's does when he is annoyed. "What will you do with your freedom?" I continued.

When Guddu is in Shagduk's form, I can never read his expressions as clearly. Guddu's face can be fairly expressive, running the gamut of human emotions. Shagduk's bears the more permanent scars of malice and ill humor, with a hint of the whipped cur.

"You can write that book you were talking about," I said, clutching at straws. "On your beautiful typewriter you won fair and square."

Shagduk continued to stare me down with his yellow eyes. "Fair and square," he said at last. What a rube. I noticed he was wearing my "100 Proof Irish" button I had misplaced after St. Patrick's Day. Shagduk the Leprechaun! The absurdity of it was too much.

"You know it to be true. In your heart." An appeal to an imp's heart is a shot in the dark. I doubt he has one.

"In my heart," repeated Shagduk, as if the words had meaning for him. Now I had him. The rest was comparatively easy. But as soon as I was sprung, some guy in a nearby cell started yelling and banging his cup on the bars. He was one of those reptilian types you take one look at and just know. They take one look at you and they also know.

"Hey you," I said, ignoring my "fight or flight" instinct as only a human can do. "What are you in here for?"

"What the fuck do you want me to say?" said the reptilian type. The way he was talking, it did not seem like he could see Shagduk. "That I beat the shit out of the woman I loved? That I stuffed her lifeless body into the dumbwaiter? Or, wait—what did you call it? The trash hole? Naw, that's cold, man."

"If you did that then you deserve worse than jail," I said.

"You'll never make it past the guards!" sneered the reptilian type. When he started banging on the bars again, Shagduk *Shushed* him. For good, by the looks of it. But I was in no position to quibble.

The imp displayed an awkward eagerness that was endearing, if that can be said of such a horrid-looking creature. It was astounding, the ease with which he unlocked every door with an almost imperceptible flick of the wrist. By some stroke of dumb luck, we encountered no one.

We found ourselves in some sort of utility corridor. "My mansack," I said.

Shagduk nodded then scampered away. I nervously assumed he intended for me to wait. He returned with my mansack slung over his shoulder. Due to his small stature, it dragged behind him. If he only had a clue what was inside. But of course he knows. The only secrets that are safe from Shagduk are the ones in my head.

The corridor ended abruptly into a small room lined with meters and humming panels. By the dim glare of a naked bulb, I watched as Shagduk traced a rectangle over a portion of the wall opposite. An opening came into being. The imp padded into it, then turned and beckoned to me. "This way, master," he insisted. He scrambled along, evidently quite at home in the subterranean gloom. Why call me master only now, after all that has transpired between us?

"I can't see!" I hissed. For guidance, I ran my fingertips over some pipes to my left that ran along the length of the hot, stuffy passage. I followed the slap of Guddu's footfalls, bumping my head repeatedly on some hard protuberance or another. How painful scalp injuries are! A dog leg, then a halt. There was a click, then the sound of wood sliding against wood. By the smell of mop water and Lysol, I judged we were in a janitor's closet. We emerged into a spacious area. Large windows admitted enough city lights to provide a view of our location: behind the circulation desk at the main branch of the public library.

Now it was I who led. We hastened along the deserted sidewalk. At Burnett Park, I stopped behind a yucca tree to catch my breath. I observed there a weathered flier for our May 10 gig at the Knight Spot. A squad car passed, then stopped. My eyes darted to and fro, seeking an escape route through the tall monkey grass. But there was no point in running now.

A flashlight beam blinded me. "Let me see your hands," said the cop. He approached me. "What are you doing here past curfew?"

"My old lady kicked me out of her car," I said. Which was vaguely true. I had done the same to Loretta exactly one year ago today. Not far from here, as a matter of fact. When she chased me on foot, screaming my name, I almost stopped. That I did not is one of my proudest moments.

"Women," he said ruefully. "The most dangerous of all sports. Your I.D., please."

I cautiously lowered my hands, then patted my pockets disingenuously. "My wallet's in her car."

"Mmm hmm. Name?"

"Mantee," I said automatically. "Duke Mantee."

The rules enforcer jotted it down in his little notebook. "Are you aware that this park closes at ten o'clock, Mr. Mantee?"

"Does it? I was just passing through."

"Hop in. I'll give you a ride home."

"If you don't mind, I'd rather walk," I said. "Helps me clear my head."

The cop looked me up and down. "Suit yourself. You have a good evening, now." He paused before adding, "Mr. Mantee."

The squad car's tail lights rounded the corner. Shagduk reappeared. Ah, to simply boink yourself away like Jeannie whenever there is trouble. Something to think about. The imp and I zigzagged our way along side streets to avoid further brushes with the law. From the levee I cast a glance at red and blue flashing lights moving along the Lancaster Avenue bridge. Perhaps it was the same cop. With the aid of a small, conjured boat, courtesy of the imp, we crossed the Trinity. I regarded the still, murky waters and recalled the thing Randy and I had loosed upon the west side what now seems a lifetime ago. Let us hope there were not any others. We traversed the park. The imp moved with a purposeful stride, humming softly to himself a tune I identified as "Tokyo Joe." How the hell would he know that song unless he was there that night at the disco? I do not imagine he listens to the radio. Soon, I will not have to worry about him anymore.

At Farrington Field, I prepared to hotwire a Frito Lay van. Loretta's old stomping grounds beckoned from across the street. The theater's distinctive round stage would be an impressive *mise en scène* in which to banish the imp once and for all. According to the marquee, *My Fair Lady* had opened earlier this fair evening. Too bad the audience did not stick around for the encore.

Pushing and pulling in the right spots on the back door, and I was in. A trick remembered from Loretta's Casa Mañana days. Try as I might, I could not locate the panel for the stage lights. Fortunately, I found one of those Eveready lanterns mounted on the wall next to a fire extinguisher. It would have to do. For the ritual, I needed a few simple material components. Witch hazel and a bobby pin were readily found in the rehearsal and dressing room area.

"Dark theaters are suitable for dark deeds." I pointed the lantern toward the center of the stage. A small rectangle of masking tape was succeeded by other cursory preparations. Naturally, I took certain precautions.

With a mic boom I tapped into the center of the rectangle. Shagduk dutifully stepped into it. The film canister of his slime proved useful. "Essence of imp," I said, holding it aloft for him to see. Shagduk's eyes narrowed. They followed my hands as I prepared the boom. I then pronounced the requisite words, slowly and in proper sequence, tapping the designated points with the mic in succession. Such elocution! If only Professor Henry Higgins from *My Fair Lady* were here to witness this terrible curtain call. It is amazing what one can accomplish with simple phonetics and the science of speech. The imp seemed to realize too late that I was not setting him free, after all. My conjuration will send him crying back to his erstwhile master with his dracotine tail between his legs.

Despite my efforts, the imp could not, or would not, cross the rectangle's edge. He scrambled frantically back and forth, ricocheting off the invisible walls marked by the tape. "You promised!" he pleaded. I had intended to throw in an *Iron Claw*, but I did not have the energy to spare. During the ensuing battle of wills, we were joined by a third, much more powerful will. The Fear welled up within me. I dropped quivering to my knees and stared at the scene in mute horror. The imp's eyeballs turned solid jet. He lurched sideways, then back, like an animated corpse. His long shadow produced by the lantern danced mockingly among the empty seats. Shagduk's pompatus slurped and hissed, then spoke through him in a voice I remembered well.

"Where is it?" it croaked. It then uttered a caw of savage laughter. On account of the Fear perhaps, I, too, cawed. Laughter gave way to shadow. With a shaking hand, I pointed the mic at the Wurlitzer. It sounded in D major, that rumbling key of triumph, of Hallelujahs, of war-cries, of victory-rejoicing. The imp went limp, as if released from an unseen grip. He shrieked "Master!" then dematerialized in a burst of black flame. His shriek ping-ponged across the silver-pillowed ceiling, its reverberations magnifying into a ear-splitting crescendo. The stage lights went from dark to piercingly bright before shattering. Bits of jagged glass rained upon my head. A fitting finale to a farce that had gone on far too long.

Someone was prodding me with the lantern. I found myself in the orchestra pit. Summoning what little strength I had left in me, I stood up, then made for the exit, broken glass crunching beneath my feet. "Hey you, boy!" cried an elderly voice, probably that of the janitor. "Come back here!" Only time will tell if the ritual was a success. But I believe it was.

"*Kha-Shagduk haka*," I said to myself. "Shagduk is yours."

Tuesday, June 14

Vee's rolling fishbowl was in the driveway. To my infinite disgust, there was a fluorescent Mr. Yuk sticker on the bulbous window. I scraped off its sickly face with my fingernails, then stood there with my hands on my knees. Was she really gone? Weeping, exhausted and hungover, I made my way to the front yard. An x-roxed "Keep Out" sign flapped gently on a sawhorse on the porch. Guess the cops did not realize Vee and I shared the front door. I used the key under the flower pot. Was the house being watched? If so, they would have nabbed me at once.

I stepped over the mail. From upstairs I heard pacing. The Doom Hippie, perhaps, returned, to quote, "burn this sucker down." I recalled the early days of Collinwood before Vee and I had met. How her footsteps had driven me nuts. Until I saw the legs the redhead's feet were attached to. Then I no longer cared!

Vee's place was dark and freezing cold. The air conditioner was running on full blast. Roaches scattered when I turned on a lamp. Besides a missing rug and what looked like blood droplets, nothing had been disturbed. Perhaps the investigators thought the roach-clipped fox tail was Vee's but I recognized the vile totem at once. Evidence that might clear my name, but I had no time for that now. I placed it into my pocket.

The Doom Hippie's words echoed in my mind: *I'm going to find out what you love and make it cease to exist.* But how did he know I loved the gracious, intelligent, glib Gemini? I did not even know I loved her, until now. As a friend, that is.

With tears in my eyes, I collected Figgy's food, medicine, litter pan, and turtle. May as well nab that bottle of Galliano. The overdue Robert Byron book I left on the bedside table on top of a Civil Service Exam study guide. Late fees were the least of my worries. I scooped up Vee's dirty things and buried my face in them, sobbing. Her strong scent conjured up wistful memories. *Welcome to Margaritaville, population: one.*

Before I left, I went into Vee's bathroom to drain the lizard and wash my face. I regarded myself in the mirror. I was covered in bloody cuts from the falling glass at Casa Mañana. So that had really happened. I called the imp's name. Nothing. So that had really happened, too.

Movement caught my eye. I spotted a face staring back at me in the mirror. Shagduk! I turned around and ripped open the shower curtain. The DDT kid shoved past me with a flipper and took off down the stairs. To discourage him from returning, I retrieved Todd Rundgren from downstairs and placed him in Vee's window. That ought to freak him out, Todd staring out the window like blind Father Halliran from *The Sentinel*. A somewhat apt comparison given Todd's eyes were gouged out from my *shuriken* practice.

The Rambler was where I had left it behind the Showdown. I parked in front of Collinwood, then hastily loaded the car with armloads of clothing, books, Brannock device, nut cracker, boot jack, and a cigar box of keepsakes. Whatever seemed important. Had a bulky safe not been taking up half my trunk I could have taken more. Should have had Shagduk get rid of it.

Nothing from Randy in the mailbox. What else was I forgetting? The amulet! I raced back inside. Could not find it at first because I had forgotten I had hidden it in a half-full tin of Nestlé Quik. Frantically, I dug through the sweet brown powder before dumping it out onto the counter. At first I thought Guddu had taken it. I concealed it inside the 76 ball on my antenna so I could keep my eye on it. The horizon glowed orange. As I gazed upon Collinwood one last time, I observed that Vee's bulbs were coming up.

Made a quick detour to look at Sherwood's place. I found it in shocking disrepair. The windows were broken and the roof was partially caved in. It is as if the Fox Emeritus himself had been propping it up. And now he is gone.

A feral tabby stood guard on the porch. He and Figgy locked eyes and stiffened. "It's you and me now, Figs," I said. Figgy leaped out of the window. Both cats raced around back.

The tornado shelter had collapsed. I peered into the rubble and recalled what Randy and I had found—the shattered mirror, the runes on the wall, and Sherwood's cane. The mystery of the professor's disappearance has only deepened since then.

Spotted Figgy perched upon the garage, growling. I approached slowly until I was beneath him. There was no time to mess around so I uttered a charm I knew. I assume it worked because I was able to grab him. The black and white cat relaxed in my arms and began purring. I considered trying the back door but could not risk getting caught now.

Time to take stock. Twelve hundred miles to Vegas, a pack of Kents, and an orphaned cat. For some ridiculous reason, I ruminated on my New Year's resolutions to travel, be less aloof, and get laid. It all seems so trivial now. The terror and delight of a new beginning! If I could only pause this moment. But I must go on.

I suppose Porteous will mail my final paycheck to Collinwood where it will do me no good. Safe to say I will lose my deposit with Hawlie. Apart from my hoard of two-dollar bills, there is probably twenty bucks in the wallet Jenny gave me. Cashing a check was not an option. They will be looking for me.

Did not realize until I was well on my way that the Rambler was so stuffed with crap that I could not see out of the rear view. I pulled over and abandoned a couple of boxes on the side of the highway. I did not even look inside. A full saver book of S&H green stamps fell to the ground. A Libbey eight-piece wine caddy set or Treasure Craft ceramic bull never seemed less important than they did now.

The radio came on by itself. A jingle emerged from the static. Unless I am mistaken, the disco tune is in the key of B major—every burden of the heart lies in its radius.

*Studio 6333. Dedicated to decadence.*
*Committed to the pursuit of pleasure.*
*State of the art disco.*
*Live the fantasy.*

Guess the Doom Hippie's dad dubbed the narration in Bobby's studio. A woman moaned suggestively in the background. I hoped it was not Bonnie. The jingle ended. The discotheque should at this moment be collapsing upon itself. For a moment, I prayed no one was inside. I was chiefly thinking of Amber, but what of the innocent janitor? If the Doom Hippie was crushed, well, would that be such a great loss?

The ad was followed by a burst of static which soon gave way to a familiar voice, the DJ from *The Fringe*.

"This next song is dedicated to Steven Miller, Esquire, Master Cataloger, from Krolok, eerie master of illusion. Krolok says, 'To my brother in karnic arts, Fate has favored you. Together, we will wield great power and receive great rewards. Come to me, and let us share in the glory and riches of Yaat, our ancient kingdom. Our success depends on your skill and secrecy. Do not fail me. You know what you must do.' This is Fox on the Run."

"Our ancient kingdom"? Who does he think I am? I winced at my first and only attempt at song lyrics. Worse, however, was the sound of my name going out on the airwaves. Time for a pseudonym. Maybe "Richard Kimble," the guy from *The Fugitive*.

I felt an emptiness in my stomach, a sudden pang at leaving Collinwood and the brown lawns of the west side. A fishtailing trailer of children caused me to swerve. Physics is not my forte but I know that those damn kids need to move closer to the hitch before it flips. Functioning tail lights would also not be remiss. In the rear view mirror I saw nothing but madness. Traffic was sparse heading out of town. I drove like a bat out of hell—a bat that did not exceed forty-seven miles an hour. When possible, I took back roads. The only obvious hazard was traps, not for speed, but for the violation of any law no matter how arcane or fabricated. For some jerkwater counties it is their only source of income.

Mundane thoughts distracted me. Like the Nestlé Quik all over the kitchen counter. That is going to attract ants. Nothing I could do about it now. Then there was the matter of Ron Wooten's Dataman. I should not have ruined it. What he did to me happened years ago. We are both adults now and neither one of us are the same person we were then. I am not the same person I was last year.

Blew a tire outside Cross Plains. Wrestling the spare from under the safe was no easy feat. Where was my dogsbody when I needed him? I was already starting to regret banishing the imp. The jack slipped and I hurt my hand. I relented and summoned an elemental. But I could not look. Instead, I took in the rugged beauty of the countryside and cloudless sky. The only sound was the shush of Indian grass and the soft crunch of gravel under my restless feet. When I turned around, the tire was fixed.

A sedan followed me. Most traffic would have passed me by now were I driving faster. The old paranoia was back. I pulled into the crowded parking lot of a diner. The brown Centurion gunned past.

Parked under a shady pecan. Figured I may as well try to finish off the forty-eight-ounce T-bone. If I succeeded, it was free. Sat by the window to keep an eye on the cat. He stood with his paws on the steering wheel, mouth open in one continuous cry. Whether for Vee, his circumstances, or simply existential feline anguish, I understood. Let it out, cat! Lest it get too hot in the car, I two-fisted the steak. My jaw became sore from all the chewing. Since I only had a half-hour to eat the whole thing, I abandoned the salad and potato. I quickened my pace and finished with two minutes to spare. The waitress treated me like a minor celebrity but when I caught a glimpse of the manager he looked mad. The power of the T-bone surged through my body. I felt invincible.

When I opened the door to the Rambler, Figgy made a run for it through the gummy lovegrass. Caught up with him in a derelict cemetery. He was at a loss for where to dash among the slender tombstones. He just gave up and cowered to the dust.

Back on the road, the freaked out cat would not settle down. I let him out of his carrier. This proved to be a mistake. All he wanted to do was get between my feet and the pedals, which I could not abide.

Figured my records were doomed on account of the heat. Stopped at a secondhand shop in Lubbock where I unloaded some early Elvis on Sun. The ones that were not warped, that is. Considered offering Hitler's bookplate from *Die Tür* but the provenance might arouse scrutiny. *The Hobbit* was rejected. Not a first edition. Forty-one bucks to the good. And a psaltery. The proprietor did not know what the instrument was called. It is compact and easy to play for when I get the itch.

Got pulled over near the state line. In the side view, I watched the officer approach, whacking his palm with a baton. He sidled up to the driver's window. He tapped it with his baton. I slowly rolled it down.

"Driver's license," he said. He studied it then studied my face. He walked back to his motorcycle. Figured the jig was up. I mentally ran down the list of spells that would get me out of the situation. The only one that made sense in this context was *Hinder*. Evidently, it prevented him from using his radio.

The cop paused to kick out my tail light. He issued me a citation for it. "Twenty bucks," he said. "Payable to me." He spat chaw into the sandy loam. When I produced my checkbook, he added, "Cash only, son."

I was shaking as I pulled away. I felt like I was stuck on a pin. With nothing but static on the radio, I tried to distract myself by singing. *By the time I make Albuquerque, she'll be working*. Dawn would be at the museum. I tried to imagine the conversation. "It's me, Steven. I'm afraid I have some terrible news. It's Vee." Of course, Dawn already knows by now. It is best I never make that call.

Flashing lights appeared in the rear view. The cop was back. I put the hammer down. I had no idea what would happen if I took the Rambler over forty-seven miles per hour but I would find out. The faster I went, the more the poor car shuddered. At seventy-seven, I thought it might shake apart. The cop glided up alongside my car and motioned for me to pull over.

There was no way I was going to let him take me in. I did the only thing I could do. The effort would take a lot out of me. I prepared the best I could, which meant I had to take my hands off the wheel for a minute. I steered with my thigh. The cop stayed on my ass. At last, I was ready. I did not hear the words of power as I sang them, such were their potency. As I sustained the final syllable, the cop suddenly swerved and slowed. The distance between us increased until I saw him pull over. He doffed his helmet and let it fall to the pavement. His teeth would be jelly.

Pit stop near a missile range. The sign flashed "The World's Edge." Derelict saloon with a row of choppers out front. The interior was illuminated only by the sunlight admitted through the open front door. Inside, a chick right off the cover of *Slave Lord of Siluria* was swaying to a mournful country ballad in her mind. An emaciated donkey stood with its nose in the corner. It had no tail. Some burnout bikers stopped shooting pool and stared as I rounded their table with a "Pardon me."

"You guys don't sell Chap Stick here, do you?" I said to the bartender. He just looked at me. In retrospect, I guess it was a dumb question.

Had just begun to drain the lizard when the door opened behind me. Someone turned on the faucet, ostensibly to drown out my cries for help.

This person then lathered up at the sink for several minutes like Trapper John prepping for the O.R. I stared straight ahead through the bars of a tiny window, determined to play it cool. Just in case, I readied *Invisible Wedgie*. Tired of waiting, I slowly turned around. By the looks of him, the biker had never bathed in his life yet he chose this moment to thoroughly scrub his entire arms. He sneezed. "Bless you," I said without thinking. I hauled ass and did not look back.

At first, I thought she was one of the biker's old ladies. Her features were gaunt; her cheeks sunken. She must have been wearing a pound of makeup. A sheer scarf contained a pile of brittle blonde hair. She leaned forward in the passenger seat, nonchalantly fixing her false eyelash. I stood there slack-jawed. Ursula of Ulm summoned me to get in.

# NO COVER
# ONE NIGHT ONLY

Sonny Side Up at The Piano Bar

Tuesday May 10

at **The Knight Spot**

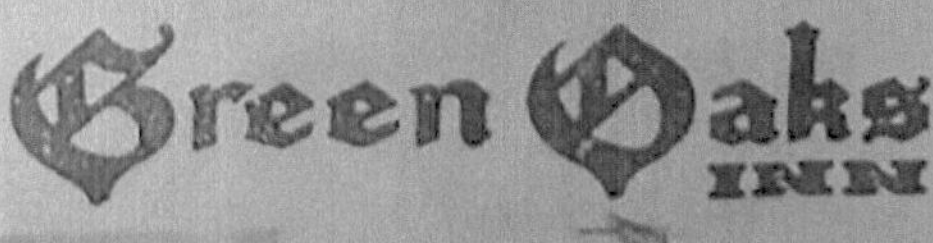


FULL

MENU

*Mashik baya!*

Krolok thanks (in no particular order): M., Norberto, Eddie Black, Sky Hernstrom, Paul Rhoades, Robin Whealdon, David Bullock, Jeffro Johnson, Bastien Pilon, Daddy Warpig, Peg Roth of Time Frame, R.J. at Critical Blast, Susie Corbett, Emily Hixon, Lloyd Llewellyn, Ernie Gygax, Jr., Kevin Bazzana, Dr. John Parce, Erik Waag, Kirston Fortune, Darius Garsys, and Gagan Boparai at Wilibees.

Did you enjoy the book? We really hope you did!


Three ways you can help Pilum and JB Jackson:

1. leave your reviews on goodreads.com and Amazon.com;
2 Buy directly from the pilumpress.com site;
3. sign up for our mailing list—this way you'll be the first to know all Pilum and JB Jackson news!

www.pilumpress.com

www.ingramcontent.com/pod-product-compliance
Lightning Source LLC
Chambersburg PA
CBHW031443200726
48289CB00007BB/2189